FISHING THE NET

By

Rod Wood
with
Jane Reeves

Copyright © Rod Wood & Jane Reeves 2016
This book is sold subject to the condition that it shall not, by way of trade or otherwise, be lent, resold, hired out, or otherwise circulated without the publisher's prior consent in any form of binding or cover other than that in which it is published and without a similar condition including this condition being imposed on the subsequent publisher.
The moral right of Rod Wood & Jane Reeves has been asserted.
ISBN-13: 978-1535406796
ISBN-10: 1535406798

Helen and all the ladies who have sought the internet to find the one of their dreams.

CONTENTS

PROLOGUE 1
PREPARING THE LINE 5
BACK TO SPAWNING GROUNDS 39
SETTING THE BAIT 43
THE RULES OF ANGLING 54
HOOKED 62
THE PIKE AND THE PIRHANA 79
NIBBLES, BITES and THROW THEM BACK 95
THE PERFECT CATCH 156
THE BLOW FISH 183
CLOSED SEASON 187
WORLD RIVERS/BRINGING IN THE CATCH ... 229
OPEN SEASON 251
GAME FISHING, SPINNING my LINE 282
THE HADDOCKS AND THE HADDKNOCKS –
LOOKING FOR NEMO 294
IN SEARCH OF A LOST SOLE 311
HOOK, LINE AND SINKER 319
REFLECTIONS ON THE WATER 417
TACKLE, BAITS AND LURES 436
WADERS, NETS, THE END OF THE LINE 451

This is a work of fiction. Names, characters, businesses, organizations, places, events and incidents either are the product of the author's imagination or are used fictitiously. Any resemblance to actual persons, living or dead, events, or locales is entirely coincidental.

PROLOGUE

The Catch

As my eyes gently opened, I felt the warm breeze against my face coming through the open bedroom window. The curtains moved gently as the warm air wafted past them. A noise, the gentle flow of running water came from the ensuite, he must be having a shower.

As my eyes circled the room, I saw the memories of last night – my stockings now hanging limply over the end of the bed, my black bra dangling from the dressing table chair, my dress lying in a heap on the floor by the side of the bed. What was my thong doing hanging from the lamp shade? I smiled to myself, recalling the previous night, a night of love and of passion. I pulled the sheet up over my bare breasts, noticing my hands still bound very loosely by long strands of red ribbon to the bedstead. What was it he said? He didn't want to prevent my hands getting up to the tricks they usually did. As I snuggled in under the cotton, closing my eyes again, I tried to recall the events of the past few hours, what had been a romantic evening, perfect evening.

An evening which had begun at our favourite restaurant, sharing a candlelit dinner. That little black dress, that which every girl should have, had come out for this special dinner. I had so wanted to make a good impression, show myself off.

Though I say it myself, I looked a million dollars, and appreciated his flattering comments about me.

A wonderful meal, tucking into spicy king prawns to start with, followed by what seemed the most appropriate dish on the menu, 'catch of the day', a gorgeous piece of Hake (it could have been me, catch of the day!), then a little cheese to finish off, and a lovely Chardonnay to swill it all down with, hoping that I would be the afters later.

As all good meals should be, we were not rushed, and chatted while devouring this wonderful food. We talked about anything, everything, enjoying each other's company and the whole romantic setting of the evening. My hand reached across the surface of the table, and was met by his, a gentle squeeze in his palm, and a knowing wink from his eye. Is this love as I want it to be? Oh, yes!

He paid the bill, and we walked hand in hand out of the restaurant and to his car. A click of the key, and he opened the door for me to get in, but before getting in, he drew me to him, into those muscular arms, stared into my eyes and then kissed me, long and hard. The air was draining from my lungs, but my lips didn't want to let go. Breathless, we separated. Our eyes met again knowingly and he released me to get into the car. Home, to my place, and I asked him in for coffee, but I was expecting more, a lot, lot more.

Coffee, yes, we were going to have coffee, so I pulled myself away and went into the kitchen and switched the kettle on. It started humming as it started to get warm, but as I stood there waiting, I felt arms around me again, turning me to face him and we were kissing again. A hand fondled my left breast. Did I want to push it away? No, I didn't, so my hands explored his body more, running down his chest and down to his crotch. Something was hardening, firm in my hand beneath the fabric of his chinos.

Fuck the coffee, we were heading upstairs and into my bedroom, and then in each other's arms again, but this time feeling, exploring, undoing zips, buttons. He released my dress slowly from over my shoulders and it slipped down over my body, down my legs and fell in a heap on the floor. His trousers followed the same route down, and I peeled his shirt from him too.

There I was standing in front of him, stilettoes, stockings, a skimpy thong and my black satin bra. And then I was lying on the bed, and he lay beside me. We embraced again, kissed, long and hard, and it was now full on. Hands exploring, roaming over each other's bodies. Phew, it was getting hotter and hotter.

He caressed my breasts, gently, very gently, and as my nipples were aroused they got a little tweak as well. I was getting more and more excited, my breathing getting heavier and heavier. I could only do one thing and reach down between his legs. Didn't have to go that low as he was excited and now I was going to arouse him more, pulling back his foreskin and massaging his manhood firmly up and down. We were getting more and more into a frenzy as his hand slipped down my body, down to my womanhood, now getting moister and moister. Oh fuck, I was his, really his as his finger slipped inside me and gently stroked that special spot he had managed to find straight away.

I needed him inside me, and pulled him gently over, encouraging him to mount me. That object I had been stroking, I directed it into where I needed it, deep inside me. Wow, as we thrust together, up and down, over and over, I was going to come, I had come, and yes, he had too. Those wonderful sensations rippled down my body, but he hadn't finished, not yet, as he slipped out, rolled me over and entered me again from behind. Woof, woof! Bliss, this was bliss, as by buttocks were smacked by his thrusting thighs.

And then, back on my back, he found some red ribbons from

somewhere and loosely bound me to the bedstead, but my arms were on long leashes, not constricting me so much that I couldn't use my hands on him. We loved again, and then time to sleep. At some stage I had lost the rest of my clothes, my undies, who cares? That was marvellous, and I – we – were both spent.

Sleep came easily as we snuggled together under the sheets.

And then I woke, the sound of the shower running, the curtains shimmering in the breeze. What a wonderful evening.

But what was that noise? Sod it, it's the bloody alarm clock. Blearily, I rolled over and switched that horrible noise off. I got out of bed and wandered into the bathroom, switched on the shower and after removing my pyjamas, stood under the warm running water.

Bugger, bugger, it was all a dream. Does this show me how I really, really need a man, a man of my own to share my life, to live these dreams for real? To be bonked when I want, to love, to be happy.

Stepping out of the shower, water dripping over the floor, but my mind elsewhere, I resolved to myself that I must do something about it, to fulfil my life, and I must do it soon.

PREPARING THE LINE

The Angler

I should introduce myself.

My name, Gill Finn, divorced (twice), a mother of three, now fifty-something, alone, returning to the town I had started my adventure called life. The town I had met my first husband, brought up two of my kids; the town I had deserted all those years ago to pursue a life the other side of the world. Life had turned full circle, now I was back.

In years gone by I used to enjoy fishing, especially sea angling. Now as I reach middle age, I need to start again. Life is passing me by, and after unsuccessful relationships (my children have grown up), I now need to find the man I want to spend the rest of my life with, to have companionship, love, holidays, as some of the lonely hearts columns describe, and a little bit more.

I am giving my experiences in trying to find Mr Right in those waters I chose to explore and pursue my prey, the Net! Many couples have met, evolved a relationship, married, and to this day have lived happily ever after. But it can be daunting; there are many pitfalls out there and I want to share my experiences with you – the highs, the lows, the perverts, the Lotharios, all sorts out there. This has been an adventure, an insight to life and to how others think and act to try and get what they want. Genuine men, the fakes, those that perhaps should look more closely at themselves in terms of appearance and bodily hygiene. The ever increasing use of social media and social networking opens an array of people looking for that special someone, or just a quick bonk. An opportunity to sell yourself, metaphorically speaking, to a wide audience of likeminded people also looking for their soulmate (or a quick bonk), on a forum that breaks down the barriers of walking into unfamiliar or uncomfortable surroundings to do that first meeting. The opportunity to sift through the shoal, and sift out those who you know are an unsuitable catch, without having to meet them face to face, and the embarrassment of having to put them back into those waters they have swum from.

In these waters, I have loved, I have loathed, I have been hurt, I have laughed, I have cried. I have seen sides to people never experienced before, and I have seen the baseness of some members of the opposite sex (by which I mean men, not members, if you'll excuse the pun). Have I found what I was fishing for? I thought I had, then I hadn't. Some wouldn't leave my bait alone, others struggled to take the bait at all, so as with all good fishermen I would have to change my strategy. Like all days angling, there are good days and there are bad days, but you persevere until you find what you are looking for.

You will now have to read on to find out if I succeeded in my landing my catch.

Ladies, if some of these men remind you of your husbands, maybe are your husband, I can only say sorry, but it wasn't my fault. With the right bait, it is surprising the bites you get, some of them whoppers!!

'Fishing the net'. Don't get hooked, let the competition commence!

The Specimen Fish

In the beginning (is there another book that starts like that?), the genesis of Gill's interest in fishing started like so many kids, with the odd trip with Dad and her sisters. Nothing too sophisticated, just a nylon net on a pole that you could buy from any seaside shop for not more than a few pence. We are talking sometime back here, not the *beginning*, beginning, and armed with these over our shoulder we would set off across rock pools looking for, and trying to catch, those elusive little fish we often see but rarely snare. Perhaps the odd shrimp, but nothing to get fat on. Of course in those happy times, males were off the menu and if anything, would be considered a bit of a pain in the bum.

Memories, memories of summer days by the beach. But as I got older, and we graduated onto more 'grown-up' pursuits, it was then that Dad would take me along to car rallies and treasure hunts, as he was very interested in this when in the RAF. And it was on one of these expeditions that I caught my first real fish. A little pool by the side of a river gave me the opportunity to try my luck. Nothing fancy in technique, or equipment, but I hooked a small trout, a rainbow, and as it was the first, we made up a campfire and cooked it there and then. I was hooked, so to speak.

School holidays would take us back to the coast and here I would happily spend hours sea fishing, trying to catch myself a few mackerel that we could cook for dinner. Joy, those distant childhood memories when you didn't have a care in the world.

Like a lot of hobbies as one gets older, they tend to go on the back burner – school, further education, marriage, and then kids of your own. A cycle goes round as the nets come out again, and back to the rock pools.

As life progressed, my journey would take me with my army life, with husband, to the other side of the world, to Brunei where I would catch barramundi, and eat them. Barramundi, to all you fishing aficionados, *Lates calcarifer*, the Asian sea bass, a fish ever increasing in popularity, especially in Oz, known for their fighting ability when trying to catch them, and on my barbeque, would produce a white, flaky flesh that would be good if added into Thai cuisine. Wonderful days.

Many happy hours I would fish for the barramundi, and then I was off to Australia where they are also very popular (with crocs as well), the Gold Coast, where I would get into serious fishing during the holidays. Big game fishing off the Barrier Reef, a truly exhilarating experience in a really beautiful part of the world. Out on the ocean, fast boats, strong rod and safety harnesses, the works, as we searched and tried to catch that huge fish. Hook them, play with them till they tire, and then draw them into the boat to 'land' them. That marlin on the end of the line, and bringing him in to land, very tiring for a little lady, but one of those lifetime experiences, great fun not to be forgotten.

But as I return to home shores, then it is now time to cast my line again.

I think a lot of anglers go out looking for that perfect fish of any given species, what they call a specimen fish. So now I am out looking for just that, but in the muddier waters of back home, it is no longer marlin I'm after but Martin, or Tom, or Dick, or Harry. So I will begin here on my search for my specimen fish, if he is out there at all!

For this, I have bought myself a net, the internet, to search those hidden waters for my perfect catch. For now, I have used the paid sites for here I feel it is more likely that I will find what I am looking for, more quickly than other sites where there may be a lot feeding but none really looking to take my bait.

So here goes, I have cast my bait and floating myself online, I will see what I can hook and bring to my trophy bag.

Lobster Pots

So, here goes, time to switch on the computer, log

in to the website, and see what comes up. Yes, there are a few bites so let's have a look at what is nibbling. This one looks interesting, read his profile, yes, definitely interesting so let's see if we can start chatting to him online. His light is on so here goes. A conversation starts between us, type a bit, read the reply, answer his questions, then fire a few back of my own. A slight pause to see if he replies – yes he has, more questions from him, more answers and then from me again, as we try to find out what we can about each other. There are of course, photos online in his profile. How much like him are they really? So my quizzing of him is trying to build a picture in my mind of whether this person I am talking, chatting to, is actually the face staring at me on the screen.

The fishing has begun; could this be the man for me? I am a little naïve at this type of course fishing, so am a little nervous about what I am doing, but can only wade into what I hope are safe and productive waters.

We have chatted for a while, and it seems a natural progression to try and break the ice, see if we can meet up, the only way that I can see if there is that spark that I am looking for between us. I know where he lives now, and him likewise with me, so it only seems logical that we should meet halfway, as he is just over an hour away from me. I will be far happier playing on a neutral venue, but he seems keen that I should go over to him, meet him in his shop which I have ascertained that he has got. Am I happy with that? I am getting out of my comfort zone, and feeling just a little uneasy at this, partly for the obvious reason of female safety – a girl on her own should be careful – and partly in that the further I have to go, with my sense of direction and a crap sat nav, my chances of actually arriving there become less and less. If he gives me directions, oh help, it will probably be that his right is my left, and vice versa, I am that proficient at it.

Much discussion, but the barriers come down, and indeed I am persuaded to go over to meet him on his home ground. My first internet date is arranged, in at the deep end. Those girly decisions of what I should wear, make-up, etc., to show myself off as best as I could. Yes, he has seen my photo, but I am not very photogenic, so now have to sell myself. Smart ironed jeans, blouse, and some make-up should be ample, after all this is only for a coffee and a chat, it's not as if I have to be in a mini skirt and revealing a full cleavage; that might be classed as entrapment.

Smart, but casual will do nicely as I get in the car and set off towards Staffordshire. Yes, a little nervous but I am a confident girl, especially in myself. But that doesn't stop me wondering what I have let myself into, as my destination draws closer and closer. A reminder of what I am looking for, a man, interesting and with a business or good job, his own property, a man of means that I can settle down with and live a comfortable life.

What do I know of him? He does tick some of these boxes. I know his favourite colour is blue, though what effect that has on the price of fish I don't know! He likes cooking, as do I, so there is a mutual interest, his favourite food being duck.

For once, my navigation takes me almost directly to him, or should I say his business, a shop in the outskirts of town, an electrical repair shop. I park the car and, here goes, enter through the shop door. Deserted – this is a good start. I call out, "Hello? Hello?" hoping someone, preferably him, would answer.

And indeed a voice from the back says, "Hi," and, "is that you, Gill?"

"Yes," I reply.

"Come through to the back," he says, and a bit apprehensively I go into his workshop behind the main shop. Benches with electrical goods on, a couple of TVs on, a bit gloomy, but I'm here so here goes.

He appears from the back of the workshop, tall, six-two, six-three, thin, a good crop of hair on him, and wears glasses. If I were to tell you he was ruled by his daughter, long, thin and battered, fish finger.

Yes, the guy in front of me, Tom, was just a normal-looking, average guy. A friendly greeting, a quick peck on the cheek and offering me a seat, we started to chat and get to know each other better over a cup of coffee. As my first date, my intention was for this to last an hour or so before we went our separate ways, and I could then consider in my own privacy whether to go on to date two. It was nearing his lunch hour, so he asked if I wanted something to eat, and he would nip out to the local fish and chip shop and get whatever I wanted. This he did, though I don't know why but it was me who paid, and as I tucked into my sausage, we chatted more on mutual interests, which looked as if cooking was the bait. My time limit was drawing to an end and I was ready to wind my way home, so we exchanged pleasantries, and after seeing me to my car, another quick kiss, we went our separate ways. A nice kiss, nothing sloppy about that, a positive. My thoughts as I drove – I think if he wants to, then I will see him again. He seems very interesting, had kindly said I looked better than in my picture, and a little flattery always goes a long way. A good start to this net thing!

We had each other's phone numbers, just in case I had got lost on the way there, so having broken the ice, we decided that we would like to keep the communication going. It was natural now to continue by phone, be able to hear each other, and move the young relationship forward. Through these conversations, we had decided that we would like to meet again, and he invited me over one evening; he would cook for me, our mutual interest. So, now a new destination as I had to find my way to his house, but this accomplished, we settled down for our first 'date' proper. He had a nice house which he shared with his teenage daughter. It would appear that she ruled the roost as she monopolised the living room, us confined to the kitchen. A slight drawback for me as I did not want to inherit a family, I had done my maternal bit. Early days, let's see where this goes.

We sit in the kitchen chatting while he prepares the meal, duck, his favourite. He tells me he is thinking of moving his workshop here into the house, it would save a lot on the rent of the shop.

In this house, how many freezers are there? Five in total at the moment. He is a hoarder, and would go to the shops, supermarkets, and buy up all the food they were selling off cheap at the end of the day, bring it home and freeze it. If he had filled all this freezer space, then rather than stopping buying more food, he would just go out and buy another freezer, so not saving himself any money at all. He also had three vans parked outside his detached house, and his estate car, though only one of the vans was taxed. Add to that the piles and piles of wood, pallets, logs that were also in front of the house waiting to be used in his wood burner. Yes, a collector. No, I was right first time, a hoarder.

Well, I can say he was a good cook, the duck was cooked perfectly for me and it was a really nice meal over a glass of wine, and good conversation as we dismantled the barriers between us, which weren't that high, and we started to look forward to developing a relationship between ourselves.

When it was time to leave, it was a very nice cuddle and smooch before I returned back home, and yes, we would be seeing each other again.

Why did I think this may be the man? Well, he had property, a business though only small, we had similar interests, and he was very presentable. My one reservation – the daughter. As I have already said, I have had my own family and now felt this was my time, not time to look after someone else's kids. I hope that doesn't sound selfish, but it is time to enjoy myself, especially if it is with the man of my life, and I didn't want anything to interfere with that. I didn't want to become a step-mum.

Our relationship is developing. Frequent telephone calls, I like to speak to him every day, and texts, lots of! The road to Stoke is becoming a familiar path for me now as I get in my little car and tootle over to Tom's, trying to spend more time together and develop our common interests. But all the time the daughter would rule the roost, her watching television or playing games in the living room while we would be confined to the kitchen. You could set your clock by it, at the time the shops were closing he would nip out and see what cut-price bargains were going down in the local supermarket, and then bring them home to put in one of the freezers.

We would spend evenings cooking together, though at times I would take it upon myself to batch cook, whether it be pork, or lamb, or beef, just to get rid of some of the collections of meat in the freezers, some of which were getting to be museum pieces, and some with quite a lot of freezer burn which I would have to trim off, and discard. Typical of a hoarding man, I thought, but despite the freezers we were enjoying each other's company more and more. Cooking soirees, sometimes a stroll down the street to his local; life was becoming quite fun.

To save these constant journeys, it became a natural progression that we reached the stage where he asked me to stay over for nights. Separate bedrooms, so no hanky panky. This allowed us to enjoy long weekends together, with the freezers. We would cook, and daughter would come into the kitchen, fill her belly, then ponce off back into the sitting room, leaving us with the washing up, and a couple of chairs. She would dress up in the most outlandish costumes, looking more than a bit of a tart, but Tom would say nothing and just let it wash over his head. When she eventually would slope off to bed, we could have the sitting room at last and get down to some serious kissing and cuddling on the sofa.

So what of the net now? My rule is that I am not going to see anyone else while I am going out with one person. A pity perhaps, as this site is costing me money, and that perfect, that specimen fish may still be lurking out there in this pool of men. But I have to be fair to him who I am seeing, and not complicate my life. It may become a double life, juggling with too many dates, and fitting in work as well. Different sites have different mechanisms for hiding, while still being on the site with your profile, but I press a button that means until I reactivate it, then I won't see any messages sent to me. At the moment I am unavailable, and Tom has my full attention.

Cooking certainly was what we did most together, both mucking in together, preparing different parts of the meal, and it all coming together for a successful gourmet night.

At last, one night, daughter had gone out for the evening and a sleepover at a friend's house, so we were alone. Yes, we even had use of the front room, and it was after one of our meals that we were able to settle down in front of the fire on the settee, cuddle up together, and get down to some serious snogging. A warm feeling, in the light of the burning logs, as we were able to enjoy the feel of each other's bodies without the worry of being disturbed. Hands started to explore parts that hadn't been felt before as our embrace became more intimate. I think this is going a bit further than a cuddle! As time progressed, clothing started to be loosened, and it only seemed right that the belt holding his trousers up should be loosened, and that the object which seemed to be stirring beneath should be released. Hands were exploring me, my covered breasts, and that place I keep secret, my womanhood.

What appeared out of his pants, well, I can best describe as a new 12H pencil – long, very long, but also very thin, and certainly looked like there was some lead in it. It was not long before this snake, this pencil, was working its way through my bush and entering my inner sanctum. Not that comfortable on the settee, but those carnal pleasures of sex, making love, begin, work their way up into, well I can't say a frenzy, but yes, a messy climax as he comes inside me. Me, I may have hoped for a little more, not in length of pencil, but certainly in terms of time and satisfaction, but he is spent and as he lies back on the settee, and his implement rapidly diminishes back into its pencil case, a barrier has come down. Not naked sex, but we have done it. Where will this take us now? Time for bed, but it will still be me in the spare room, and him in his own.

But, it will now be a natural progression, as I won't sleep with anyone in their own bed until we have enjoyed each other's bodies, that I can now go into his bed knowing what to expect. There is no pressure from him but I am comfortable with this now.

Time passes by; we have been seeing each other for a few weeks now, cooking together, going down the local, and now sleeping together. Things seem to be progressing along fine. He has his attributes, the business, the property, and he is pleasant company, but all my spare time from work is going over there. I hope we are not getting in a bit of a rut.

Christmas is approaching and Tom suggests it would be good to have a weekend in Birmingham. We could get a train in and stay over in a hotel as he collects vouchers, so should be able to pick up a bargain easily. The hoarder in him again, look after the pennies, you know the rest. Sounds like a good plan, we will do it, something to look forward to.

Sex is going okay, but I would only score it at five out of ten, I could be satisfied a lot more. Our kissing and cuddling downstairs would sometimes progress to a quick bonk on the floor, as that long pencil scribbled its lead inside me, but never a prolonged climatic session, usually foreshortened by him as once he was spent, he would roll off and that would be it. Me, I was hoping for more, but would have to be satisfied with what I had got.

Time to go to Birmingham, a short train journey arriving at New Street, and a short walk to our hotel to check into our room. The German Market is quite traditional, lots of stalls selling Christmas knickknacks, decorative candles, decorations and crafts, and it was nice to walk round hand in hand looking at the fare. When dark falls, it takes on a different atmosphere as it becomes more a social event, friends meeting up to enjoy a drink or two together, and tuck into a German sausage or two. There was only Tom and I, but that didn't mean we couldn't enjoy our own sausage, and tuck into the Glutwein, very warming in this cold winter air, and very moreish too. It gives a romantic feeling, us wrapped up in our gloves, warm coats, and scarfs, walking arm in arm, our frosted breath in front of us, enjoying the ambience of this joyous time of year.

Perhaps time to go back to the hotel to finish our evening with a bit of rampant ardour. A drink to take up to the room with us, and we are soon undressing each other, as the sheets awaited our arrival. We kiss and cuddle, start to envelop each other's bodies, entwined, rolling from one side of the bed to the other. My temperature is rising, my body needs to be entered. I'm rampant, wanting to satisfy my insatiable appetite for sex, for making love.

I lay back, legs apart, waiting to be taken, to be pleasured, to be his. Expectantly I wait, and wait as he fumbles under the sheets. Surely he knows where I am. Come over because I want to come, and come soon. But, there seems to be a problem, Houston! All this fumbling, what's going on? And then he mounts me, pleasures me briefly, very briefly, as that 12H pencil seems to have softened to a 6B, and no lead. I'm disappointed, he a little embarrassed, and so the evening didn't quite reach the climax I had hoped for. All we could do was lay in each other's arms and drift off to sleep, me dreaming of being taken by a colossus, and if I cried out in my sleep, in was from the pleasures running through my mind.

The morning saw us walking the canals, visiting the old Post Office, and then it was time to go home. Back in Stoke the next night, and when we went to bed, again this fumbling started before our naked bodies met in the centre of the bed. There is a problem, Tom can't keep it up as well as he used to. This fumbling is him trying to entrap his privates in a rubber band, to help his member, his penis, to engorge and enter me long and straight. It would seem the ravages of time have created a little problem downstairs, erectile dysfunction.

Chastity belt! Where did that pop up?

He was obviously embarrassed and hoped in the future that part of our foreplay could be me popping him in rubber at the appropriate moment, it would make it a less sensitive issue for him if it became a natural process for me to do. Never said anything about this when I was told the birds and the bees – help! I hope this doesn't mean I will be searching the path after the postman has been, looking for those discarded rubber bands, they drop everywhere.

This may throw a spanner in the works, we will see.

He did introduce me to a website, Love Honey, which had an array of gorgeous sexy lingerie, as well as toys to enjoy ourselves with (and rubber bands and chastity belts – there it is again!). For me, I acquired a gorgeous black body stocking, nicely ribboned down the front… and crotchless. I hope to have some fun in this.

This problem down below did evoke some discussion between us, but we would persevere with me applying the 'band aid' at the appropriate time, to take some of the pressure off Tom (though the pressure was needed in his cock), to ease his embarrassment and to involve myself more in the process of helping him to satisfy himself, and subsequently me. Our sex some days would be okay-ish, other times, more than a little disappointing for me, but I had to try and hide that from him, or he would be more uptight about it. Not quite what I had envisaged. I know it is more and more a problem in older men, but that wasn't going to give me satisfaction. With the enjoyment I hope to get out of sex, and I love it, obviously I am disappointed and can only feel for men with this problem who are continually disappointed with their efforts – utter frustration. Perhaps I should check it out on the net, perhaps those little blue pills would help.

Winter progressed and as spring approached, Tom asked me if I would like to go down to London with him to stay with some old friends of his. This would be nice, a change of scenery, relaxation, and a chance to get him out of his own environment and forget his problem.

A long weekend was planned, going down by car, the taxed one, after work on Friday night, and coming back on Sunday. No driving for me – great! Not the back and forwards journey to Stoke.

Just a small suitcase would suffice, and my make-up bag, should be ample to see me through the weekend okay. Even on a Friday afternoon, and he did shut up shop a little early so we could get away, the journey wasn't too bad once we had got past Birmingham, and our destination in North London greeted us in the early evening. A basement apartment in a crescent looked a lovely setting, as we were welcomed in by Dave and Alice. Long-time friends of Tom's, happily married for many years, and like us, in their fifties. They settled us down with a glass of wine after our journey. They had times to catch up on with each other, but tried to involve me as often as possible, so were wonderful company for me in this new environment. Alice retreated to the kitchen to prepare our supper, a quick pasta dish, so I went with her and left the men to talk about whatever men talk about.

Over a pleasant meal the four of us chatted on through the night until it was bedtime, but it had been a long day so it would just be a kiss and a cuddle as we shared his friends' spare bed.

Saturday saw us up for breakfast, and then off to do some exploring, see some shops, a walk in the park, one of those nice days that London is nice for. We filled our time easily, a lunchtime drink in the local, and a little nap in the afternoon.

Our hosts had invited another couple of friends round for a more formal dinner party that evening, John and Anne, not a couple but were friends themselves, and together we would make a nice six. John turned out to be a lovely man, very interesting, and over the course of the evening paid me a lot of attention. Interestingly I warmed to him, and responded in kind, laughing, joking with him. Perhaps I gave him a little too much attention, but Tom didn't notice. Over a lovely four-course meal the evening passed us by, plenty of wine consumed, until it was time to call an end as John and Anne bid their goodnights to us. As he departed, he gave me a little peck on the lips (that was nice), saying we would all do it again sometime soon, if we were back down from the sticks.

A quick chat with Dave and Alice, and it was time for us to turn in as well. A tiring but very enjoyable day and evening, it was fun. I got into bed, and was wondering with my interest in John that perhaps Tom wasn't for me, if my eyes were wandering towards other men. Food for thought! Chastity belts. There it is again! We were lying in each other's arms, and no, I hadn't imagined it, it had come up (and let's face it, it was all that was going to come up tonight). Tom had mentioned chastity belts, or more specifically chastity cages, COCK CAGES. Cock cages (like a lobster pot with him within!). Where is this going? At least he is talking of something for him, but what is all this about? For the time being, I will let this pass. "Goodnight Tom, sleep well" I whispered in his ear, then a kiss.

'If you get up in the night, please don't wake me,' perhaps seemed an inappropriate comment. I snuggled down and drifted off to sleep, and couldn't deny that a little dream of John doing something to me which Tom couldn't may just have caused the odd sigh of satisfaction in my slumbers. Hope I wasn't talking in my sleep.

We journeyed back to Stoke after breakfast the following day, not quite so chatty as on the journey down, but all things considered, it had been a lovely weekend. It had, though, left a few thoughts in my mind. Was I beginning to doubt this was heading in the direction I was looking for? A pensive drive back home from Stoke, perhaps we are coming to a crossroads.

My trip over the following weekend, after an arduous few days at work, and we resumed where we had left off, that night cooking a meal together before popping down the local and then back home for a kiss and cuddle on the settee. Time for bed, and as we covered ourselves under the sheets, our lovemaking recommenced. It was semi-exciting but all the time in the back of my mind was the rubber band under my pillow, when to put it on. Was this really how I envisaged satisfying myself? Well, each other, but especially me. *Ping*, it was on and he briefly entered inside me, but it wasn't going to last long before this droopy thing slipped out, leaving me unfulfilled, AGAIN.

We lay back, a little tension in the air from the

disappointment experienced by us both. After a short period of silence, Tom opened his mouth to speak, and out came chastity cages (there they are again). He thought that if he wore one of these cock cages, it would turn him on, and solve his problem.

His idea was that we should meet up and when I would put it on him, lock his cock up for safe keeping until at another meeting, I would unlock it and remove it from him. I would be the key holder, so I would have total control over him

At my age, and he now expects me to become a dominatrix? Me, a young girl! I could leave it a week, six weeks if I wanted, my total control, and if I desired, I could be a right bitch over it, but then perhaps that it is what he wanted. We could wine and dine each other, he remaining entrapped under lock and key, until I said, 'Drop 'em, it's coming out to play.' What was he expecting, that after a period of solitary confinement (and not being an expert on these things, God knows how he's going to pee), release THE BEAST? I would unleash his cock, which would make a bolt for it, looking for somewhere moist and dark to hide for a good time – my fanny!

And what happens if I lose the key? I'm not taking him to the local locksmith. I would have to admit that I found all this a bit unnerving, me in total control; me, his madam, he my slave. All very weird. I like my sexy lingerie, but this... I find myself reaching for the messages button on my fishing site. Who else in the net would like a bite? Was I shocked? I don't think so, but like other things, our relationship had gone more than a little limp, and just petered out as we just didn't seem to meet up or speak very much anymore.

That was Tom, that was an experience, and I don't have nightmares about those cock cages.

Back on the net.

Nibbles: A carp introduced into other waters, but interfering with the ecosystem!

On goes the computer again, finding my dating site again. Let's see what fish there are in the sea now that my bait has been out of the water for some time. My profile would still have been on the site since going out with Tom, but I would not have been able to read any messages for me, as I had taken that option. There will be some I was chatting to before, pre-Tom as it were, and had informed that I was now seeing someone (Tom), some who I had chatted to for some time, some just a short while. To be honest, at this stage of my 'fishing' career, I would have to admit I was more than a little addicted to chatting online, and would spend far too long doing it while I could have occupied my time better doing other things, but how desperate was I to find that lifelong partner I was looking for. But, I suppose in my naïve state at this time, and wanting to get my money's worth on this site, I spent hours chatting to different men, to reassure myself that if we did date then I knew as much as I could about him.

Dick was someone I had been chatting to over a long period of time before I started going out with Tom. What did I know about him? A man of similar age to me, living in a council house in town, which he had had the opportunity to buy, but had turned down the chance. He had added a conservatory, and lived there alone with his dog.

Having chatted for some time online, we did decide to meet up. We both wanted fun and a relationship, and there seemed to be possibilities here, from what I could see from our interactions.

We decided to meet in the local town park, a large expanse of parkland with lakes, walks, trees, and a large play area for children, situated close to the town centre. I waited on a park bench for his arrival, knowing roughly how he should look if his profile picture was accurate. He came into view, yes, probably slightly older than myself, but very upright, dressed smartly in shirt and trousers, with a yellow jumper hanging around his shoulders. I was impressed, liked what I saw. Having met up, we went to a café on the edge of the park, to chat and get further acquainted. His hobby was walking the dog, which he did twice daily, keeping him fit, and he did look good for it. He was semi-retired, at the moment fighting a wrongful dismissal claim, and was expecting to get a lump sum pay-out at some stage. Sounds good to me (though please don't think that I am a gold digger).

While enjoying our coffee, I did notice his teeth. I have a thing about teeth in that they have to look good and well cared for, no halitosis, and commendably though not the full set, they were clean and obviously cared for. We really did enjoy each other's company, and so decided that we would meet up again the next day, same time, same place. Again, a thoroughly enjoyable couple of hours spent in his company, getting to know him better, about his past and what makes him tick. He was divorced, but had a daughter close by, and grandchildren. He was very nice, and so when time came to go our separate ways, we agreed to meet again the following day. I was happy that this relationship seemed to be going along the right path, no pressure, enjoying each other's company as we found out more about each other.

Then again, another meeting the next day, by which time I had been round to his house, met the daughter, the neighbours, and all seemed good. We hadn't slept together but things were progressing well.

And then he was busy; I didn't see him for a few days, and heard very little. Pause, then there he was again, and we would meet up again, day after day, visit his place, go out for meals, to the pub, and have a lot of fun.

Silence again, he was busy. I would wait patiently and then he would be in contact again, and we would see each other, again have fun together, enjoying ourselves. But still my body remained uninvaded.

It was on one day when I was visiting after another short period of silence that when I was walking up the garden path, the neighbour, Rita, who I had got to know quite well, stopped me and asked me if I would like to come in for a cuppa in the near future – she would like to have a chat. I would like that, and went in the next day.

She sat me down, and over a cup of coffee said, "I like you, but don't want to see you get hurt. Dick has a married woman around at least twice a week, and she stays overnight. What's more, he had even been seeing this woman while he and his wife were still together, happily married."

Well! You can imagine my reaction. Those busy days of silence, does this explain all? He is having a nibble here and a nibble there if he can!

What shall I do? Confront him straight away. So on entering his house, I have it out straight away. He denied all of this to start with, but he can't deny what Rita has seen, and yes, hands up, guilty as found. "Get rid of her if you want to see me. Finish it now or I am gone," I tell him, and storming out, I ask Rita to keep me in the loop.

Oh, what disappointment again.

The next day Dick phoned me. "She's gone, I promise you she has gone," he says.

I did like him, I liked him a lot, so I did agree to meet up with him again. We resumed as if nothing had happened, with him becoming even more attentive of me, more caring, and nothing was too much trouble for him to do for me. Once my headlight bulb in the car had stopped working so he went off to Halfords to get another one, and then fitted it for me. I had returned, and we had more fun times, though I still didn't sleep with him as I didn't altogether trust him after our previous incident, and a relationship in my eyes has to be built on trust.

And so we continued seeing each other, more meals, nights at the pub, walking the dog together. Yes, we were having a good time together, and it was fun. Then history repeated itself again, as Rita stopped me after about four weeks and told me this lady was back round again. Naturally I was devastated that he had been unfaithful again, and seemed to have an obsession with bonking this married woman. What could I do? Only finish it again. That was it. If he did get rid of her, he could try contacting me, and I would see how I felt. Thus, we parted again.

It was winter now, and my family were also going through a crisis. My granddaughter had been ill for some time with a rare form of cancer, and sadly had died in a local hospice. My family came together in a period of great loss to us all; we were devastated that a young life had been so cruelly nipped in the bud.

We decided as an act of remembrance and as a token of thanks to the hospice that we would organise and carry out a sponsored walk, to raise money for them and as a lasting memory for us. So on a cold winter's day we set off from the local community centre on a five-mile walk to the top of a local hill, a landmark in the area, down the other side, and then to return to our vehicles back at the centre. It was freezing, and after an hour and a half I was so cold I just couldn't go on. What could I do? Ring Dick, I thought, and see if he was free to come and pick me up.

Of course, he would do anything for me despite his indiscretions, and he soon arrived to take me out of my misery. So kind.

Yes, you guessed, we did start seeing each other again. I'm turning into a bit of a yoyo here! He reassured me that his married lady had parted, he had packed her belongings into a bin bag and sent her on her way. Certainly some of the evidence, embroidery etc., which was in hindsight obviously hers, was now gone. A fresh beginning? We shall see.

There was little trust from me now, so I would have to admit that I did go online again, started chatting again to other men, but hoped that he really had given her up for me. I got to know his daughter and her children over this time, really got to know them really well, and became very fond of them.

But history had to repeat itself again. He saw her again, slept with her again. How can he keep doing this to me when he says he is so devoted to me? The best thing that had ever happened to him in his life. Rita told me I was far too nice for him; he didn't deserve me. Was that any consolation? His daughter found out too, and was also livid, bollocked her dad big time, and threatened to go round to this woman's husband and tell all unless he sorted it all out. People were getting hurt – me, mostly.

Again, and under this much pressure, he did draw an end to it and settled down to a solitary life, though he did keep chatting online and would ring me quite often. I really, really didn't trust him, but did keep the lines of communication open, as I said earlier, he couldn't do enough for me, would do anything, nothing was too much trouble. I was wonderful, he worshipped the ground I walked on, please, please let's see each other again.

Reluctantly, I agreed and one evening, some four months and a lot of heartaches since first meeting him, I did go round again. A quiet night in was all that was planned, and I knew he had wanted to bonk me from the start, but tonight I was going to be naughty. Let's face it, I hadn't had it for weeks and really could do with a serious bonk.

We settled down in front of the TV to watch a film,

but knowing he had a small TV on the wall in his bedroom, I suggested we could go upstairs and cuddle up in bed and watch the film there. Upstairs we went, slipped into our night things (and even in his PJs you could see he had looked after his body), and with a glass of wine we continued to watch the film.

But tonight was on my terms, as I cuddled into him, and as the film progressed started to caress his member. Well, what there was of it, certainly had seen a lot bigger. He wanted me, and had soon risen to the occasion; he was gagging for me. Fuck the film, I had him on his back, undid the cords of his PJ bottoms and there stood his manhood. I climbed aboard and I rode him, and I rode him, and I rode him until saddle sore was setting in. He was spent, literally, exhausted, didn't know what had hit him, but his appetite was whetted for more.

There mate, now you know what you have been missing with all this fucking about. You could have had me but now it is too late. I don't trust you one bit. I think perhaps that he didn't want a serious relationship, just a bit of fun. He wanted his bake and the fish, so he could bonk any woman he fancied, including me, but no way Jose, I don't trust you at all, and that is it for me.

Yes, I was naughty, but I had satisfied a need while proving a point. How he wanted me now. But if I hadn't got on top, I don't think it would have been that much fun. Average cock, and average sexual partner. She can have him.

Time passed by, as I went online again, and started seeing other men. He would follow me on Facebook, and make sarcastic comments about me seeing other men. Always there was a comment, especially when I entered one very serious relationship with a man I was besotted with. Sly remark, silly comment, but without fail, always something. It got to the extent that my daughter, also a keen Facebook user, at one stage asked if I thought he was stalking me. Fair comment. He had plenty of time to contemplate, after being ridden so hard, what he was missing.

His fault.

He truly was a wonderfully thoughtful and kind man, and that part I was looking for.

I did go out with him again a couple of years later, just once, when he took me out for a meal, a pub lunch. But that debonair, smart man of before was gone. It transpired he had been taken in and scammed by another woman looking for his wealth, taking a considerable amount of his money. A harsh world! Here he was in scruffy jeans, and when he opened his mouth... those teeth, or lack of, and the halitosis. No, not for me. I have to go, go hungry. Goodbye Dick, and this time it really is.

But I hope the memory of me on top of you, Dick, lasts forever and comes back to haunt you, more times than you ever came with me!!

Fillets

So that was Dick, and yes, I had been looking on the net again over the later part of our 'relationship', chatting to a few men.

One of these was a guy called Harry, and I had been talking to him for a while online but now I was available again, thought it may be good to pursue this line, again looking for fun, but a steady relationship (as the dating pages say), hopefully leading to more.

The usual beginning, meeting up in a coffee shop in town, and having a pleasant chat over a couple of Americanos. What had he got to tell me? He was younger than me, about seven years, but I am a mere girl, used to going with younger men so that should be no obstacle. He wasn't long out of a marriage; sadly his wife had suffered from cancer, but that hadn't stopped him having a little dabble in other waters while she was still alive. These men! Now he shared a flat with another man, a friend, that is. Even while we were chatting an older lady walked past us, giving us no attention, but Harry said he had been out with her, though her photo online didn't show her as old as she was. I said I hoped mine was a true reflection of me, though I don't take a good photograph. Is this guy, Harry, going to turn out to be Don Juan?

We passed the time chatting over our coffee, must have been getting cold by the time we had finished it, but on a time basis it was good value for money. It was getting towards late afternoon, but it was pleasantly warm so we went for a walk, a gentle stroll before finding a park bench where we seated ourselves. Hey, this guy isn't backwards in coming forwards, as soon we were kissing and cuddling. Wow! This takes me back, back to my teens, feeling like a sixteen-year-old out on her first date, having a snog when no-one else is around. Eventually we untangled ourselves and it was time to go our separate ways.

Our first date seemed to have done well. No, let's just call it a meeting, a coming together. What else had I found out? He had a daughter, away working in Europe somewhere. He was of average height but well-built, looked after himself, and went to the gym regularly. Very well dressed – even in casual clothes, he was fit.

We arranged to go out again, the cinema this time, and then the pub. But he didn't drink, perhaps because he was a fitness fanatic, but throughout all our times together, on reflection, he never had an alcoholic drink. More walks in the park; on one occasion, engrossed in each other as we relived our youth, snogging on another bench, we forgot about time and nearly got locked in. We just got out before the gates were locked. I can't imagine climbing over the fence at my age, as I carried one or two more pounds than I ought to.

He had been an engineer, but hadn't been happy in his work and so had decided to take a completely different direction, and decided feet were for him. He studied hard and qualified as a foot practitioner, and now enjoyed going house to house plying his new trade.

We had seen a lot of each other over our first fortnight, and I asked him if he could do my feet.

"No problem," Harry said. "I will come round and do them for you."

He brought his chair in at my house, and sat me down to prepare for my session. He started, but to my embarrassment I ended up getting cramp in my feet, so the session had to be abandoned. That had never happened to him before.

He had made it plain that he wasn't really looking for a serious relationship right from the off, but this guy was in my eyes a bit of a hunk, and I rather fancied him. I suppose I was seeing if I could persuade him that a relationship with me would be good, but I was also a little in awe of him, being younger than me and so fit in all aspects, that I couldn't understand why he wanted to be with me. After Tom and Dick, and other events in my life, I suppose that my self-esteem was on the low side.

But if the foot session didn't come off. Well, we had a sofa and we weren't going to be disturbed. Oh, to be sixteen again, but that didn't stop us as we kissed and cuddled, under the dim lighting of my front room. Fumbling fingers undid zips, buttons, and there we were in each other's arms, with not a lot on.

As his hands caressed my breasts, I stroked his body, down, down, until reaching those areas where I expected a big response. But what's this? As my hand went further below his waist, bare, completely bare skin. I knew he shaved his head, was completely bald (from shaving), but now I find there is not a hair on his body, that he shaves literally all over. He must be proud of his body!

Not me, I've have ever since giving birth at seventeen years old, been very self-conscious about my body, and hated being seen naked. Body image, those stretch marks from pregnancy that have remained with me. Lights out and at a push I could cuddle up naked, but not with them on. As I have got older, I now find I enjoy having wonderful sexy attire for making love. It's still an issue for me to be naked, but if I am dressed in silk or wonderful basque sets and flowing silk, I feel sexy and confident, a different woman.

That was a bit of a shock, but whatever, each to his own. Our foreplay intensified; he knew how to arouse a woman and his hands were certainly having that effect on me. What I had in my hand also seemed primed for action, and before long we were as one, with him deep inside me, thrusting powerfully with that well-tuned body. He came, I came, that was wonderful.

Then a cuddle, he dressed, and was gone.

That is how our relationship continued from then on. He would come over to me, and we would make love. Long, passionate, dirty sex.

He was so good in bed, knew what he wanted and how to pleasure me, to take me to the heights of passion. It would be no issue for him to go down on me, and I loved it, a real way to arouse me in our foreplay. We pleased each other greatly, exploring each other's breaking points, wandering hands, exploring hands, over each other's bodies, and within.

All was good in our sex, though he still preferred to try and get me to be naked. In his eyes, anything worn in bed just gets in the way.

This was one hell of a guy, and I really fancied his body, but there was no way he wanted a relationship. However much I tried to show him what a fantastic partner I could be for him, it was not going to happen. Reluctantly, I decided that I wasn't going to go out with him, and it was time to renew my fishing licence, press the button, and re-enter the pool.

There we are, back on the net again.

But then, one day, Harry rang me to ask how I was. I was fine, I told him. Straight to the point, he asked me, "Are you getting any?"

"No," I said.

"I'll come over for a coffee," he said, "see you in half an hour."

There was a knock on the door, and there he stood.

"Come in. Coffee? One ball or two? I mean, sugar."

We were at it again, cuddling, fondling. Fuck the coffee, we have some serious fucking to do! We explored each other's weaknesses, found different ways to arouse each other.

Oral sex was a pleasure for both of us; he was a big boy and to wrap my lips around that, especially if he was down on me – bliss. I had learnt to climax again, and how I did, big time.

That is how we went on. If we were not seeing anybody, and we needed some company (sex), then we would just phone up and arrange to meet up again at mine, and yes, we would bonk again and again.

He was so good, gave me confidence in myself and my body to the extent that I could have made love to him completely naked in maximum daylight. He knew what he was about, how to arouse me and how he wanted to be aroused. At times a bit apprehensive about what he wanted, sticking my finger up his arse wasn't quite my thing but if he liked it, eyes closed, here goes. Didn't enjoy that, but he certainly did. Reminded me a bit of my friend who is a farm vet!

A great lover, but not the man I was looking for to share the rest of my life. A shame, but time to move on, but with the knowledge that he would be my friend with benefits. A good, non-complicated way of getting a nibble whenever I wanted. I never did get him to like sexy undies (but I know a man who does), but he was a very attentive man. We enjoyed a good time, satisfying, and he gave me a lot of confidence in myself again.

There we are, I have come to the end of my paid subscription. Has it been worth it? I certainly have had some experiences. Rubber bands, deceit, motivation in myself, very good sex – a lot... and how could one forget the COCK CAGE? What a blessing the keys are not my responsibility.

Tom, a man of means, property, a house owner with some really nice friends (and no, I'm not going to mention it again).

Dick, a deceitful tall bugger, but so attentive, caring, would do anything for me (but alas now, the teeth).

And Harry, I shall say no more other than the satisfaction he could bring to a girl – me.

Between them, put them all together and you will have my specimen fish. IF ONLY Tom had had Harry's Dick.

Fish on.

BACK TO SPAWNING GROUNDS

Life had taken me around the world, to the Far East, to Australia, as well as different parts of Europe and the United Kingdom. But had life been kind to me? A happy childhood, though Mum and Dad were divorced before my teens, doing everything fun that kids do. Married early, probably too early, but having two wonderful children, divorce, remarriage, another child, and it was here that I saw the world with some wonderful experiences as a military wife. But things don't always work out for the best, and if yet another marriage has come to an end, I have reached supposedly the best years of my life, but there is something missing in my life.

Australia brought me back to England where the inklings of happiness looked to be appearing, firstly through a distant Scandinavian relationship, seeing each other when we could, and then taking the plunge and moving over there to buy a house and for a new beginning with a new man. If this was the start of my relationship with the web, our first contact was over gaming, a hobby also enjoyed by other members of my family – a bond between us all. If for a while, life was wonderful, enjoying the wonderful scenery of the Scandinavian lakes. It was too good to be true love, but the effects of living with an alcoholic slowly started to dawn on me, to the extent that life and love came harder and harder to the point where I could not cope anymore.

The break was made, and if a lot of my life savings were lost in this failed relationship, once again, it was time to start again. Leaving the lands of the north, it was back to England once again to start yet again.

My profession gave me the financial stability to be solvent, a career that means I am always in demand. That gave me a good footing to launch myself again.

Like any salmon returning to breed in its own spawning ground, I headed back to the town I came from to have some familiarity around me. Family, one of my children, my mother and stepfather, stepbrother and sisters.

But, I want love, and I want romance. I have passed my fiftieth year and I need to start anew. But when you have been away from your comfort surrounds for many years, when you return, you often find things have changed. Friends from your early days are now married, have their own lives and have moved on. I have lost all my old contacts; again, they have moved on to carry on with their own lives here and afar. I have a comfort zone back home, but yes, I feel like a fish out of water.

I need to meet people, I need to reel in that big fish out there somewhere who I know is perfect for me, my specimen fish. But how do I catch him? Through muddy waters, I need to cast my line, spread my net, then reel him in. But how, but how? I am a gorgeous lady looking for love, but what streams can I follow to find my man? Can I walk into a pub on my own? Can I be that obvious that I am on the pull? Would I look desperate for love? Are there too many sharks out there looking for a vulnerable woman? No, this is not me and I will have to find other ways to find my catch. For the older woman it can be difficult to meet a prospective mate – it can be a very daunting process. I have spoken to other ladies who have gone on sites, agencies, but were too scared to follow anything through, often being charged money to access 'the chance of meeting Mr Right.'

Since the start of mankind, man and woman have paired off to reproduce, and in closer times marry and live happy ever after. I have had two goes by the conventional method of boy meets girl, go out, marry and live happy ever after. I wish! So where to start this time round?

There has been a catalogue of ways to create meetings. Dating agencies, lonely heart columns in magazines and papers, etc., etc., singles clubs, and of course more recently the internet.

To say that I am a technophile would be an understatement. If anything is electronic I have to have it, and I mean anything!! So I am up to date on anything on my computer, try to have the most up to date phones, all the apps (alas not a 'find the perfect man' app), thrive on high-speed broadband – in fact it is a must for me. Social media, Facebook, Twitter, I am on them all the time. It therefore seems logical that this will be my chosen route of netting my fish.

But what is out there? Free sites, sites that charge. There are chat rooms, but are these full of paedophiles, and blokes wanting cybersex – a whole can of worms!

Match.com, a fee-charging site, or the free sites, Plenty of Fish, Badoo, or Oasis. They sound tempting, don't they? And the huge sites claiming they are local, having their own, e.g. Shropshire or Surrey dating. It is geared up to your area, so if you are looking for someone local, you will find them. So I would take the time to do a little research into how many sites there are, and then as to which I would use.

SETTING THE BAIT

Bubbly lady looking for long term relationship. I have dual nationality. Ask where from? I have been divorced seven years, and am looking for someone to spend the rest of my life with.

Six months in Australia, six months in the UK, can't be bad!

Interested? Let me know.

That's me. Now to get going, set myself up and get ready to prepare my catch, sort the tasty ones from those I will just throw back in. Trawling, angling, playing the sport, a-fishing I will go!

But first I have to decide where, and having done that, what am I after and what I am going to try and catch him with. New waters for me, but I am a confident girl, and I consider myself to be well versed in using the web, the net. So having made up my rules to safeguard myself, I hope I can navigate through the shoals of fish that hopefully come my way... and fingers crossed, I am going to catch a big one, the one that I am looking for.

Where do I start? There are many sites out there,

but I was a beginner. What did I know? To be honest, not a lot, but had heard of one site from talking to friends, and that was Match.com. This is where I decided to start. Out with the computer and I find their site. Soon I will be up and running. At this stage, I only knew of paid sites, not knowing there were free ones, but it was a start, the beginning of what I know now is a learning curve. If I knew then what I know now, life could have been a lot simpler and I could have saved myself a lot of heartache. Oh well, never too old to learn!

A paid site, so I have to pay a subscription which ties me in for six months. But basically, I found myself writing a profile of myself, above, and then going into an intense list of questions. Depending on the list of answers I give, the site then tries to match me up with someone who matches my profile, or may have ticked some of the boxes of interests I have put down, maybe only one. This match will also depend on what I am looking for – long-term relationship, friends, or dating. They have the information for their search, and through the wonders of science, they come up with the prospective man of my dreams. That's what I am hoping for anyway.

A two-way process, so at the same time, I will be coming up on men's searches, and it is from here that contact can be made.

I can begin sifting through them. Some I can rule out straight away, some of interest, others definite possibilities. I can delete the no's straight away, but will still remain on their search. I can only hope they don't become a pain in the arse.

The yesses, I'm on a paid site so I can talk to them,

message them through the site, and where we go from there is very much up to us.

Tom, Dick, and Harry, they were found on this site, and we have heard about them already.

I then found there were free sites, a whole multitude of them I now know of, where you can meet anyone who happens to be your genre. Sites for the older generation, for those who may wish to find a Russian lady, Oriental lady, SugarDaddy.com – a site for those rich blokes who may wish to have the attentions of a very young lady (and I know of one gentleman who used this site a lot locally, and dated many females. He was old enough to be their father, which was fine until his wife found out!). Gay sites, military sites, they are all out there somewhere, it's just a matter of what you are looking for.

The ones I heard about and thought I would give a try to were Badoo and Plenty of Fish, though it may have been chatting to a bloke on one of them that I found out about the other. Certainly Badoo was a lot less complicated to set myself up on; easier, I found, to use.

Again, I have to go through a registration process, and put my profile on again, so now I will try to be a little more forthcoming in what I shall say about myself, and what I am looking for.

I am a happy lady. I work hard and would like someone to share my life with. I have dual nationality, UK and Australian. When I retire, I would like to spend some time down under, a perfect solution to a good retirement. I would like to find a non-smoking man, or at least one who is looking to give up, who is solvent, even tempered, sociable, and tactile, holds a good conversation, and would like to spend some time in Oz. Not much to ask?

I think that rules most dragons out!

To continue:

I like to go out to the pub for a meal, or dress up to attend a Summer Ball, and a cuddle on the sofa is a must. Science fiction is one of my favourite subjects to watch on TV or film, and when I have time to read, I like James Patterson. I love my Kindle, I like gaming online, e.g. World of Warcraft. I also play Bridge, and love all types of music, Motown, Pop… although I find some Jazz can be baffling. That's me.

Looking for a man who is: -

Solvent

Not living with anyone as a partner,

Happy

Working.

Then there are lots of lists to choose from. What you like, food, cooking, music, hobbies, favourite holiday types and destinations, sports… lots and lots of options.

Things about myself:

Relationships: Single

Sexuality: Straight

Height: 5ft 4
Weight: Could be a pound or two lighter
Body type: Average
Eye Colour: Blue
Hair colour: Red
Living arrangements: Alone
Children: Grown up
Smoker: No
Drink: Yes, please
Language: English.

You can probably picture me now already.

My age is important as people will be looking for their 'mate' in a certain age range, and likewise for me. We will try forty-five to sixty-five years old, and see what that brings up.

There, most of my bait has been set. I just need to add photo of myself, to show myself to the world out there, and wait for the fellows to start chatting.

Only problem is, I hate, hate, hate having my picture taken, and more often than not don't even like any pictures anyone else has taken of me. I decided to do my make-up and using my camera, take a load of photos so that I could use them on my site. Ready, count to ten, then pose, flash, and job done, I hope. Of out of any ten photos I took, then perhaps one would be good enough, I considered, to use, or that I would be happy with. I took photos on my webcam whenever I was ready to go out, got my friends to take photos of me, but to be honest I was never happy with any I put on my site.

It became a common comment when I was up and running, that I looked much better than my photo, which was true, but a little bit of flattery never hurts to steal this girl's heart.

But the photo was very important to me, and I would never consider chatting to anybody unless there was a picture on his profile so I could get some idea of what he was like. More so, as I have said earlier, when I was able to recognise those false pictures, those old pictures, selfies in mirrors, distant images, those sneaky little bastards who had something to hide. Be it that they had two heads, were married, or already had a partner, and were looking just for a little extra on the side, there would definitely be something. They are all out there, trying to wheedle their way into your hearts and your mind, but at the end, only one person will get hurt and that will be me, or you. Yes, that photo of who I am chatting to was very important.

Press the button, profile loaded, I'm ready to go. Tackle in place, bait set, line out. I've chosen my stake, and am ready to cast into the wind, into the pool of men that will find a match with my profile. Exciting, apprehensive, and ever hopeful that what I am looking for is lurking somewhere in that deep, unknown pool.

The competition has begun, and as all good anglers, and I have enjoyed fishing in my time, both sea and course, I now have to wait patiently for a nibble. But on these free sites, no license needed to test your tackle here, there are plenty of fish just looking for the bait they desire. I have shown my interests; my hook is in the water and now my match fishing begins. Who has a similar taste in the bait I am dangling? How many will coincide with these? Surprisingly, there must be a lot of hungry little buggers out there because no sooner than I am live, my bait is in the water, than the nibbles start. Pictures of men and their profiles come up almost straight away. A net full already, if only real match fishing were that easy.

I can look at my leisure. No, don't like the look of that one so throw him back. This one? Yes, possibilities here. Mr Dace, too chubby. Mr Eel, he looks a bit slippery. Mr Perch, interesting. Mr Roach, looks smooth. Mr Bream, he may tip the scales. Mr Salmon, he's a dental surgeon. A mixed bag here to sort through and decide if I want to try and start chatting to them, exchanging messages as we try to find out about each other, what we have in common, our mutual interests.

Those in my net, I have a choice. In my early days online, three choices, but now only two. Onscreen, a heart, press for like; a cross, no, don't like this one so I can throw him back, and there used to be a 'maybe' but not anymore. Welfare, you can't keep one of these fish in your net indefinitely while you decide whether to take him home or throw him back.

So I can reduce the numbers in my net, but the exciting thing is, after seven days, my net fills again; another ten to go with what remains of last week's catch, and in another week, another ten, and then another. Therefore it was important to keep reducing my catch, so that I could remember who I would be talking to, when chatting online. Once a fish was thrown back, he couldn't take my bait again, unlike in the days of maybes when the greedy little buggers could come back for a second bite. Others if put back, could however reappear, as they had put several profiles of themselves on. Reject one and there he is next week as someone else. I had one of these especially who kept reappearing. Where are you, George the Mirror Carp?

It soon becomes obvious that some men don't bother to read your profile, just seeing a picture, and perhaps thinking, *I would like to have her.* Why did I bother to pour my dreams out, my hopes for the future, all on my profile, but then have to spend ages answering all these questions about myself that are already in print? The genuine men, I soon learnt that I could tell, because they had read about me, my profile, and so we would be able to converse about ourselves with the knowledge we already had of each other, getting into more personal detail. It made me think that this man was interested in me and straight away knew what I was looking for.

At times, I would find myself chatting to several men at the same time. They would, as individuals, think I was only speaking to them, but being an accomplished typist, it was easy to keep up with a conversation, except that my memory wasn't so hot, so occasionally could suddenly mix up a conversation with the wrong man. On a lot of dating sites, there is a note-taking section, so as I chatted I could write myself little notes, little reminders such as 'nice car', 'owns his own business', 'small children', 'naughty speak', so that when returning to a conversation another evening, my poor memory would be jogged as to where we were last time.

Nobody said it was easy, and perhaps this could be described as getting my line caught in the reeds, needing myself to untangle what was before me, but no probs, usually managed it and got my line back where I wanted, waiting for the nibble to turn into a bite. Fishing is fast coming back to me, and fast becoming a little bit addictive.

Chatting was never a problem for me; I'm not shy and certainly promote myself very well. I have plenty to say, and with my typing skills, can put a lot down quickly. Easy topics of conversation: How long divorced? Holidays, where do you like going to? Your favourite places, and what you like doing there, and that can tie in with my wish to spend time here in England, and in Oz.

And the conversations back, they could tell you a lot about the person you were chatting to, along with those false photos, which to me are a lie, and I hate lies. How often with these would their conversation start, "Hello sexy," or, "I like the larger lady." These men were usually trouble, but I would give them a chance to talk normal, if you like. But if they continued to escalate things, continued with the innuendos in the Text Box, asking questions like, "When was the last time you did it?" I would pretend to misunderstand. If he seemed nice or I thought I might fancy him, I might play along a bit, tease a bit, saying that's smutty talk. But a lot of them were trouble. Reject, throw them back in for some other unsuspecting angler.

This was match fishing, but there were also other

ways of trying to catch that male. Another option was to go onto 'Encounters'. Here, men wouldn't be quite such perfect matches, but the computer would find one or two common interests and flag up these men on your site. This was like trawling; my net was brimming overfull with the weight of fish, and it would take a lot of filleting to sort the good from the bad. A far wider choice, some good-looking, hunks, and some just downright ugly, but the same process of heart or cross, yes I like him, no I don't. I'm getting the hang of this now, and I can sift through a catch quite quickly.

It was perhaps looking through these encounters over time that I realised that the good-looking ones, were quite often flawed, old pictures, or just thought so highly of themselves that all they were interested in was getting me between the sheets. You began to realise that the 'matches', if they didn't look so good, it was often the case that they were a lot more genuine, and looking for the same thing as me – a long-term relationship.

The computer site also gave another couple of options, 'Favourites', and 'Superpowers', though I never used this one. If you had pressed 'heart' on a bloke, he stayed in your – my – matches until I threw him back, or chatted, maybe even saw him, and then found if there were grounds to go forward, so he stayed as a like. 'Encounters', I could also keep as a 'like', so I could have an ever-increasing bag, net, of fish to chat to.

Favourites allowed me to mark one, or several of these men, and this had two advantages. Firstly, he may actually be a favourite in that I actually thought there were strong possibilities of taking this forward. Secondly, it just acted as a bookmark so I could come back to him easily amongst my likes, and chat or whatever, without having to scroll through everyone again. This would often save a lot of time for me, more so when I was starting to get addicted to this online chatting.

With these 'favourites', it could be a two-way process. If he also had you as a favourite, then there was a definite match as far as the site was concerned. I would know if I had become someone's favourite, but would not know who that person was. I could pay on the site, to find who he was, squinting through blurred pictures to see if I recognised him from pictures that were on original profiles. A little detective work before I may commit this person to be a 'favourite' of mine, or not.

Lastly, 'Superpowers' allows you to look at these 'favourites' for free, but the price is that you have to open your Facebook to six friends for a week, the aim being that they will then join Badoo too, increasing the number of people available to match. For me, though I was really looking for Mr Right, I didn't want my friends to know that I was on a dating site, so 'Superpowers' was not for me, hence not using it.

That very much wraps up my setting the bait. I was ready to fish, and see what came my way.

But firstly…

THE RULES OF ANGLING

In any sport there have to be rules, and if I am to start big game fishing then I have to set out the criteria in which I am going to undertake this. As I have already said, I am past my fiftieth year, but have my looks, a sense of fun, am a good conversationalist, and have experienced a lot of the world. Different holidays, cruises, sun, the casinos of Las Vegas, a great variety of experiences to make me a woman of the world, which should make me very desirable when I find – catch – Mr Right. It would also be wrong not to say that I enjoy sex, but not with any Tom, Dick, or Harry out for a quick bonk and that's it (though Harry had his benefits).

With my experiences over the coming months and years, it certainly would be true to say that I have found myself more than a little naïve in this Internet Dating and what comes over on it.

For this reason, I therefore had to establish a set of rules to protect myself from whoever is out there, for my reputation and my welfare. Somewhere out there is someone special and I don't want to get hurt in finding that person, both physically and emotionally. Too much time is spent hearing of crime committed by grooming on the net, and I didn't want to be part of that. I want to be confident that the person I may be meeting really is that person, as best as I can tell. I want to be sure I am protecting myself. Gosh, Health and Safety and Risk Assessments when I am going out to meet someone. I have to look after myself, so the rules:

Rule 1:

My first rule I call the Two-Week Rule. I would want to meet a man three times in a minimum of two weeks before I decided if I would seek to pursue this acquaintance into a more regular and steady relationship. This would even mean that if I saw, met this person every day, past the three meetings, it would still have to be two weeks before making a decision. At the time I started on this quest, I had a job which revolved around a regular shift pattern where I worked for a number of days, then had a similar number of days off, usually four on, four off so that when I was off, I could spend a lot of time chatting online. This, as I will explain later, had its advantages and disadvantages, but the longer I got used to the net, the more I realised that meeting up sooner than later if the chap sounded interested, in the end would save a lot of time and again, why, I will explain later. But when you were chatting to one bloke, other fish were nibbling at the bait; in the long run it often saved a lot of wasted time.

A lot of time could be spent talking to a lot of gentlemen, and I could be putting off a lot of prospective mates in targeting my chats to one man only to find that when I had plucked up the courage for us to meet, he was nothing like he said or looked like in his pictures. Wasted time. Get your line in the water sooner than later, hook him or let him go pretty damn quick. Although you want to meet the right man as soon as possible; life is passing by and I don't want to waste time as well. As they say, there are plenty of fish in the pond, but I don't want to wait an eternity, bait them, hook them and throw them back if they are not what I am looking for.

Rule 2:

So I have plucked up the courage to meet this person, but with my three meetings, two-week rule, there has to be a sensible scenario that if we are only meeting for a coffee, and that is all that the first, even second and third 'date' will be, then there has to be a finite distance that I am willing to go for a quick cuppa, and there I mean only a cuppa, not whatever else you may be thinking! So I set a limit of a forty-mile radius from me, which took in some major population areas. Surely there has to be someone in that radius. But at least it meant, as it became apparent to me, that not everybody was as mobile as me. I have my own car, only little, but can get me there in less than an hour; obviously not everyone drives, and one couldn't expect some poor gentleman to catch a train for a quick cup of coffee, only to find that he has to wait four hours for his return trip. Even more so, as I am sticking to Rule 1 implicitly.

So forty miles it is then. And then depending on

their profiles, background that they have given me chatting online, what type of water we would arrange to meet in – a dark backwater or a fast-flowing expensive trout stream.

To protect myself, wherever I would meet, it would always be at a coffee shop, somewhere that would be crowded with other people so that if I cried for help, or found myself uncomfortable in the presence of this man, then I could at least make a safe escape. It would always be for a cup of tea or coffee, nothing else, though a decaf could be on the menu.

The categories I would put men in were those who may be unemployed, disabled, and needed an easy access. If I found them interesting, then I would arrange to meet them in a Tesco or Asda superstore. Comfortable, but not expensive, and old fashioned values. I did expect my coffee to be paid for in exchange for my company. This meeting place would also do if I was just bored and wanted to meet someone face to face. Surely my wonderful company was worth something.

The tradesmen, plumbers, builders, mechanics, I would go slightly upmarket (in my opinion though others may disagree) by going to a Sainsbury's or Waitrose cafeteria.

Lastly, for those self-styled businessmen, professionals, those who boasted posh cars, and owned their own houses, then let's go wild, how about Nero's or Costa Coffee? A bit more luxury and if they want to meet the wonderful me, then why not?

Rule 3:

My third rule was for the need of a photo, which served several purposes. This of course should be on their profile, but underlined some of the pitfalls that can occur on these chat, dating sites. It would also reveal a lot if and when I would meet these gentlemen, in that it would show how honest they had been when chatting. One could spend hours and hours, even weeks typing to one particular person, only to find that the photograph was six to ten years old, or that they were married. Some with these old photos would be looking for a younger woman, pretending they were younger too, but when they had been on the site for a long time and had not found the woman of their dreams (for whatever purpose), they would then revert to looking for someone of their own age.

Some would lie about their age, some would use someone else's photograph, make up a different profession for themselves. Some would take a picture in the dark, in bad lighting or from a distance, all to hide their true looks. Some would put no photo on at all. Then there would be those I would recognise as technophobes, those who didn't know how to choose one photo to post so they would have all their Facebook pictures on their profile, and all that they might reveal the family, the kids, and a lot else.

I found here the paying sites where you have to pay sixty to eighty pounds for a six-month subscription, you tended to get more genuine people, correct photos, a far more honest gentleman. These people you would find, the more genuine ones, would have read your profile to the end and also expected you to have read theirs.

But the free sites, there would be many who thought themselves God's gift to women, said they were looking for a relationship but all they wanted was to get their leg over.

I, myself, do not take a good photograph, but at least I try to be honest with the picture that is on my profile; what you see is what you get. If we do meet, there are no surprises from me. If only that were true the other way, but at least if you have seen a picture and it is not what is standing in front of you, then you may only have wasted a little time, and he can be dismissed promptly.

So, the three rules work hand in hand to save time, anxiety, and for my personal welfare. I am gone fifty and I need to find the right man.

That is not to say that there were no other pitfalls along the way, and I can only look back on perhaps how naïve I was in some of these chats, but more of that at a later date. I also added other rules as time went on. There would be men who said they were looking for a relationship, but were already in a failing marriage or other relationship. How genuine were they? Or were they just another bastard looking for his own fun at my expense, with no future in it for me? So no dating married men, or men in a relationship. And also kids, no disrespect here. I like them but I have done my stint of child rearing, and in my later years, it is fun and a relationship between two people I am looking for, not a shoal following us around for years to come.

I can only now see how this works for me, and I

may have to adjust along the way.

I have laid my bait, and set the rules that I intend to follow to look after myself in my quest for my man. What else do I have to do?

I think the only thing left is how I was going to present myself on these first encounters. As I have said earlier, I am not the most photogenic of people, and don't like posing in front of a camera, so with the use of friends' pictures, catching me when I'm unsuspecting of my photo being taken, and any others that came my way, I would update my profile pictures when I thought better pictures came along. But, that meant that when I did meet up with a fellow, I wanted to look my best without seeming as if it looked like overkill. To this end, how was I going to dress, what make-up should I wear? Rule 1 – meeting only for a coffee, for an hour or so, but I wanted to show myself off in my best light even for such a casual meeting.

Dress would be casual, but smart. Jeans to show off my lovely bum, so reasonably tight-fitting in that region, with a nice crease down the leg. Smart but casual shoes or sandals with small heel (or whatever was appropriate for the weather), and a nice blouse or shirt. Again, depending on the weather, a jumper or casual jacket or anorak.

Make-up, I always used this but not so much that I looked tarty. Lipstick has always been an issue with me, finding that if I used a dark colour, then as the day wore on, it tended to get on my teeth. I didn't want red teeth, as if I looked like a vampire; I was looking for a partner, not someone who I could suck their blood. So, usually it would be a natural colour or lip-gloss, some eye make-up, and I always wore a perfume so that I smelt nice, not that I don't anyway. But I wanted to make a good impression from the start.

Hair, well groomed, whether hanging naturally to show my flowing red locks, or up in a bun.

Yes, I think I look good, though I say it myself, and was frequently flattered as I have said before, that the comment would be made that I looked a lot better than my photo on the site.

All is done, and it is now time to cast my line out into the wind, over the water, and see what I can bring to my bag.

Let fishing commence.

HOOKED

The Barbel

Enough of the chatting, it's time for action. I need to get meeting some of these blokes, see who tweaks my line, takes my hook. I have been chatting with this one guy now for a while, so I float the idea that we should meet up, just for a coffee to begin with, and see where life takes us.

We come off the site as a match, so there must be something that can ignite a bit of chemistry between us. Certainly from my point of view, he's a nice-looking guy, looks as if he would be a good catch, and there are other things in his profile that suggest that something could kindle between us.

So I have taken the plunge, into shallow waters to begin with. It's arranged, we are going to meet up.

I have set my rules, and have to stick with them from the start. A problem straight away in that he lives right on the periphery of my distance limit, and doesn't drive. Easy enough to solve, he will meet me about halfway, and will come by train. Sorted, that keeps me in my boundaries, and it will still be neutral territory, where I can feel safe without being whisked off to some hidden love nest.

Our date arrives. It's been circled on my calendar for a few days, but now it's here. This is what I started Internet Dating for, to meet Mr Right, so I can't back out now. I have a nice half-hour drive, through pleasant Shropshire countryside up to Wem, where I will meet him off his train from the Potteries.

I was more confident of the men on paid sites, because they too had paid; my mind told me that they would be more genuine people. This guy, from a free site, looked nice but only time would tell, so as I made my journey I would have to admit to feeling more than a bit apprehensive. This despite me being a very confident and positive lady. But a station should be safe, unless he decides to throw me under a train. But then again, this is Wem, so he might have to wait a while for the next one to come.

I'm at the station, waiting on the platform for his train to arrive. It pulls up and a couple of carriage doors open. Recognition shouldn't be hard, it's not as if it's Euston, or Waterloo Bridge to pick out one fish swimming by out of a whole shoal. I have a choice of two, and it is a simple choice as he looks just like his picture on the site. Me, I obviously look better than my photo, but then I'm the only woman waiting there. I hope I don't look too desperate.

As he walks towards me, yes, good, he does look smart. It is a warm summer's day, and he strolls towards me wearing smart shorts and a shirt – cool look! He is now standing in front of me, an introduction. Who goes first? "Dr Livingstone, I presume."

Don't be silly Gill. I put out my hand to greet him, and smile, and say, "Hi, I'm Gill. You must be George Goby." He takes my hand, opens his mouth, and grins.

OH DEAR! Look at those teeth. If they were all there, if they were clean, if only…

I have a thing about teeth, and know at once this is a non-starter. Standing in front of me, I have a Barbel, with long, ugly teeth.

But I have to be polite. This is Wem and the next train back for him (though I wouldn't now care if he took the next one in any direction), is in three and a half hours. Oh no! What can I do? I can't offend him. Diplomacy, Gill. That is what I must do. It can't be a quick cuppa and about turn.

It is approaching midday, so we decide we will find a pub near the station, and have some lunch; that will kill some time and give me a meal. Hey, multitasking again. We find a typical town pub, with a fairly basic menu, but it will suffice, and we sit down at a table, me trying to keep my distance from those teeth.

We order and it is only polite to chat, even if I want to run away as fast as I can. In our chatting online, he had told me about an unusual hobby he had, but said he would tell me about it when we had met up. Well, that's something to talk about, and should help kill some time, though I have to admit that I was genuinely intrigued by this mystery hobby.

"Time to confess," I say.

He opens up that he is a train spotter, an anorak, a dying breed of people he thought despised by many for their interest in watching trains go by, riding on trains.

Me, I like gaming, that's my hobby, so I can't fault him for his hobby – each to their own.

He explains that the reason he doesn't drive is because of his love of trains, and he prefers using that network to get him from A to B as far as he can. Great, and now I am stuck with him for three and a half hours, lucky me. It will be okay as long as he doesn't open his mouth, but that can create problem with eating.

Lunch wasn't that bad. By positioning myself to his side, I didn't have to look into those choppers all the time. But it was now over, and I have only two hours to kill.

I know, I can offer to take him to another station where he can catch a train back home sooner, I'm sure he will know the local timetables off by heart. Sadly, a non-starter as there are no earlier trains, and being a polite lady, I can't just abandon him alone on the platform till his train arrives. Even for a train spotter, the number of them passing isn't going to keep him enthralled.

There is a park nearby, perhaps we can go for a walk. The sun is still shining (though not in this potential relationship), and it would be a pleasant way to use up that remaining time before he has to catch his train. We walked slowly, enjoying our surrounds, enjoying the sunshine, but then I felt a hand reaching for mine. I think I know where this is going to go – the old routine. Sit me down on a bench, his arm comes round my shoulder, and then he leans forward, his lips craving for mine.

Those teeth. What do I do? I don't want to push

him away and hurt his feelings, BUT I don't want my lips anywhere near those teeth.

Diplomacy, Gill. Diplomacy.

"Your teeth," I blurt out. "Teeth missing, teeth rotten, smelly breath, teeth all stained. Why?"

How subtle can I be?

Taken a back more than a bit, he explained to me that when he was young, he had a problem with a couple of his baby teeth, and they had to be extracted. The procedure hadn't gone well, had been very painful, and had left a lasting impression in his mind about dentists, to the extent that he had a phobia about them ever since. Anyway, HE didn't think they were too bad.

I must get this guy a mirror.

Time was passing, perhaps a little slower now, but it was time to make our way back to the station. A silence had fallen on us. *Yes,* I thought to myself, *he is nice, and I don't consider train spotting to be an unusual hobby, just boring. But, and for me a very big but, those teeth.* I have a thing about men having good teeth, and these choppers did not fit the bill.

We reached the platform and as the train pulled up it was time for us to go our separate ways. He tried to kiss me, but not with those teeth, oh no! What did I want to do? He was nice, but...!

I said that if he would do something with his teeth then I would see him again, but only if. Sorry, but that had to be my condition.

He turned and boarded his train, and as he departed I stood on the platform wondering, wondering, if only.

Then as the train disappeared into the distance, I turned and skipped all the way back to my car – an escape.

REMEMBER Gill, next time, always in the future, try and get a look at their choppers, their barbels, and save yourself some trouble.

I never heard from him again.

Me? Back to the drawing board. Who shall I see next? There are still plenty of fish out there, and I am going to find the one I am looking for, even if at times it is like pulling teeth!

Cast out and see what I can bring in next.

But for sure, in the future a de-scale and polish was a prerequisite of any fish I would chase.

Gill, this is going to be a learning curve.

Fishing the Dyke

I was becoming addicted; finding my soulmate was starting to dominate my life. Any spare time, when not working and doing those everyday things like shopping, washing, ironing, then I would be found looking through my matches, chatting online, or out hopefully meeting Mr Right. The only problem was that as yet he was not forthcoming. Why? I am a lovely lady, wonderful bait for any gentleman looking for a long-term partner, especially if they want to spend time down under, that is, as in Australia for a few months each year. Surely this must appeal to someone out there, but as yet, a few nibbles but no real bites, and I won't say I'm getting desperate – yet, anyway – but I'm not getting any younger and I want to settle down.

An idea occurs to me. I'm in a match but haven't studied the form of the competitors, could I be making myself more desirable (if that is possible)? Could I be making more of a play of myself? Yes! I need to find out what I am up against. So what if I try and find out who else is out there looking for the men I am after, and how many men may be chatting to other women, not me.

What if I try and find out what the competition is? And my cunning idea is to do just that. I will look at other women – yes, good idea.

I go back online, setting new parameters for myself. Looking for a friend, yes, a friend or friends, but this time female. An innocent enquiry, my profile unchanged (but naïvely still saying looking for a partner to share my life with). A friend, female, fifty to sixty years old. That should flag up the women I am tussling with to find my man.

I am on the site now, looking for a female companion, or that's what I think, and am astonished now by the number of likes I am receiving. With this I think I can scan the profiles of my competition, those women who are preventing me from finding and catching Mr Right.

I'm a woman, so now start being a bit catty, or perhaps I should say a bit catfishy to these potential rivals.

Blimey, she's a lot older than the picture she has put up!

She's dyed her hair!

Wouldn't put my photo up with my roots showing!

Wouldn't have my hair like that, especially at her age!

I find myself making comments to myself about all of them, is this what I intended? Well, I think I now know what I'm up against and in my own opinion, not a lot.

The next day, I am back online trawling through these women, and horror upon horror (this isn't what I expected), I am getting messages from gay ladies. How did that happen? I only put I was looking for a female friend, a companion – oops – to share my life with. Big oops, that's not what I meant at all.

Lots of questions being asked of me.

"Hi, what you looking for?"

"Hi, how long have you been gay?"

General comments, questions like that.

Surprised? Oh boy, yes. I nearly fell off my chair.

What shall I do? After some thought, I decided the best out was to be honest and tell the truth.

A couple of the ladies I had been chatting to, I thought had got to know quite well, or as well as you can online, and so was now honest with them and told them I wasn't gay. One I messaged, and her, I never heard from again. The other, who I chatted to for a while and had more than a bit of a laugh with, sounded a very nice lady.

We chatted about relationships, what we were

looking for in life, what we wanted to do, my Australian ambitions, lots and lots of things, but I guess this wasn't going to go any further than this. We would reach a point where contact would cease, as it was never just going to be just a friendship.

I guess, just as I was looking for my man, she was looking for her soulmate, but female, and if I was a match for her, she could only try and pursue her dreams.

We were coming to an end but one last try from her.

"Did you want to have a dabble, test the waters, stick your toe in, and see what you thought?" she asked.

"Flattered, but no thank you," I replied. Have I ever felt so much like a fish out of water than I did then?

"Okay. But you don't know what you have missed unless you have tried it."

That was it. I quickly took myself off that profile, and headed back to the waters I was comfortable in, where I knew what my catch should be, if only I could hook him.

I hoped I hadn't hurt anyone's feelings in my naïvety in trying to find out about my competition. A learning curve, this Internet Dating, and I was quickly finding out what a tangle you could get yourself into.

Back to man-fishing for me, my resolve all the stronger.

The Loach

I was getting more confident with this online dating lark, and was spending more and more of my spare time chatting to this bloke or that – perhaps too much of my time. Was this a sign of my desperation in wanting to find a man, Mr Right, as it were, or just my growing addiction to these sites? Certainly, if I felt life was passing me by, and I wanted to live a little before I was too old, then I needed to turn these chats to meeting, to relationships, to marriage, to living happily ever after.

I had been chatting to a guy from the East Midlands for a little while, from Nuneaton in fact, and from the sound of him, we had a lot in common, especially in that we both liked gaming. Could this be the one? A hobby we could enjoy together would be an excellent start.

Rules are rules, and technically, Nuneaton just dipped out of my forty-mile rule – Rule 2. Should I make an exception so early in my dating career? I would like to meet this guy, Joe Loach, but he is just that little bit too far, and if I say okay, I'll go another five miles, then I might just as well go another fifty.

A compromise is called for that allows me to keep my rule intact. We decide we will meet up, but at a neutral venue. We could try meeting in Wolverhampton, not the most salubrious place as far as I am concerned, from my own history, but it was easy to get to for both of us.

The meeting was arranged. We would go for lunch in town, meeting up in the Beatties' car park, say quarter past twelve, so we could spend a bit of time, and this time sticking to my rule of an hour or so on a first 'date'. An exchange of mobile numbers would allow us to find each other, and of course we had seen photos of each other on our profiles.

Contact was made and from my first sighting, this guy was good-looking, just as his photo suggested, but was a little on the chubby side. But then, who am I to talk? I carry a pound or two more than would be my ideal. First impressions, very good. Over the course of a pub meal close by, and a glass of wine, we chatted about this and that, hobbies especially, and got to know each other more personally than a written conversation online.

I did enjoy this rendezvous, and as we parted company and I made my way back to my car, I was pleasantly surprised by the man I had just spent the past hour or so with. No firm arrangements were made for a follow-up meeting, but in my mind, I probably wouldn't say no.

When back home, and over the coming days, quite a few days, we chatted more, and talk of a second meeting did indeed come up. But now we have a problem. I am living in shared accommodation. I have a room in a friend's house, which gives me some privacy, as we work in the same establishment, but on different shift patterns, sharing the kitchen and lounge/diner. It is a long way for him to come from Nuneaton for an evening out, without offering him some sort of accommodation for the night if necessary. I just don't have any and I'm certainly not going to offer the sharing of my bed at such an early stage in our relationship.

Joe's solution was that I should go to Nuneaton, not in the non-speaking sense of course, but I could stay with him, and he would sleep on the settee, giving up his own bedroom to me. My standard reply to anything like this was to say, "You could be an axe murderer for all I know."

He replied, "Of course I'm not."

And then I said, "Well, an axe murderer would say that, wouldn't they?"

I decided I would take the plunge and go over there. It would be the first time on this dating site that I had committed to a weekend meeting. I packed myself an overnight bag, to stay over, but thought if I didn't like him on his home territory, then I could just get in the car and head back home; no commitment, obligations, just back to the sanctity of my own surrounds.

Saturday came, and after I had done all my chores at home, I headed off to Nuneaton down the M6, in my car. Yes, though a confident girl, I did feel a bit of apprehension as I set off into the unknown. A little over an hour, and I was there, just looking for where he lived, but even my poor sense of direction soon got me to outside the shop that he said he lived above. Parking up, there he was outside to greet me and take me up to his one-bedroomed apartment. The entrance was actually behind the shop, and up a steel staircase, and he kindly took my bag and carried it up for me.

A kitchen well-cluttered with his cooking from how many days previously? There was enough still clean, however, for him to make us both a cuppa, and the rest of the flat looked very tidy. I could sit there opposite him taking in my chub in his own waters. Good-looking, yes, and as I thought last time carrying a slight excess of poundage, but well groomed, almost certainly five or six years younger than me. Hey, a toy boy, that would be something to tell the girls at work when I saw them next.

I found out that he had been in work, but at the present time was unemployed, waiting to change jobs. He was a very clever man in his field of electronics, having had a job fixing handheld scanners, as used in supermarkets.

He rented the flat, had a car, and had enough to live on quite easily.

This all sounds very promising, I think to myself. *He wants to look after my every need, being very attentive, and concerned I am comfortable and happy being in the same room as an axe murderer.*

Next on the agenda would be something to eat, so we went out to get a take away, and then back to the flat to eat it. I like my Indians, so that went down very well.

The meal gave us the opportunity to chat further. He did have a very pleasant personality, and I was surprised he had not found anyone earlier, because despite the extra poundage, he was a really nice person. He told me that he was fed up of being on his own, and dearly craved the chance of some permanent company. He even came across as being a bit desperate to find a woman.

It was an opportunity to try different things, see what each other liked, so we went for a gentle stroll after our take away, enjoying the pleasant weather we were having. Again just talking, no holding hands, no whisking me off to a park bench for a quick snog, in every way a perfect gentleman.

Back from the walk, and we cleared his kitchen away for him, it was only polite to wash up after the meal, so it seemed right to help clear the other stacked-up plates as well.

I still wasn't sure if I wanted to stay the night, but I did fancy a glass of wine or two, in which case I wouldn't be able to drive. He assured me that there would be no hanky panky, I would be perfectly safe in his bed, and he would stay on the settee if I did decide to stay. Okay, he did seem genuine, a nice man, and couldn't do enough for me.

Reassured, I decided to stay, so we settled down to a mutual interest, our gaming. Me, my game was World of Warcraft, he was more an Xbox man, so we had a go on that for a lot of the afternoon. Strange for me, using these thumby control things, but it was something we had in common, and even if they did start to ache, it was good fun, sitting on the end of his bed where he had his big screen and just gaming. I also felt very safe.

Evening came, and he showed off his cooking talents, a stir fry and more wine, and then we settled down in front of the telly for the evening. He even found a chick-flick for us to watch, so yes, very attentive and thorough in his desire to please me.

The day had passed with nothing for me to have worried about, going away to a stranger's house, and I went off to his bedroom to settle down in my pyjamas and dressing gown, leaving him to enjoy the comfort of his settee.

A peaceful and comfortable night; no visitations from any axe murderer, I slept well and got up in the morning feeling very refreshed when I heard stirrings from the other side of the bedroom door.

I dressed and joined Joe in the kitchen where he was cooking me breakfast, a full English. Yum, yum. A further conversation over my bacon, and it was time for me to depart back home, all in one piece, and it had worked out okay.

We spoke again on the phone, and chatted online. He wanted to see me again, for me to come over again, but with my shift pattern, that mainly restricted me to weekends, so it wasn't going to be on a regular basis. When I could manage it, which was a fortnight later, I did go over on a Saturday lunchtime, and leave on the morning of the Sunday. He did look after me, splashed the boat out in his desire to please me. We talked, we gamed, we would watch films in the evening, and then I would retreat to the sanctity behind the bedroom door, leaving him to his settee. Then in the morning, I would come home again.

That was fine, but was there a burning in my heart, something igniting in me? As yet, no.

The trouble was as time went on, he became even more attentive, and I had that growing feeling (the same feeling occurring in his y-fronts) that he wanted to get into my knickers.

He wanted to see more and more of me. Could I come over after work, stay the night and go back to work the next day? No, that was too much for me, too tiring with the journey, especially as nothing was happening for me. Flattered that a younger bloke was after me, but nothing, absolutely nothing.

We had got to the stage that we would kiss and cuddle, but there was no stirring in my loins, no sexual attraction to him at all.

But he was getting even more demanding in wanting to see me as often as he could, even to the extent that he wanted me to drop everything (including my knickers), and move in with him.

He was nice, but this was becoming more and more overbearing, so I was going to have to call an end to it.

It was a Dear John phone call. I said that I didn't think this was going to go any further than where we were now,

"Couldn't we give it more time?" he asked.

"No," I said, "there was no bite, no spark happening as far as I was concerned. I've had a nice time, but we should both move on and search elsewhere for the right person for each of us."

He had fallen hook, line, and sinker for me, but no. Someone who did want to keep me forever, locked away with a chub. The first who wanted to marry me, which was encouraging for me in that there were those out there looking, fishing for the same as me, but my search will continue.

And I've managed to keep my head on. Guess he never was going to be an axe murderer, but you never can tell, you hear too many stories of internet dating that have tragic consequences, so from now on I will strictly stick to my three Rules of Angling.

He did text me at a later date to see if I was okay, which was nice, and later sent me a message to say he had met someone new, and that they were really happy together.

I was really pleased for him, and wish him well. That was the last I heard from him. Farewell.

THE PIKE AND THE PIRHANA

Walk round any pond, lake, along a river bank, along the sea shore, and somewhere you will find warning notices. 'Beware deep water', 'Beware overhead cables', 'Deep water', 'Strong tides'. For sure, there can always be a danger lurking somewhere. For some small tiddlers in the water, that danger may be predators, for wherever there is wildlife, there will also be something, somewhere wanting to hunt it. In our environment, the water, there are sharks, orcas, a whole mixture of different fish feeding on one another. The law of the jungle, the wet jungle.

For me, I cast out still looking for my perfect catch, my soulmate forever, I hope. My bait is in the water, still waiting for the big bite. But are there hidden dangers posted around my pool? I certainly didn't see any.

I'm back on the net, chatting to a few people – men – again seeing what's out there in those murky waters called life. Again using a free site, of which there are many, one lonely evening a chap started chatting to me. Nothing unusual in that, but being probably more than a bit addicted to this online chatting and dating, I was probably more than a bit naïve, and many would recognise the story I am about to tell, for you may well have been there as well.

So to that end, it looks like I am after a big one now, a PIKE, and for that it may take live bait.

If you recognise my opening gambit, you have already been in the same pond no doubt.

My guy, a US army man, serving in Afghanistan, comes online and starts chatting. He has been posted out there now for four months, not his first tour of duty out there, and may not be his last, but he has plans when he leaves which sound interesting to me.

Name, 'Samuel Johnson, Sir!' It transpired through our first time chatting, that he had been married (haven't they all?), but his wife had died at a young age of cancer, leaving him with a son. He had dual nationality, American and British, and had himself a house in London, Chelsea in fact, so must have had a bob or two somewhere. His son, so as not to disrupt his life too much, had remained in the States with his mother, to give him a more settled and stable life. He thought that best for him.

He had three months left on this tour then he planned to return to London. He had plans, he had visions for his future, and some of these involved setting up his own business in the capital – a jewellery shop – and to that purpose he had started designing and making his own lines. After a couple of chats, he sent me pictures, photos of some of his designs, five pictures of what looked lovely but modern jewellery, just to whet my appetite as to where he planned to go with this.

I don't know how much downtime they have on their tours, but he seemed to find a lot of time to chat to me online, and we would pass away hours exchanging comments, plans, generally trying to find out more and more about each other.

And poems, I mustn't forget the poems he would send me, written himself, sounding so eloquent.

I was very keen at this stage. Having checked the Chelsea address out and finding it to be authentic, yes, I was keen. He sounded nice, talkative, ambitious, and sounded well off. Moreover, he sounded very keen on me. I was not suspicious of him at all. He would be back in three months and he would like to meet up with me, when grounded in the UK.

Dare I say at this stage how much I was getting involved? To the extent, was I falling in love with him? I don't know, watch this space, and all the time as we chatted more and more, those days were ticking by, ticking away until I could meet him. Even better, he wanted to meet up as soon as he got back. Have I found my man at last? I think I may have and am falling, falling more and more for him. He has cast his line, and I have leapt out of the water and taken the bait.

We set up Skype between us so that I could see him as we talked. Though he was always a little distance away from the camera, he looked a bit of a hunk. Still no suspicions as to why he was always so far from the camera. I stopped chatting to all other men online as I was really keen on Johnson. I was the fish on the end of his line and he was starting to reel me in.

We talked about feelings, and he said that although it was strange for him with a stranger, he was starting to develop strong emotions towards me. *Yippee*, I think, and looking back now, would have to say how naïve I was for all that was going on in my life, starting to change my life.

I was sure I had fallen in love with this guy, Samuel Johnson, and as we talked for hours on the net, I found it hard to drag myself away from him, from the computer which was the link between him and myself, where he talked of us settling down together in his Chelsea residence. I cannot be serious, I have fallen in love with someone, a man who I have never kissed, never made love to, not even ever met. He really has me hook, line, and sinker.

It was here that it really started to affect me; I wanted to make myself perfect for him. I wanted to lose weight, and started going out for long walks, tone those muscles up, and slim the waist. I burnt up the paths in the local park as the pounds were shed, and if my breasts were perfect already, then the rest of me started to become shapelier. How I wanted this. I was getting obsessed with this man, this stranger, my love! The time is ticking by fast. We chat, I exercise, my excitement is growing as soon I will meet him and we will go on holiday together, then I can really get to know him and show him my assets.

We are now only three weeks away.

At this stage in my life, and my profile would have

said so, I am trying to set up a business of my own. I am qualified to look after people with disabilities, and in Age Care, so I thought I could start a business offering respite care to those who need it, so the carers, parents, family, could get away for a couple of weeks from time to time, leaving their dependents in the capable hands of myself. With an ongoing tragedy in my family, it had become clear to me there was a niche in the market to be filled; someone offering this service would be a godsend to a lot of people. That was the business I had planned, was trying to get off the ground, and I suppose my online profile would have said, 'fun-loving single businesswoman looking for a relationship', and the predators would have been circling. I suppose on reflection now, Johnson would have seen this – a vulnerable woman, businesswoman – and his interest was raised. But the business was me, only me, and as yet, I didn't have any money.

The weeks continued to pass, and daily we would speak. Not long now before I could be with this man I had fallen so much for. Another day gone, another day crossed off, and our time was drawing closer and closer.

Then, only seven days to go, and out of the blue he tells me that he is going to be sent out on one more mission, twenty-four hours out of camp, then that would be it, time to come to my welcoming arms. However, whatever this mission was, and he couldn't tell me, there was danger involved.

He was off, and I waited patiently by my computer, waiting for word of his safe return. There I was worried sick that someone I had never met, someone I had all these feelings for, was going to get hurt, oh my god! Imagine me here, three months chatting to a bloke who claims to be in love with me, and I am definitely in love with him, besotted in fact, waiting for a Skype call to tell me he is safe and well. Could I sleep? No chance!

Twenty-four hours passed, then another, and nothing, except I'm now not sleeping, not eating, and cried off work. I was just so worried about him, wanted to hear his voice again, to know that he was safe. Nothing.

Monday morning, and at last the Skype rings, and yes it is Samuel Johnson. He can't stay on long as he is injured and is awaiting the doctor to come and dress a leg wound, and then to debriefing. He would phone again as soon as he could.

I was just so relieved. I felt elated, thankful that he had got back safely. A time to reflect on it all, so I took myself out for a walk, to clear my head, collect my thoughts, and give a little thankful prayer to whatever god I may have.

I returned back to receive another call from Johnson. He was asking me if I could do him a little favour. I would do anything for this 'stranger' that I loved, so fishing for any way I could find to help him, and of course I would help him. I loved him; my heart was bursting with love for him, and he said it was easier for me if he emailed me what had happened, as the doctor was returning again shortly. Then he could ask me what he wanted me to do.

More waiting but eventually the email arrived from him. The gist of his mission was:

To rescue the son of a tribal leader who had been

kidnapped ten years earlier by another tribal faction.

This was his last mission before returning home.

The mission was successful in that they had rescued the son, but he had lost two of his men, and had been injured himself.

The second part of the mission was to return the son, now an adult, to his father, who was so grateful he had given him a reward, which was in a case and now he had to get it into the UK.

It was worth a lot of money.

My first feelings, despite my love for him, was that I would not do anything illegal. I have always been an honest girl, so quizzed Samuel Johnson regarding the legality of it all. He assured me it was not drugs or anything bad so I agreed. How trusting you can be when you are so much in love.

What was I to do? He would send me the telephone number of a chap who will act as a middleman; Johnson had given him £4,000 to get his flights, and this man had diplomatic immunity so he would be able to get on and off planes when and where he wanted. He would get the courier to let me know where he was and when the case would be delivered into this country to me for my safe keeping, until Johnson also returned to the UK.

I'm naïve at this stage. I take it all in, believing it all.

So let's recap. Here I am, been chatting to an American soldier online for three months, have fallen madly in love with him, to the extent that he now affects the way my body functions. I have gone on a fitness campaign to become Miss West Midlands for him (well perhaps Glamorous Granny West Midlands), though if I haven't figured it out yet, if he is in active service, he has to be considerably younger than me. Now I am considering, no, have agreed to receive some dubious parcel for him until he returns to whisk me off my feet, take me off on holiday and live happy ever after. I can see you trying to check out my profile by finding a photo of an ass. Yet, me no suspect anything dodgy yet, Eeyore!

It seems there is some urgency in getting this package back over to England; Samuel Johnson seems to want to get it on its way as soon as possible. He tells me that my contact, his courier, is called Marcus. He will keep in regular contact with me as he travels with parcel across the continents, carrying his precious cargo to me in London, for me to keep until Samuel Johnson arrives back safely.

Samuel Johnson and I continue to chat at regular intervals, when he can get free from his debriefings and medical treatment. He is doing okay after his injury, but it is still requiring regular medical attention. He tells me he is really looking forward to meeting up with me in only a few days' time, how much he loves me, and that soon we will be together. Oh my god, he has got me really smitten, how I love this man, this man I have never met but look forward to spending the rest of my life with. How I want to help him; whatever this thing is could set us up to start our time together.

He tells me that his friend Marcus will be departing in the next twenty-four hours, and to await his call. Of course I will, and will do whatever I can to help him, though I'm not sure what I can do. He must go now, as the doctor is back round again, but will keep in touch, and looks forward to hearing the progress of the package.

We sign off and I wait to hear from Samuel Johnson, to hear from Marcus. I am nervous; this could be our future together, and I want all to go smoothly.

Silence for a while, then a call from Marcus. "I am in Dubai," he says, and, "all going well so far, no problems, and will soon be on the next part of my journey."

Silence again.

"Hi Gill, Marcus here," a call comes through my phone. "I have a slight problem, I am in Ghana, and there is a hold up, but I will keep you informed what's going on."

"Hi Gill, me again," Marcus says down the phone a few hours later. "I'm in trouble, I'm stuck here," he says. "I have had to use the £4,000 that Samuel Johnson had given me already, bribes to officials to get me back on track. You have probably heard how corrupt some of these officials in African countries can be, cough up or get arrested on some trumped up charge. Honest to God, I am telling the truth, I need your help."

I listen to his story thinking, *How can I help, contact the Embassy? What does he want me to do?*

"Gill, I have run out of money. I need to you send me another £4,000 for me to get through customs, then next stop would be Europe and the rest would be plain sailing."

I told him I hadn't got any money, and that he should contact Samuel Johnson. "I will try as well, see if he can wire some money out to Ghana. He will see you right, I am sure. Keep in touch."

"Okay," he says, "speak to you soon."

I tried over and over again to call Samuel Johnson, but whether he was in debrief, having his medical attention, or was starting to pack for his return, I don't know, but my attempts at contact were all to no avail.

"Marcus here again," comes on the phone a couple of hours later. "How have you got on? Have you spoken to Samuel Johnson?"

"No, I've tried and tried but no reply."

"I'm still stuck and desperately need some money, to get things moving and get out of this country."

I suggested that he tried to find a locker where he could leave the package, and then Samuel Johnson could pick it up when he was returning home.

Marcus kept telling me it was our future together, Johnson and I. *What can it possibly be?* I wonder. I worry that Samuel Johnson is going to be angry with me, and get more and more upset as our conversation goes on. Marcus explained he had now run out of money completely, and couldn't even afford the locker, couldn't contact Johnson, and I was his only hope now. I was a businesswoman and please, surely I could help him out of his predicament. "Please send £4,000, or as much as you can."

I agreed to send what I could. I wasn't rich, my business was in its infancy but I would do what I could. This was £125, all I had, which I went into the post office to send by postal order, a form of money transaction acceptable all over the world. The counter assistant asked if I was sure I wanted to do this, to send this money to Ghana. Had she seen this before?

Yes, send it, I implored her. But something in the look on her face, at last the penny was starting to drop. EEYORE, Eeyore. I think I have been scammed. How naïve have I been.

That was the last I ever heard from Marcus, Samuel Johnson, the whole fucking US army.

The money, not a lot I grant you, but a lot to me, was gone, lost forever. Idiot, idiot, what a fool I have been. How foolish, how stupid have I been?

The warning signs, 'DEEP WATER, DON'T GET OUT OF YOUR DEPTH', I ignored them all as I blindly fell in love with this man I had never met. Undying love, a life together, so many promises and I swallowed them all. If 'fuck Samuel Johnson' had a few weeks, days ago, been a big wish, now 'fuck Samuel Johnson' had a completely different meaning! Eeyore.

That pike, the largest predator in home waters, nearly got me but I have escaped to fight another day.

Piranhas

So back to the pool I go, chastened but my search for that eternal partner as yet is undiminished.

Not long after the Johnson saga, changing my bait from Plenty of Fish to Badoo, another free site, I started chatting to another man, an adopted son of a Scotsman who strangely enough lived in Scotland. We chatted online for a while, then exchanged e-mail addresses. He told me something of himself, his background, his plans for the future. His stepfather owned a business in his native country. He had a son who was not at all interested in the business, so one day this chap, Karl, hoped that he would inherit, that it all would become his. I liked the sound of this, a man with a future, an inheritance.

Better still as we chatted about ourselves, our interests, my family, of my dual nationality, my history of travelling, what I had seen of the world, we found we enjoyed each other's company more and more. Things were going well.

We had chatted electronically for a while, and it was now that I suggested that as I had a contract phone, I could phone him whenever and it wouldn't cost me anything, just let me have a mobile number and I could ring. How nice it would be to hear a voice from this man, Karl, who I was getting to know and sounding as if I liked him.

He told me he worked long hours and was not always readily available on the end of a phone, almost seemed like he was putting me off. I was getting a little fed up with all this typing, e-mailing; how nice it would be to talk properly. I suggested another communication, and asked again for a number, it wasn't going to cost me anything to speak to him. "Please let me phone you," I implored Karl.

We continued to chat online, work interests etc.

Oh, his business, well would you believe there is a Scottish rice industry? It may sound hard to take this one in, but there is. More specifically, Karl's firm bought in rice from China and other rice-growing countries, repackaged it and then exported it to other destinations. A growing business, it would seem.

He still seemed reluctant to send a phone number, but eventually relented and said he would e-mail it tomorrow. I thought tomorrow would never come, but then a number appeared on an e-mail from him. I was so excited, I felt we were getting closer, AND perhaps this was the proof I needed that he wasn't overseas somewhere, in some far-off land, inaccessible to me. After Samuel Johnson, I had had enough of faraway prospective life partners and heartbreak.

I started to get excited, when could I ring him? He kept saying tomorrow, tomorrow, but at last tomorrow came. He said I could phone him at seven in the evening when he had got home after work.

Excitement. He said he was getting very fond of me and after weeks of chatting, swopping stories, telling each other about ourselves, I would be able to put a voice to Karl, this man who sounded more than a bit interesting, and interested in me.

Scared? I don't think so, but as the time approached, my heart was beating faster, and I was feeling nervous.

Seven o'clock arrived and I pushed the numbers down on my mobile, waiting for the dialling tone and knowing I had an hour of chat before there would be any charges.

Ring, ring – no answer. Disappointment, but

perhaps he was late back from work. I will try again in five minutes.

Five minutes pass and I press redial. "Hello, hello," a voice replies, he has picked up. A quiet voice with an accent speaks to me. "Hello love, hello baby," he says.

That should have caused me to think (warning signs again, but no), but I was so excited about hearing his voice that I took no notice.

We talked but his responses to my questions, my banter, tended to be short, one-worded answers. He did say that he was European, English wasn't his first language.

"How are you?" I asked, to which he replied, "Very tired, have been working very hard."

I told him about my planned business, that everything seemed to be progressing well with it, and he told me more of his rice business. Importing at low prices, bringing in into the country in large container ships, repackaging and then selling it on. Yes, it was making very good money.

The conversation went on for some half an hour. I tell him he doesn't sound Scandinavian, and Karl tells me, no, not Scandinavian, but he is from Belgium.

Then he says, "Okay, I go now," and the penny starts to drop. The more I speak to him, the more I think he is not European at all.

"Bye baby, speak to you soon, love," he says and he is gone.

Oh no, we have finished on the phone for the first time, but I sat back and thought about what we had said, and what his voice was like. Was I having doubts about this man? I don't know, but something in my head said check this out.

How much money have I left on my account? How many free minutes left on my account?

Oh no! Still over an hour of free time. Which means that… This call has all been added on as extra.

Press on Three account, added extras, £37 in call charges.

Not again. I have been scammed, a phone scam this time.

The warning signs were there again, but I chose to ignore them. Stupid, stupid woman. Will I never learn?

The scammers are circling me, like piranhas waiting for their supper. Me again. Am I so gullible in my search for love?

Write a hundred lines.

"I must stick to closer men to meet, so I can have a cup of coffee, a chat, and decide if they are true."

"I must stick to closer men to meet, so I can have a cup of coffee, a chat, and decide if they are true."

"I must stick to closer men to…"

Beware the scammer, and so from now on my rule is never to speak for long before meeting up for a coffee, to ascertain that they actually exist, are real people. They may turn out to be plonkers, but at least I know.

I have taught myself to recognise the scammers straight away now, spot them a mile off, see what they are like compared with their photos. There is always a reason that they do not use an up to date one. No longer chats on the phone, no more e-mailing, and no more scammers.

Get the bastards in front of you, see they are for real.

Yes, pikes and piranhas are predators, avoid or get hurt.

Me, I am now chastened, but wise. I am also still looking!

NIBBLES, BITES AND THROW THEM BACK

I have said before that at times I would become addicted to chatting online, looking for that perfect catch, the reason why I was doing it all. But there were times when I went online because I was bored, feeling a bit down, or just wanted something to do. You never know, even if there was no obvious catch on view, just by chatting to others, I may have found something I was looking for. After a time, I realised that perhaps I should lower my standards, the good-looking hunks were either unreal, or just looking for a quick bonk, probably extramarital. Look at the next section down; they may be more genuine, and be looking for a life partner like me, not just my body as a one-off.

I had no great interest in buying lots of clothes, or other shopping, and with my shift pattern of four on, four off, it would often be difficult to organise much of a social life with friends. Therefore, I would just meet up for a coffee and a chat with someone I had seen on one of the sites, and had exchanged the odd communication with. Coffee didn't exceed Rule 1, so I felt happy with this.

I didn't have my own house, being a lodger in a friend's house, so bringing people back was difficult – impossible – and it helped me appreciate how others felt who were unemployed and in a council house, or in lodgings themselves. It did not worry me meeting some of these people, as long as I felt they were looking for their future, to help themselves, to push their lives forward. Who knows? One of them could be the person I am looking for, so I have to give them a chance.

On one such occasion, I had arranged to meet a gentleman at Tesco's for a coffee, and a chat. As was the norm for me, I had cleaned myself up, a little bit of make-up on my face, a little eau de toilette, and I thought I was dressed reasonably smartly. I got myself a coffee, and waited, waited for this gentleman to arrive who was seven years younger than me, but looked okay on the site.

I noticed my coffee partner suddenly arrive – decked in tracksuit bottoms, and he hadn't just dropped in after a run. Well, I like to be comfortable, and will often do my housework in my trackies, but to meet someone for the first time, with a possible view to a relationship, this guy is taking the pee. "I think not."

A very brief encounter, a very quick cup of coffee and I'm gone. Needless to say Mr Tracksuit man did not even get a consideration for a second meeting.

A nibble, and one to throw back into the pool.

Sid Flounder, Coffee Man

It was back online again, and I started chatting to another man, for quite a while in fact. What he started with was a rather vague profile and a blurred photograph. He said he was over six foot tall, so he claimed to drive an estate car to get all of himself in, not a van, needed the space to squeeze as he was a repair man for the council. This sounded an exciting conversation didn't it, if we talked about how to get in cars, but I was not succeeding much in finding my man, so any conversation was better than nothing, and maybe the start of something, who knows? This could be a very big fish by the sounds of it, whale proportions, so the interest was held.

We arranged to meet at Tesco's for coffee one day, just before lunchtime. I waited patiently in the coffee shop, to be greeted by this man vaguely looking like that blurred photo. Six foot? This guy was a giant, standing at six seven, towering over me by a foot. *If this works out*, I thought to myself, *I don't think we will be going out in my car.* The old joke, 'How do you get an elephant into a car?' came to mind. But just there in the back of my mind, alarm bells were ringing as to what else might be untrue in his profile. Yes, he was six foot, but six foot and a lot. The blurred picture of him, yes it did look like him, but how long ago? Be careful Gill with this one.

Introductions and then ordering some coffee, we started to chat and find out more about each other. I was now thinking perhaps that an articulated truck may be more appropriate than an estate car. Having exchanged formalities, I thought it important right from the start to tell him of my two-week rule, and my hopes for a long-term relationship, which is why I had joined the dating site.

He wasn't too keen on my rules, but I said that was how it was going to be. Reluctantly he accepted it. We continued to chat, finding out each other's interests, my hope to share a life here and in Australia, my family, and I tried to find out about his.

He was in work uniform, so had obviously managed to pop out from work for a break to accommodate me and our date. It was time for him to get back, so we parted, me saying I would get in touch.

I did get in touch again, and we met up for another coffee date; again, it must have been break time as he was in uniform. Things seemed to be going along okay, so on another day off, I invited him over to my house for a coffee and more chat. We sat on the settee chatting, and before leaving, because he again was in uniform, we ended up having a bit of a kiss and a cuddle. I was beginning to like this guy, but was still a little cautious, a little suspicious. Why couldn't we go out in the evening?

He sent me a picture of his garden, and the bungalow he lived in, but when I saw him next, during the day in his uniform, I did ask him if he was married.

"No, I promise you I am not married," he assured me.

Silly me, at this time it did not occur to me that he was in a relationship, had a partner, or was probably living with someone, so as I was being blind, I thought I would give this man a go, see if we could have a future together, he may be Mr Right. Let's look at the facts – he had a good job, with a pension attached, owned a nice bungalow, was a hard worker and seemed keen on me. I would carry on seeing him but try to avoid dates at my place for a while.

I wanted him to take me on a proper date, a dinner or lunch, somewhere nice. I was still in my two weeks so was strictly keeping to my rule book, and would see him when I could for coffee on my days off, but four nights on, four nights off was somewhat limiting in finding time to go out.

So life continued as before, passing my two weeks, but our relationship carried on basically over coffee, and in uniform. Life, what he liked to do, Australia, holiday destinations – all topics we chatted about.

But how I wanted to go out to dinner with him. It would have meant a lot to me to have proper time with him, and he said he would like that to happen as well. But somehow we never got that far.

He came over for coffee one day, and you guessed, in his uniform. We were sipping our Gold Blend, and in between we would start kissing. I liked him kissing me, even if I could have done without the coffee at the same time.

"Oh, I want to make love to you," he said.

"What?" I said. "I have only had coffee with you, only seen you in your uniform, your working clothes. This isn't a relationship, I need more than a man in uniform and a constant supply of diuretic over five weeks to keep me awake. And only in daylight hours!"

I wanted a proper date with him, I told him, or that was it for 'coffee man'. Last chance. He would agree. Okay, okay, yes he would, and agreed to take me out for dinner that Saturday night. Success at last for me, I was going to see the proper him.

Saturday night came and I was going through my wardrobe, deciding what to wear and thinking that at last things were moving forward. A step in the right direction, this really could be Mr Right.

Then, my mobile was ringing – him!

"Hello Gill. I'm really sorry, something has come up at work, they have rung and want me to come in. I can't make it tonight but I will make it up to you, perhaps meet up for a coffee tomorrow."

"Don't bother," was my reply, and that was the end of 'coffee man'. He was no more, and my frequent visits to the loo after so much coffee diminished as well.

Disappointed, yes, but at last I realised he was just playing me. Almost certainly in a relationship, he just wanted me for a bit of fun, my body, and of course sex. Oh, and coffee!

I will enjoy my coffee, but not in such copious amounts, and won't have to worry about legs protruding way, way out of my bed. I have reinforced my need for my two-week rule, and will now, hopefully, recognise this type of player again.

A week or so later, I had worked my four days on and had returned home for a rest. The only way to see out of my house was through the kitchen and front bedroom window. I needed a wee (no, not after more coffee) but wanted to see what the weather was doing so made my way to the front. Looking out of the window, it was raining. But who was that parked outside my house, staring in? It was coffee man. I texted him to say don't park there again.

But I think he still parks there, is that stalking? Even months later I still see him driving past from time to time, stopping opposite.

He was another man who only wanted sex, but he wanted coffee too!

James Chub

Back to chatting online again. *Perhaps,* I thought, *I am setting my expectations too high.* The chances of finding everything I was looking in my life partner were too unlikely. It was lucky that I enjoy fishing, but I think I may have to change what I was looking for. As they say, there are bigger fish to fry. Don't be so choosy, Gill. Some men are overweight, so don't be so shallow about those larger men, one of them may be very nice, and we could always engulf ourselves in a healthy eating regime, especially as I did like cooking so much.

So I started looking for larger fish, whales, whoppers. Let's face it, I have had a few whoppers in some of the lies men have told me, but hey, let's have a go at what I can hook after I adjust the breaking strain on my line.

So I started chatting to a chap, James Chub, who was a little younger than me, but sounded very pleasant, and there was certainly no smutty chat. Someone genuine I hope.

I wanted to meet him, and following the rule book, it would be coffee first. We arranged to meet at a lakeside café I had been to before, a lovely spot where we could enjoy the nice weather we had been having. I had met another chap here in the past, and enjoyed watching the swans, the ducks, and other birdlife enjoying the warmth that early summer was bringing. It was a nice day as we had hoped, and with this, the car park was full, as other people enjoyed the pleasures of our surrounds. I had to park a little way away, but that was no problem, giving me a chance to stretch my legs, and take in that fresh air surrounding me.

I walked to the café, as usual a little early, and sat outside waiting for my Chub to arrive. I wondered if I could bring my rod here and participate in my now keen hobby of fishing. Good idea, I thought, and as I was imagining what I could catch, my chub, James Chub arrived.

Oh boy, was he puffing and blowing. Was he really that unfit? He would need my culinary skills. A thought entered my head (jumping the gun a bit here) that he would not be able to take any weight on those chubby arms, if we did get as far as bed. Poor me if he mounted me, poor bed for that matter. Back to reality, Gill, you have only just met him.

Otherwise, looks, quite presentable as he stood before me in smart trousers, struggling under his overflowing tum, a smart shirt, dress shoes, but no jacket. That may be too formal for a park meeting.

We ordered a pot of tea, and sat in a comfy chair overlooking the water. I was mum and poured, and as we drank we started talking about our past. Previous marriages and travel took a lot of our conversation.

He had not been overseas so being very interested in all the parts of the world that I had seen, our conversation lasted a long time.

He lived on the ground floor of a council house by himself. We had talked for so long that the pot had run dry, but I took no notice that he didn't get up to get a refill. He seemed very nice and seemed quite smitten with me, more so at this stage than I was with him. I paid the bill and we got ready to leave.

Time to go and I had enjoyed our meeting, I told him, but I would have to think as to whether we would meet up again. He was very keen to, I needed to think about it. I got up to go, and watched him struggle out of his chair. He had seized up in his chair, but did eventually manage to get himself up, easing the vertebrae in his back into a working position. But then as we started to walk towards our cars, he started to limp, quite noticeably.

"Are you okay?"

"Yes. I haven't told you I am registered disabled. I have to walk to my car now. I should have parked it in the closer disabled spaces, but I didn't want you to see me struggling."

"I wouldn't have been bothered at all if you had told me, I still would have come."

I phoned him the next day to tell him I didn't want to see him again. If he had told me the truth straight away when chatting, it wouldn't have been a problem, but hiding the truth wasn't a good start to a relationship, which should be built on trust.

Sorry.

I have spoken to other ladies who have dated online, gone on a date, only to find that the bloke they were meeting couldn't get out of the car, or there was some other problem that restricted them. Their feelings, unfortunately, the same as mine – if the truth had been told straight away, there wouldn't have been a problem, but not being honest was a no-no. I suppose from their point of view, they would think no-one would be interested in them if they told the facts. A dilemma for all.

Louis Calamari, London Man

London man had first gone online some four years previously. He had been working in London for some years as a businessman. He had just moved into the area with a change of jobs, squids in with salary, and had started going online again looking for a date.

What sounded exciting about him when his match came up was that he was Italian, an Italian stallion, may be worth a look.

No point hanging around, so rather than chatting for a long time online, I thought, *Let's meet up and see if there is a spark*.

He was keen to meet as well, so we arranged an assignation, to meet up at the café at Sainsbury's in town. I sat myself down and waited… and waited… and waited. Where was he? This was a change from earlier, coffee but no man.

I of course wondered where he was, and decided to give him another ten minutes. I hadn't been stood up yet on one of these meetings, but was it about to happen. I hope not, fingers crossed. Then I noticed him passing he window, and did he look worried; he looked shy. I don't think it said 'dragon woman, eats men' on my profile, but that is what it looked like with the expression on his face.

When I had spoken to him on the phone, he had sounded confident, comfortable talking to me, and as a businessman one assumed he was well used to meeting total strangers. But I suppose chatting online for a partner is totally different to meeting someone for the first time, especially if you are hoping this person will be the person you want to share your life with. Me, I am very confident so it had never been a worry to me.

He came in, looking very nervous, and said he had been very worried about meeting me – anyone. Here he was standing in front of confident me, in a Crombie and cravat, looking very dapper, but nearly shaking, and arriving nearly thirty minutes late.

He introduced himself, "Hello," almost in a whisper, but did start coming out of himself when we got talking. Motown, he loved motown just as I did, and also loved to go out to dances where it played. We had a topic of conversation we could talk at length about.

He came out of himself after this, and we chatted over a couple of coffees before it was time to go our separate ways. I don't think he left feeling he had escaped that female dragon.

We did start seeing more and more of each other over the coming weeks, and he would come round to my rented accommodation, where we would kiss and cuddle.

But it never got any further than that, and gradually just petered out as we lost touch with each other.

Perhaps it just wasn't meant to be, and I resigned myself to not being able to ride a stallion, but then perhaps…

I was shopping in town one day, a long time afterwards, looking for some new sexy underwear, when in the shop window he appeared. He came in and said, "Hi Gill."

I didn't recognise him, he now seemed so confident, and I racked my memory trying to recall his name. Italian, Italian, it was there somewhere. I did at last recall it.

He was busy just then but we exchanged phone numbers again, him saying he would ring me.

I did ring him once at a later date to say sorry but I was no longer a free lady. Well, I hoped I soon wouldn't be, but I could introduce him to a friend.

That underwear shopping, a lovely basque and thong, was part of a fishing strategy I was putting into place to help me catch something special!!

Simon Perch

At times this fishing would be compulsive, addictive, but then I suppose if my goal was to find my life partner, and I had already found that he wasn't going to come knocking on my door, I had to keep at it. If my chosen method to get a catch was my fishing route, then sometimes, quite often in fact, if I wasn't seeing anyone, then I could be chatting to several men at the same time, and if I wasn't seriously going out with anyone, then I could actually end up meeting a couple of men at the same time. Not at the same time literally, that could get a little embarrassing. What I meant was seeing several men at different times, but concurrently, sticking to the two-week rule to see if any were worth further pursuit.

It was during one of these quieter times, chatting but not actually dating, that I came cross one interesting chap. Why was he especially interesting? It was because his background was very similar to mine in that he also worked in people-caring, albeit that he was in child care, my responsibilities being older, but we would have a lot in common through work. Even better, he was local, so it seemed sensible to me to meet this guy, and see if we would hit it off and possibly find a future together.

So it was with a little hope that I arranged to meet for coffee, as in my normal fishing regime, meet up for an hour or so and see where we would go from there.

We met, and there, sitting in front of me was a very pleasant man, looking very fit, he obviously worked out, and those bits of flesh I could see, were heavily tattooed, but that was okay with me. He was in fact very presentable, one of the better-looking blokes that I had met up with. And better still, at a first-off meeting he seemed very pleasant, though there was obviously a lot of baggage that accompanied him. He was divorced, and worked very hard to earn himself a life and a future, but sadly for him, every time he accumulated some money, then his ex would come knocking on the door, demanding half of it or more, and as he had no record of what he had paid her out, he was obliged to, and did pay her. He therefore worked very hard for very little reward, which was very frustrating for him. One would have thought he would have learnt, because he had been married several times, and would seem to have had many skeletons in his cupboard. That didn't sound to promising to me, for a future, because the past would always be there to bite back, but I had to give him a chance, especially as nothing else was looking too promising. My fishing quest at that stage was looking more than a little barren; nothing was taking the bait, or I was setting the wrong bait for what I wanted to catch?

I decided to give him a go, so after another couple of coffee meetings, we did start seeing each other as a 'couple'. We had a good start in that with our jobs being so similar, we had a lot in common to start with, so conversation would always be easy. Our shift patterns may make life a little awkward, but it was nothing that couldn't easily be sorted out, and he lived locally so we didn't have vast distances to travel.

Our first dates were just casual affairs, meeting up to go to the pub for a drink, or even better sometimes to do a pub quiz which I really enjoyed. We would chat about work, and about his past, and his ever-demanding ex-wife stinging him for every penny he earnt, and he did work very hard. It was a shame for him because he was never able to give himself a new start in life, as just as something became obtainable, then it was snatched away from him by his ever-greedy ex. If it painted a gloomy picture for our future to me, at least I could see if I could help him by getting some forms for him, and helping him fill them in which may let him escape from his predicament. The hard thing for him was that the she had gone off with another man, and he was paying for it.

I suppose that meant that we both knew we were only killing time together; we would enjoy each other's company for the time being, but it wasn't going to last, and sooner rather than later we would go our separate ways. Me, I wanted a more stable and sound financial background, and him, to be honest with his highly toned and tattooed body, he was really looking for a more 'fit' woman than slightly overweight and couch potato me.

But while it lasted, we were determined to try and make the best of it, and I certainly had a lot of fun while with him. He had a flat in town, and me my house out in the sticks, but we would often, as we got to know each other better, stay over at one another's, so we could drink, watch videos, or whatever else took our fancy.

He had a Mini which I loved, and would be my ideal car, and he also had a motorbike, which he would take me out on. It was my idea to have a go on the bike, a big sporting motorbike, though he didn't have any spare kit – helmet, leathers etc. It was arranged, he would pick me up and we would go out for the day on the bike.

I would have to admit that it had been some years since I had been on a bike, my only experience being when we were based in the Far East. I did have a little moped to get around on when I was in Brunei. Low-key stuff, putt-putting around there.

I borrowed a helmet off my son, which thankfully fitted me very well. No leathers so I would just be wearing normal clothes – jeans, a sweater, and a leather jacket I had. I patiently waited for Mr Perch to arrive, starting to feel more than a bit apprehensive. He arrived, dressed the part in his leathers, and ushered me on board, riding behind him. We were off, and he did travel at a fair speed, which meant if my hold of him, arms around his waist, was firm to begin with, it became more and more of a bear hug the further and faster we went, until I was starting to crush the life out of him. Yes, it was exhilarating, but my lack of experience of bikes, especially at this speed, made for more than an interesting journey.

Never a problem on my moped, fast cornering created more than a bit of a problem. When he leant into the bend, I was trying to go the other way. Was that a wobble of the bike? Yes, I think it was. We drove, rode, for an hour or so and then stopped for a pub lunch, and for me a much-needed drink to calm my nerves. Then we were back riding again, but our co-ordination was still not in sync. It was not an understatement that by the time he had dropped me off, I had decided I wasn't going on the bike again, and he that he wasn't going to take me on it again. True love would have to find another way to travel. Leathers may have helped. Would I have looked good as a biking chick? To be honest I could see myself in more appealing leather attire, which could whip my man into a frenzy (only joking about the whip).

I would visit his flat where I found he had a big interest in collecting skulls, as in, being embossed on belt buckles, on miniature motorbikes. He had motifs of them, a whole display. Not for me, but if that was what he wanted, who was I to stop him? Even with a collection filling any space it could in his flat, he did keep it very tidy, especially for a man. The only thing that I could fault him on was his choice of linen for the bed. I like, always have liked, expensive, top-quality linen, sheets, pillow cases, and duvet covers, and it was rather against the grain to be sleeping in these old, cheap sheets, with all the material forming bobbles. As our relationship got more intimate, which as you may have guessed it did as we both had needs, then for me to enjoy his bed I did find it necessary to go out and buy him some 'decent' bedsheets.

It was summer, so we enjoyed getting out, going places whether on the bike (the once) or in the car, the Mini. We had a lot of fun, and one weekend even took ourselves off to France on a wine run. Could you blame me? I do love my wine, and it would combine a weekend away with purchasing something I – we both – enjoyed drinking, and we would be able to squeeze quite a lot even in a Mini.

This French trip was my idea. We set off on the Saturday morning, sharing the driving as we made our way down to the Channel Tunnel. Not a bad trip as it was all motorway, and waited patiently for our turn to board the train. I had driven on the Continent before, so this was not a new experience for me. All I had to do was to remember to drive on the other side of the road when we got to France. Whatever you may be thinking, we were not about to have a disaster any time now, but just disembarked from the train, and had a short journey down the coast to the hotel we were staying in, in a little village called Coquelles, literally just a stone's throw from the Channel terminal. By now it was late afternoon, early evening, so we weren't going to do much other than book into the hotel, which I had organised and paid for, and then find something to eat.

This was France, renowned for its fine food and wine, so what better than the Grill House across la rue? Were we about to tuck into entrecôte and pomme frites – no, we were English abroad, so steak and chips was good enough for us, but of course with a bottle of vin rouge. C'est la vie, we were in France and having a good time; it had been a nice drive down through England and then under the Channel to be here, we had enjoyed each other's company.

Time to retire to la chambre, and I hope it doesn't sound like I was prostituting myself out, but was I going to pay for the room if I wasn't going to get a bonk? Not on your life. If I had just had my steak medium rare, I was now hoping for something tougher, harder, with a lot of beef behind it. Branded with tattoos, my bull was about to perform for me, service with a smile. I lay on my back and for a brief time enjoyed the pleasures of France, le boeuf then le bonk. Then c'etait les temps a dormer, pardon my poor French.

Our crossing back to England was not until four in the afternoon, so we had time to kill. Le petit déjeuner of croissant and coffee, enjoyed, then time to get our wine. There were several outlets to get cheap wine, and that task was soon completed, so we took the brief road down to the sandy beach, and enjoyed the sunshine, walking with sand in our toes, and skipping through the gentle waves. Typically English, and childish and fun, but it was nice to walk hand in hand along the shore.

The hours soon passed and it was time to head back to the Channel terminal, board and return back to England, and home.

It had been a lovely, if tiring weekend, but we had enjoyed the sun, each other's company, and I most importantly had restocked my 'wine cellar'.

We enjoyed each other's company very much, but as I said earlier it wasn't going to last long. I wasn't really his type of woman in body shape, and as we spent more time together I found him too set in his ways; there was never any compromise in anything we talked about or did. He wouldn't except my viewpoint, or adapt to any suggestions of doing something better that I may have suggested, trying to be helpful rather than interfering.

We made love together on several occasions, hence my need to get linen I was happy to sleep in, and have sex in. It was good; he was a fit man, and if he would take me to bed in my nightie, we would entwine, wrestle as we explored each other's bodies, toying, arousing, exciting each other before with his cock erect he would mount me, enter me, and energetically thrust away until he was spent. But what about me? I wanted to come as well, bigtime, so although when he was inside me it was good, it was never enough for me, as his penis quickly drooped away, and me, I was left frustrated once again. Jesus, would I have to go to Boots again and get some more batteries for Buzz Buzz? The bloody rabbit would soon be worn out.

It's a common problem among men of the age I was likely to date, but this not being able to keep it up was frustrating me, big time! Again, here though, there was a selfish element in him in that he had got his satisfaction from me, had shot his bolt and that was good enough for him. It didn't seem to matter that I lay there being frustrated yet again.

Yes, we did have fun together, but through a variety of things — no money, a council flat, no real prospects, and his unwillingness to adapt or change to accommodate me — we slowly petered out and were back online, out to catch another.

However, unlike a lot of the men I had met and chatted with, we did remain friends. In fact, he did help me move house, which he didn't have to do, and even to this day he does write on my Facebook, seeming genuinely pleased when I put up a post about being out somewhere with my latest, hoping that I am happy and wishing me well.

No great romance, but I did gain a friend, so to that end a worthwhile encounter. It was also the first of my dates, online dates that is, that I ventured away from our home shores, even if it was only for a weekend away.

Elvers Rose

I didn't seem to be getting very far in finding my match. Were my expectations too high? I don't know, but perhaps this was the time to step back and review where I was going, what I wanted, and how I was going to achieve it. Was I setting my expectations too high? Did I need to change the way I chatted? Should I broaden the spectrum of men I was prepared to chat with, and then potentially meet? A lot of questions; all I could say was that there was no-one yet who had come anywhere near what I thought I was looking for.

I decided that I would go for a slightly wider age group, and then if we got chatting online, meet up sooner so I wouldn't waste time. If they were nice we could meet again, if not suitable, I could throw them back into the pond. If we couldn't meet up straight away, I would try and get them to chat on WhatsApp, so we could exchange more 'media' like photos, etc. We could then get a better feel for each other, and progress from there. It was a bit like tickling for trout in those bygone days of when I was young.

So it was that I started chatting to this guy called Elvers Rose but on a different site, Oasis, because I was finding a lot of men on Badoo seemed just after one thing, and got very smutty early on. We chatted for a fortnight or so, and then it seemed a natural progression to go onto WhatsApp, and then to exchange telephone numbers. That thing called work did get in our way, as to when we were able to chat to each other, but I did think it would be an idea to record how some of these conversations went, and how events would unfold – some good, and some bad.

Here goes.

12/05/2012, 9:32 pm - Elvers: Hi u not forgotten me have u X

12/05/2012, 9:33 pm - Gill: Nope. I like this chat site. Just going to work. X

I slept a long time lol, chat after 11 if you're up still x

12/05/2012, 9:35 pm - Elvers: No sorry tucked up in bed at ten

12/05/2014, 9:37 pm - Gill Finn: OK chat soon x

As one can see, I was getting a far quicker reply on this, like on a phone but in written word.

13/05/2012, 10:41 am - Elvers: Hi

I would have been doing a night shift so when Elvers called, I would have been tucked up in bed myself.

13/05/2012, 2:15 pm - Gill Finn: Hi Elvers. X

I have just woken up. I needed a wee, not that you needed to know that.

Last night I booked to go to Las Vegas, I am going on 11

June for a week. Fantastic price. Wanna come, lol xx (I suppose that was quite forward, but I was going on my own, and any trip is better with company!)

13/05/2012, 2:35 pm - Elvers: Only on 1 condition!!!!!

13/05/2012, 2:35 pm - Gill Finn: What's that??!!!!

13/05/2012, 2:37 pm - Elvers: I get to become a member of The Mile High Club

13/05/2012, 2:38 pm - Gill Finn: OK x (Is this getting smutty already?)

13/05/2012, 2:57 pm - Elvers: Not sure if vital measurements would allow me entry ☹ (His profile had him nearly six foot six.)

13/05/2012, 3:11 pm - Gill Finn: Lol so if it's measurements of vital organs. I think you would be fine. Lol

I have won a laptop lol just sorting out delivery xx my son will have to wait at my house while I am sleeping. X

13/05/2012, 3:19 pm - Elvers: Lucky lady

You laugh at my vital organs

13/05/2012, 3:20 pm - Gill Finn: They are no laughing matter. X

So are we going to talk on the phone soon

Remember I have seen your undies lol x

(He had already sent me a photo of him as a baby in nappies.)

13/05/2012, 3:24 pm - Elvers: Yes, be nice to hear your voice

Oh them not undies lol,

Just winter warmers

13/05/2012, 3:25 pm - Gill Finn: OK I will phone you later. I am just booking my car parking at Manchester. X

13/05/2012, 4:09 pm - Elvers: Just on metro on way home

13/05/2012, 4:15 pm - Gill Finn: Easier than driving. Or do you not drive?

13/05/2012, 4:16 pm - Elvers: Thought you seen pics on oasis, pictures of the car ,

13/05/2012, 4:16 pm - Gill Finn: Oh yep lol x

13/05/2012, 4:17 pm - Gill Finn: But could of been wife's car!!!!

13/05/2012, 4:21 pm - Elvers: Lol with my name on reg. Don't think so.

13/05/2012, 4:22 pm - Gill Finn: So I could only see part of it what is it. Or have you told me?

13/05/2014, 4:22 pm - Gill Finn: I think my memory is getting worse.

13/05/2012, 4:23 pm - Elvers: U need Specsavers lol

13/05/2012, 4:24 pm - Gill Finn: OK booked holiday. Visa card for parking and got nectar point on the holiday lol, x

13/05/2012, 4:24 pm - Gill Finn: I got valet parking

13/05/2012, 4:24 pm - Elvers: U won lotto lol

13/05/2012, 4:26 pm - Elvers: Going to car now chat later

13/05/2012, 4:26 pm - Gill Finn: I have new glasses ordered. Should get them before holiday. One pair are reactor lights.

Weather in Vegas 32 degrees nice and pool

13/05/2012, 4:28 pm - Elvers: Do like me throw glasses in bin have laser treatment

13/05/2012, 4:31 pm - Gill Finn: The problem is laser treatment, I don't know whether it's true but it'll only last couple of years he spending a couple £2000 pam jeffrey classic up the tree you for our age.

13/05/2012, 4:31 pm - Gill Finn: Lol that's funny that message I'm trying to talk into my phone and half of it correct and half of it not.

(The phone was picking up another conversation, hence the garbled message.)

13/05/2012, 4:32 pm - Gill Finn: I don't want to spend a couple of thousand pounds to have my eyes done. (The right message now.)

13/05/2012, 4:33 pm - Gill Finn: Sorry talking to my friend and it went to wrong chat. X Have a good journey

13/05/2012, 6:34 pm - Elvers: Shame u didn't swear to your friend lol

13/05/2012, 8:25 pm - Gill Finn: I very, very rarely swear. X Just woke up.,

13/05/2012, 9:15 pm - Elvers: Have a nice evening x

13/05/2012, 9:43 pm - Gill Finn: Thank you Hun x

13/05/2012, 9:44 pm - Elvers: Just putting nightshirt and bobble hat on for bed

13/05/2012, 9:54 pm - Gill Finn: Lol xx

14/05/2012, 11:51 am - Elvers: Good morning or Good afternoon

14/05/2012, 7:06 pm - Gill Finn: Hi. Just woke up x

I was up at 1, till 3. Sorting out new computer but went

back to sleep at 4. X

14/05/2012, 7:07 pm - Gill Finn: I did say. when I am working I would be sleep and work x

14/05/2012, 7:08 pm - Gill Finn: I have picked up sat night too.

As I am off on Tuesday and Wednesday to have windows fitted. X

14/05/2012, 3:59 pm - Elvers: Hi Gill want to see your naked selfie

15/05/2012, 5:25 am - Gill Finn: Nope. Never see unwrapped presents.

Like them wrapped.

(He is getting a little forward and smutty again, I will try and cool things down.)

15/05/2012, 7:18 am - Elvers: Lol enjoy

15/05/2012, 7:28 am - Gill Finn: Good morning.

15/05/2012, 7:29 am - Gill Finn: Last night till Saturday. Free on Sunday?

15/05/2012, 7:30 am- Elvers: Hi on tram know how a sardine feels like lol

15/05/2012, 7:31 am - Gill Finn: Really tired but got to drive 21 miles. X.

Then I will be home x

How are you Mr sardine????

15/05/2012, 7:33 am - Elvers: Ok can't complain

So have u won lotto

15/05/2012, 7:39 am - Gill Finn: Cannot say have to shred you xx. (it's my secret).

15/05/2012, 7:42 am - Elvers:

At this point he sent me a naked selfie, a Teddy Bear with his face on!

15/05/2012, 7:42 am - Elvers: Hope u like my naked selfie

15/05/2012, 7:45 am - Gill Finn: Lol x very nice

15/05/2012, 7:52 am - Elvers: Must get a new razor I look terrible (To look more bare-faced, I suppose.)

15/05/2012, 7:57 am - Gill Finn: Driving now x

15/05/2012, 8:03 am - Elvers: Know where u lived but where do u work Gill

15/05/2012, 8:10 am - Gill Finn: Work in a village some 4.5 miles from Shrewsbury. Just stopped to get milk. X driving again xx

15/05/2012, 8:11 am - Elvers: Long way. You'll be glad to get in bed

15/05/2012, 8:11 am - Gill Finn: Yep x

15/05/2012, 8:12 am - Elvers: Just starting work now ☹

15/05/2012, 8:59 am - Elvers: So how much u win on lotto

15/05/2012, 9:02 am - Gill Finn: Nothing as good as lottery. My birth father and his wife both died and I have had a few pennies to buy my house. Etc.

I also have a pension that. Is very good and index linked. That is why I want a man who is solvent.

15/05/2012, 9:04 am - Elvers: You don't want a gold digger I understand

15/05/2012, 9:06 am - Gill Finn: I have already had one. X

15/05/2012, 9:10 am - Gill Finn: I am sending you a topless photo of me

15/05/2012, 9:11 am - Gill Finn: If I have it on this phone x

15/05/2012, 9:12 am - Gill Finn: (I sent him a picture of me in our garden holding a spade.)

15/05/2012, 9:12 am - Gill Finn: Me aged 7 in Singapore x

15/05/2012, 9:16 am - Elvers: Thanks Gill, I love it

I am not gold digger as have large shovel but small pick lol

15/05/2012, 9:17 am - Gill Finn: Very droll. OK phone going off ... sleep time. Text you later xx

15/05/2012, 9:18 am - Elvers: Sleep well.

A problem here in that when at work, he is in bed, and when He is at work, then I am asleep.

15/05/2012, 9:19 am - Gill Finn: Ty

15/05/2012, 9:25 am - Elvers: (He sends me a photo, him topless and holding his belly.)

15/05/2012, 9:26 am - Elvers: Me topless 8

Sorry forgotten the 5 lol

15/05/2012, 5:20 pm - Gill Finn: lol x

15/05/2012, 6:15 pm - Gill Finn: Hello naked man lol

15/05/2012, 6:40 pm - Elvers: Hi babe, not naked just topless like yours. Think I got bigger boobs than u lol

15/05/2012, 6:47 pm - Gill Finn: Lol

Perhaps.

15/05/2012, 6:49 pm - Elvers: Joke, Whats

Hard

Long

Ejects Seamen!!!!!

15/05/2012, 6:51 pm - Gill Finn: Lifeboat lol x

15/05/2012, 6:52 pm - Elvers: Close Submarine.

15/05/2012, 6:53 pm - Gill Finn: OK I have to eat something. I slept too long. Lol

Have lots of housework to do. Son on his way, to get KFC. I was going to have a steak and salad.

When I am working nothing gets done lol

Shall I ring you for 5 mins?

15/05/2012, 6:54 pm - Gill Finn: I am also trying to download all updates on new laptop lol x

15/05/2012, 6:55 pm - Gill Finn: It windows 8. Not sure I like it

15/05/2012, 6:56 pm - Elvers: Got friends here. Friday better.

No 8 forget it 😕

15/05/2012, 7:08 pm - Gill Finn: Friday might be a problem for me. But sat early evening. Will be ok 4 me what about you?

15/05/2012, 7:10 pm - Elvers: It's a date

Hope u not offended by my naughty jokes Gill

15/05/2012, 7:11 pm - Gill Finn: No. I am fine with them x

No worries

15/05/2012, 7:12 pm - Gill Finn: Have fun with friends. I will text you sat afternoon. Just to interrupt your sport lol x

15/05/2012, 7:12 pm - Gill Finn: Might send you a naked photo of me lol x

15/05/2012, 7:13 pm - Elvers: Mmmmm interesting

15/05/2012, 7:13 pm - Gill Finn: Lol yeah x

15/05/2012, 7:23 pm - Elvers: Ok I exchange totally naked photos with you, Gill

15/05/2012, 7:23 pm - Gill Finn: No lol

15/05/2012, 7:24 pm - Elvers: It's ok, nothing to be ashamed of the human body.

I send my first

15/05/2012, 7:26 pm - Gill Finn: (I send him a picture of me and my sisters as babies, that's the best he's going to get.)

15/05/2012, 7:26 pm - Gill Finn: I am first one

15/05/2012, 7:27 pm - Gill Finn: Nope real life is good. But this has shared files lol x

OK dinners here x (My son had arrived with the KFC.)

15/05/2012, 7:27 pm – Elvers: (He sends me a cute naked baby picture, on all fours with its bum sticking in the air.)

15/05/2012, 7:27 pm - Gill Finn: Mine's real

15/05/2012, 7:28 pm - Elvers: You asking too much Gill lol

15/05/2012, 7:42 pm - Gill Finn: Lol

Cute. Right

Have to do housework x

15/05/2012, 7:42 pm - Elvers: That's not lady like sitting with legs apart lol

15/05/2012, 7:43 pm - Gill Finn: Lol. Well your bums sticking up near my nose.

15/05/2012, 7:44 pm - Elvers: Yes, I got wind lol

15/05/2012, 7:44 pm - Gill Finn: OK I will text u in a bit I have changed bed. Washed sheets. Done tidying up. Now going upstairs to do bathroom after my shower x

15/05/2012, 7:45 pm - Gill Finn: And no you cannot wash my back. Lol x

15/05/2012, 7:48 pm - Elvers: Ur BACK to start with mmmm

15/05/2012, 7:52 pm - Elvers: Mmmm nice body, mmmm!

15/05/2012, 8:13 pm - Gill Finn: A glass of white x taking 5 mind lol x

15/05/2012, 8:27 pm - Elvers: Sorry not understand any of message ☹

15/05/2012, 8:29 pm - Gill Finn: I am having a glass of wine. taking 5 mins away from housework watching big bang theory. X

15/05/2012, 8:31 pm - Elvers: U. Not working tonight?

15/05/2012, 8:31 pm - Gill Finn: So when are we going to meet?

15/05/2012, 8:32 pm - Gill Finn: Nope. Goodness me I have just Done 4 nights. slave driver. I am doing extra night sat. *As my window are being fitted on work days. (Sometimes the odd message would be delayed and so would be received in the wrong order.)*

15/05/2012, 8:35 pm - Elvers: I work 5 days looks like Sat's as well, soon to much work.

15/05/2012, 8:35 pm - Gill Finn: I do 10 hour shifts

15/05/2012, 8:36 pm - Gill Finn: But love my 4 days off.

If we do not meet soon I will fall out with you

15/05/2012, 8:39 pm - Elvers: Oh Gill don't b like that with me ☐ 😕

15/05/2012, 8:40 pm - Gill Finn: Avoiding question

15/05/2012, 8:42 pm - Gill Finn: How long have we been chatting

15/05/2012, 8:43 pm - Gill Finn: Over a week, are you shy?

15/05/2012, 8:43 pm - Elvers: That sounds serious. We only been chatting few days' sweetie.

15/05/2012, 8:44 pm - Gill Finn: OK. But I think your shy.

Or married?

15/05/2012, 8:45 pm - Gill Finn: Anyway it's not serious. It's natural progression.

I am worried for you. What if you miss out on the best thing that ever happened to you????

15/05/2012, 8:47 pm - Elvers: Gill after 23 years married. out of touch in dating, and yes am shy, not had date in years.

15/05/2012, 8:48 pm - Gill Finn: Well do not worry I

will be gentle with you. Lol. (I was at the stage where I felt a meeting would be good. He seemed okay, a bit smutty at times, but with a good sense of humour, and it would be nice to know if we were compatible. He seemed to want to delay this progression.)

15/05/2012, 8:50 pm - Elvers: Thank you. U more confident than me.

15/05/2012, 8:50 pm - Gill Finn: I am not shallow. I am 57. And I am looking for someone to be able to cook for and be able to cuddle while I sleep.

I usually meet ASAP. Then I know I have some connection to work with.

15/05/2012, 8:51 pm - Gill Finn: Someone to look after my needs. Oh don't worry I have a dishwasher.

I am even tempered. I never lie.

15/05/2012, 8:54 pm - Elvers: Hope needs are not too demanding lol

15/05/2012, 8:57 pm - Gill Finn: But I do understand.

I will wait until you're ready.

I am chatting to another chap.

But I am very fair. I hope!! If I decide to see someone a second time, then I will tell you or them and I will no longer chat to anyone else as it's not fair.

So I hope it's you xx

But I will wait until you're ready.

You make me laugh.

Funny man

15/05/2012, 9:01 pm - Elvers: Thanks for understanding

Not going into detail, when married had a very adventurous and passionate love life.

15/05/2012, 9:01 pm - Gill Finn: Did you have affairs?

15/05/2012, 9:07 pm - Elvers: NO, wasn't me.

15/05/2012, 9:08 pm - Gill Finn: She strayed?

You will have to tell me.

One day.

15/05/2012, 9:11 pm - Gill Finn: I am going upstairs. Chat later. When you visitors are gone and when I finish cleaning.

But if your asleep, no issues. X chat in morning or sat. When I am free x

15/05/2012, 9:21 pm - Elvers: Usual old story, me working long hours

She met a man at work

15/05/2012, 9:26 pm - Elvers: Hols to Turkey Greek Islands Portugal Malta Amsterdam Belgium Cyprus Egypt (pyramids) for wat O ☹

15/05/2012, 9:41 pm - Elvers: Just putting night shirt and bed socks plus bobble hat on.

What time can u chat Friday

15/05/2012, 9:46 pm - Gill Finn: Not sure I will text you x.

15/05/2012, 9:48 pm - Gill Finn: I have done All those hols. Lol lived in Belgium, lol.

Chat soon. Funny man, sleep well x I will text you in the morning x

15/05/2012, 9:50 pm - Gill Finn: Can't wait to see you

in bobble hat and night shirt. lol

But alas could be next year at this rate lol

X X

I have just restarted new laptop 100 updates lol x

15/05/2012, 9:51 pm - Elvers: Only joking sleep commando

15/05/2012, 9:53 pm - Gill Finn: Night, night. X sleep well.

Question. How often do you change your bed linen?

Lol

15/05/2012, 9:54 pm - Elvers: Lol cheeky sod

15/05/2012, 9:59 pm - Gill Finn: Lol

15/05/2012, 10:00 pm - Gill Finn: Night lol

15/05/2012, 10:08 pm - Elvers: I have shower before bed, and hope no accidents in night ☹

15/05/2012, 10:24 pm - Gill Finn: Lol x

(I was trying to push him to see me, but he at least was opening out a bit about his past, so was I making progress, even with all his little innuendos!)

16/05/2012, 7:15 am - Elvers: Good morning gonna be hot today, have to find your bikini. out

16/05/2012, 7:17 am - Gill Finn: Good morning

I have had a message from my optician's I have new reactor lights ready today. Just in time for good weather

X.

16/05/2012, 7:24 am - Elvers: That's good

16/05/2012, 7:24 am - Elvers: Oh, sitting on tram now.

16/05/2012, 7:36 am - Elvers: Did u know reactor lights no good for driving

16/05/2012, 7:42 am - Gill Finn: Why? I do have some driving sunglasses.

16/05/2012, 7:43 am - Elvers: They don't change in the car.

16/05/2012, 7:43 am - Gill Finn: So I have to stick my head out the window lol x

16/05/2012, 7:45 am - Elvers: (He sends me a picture of his smiley face poking out of sheets with his bobble hat on.)

16/05/2012, 7:46 am - Gill Finn: Was that a joke lol. I think I am clever lol.

16/05/2012, 7:51 am - Elvers: No serious I wore them.

U said last nite you wanted to see me in nite shirt and bobble hat,

Only way is in bed

16/05/2012, 7:53 am - Gill Finn: Lol, behave. Told you this dating thing has a natural progression. The only time I will ever see you in bed will be in a nursing home lol

16/05/2012, 7:56 am - Elvers: You sure about that remember I been celibate over 3 years.

16/05/2012, 7:59 am - Gill Finn: Bless you.

If you have been completely celibate for three years I will be lucky.

You certainly do not know how dating goes as we have to meet before we go into bed, and perhaps go out to dinner, go for a walk, going visit different places.

16/05/2012, 8:06 am - Elvers: Only teasing you.

Manager going out at 1 pm, so can talk if u wish.

16/05/2012, 8:08 am - Gill Finn: Sorry Hun I will be out. A friend has just bought an Audi. It's faster than a Porsche, so he says so I going for a ride. Not sure if it's a cabriolet. But it will be fun as the sun is shining x

16/05/2012, 8:09 am - Elvers: A MAN FRIEND ☹

16/05/2012, 8:11 am - Gill Finn: I have more men friends than ladies.

(Can I make him jealous so he wants to see me? I can't understand his reluctance at this stage, even if he is supposedly shy, though I was going out in the Audi.)

I told you if my relationship is not right then I always stay friends. Lol.

Anyway you won't even be classed as a friend, you're a chat person.

16/05/2012, 8:14 am - Elvers: I want to hear your voice

16/05/2012, 8:14 am - Gill Finn: Saturday I will phone you x

16/05/2012, 8:15 am - Gill Finn: Before I go to work.

16/05/2012, 8:16 am - Elvers: Long time to wait Gill

U got anymore photos please?

16/05/2012, 8:17 am - Gill Finn: I might do a selfie. In a minute I will see lol

16/05/2012, 8:19 am - Elvers: Thank you. Too hot to work today.

16/05/2012, 8:22 am - Gill Finn: (I send him a picture of the real me, just head and shoulders.)

16/05/2012, 8:22 am - Gill Finn: Me now. A selfie x

16/05/2012, 8:22 am - Gill Finn: But getting new glasses today

16/05/2012, 8:23 am - Elvers: R u true ginger

16/05/2012, 8:23 am - Gill Finn: Bottle lol sorry

16/05/2012, 8:37 am - Gill Finn: So now you're not speaking to me??

Now you know I am a bottle red and you gave seen my selfie sob sob.

16/05/2012, 8:47 am - Gill Finn: Starting my ironing x

16/05/2012, 8:59 am - Elvers: Sorry, had to start work.

Don't starch bra and panties

16/05/2012, 8:59 am - Gill Finn: (That was a bit more personal.) *Lol enjoy your day x*

16/05/2012, 9:08 am - Elvers: Never seen a ginger Bush ☹

16/05/2012, 9:08 am - Gill Finn: Nor me lol x

16/05/2012, 9:18 am - Elvers: I prefer nice and smooooooth.

16/05/2012, 9:19 am - Gill Finn: Tut tut. Calm down lol.

Your funny. Get back to work x (He was getting more and more smutty now, tried to calm him down and get onto a better topic.)

16/05/2012, 9:20 am - Gill Finn: I am going to get my new glasses x chat later x

16/05/2012, 9:40 am - Elvers: U think I funny

U not seen my briefs around ankles

16/05/2012, 9:41 am - Gill Finn: Lol x

16/05/2012, 10:23 am - Elvers: Hi Ginger

Elvers The Bolt here!!!

16/05/2012, 10:24 am - Gill Finn: Lol shopping at moment.

16/05/2012, 10:26 am - Elvers: On a break thinking of u

16/05/2012, 10:26 am - Gill Finn: That's nice lol

16/05/2012, 10:27 am - Elvers: Mmmmmmmmmmmmm.

16/05/2012, 10:42 am - Gill Finn: Petrol or diesel now, lol.

16/05/2012, 10:52 am - Elvers: Diesel

My piston gone rusty. ☹

(He has got seriously smutty now, non-stop.)

16/05/2012, 12:23 pm - Elvers: Having nice day in sunshine sweetie?

16/05/2012, 3:42 pm - Elvers:
☺☺☺☺☺☺☺☺☺☺☺☺☺☺☺☺☺☺☺☺

16/05/2012, 6:07 pm - Gill Finn: Went to the RAF museum at Codsall.

Now going to eat.

If you're brave enough we will have meet Sunday lol.

Lol. Talk later x x

16/05/2012, 6:27 pm - Elvers: Glad u had a nice day

Sorry but going fishing Sunday, as weather gonna be nice

X.

(Now he is going fishing. It's me who's supposed to be fishing, to catch my man!)

16/05/2012, 6:28 pm - Gill Finn: OK I will remember.

17/05/2012, 9:38 am - Elvers: Good morning

17/05/2012, 9:44 am - Gill Finn: Good morning

17/05/2012, 9:50 am - Elvers: Too hot to lie in bed ☹

17/05/2012, 9:53 am - Gill Finn: I have the lawn to mow and I need some shopping from b and q

17/05/2012, 10:30 am - Gill Finn: What are you doing today?

17/05/2012, 12:43 pm - Elvers: Took brother to hospital for his pre op he got op on foot next sat.

Just having a cold beer, then in garden with my mankini.

17/05/2012, 12:49 pm - Gill Finn: Lol

17/05/2012, 1:06 pm - Elvers: What you laffin at ☺

17/05/2012, 2:25 pm - Gill Finn: Mankini lol.

17/05/2012, 2:28 pm - Elvers: Ok maybe can't fill pouch plus knobbly knees.

17/05/201, 2:29 pm - Gill Finn: Just spent too much time in the garden. Going to shower then have 40 winks. Will you be sleeping early tonight or wanna chat to me at work? Extra duty. Tonight xx

17/05/2012, 2:30 pm - Elvers: Can chat now if u wish?

17/05/2012, 2:31 pm - Gill Finn: Shower then 40 winks.

17/05/2012, 2:33 pm - Elvers: Ok. Send selfie in shower

17/05/2012, 2:37 pm - Gill Finn: Lol I now am not working. Wanna meet up? I was double booked??

17/05/2012, 2:40 pm - Gill Finn: Tell you what we can chat I will have a shower and then phone you ok?

17/05/2012, 2:42 pm - Elvers: Yes, that be nice I put some clothes on lol.

17/05/2012, 2:44 pm - Gill Finn: What???? Meet up.

17/05/2012, 2:45 pm - Elvers: On my way to you.

17/05/2012, 2:46 pm - Gill Finn: You don't have my address

17/05/2012, 2:46 pm - Gill Finn: OK, shower and I will phone you xx

17/05/2012, 2:46 pm - Elvers: Lol I teasing u,

17/05/2012, 2:47 pm - Gill Finn: I know but I will still phone you. In 30 mins 'ish

17/05/2012, 2:48 pm - Elvers: Ok don't forget my selfie

17/05/2014, 2:52 pm - Gill Finn: Not on your life or if my life depends on it x

17/05/2012, 2:51 pm – Elvers: Lol just a leg

17/05/2012, 2:59 pm - Gill Finn: I am fed up that you're going fishing instead of spending time meeting me.

17/05/2012, 3:00 pm - Gill Finn: Think I will have to find a new beau.

I have 60 people on encounters wanting to meet up.

At this rate you will lose the chance!!!!¿¿¿

(I was starting to think this was all a waste of time;

he was so standoffish when it came to talking about meeting up, and we couldn't get anywhere if we didn't at least see each other once. There always seemed to be some excuse that he couldn't see me, or didn't want to. And wherever our chats went, they seemed to get on the suggestive side sooner or later. Persevere, Gill, and see what becomes of it).

17/05/2012, 3:02 pm - Elvers: Sorry but planned this over week ago.

17/05/2012, 3:05 pm - Elvers: Maybe u best delete. Me.

17/05/2012, 3:13 pm - Gill Finn: Truth? Are you married or really shy?

17/05/2012, 3:37 pm - Elvers: I. AM NERVOUS. AND SHY

Sorry.

17/05/2012, 3:40 pm - Gill Finn: I cannot bite you over the phone. I am about to chill out and play a few games on the computer. I will leave it for you to phone me. Then there are no worries. Your choice Elvers Rose. x😊💬

18/05/2012, 5:41 pm - Elvers: Hi sorry no contact!!!

18/05/2012, 5:41 pm - Gill Finn: I did say up to you.

18/05/2012, 5:48 pm - Elvers: I can see future.!!!

18/05/2012, 5:50 pm - Gill Finn: What do you see?

18/05/2012, 5:52 pm – Elvers: (He sends me a picture of two people in bed, with our faces on. There he goes again, smut again, or certainly being more than suggestive that he just wants to bed me!)

18/05/2012, 5:52 pm - Gill Finn: PMSL

18/05/2012, 5:54 pm - Gill Finn: You're not shy. I

think your married

18/05/2012, 5:55 pm - Elvers: I think it's brilliant We make a lovely couple. x

18/05/2012, 6:21 pm - Elvers: Hi look not married have only one ring

18/05/2012, 6:21 pm - Elvers: (A picture of his hand.)

18/05/2012, 6:22 pm - Gill Finn: Lol wrong hand.

(Another picture.)

18/05/2012, 6:22 pm - Gill Finn: Same hand

18/05/2012, 6:22 pm - Elvers: (A picture of his knees.)

18/05/2012, 6:23 pm - Gill Finn: Knobbly knees

18/05/2012, 6:25 pm - Elvers: ☐

18/05/2012, 6:26 pm - Gill Finn: So why not meet up. We could be wasting lots of time if we'd met up we could of been having a lovely drink and cuddle on a sofa

18/05/2012, 6:28 pm - Gill Finn: And at this rate in your mind and in your photos of ladies will be me the one you let get away.

18/05/2012, 6:38 pm - Elvers: I know the thought of me holding you. Sitting close smelling your perfume excites me.

18/05/2012, 6:39 pm - Gill Finn: But not enough to meet.!! (I was now really pushing for this meeting, was getting fed up though he was funny, and would have liked to at least have seen what he was like in the flesh.)

18/05/2012, 6:40 pm - Gill Finn: I only want to meet up due to the fact I have been scammed twice.

Both times I never met them.

18/05/2012, 6:51 pm - Elvers: We meet soon Gill

Be patient please

18/05/2012, 6:53 pm - Gill Finn: I will. But don't ask to lend any money or to phone you. On a dodgy pay line lol.

18/05/2012, 6:56 pm - Elvers: Don't want your money I have good employment

Gill please don't insult me

I not like that. 🙁

18/05/2012, 6:56 pm - Gill Finn: It was a joke

18/05/2012, 6:58 pm - Elvers: Ok going for shower now then going for drinks with brother

Need back washing.

18/05/2012, 6:58 pm - Gill Finn: OK speak again

18/05/2012, 6:59 pm – Elvers: Ok u wash my back or speak again

18/05/2012, 7:00 pm - Gill Finn: My arms are not long enough lol

18/05/2012, 7:01 pm - Elvers: Shame

18/05/2012, 7:01 pm - Gill Finn: Enjoy your drink. X

18/05/2012, 7:08 pm - Elvers: U never asked to see my ring.

18/05/2012, 7:16 pm - Elvers: Lol now who shy.

18/05/2012, 7:20 pm - Gill Finn: Lol was worried. if you have no rings there was only one ring it could be. (I didn't want to see his anal ring.) *I do not want to see that ring lol and it's not fair you're going out and I am sitting in alone.*

18/05/2012, 7:24 pm - Elvers: Lol not a BIG ring lol

18/05/2012, 7:26 pm - Gill Finn: Nope sulking now want to go out. Fed up of everyone going out and me on my own ☹

18/05/2012, 7:27 pm - Gill Finn: May 22, new X men movie .

Woohoo

18/05/2012, 7:27 pm - Elvers: Oh Gill I'm sorry

How can I cheer you up?

18/05/2012, 7:28 pm - Gill Finn: Can't. Go out. Need to plug in phone

18/05/2012, 7:28 pm - Gill Finn: Going to watch the Vikings tonight.

19/05/2012, 7:19 am - Elvers: Good morning how was the Vikings. Not too much raping and pillaging was there

Going to n hot today again x

19/05/2012, 7:22 am - Gill Finn: Good morning Elvers. It was good as far as I watched it, I fell asleep about quarter past 10 so I missed the rest but I do have it recorded.

I have physiotherapy at 8.30 this morning so I am about to get up and have a shower.

19/05/2012, 7:29 am - Elvers: I cud do with a bit of that. Busy in garden weekend

Not had time with operations

Don't forget to wash all your bits lol

19/05/2012, 7:32 am - Gill Finn: Oh busy in the garden. Lol

No time to meet me. Although my wining and dining was

nice I will post a picture of the car I was in.

19/05/2012, 7:33 am - Gill Finn: (A picture of the Audi.)

19/05/2012, 7:33 am - Gill Finn: The engine is 6.2 litres.

19/05/2012, 7:35 am - Elvers: What they say about men with big cars lol

19/05/2012, 7:35 am - Elvers: (He sent me a picture of his car.)

19/05/2012, 7:39 am - Gill Finn: Is that yours?

You will have to tell me what it is.

Lol, I am a woman. I just think they look nice or sound nice. Haven't a clue what they are. I have a son who tells me lol

19/05/2012, 7:44 am - Elvers: Ford Fiesta Titanium plus extras pack and private Reg. number.

So does size matter to u Gill

19/05/2012, 7:46 am - Gill Finn: Oh dear. Lol. Depends on what it is.

I love a big bunch of flowers.

A big bar of chocolate.

19/05/2012, 7:53 am - Elvers: CARS of course.

What u think I talking about   Twix extra-long, lol.

19/05/2012, 7:57 am - Gill Finn: Not keen on Twix.

Like bounty.

Question what do you think about taking perhaps two months out of the year in Australia when we are retired of course?

19/05/2012, 8:48 am - Elvers: I not a chocolate fan, prefers a nice passion fruit, nice and juicy mmmm

Heard New Zealand much better.

19/05/2012, 9:02 am - Gill Finn: I have dual nationality. AU

19/05/2012, 9:02 am - Gill Finn: Driving now, you at work now?

19/05/2012, 9:07 am - Elvers: Yes, from 8am.

19/05/2012, 9:21 am - Gill Finn: Lol naughty boy then. X

19/05/2012, 9:56 am - Elvers: Yes. Naughty doing this while working!!

19/05/2012, 10:05 am - Gill Finn: Lol. Right watching Vikings. X

19/05/2012, 10:08 am - Elvers: Hope u not getting to excited?

19/05/2012, 10:09 am - Gill Finn: Not raunchy yet lol.

19/05/2012, 10:10 am - Elvers: So I like a bit of ruff do you?

19/05/2012, 10:10 am - Gill Finn: Nope Lol x

19/05/2012, 10:11 am - Elvers: Just having my oats

Porridge oats that is.

19/05/2012, 10:13 am - Gill Finn: It's meant to be good for you Lol eating your oats lol x

19/05/2012, 10:14 am - Elvers: Mmm, do like my oats

19/05/2012, 10:15 am - Gill Finn: Good for your heart.

19/05/2012, 10:17 am - Elvers: Not sure about that,

takes me long time to finish!

19/05/2012, 10:18 am - Gill Finn: That's age related lol.

19/05/2012, 10:19 am - Elvers: No always been same

19/05/2012, 10:20 am - Gill Finn: Why... oats are soft. Have you got no teeth, x.

19/05/2012, 10:21 am - Elvers: Oh, sorry talking different oats lol

19/05/2012, 10:22 am - Gill Finn: Lol. (There, he is off again. Must try to divert him again).

19/05/2012, 10:23 am - Gill Finn: So sir. What if I fall in love with you through texting then you do not feel the same way I will be hurt.

19/05/2012, 10:24 am - Gill Finn: I have decided that I do not want this to happen. I want to protect myself.

If we do not meet up within a week I will stop texting. Is that a deal?

19/05/2012, 10:26 am - Elvers: Back to work now.

19/05/2012, 10:27 am - Gill Finn: While you're working think about it.

19/05/2012, 10:29 am - Elvers: If u stop I will be so upset.

Love chatting Gill

19/05/2012, 10:30 am - Gill Finn: No time to just chat. I am looking for a life partner. With all the things that go with it. Not just chat

19/05/2012, 10:33 am - Elvers: Ok sweetie.

Baby sitting next weekend brother having big op on foot so no fishing. (Even my type!)

19/05/2012, 10:34 am - Gill Finn: And no time to meet with me????

19/05/2012, 10:36 am - Elvers: Sorry

Please wait u won't be disappointed x

19/05/2012, 10:43 am - Elvers: If you wish no further contact please say

I won't bother u again Gill.

19/05/2012, 10:45 am - Gill Finn: Promise me you're not married

19/05/2012, 10:46 am - Elvers: NO, am not. But I am very demanding in the bedroom!!!

19/05/2012, 10:49 am - Gill Finn: I think men believe they are demanding in the bedroom. But when they are self-gratifying it takes not a lot of effort, but when it's shared fun it's a different matter. Lol.

Two of my beaus could not manage my demands

19/05/2012, 10:52 am - Gill Finn: I don't think you can manage me.

I will meet up with someone I am chatting to. If I like him then I will let you know.

(Now me being suggestive perhaps, but then am I trying to sell my wares, make this meeting happen or not. He could be fun, or...? I don't know.)

19/05/2012, 11:07 am - Elvers: I know how to please a lady

19/05/2012, 11:09 am – Gill: Elvers. We will see.

Enjoy your day. X text later

19/05/2012, 11:13 am - Elvers: Most men my age need blue pill or herbal treatment

19/05/2012, 11:15 am - Elvers: Ring u at 1pm

19/05/2012, 11:16 am - Gill Finn: Oh ok. Will be nice to talk to you.

19/05/2012, 11:16 am - Elvers: Ok.

19/05/2012, 11:19 am - Elvers: Promise u won't talk dirty to me.

19/05/2012, 11:23 am - Gill Finn: Lol, no I won't.

I won't talk dirty to you.

19/05/2012, 12:17 pm - Elvers: Need ice cubes down briefs

19/05/2012, 12:18 pm - Gill Finn: Lol. U busy

19/05/2012, 12:20 pm - Elvers: Yes, working B's off lol.

19/05/2012, 12:20 pm - Gill Finn: What do you actually do?

Sales or marketing or?

19/05/2012, 12:46 pm - Elvers: (He sends me a picture of a beautiful pen.)

19/05/2012, 12:46 pm - Elvers: Make pens

19/05/2012, 12:47 pm - Gill Finn: Beautiful x. 15 mins till you phone

19/05/2012, 1:02 pm - Gill Finn: After you phone, I am going to start rubbing down the paintwork. At the front of my house.

19/05/2012, 1:04 pm - Gill Finn: Shall I phone you?

19/05/2012, 1:31 pm - Elvers: Sorry sent photo of me in long johns Gill

Enjoyed our chat

19/05/2014, 1:32 pm - Gill Finn: No worries.

I also enjoyed our chat x

19/05/2012, 1:33 pm - Elvers: Plus, knobbly knees

19/05/2012, 1:37 pm - Gill Finn: Do not worry. I will delete it.

Sometime not having the same interests is good. To be introduced to other things at our age can be nice.

Would love to talk tonight

19/05/2012, 1:39 pm - Gill Finn: I am going to put on some rough clothes as I a rubbing down paintwork x

19/05/2012, 2:31 pm - Elvers: Hi Gill, I think you're a really interesting lady, yes, it would be good to talk tonight, I'll tell you what, for a change, I will Skype you, would be good to see what we really look like, in the flesh as it were. Say eight o'clock.

19/05/2012, 2.32pm – Gill Finn: That would be lovely, it would be nice to see the real person I have been chatting to, and yes I do have Skype. See you at eight, look forward to it.

19/05/2012, 2.33pm – Elvers: See you at eight, enjoy rubbing.

This sounded positive for the first time. We were going to see each other, at least on Skype – it was a start.

I got on with my jobs for the rest of the afternoon, looking forward in anticipation for eight o'clock to arrive.

I wanted to look my best, so had a shower and applied a little make-up, then waited by my computer for my Skype call to arrive.

It was eight, and there he was, he was calling me on Skype. I answered, expecting to see him on screen, but what was that? There staring at me was an erect penis, and then he started masturbating until that eel that had risen up at the screen was then spitting venom from its orifice. A voice in the background said, "Well Gill, what do you think of that then?"

It certainly looked nothing like his picture. What a prick, what a wanker, and I quickly reached for the off button.

Another disaster. Should I have seen that coming? Well I suppose I did see it coming, but not quite what I was expecting.

Elvers, up to this point, had seemed very pleasant, funny, even if at times he was a bit smutty, and I hoped I hadn't encouraged that. I could see a reluctance to meet up, even when pushed, as he made his excuses – fishing (it was me who was supposed to be fishing), or meeting his brother for a drink. Thinking afterwards, I suppose it wasn't going to work anyway; he hadn't seemed over keen on Australia, and our work patterns weren't ideally suited, especially if he was to start working Saturdays.

Did he just want to bed me, or did he just get his kicks from exposing himself? If there isn't such a word as a Cyber Flasher in the dictionary, then there certainly should be. From little elvers, they grow into big eels, staring at me onscreen.

What a waste of a man's time. Had I been very naïve throughout all this conversation with Elvers? I supposed I would have to put this one down to experience, AGAIN, and look out for the signs again in the future.

I didn't need him, I still had friends with benefits to provide for my womanly needs if necessary, and I wouldn't be put off by this prick in searching for a life partner to love and cherish.

Reel in the line, and cast further out into the pond, Gill. He is out there somewhere, and you will catch him.

Dory, Searching For Her Nemo

At my age, although I have a few long-term friends who are married, there are a lot who are divorced, some more than once. It is therefore of no surprise that most of my present friends, those that I would go out with socially, or would just meet up for either a coffee during the day at one or others houses, or even as us ladies like to do, go shopping together (even if we didn't actually want anything), are single. One or two may have a partner, or be in a casual relationship, but generally single. At our age we all, I think, have aspirations of finding a soulmate of the opposite sex, whether Mr Right to marry, or just to find a partner for life, as they say in the lonely hearts columns 'to share the good things in life, have fun, and maybe more.'

Through work, I made a few very good friends, in a workplace where men and women are equal. But with us all working shifts, some we would see just in passing, others I either worked with all the time, or as a group we would hang out together when we could. These tended to be just ladies. In any group of women, there will be clashes of personality, catty, men might say, to the point of dislike.

One such lady was Dory. When we first started in the same care home, we weren't each other's favourite people, possibly because we were so similar in personality – loud, boisterous, liked to be in the centre of things. And of course being women, we had to say the odd thing out of place about each other. Bitch!

With a change of direction though, with my career, I did stay in contact with Dory, I think first getting together at another friend's fiftieth birthday party which she organised, but I was invited as well, as it was a mutual friend. From then on we got to know each other properly, and I would now count Dory as one of my best. We have actually found we are very similar in what we like to do, the same sense of humour; we have a lot in common, and meet up frequently.

Men of course come up eventually in any conversation when a group of women get together, admiring passing bums, talking about, or moaning more likely, about their latest, and sex would be often become a topic of conversation. It was a standing joke at my workplace about who I had found online, where I had been with him, and what we had done (getting down to the nitty gritty!).

"Which one was it this time?" they would ask. "What, another? What happened to the last one?"

It would keep them amused as my ever-turning

door of men kept rotating, one out, another one in.

Yes, it was common knowledge with the girls that I was dating online.

Dory was becoming a real mate. Younger than me by nearly ten years, she too had been divorced for some time, and it was now nearly fifteen years since she had been dating, through marriage and then a mistrust of the opposite sex after what she had been through. A marriage gone wrong, though she never knew why, and once it was over, he wanted her back again. She had a frame of mind where she hadn't really the wish or confidence to put herself through it all again. But now, as life was trickling on, she was coming round to the need to find a partner herself, like me, to spend her life with, if he was the Mr Right for her. There must be a lot of Mr Right's somewhere but hopefully all a bit different.

Our friendship developed very quickly, and we would frequently go round to each other's for coffee, or shop together. Through this developing friendship, we would talk about men, and our hopes for the future, about my experiences online. She would have caught up with the latest from chat at work, so knew I was using this way of trying to land my big catch.

She is a good-looking girl, looks far younger than she actually is, very outgoing, and real fun to be with. But, no men in her life now for a long time. She was nervous of being hurt again, and like me, had the same reservations about walking into pubs, clubs, by herself to try and find the person of her dreams. And they don't come knocking on your door either, only in rom-com films!

Is was during one of our coffee dates that she got onto the subject of online dating, FISHING THE NET, and whether she should try it. She needed some outlet to get out there and meet men, and couldn't see any other way at the time, without going out with our female friends together, but was worried we may come across as a group of sex-starved fifty-something aged women who were out for a good time, and that could give the impression of only one thing – we wanted sex.

She was, still is a bit, well, a big technophobe, so was very uncertain of how to do this computer dating thing. Could I help?

I was only too pleased to give my assistance, so we arranged that we would meet up again at hers in a couple of days, and spend the evening getting her an account, and getting her started. I really felt our friendship had come on when she asked this of me; she showed a level of trust that I would help and look after her in what was a form of media she didn't understand.

I had suggested to her that I could get one of the men I had met to text her, and see if they wanted to meet up. He wasn't quite for me, though was very pleasant, but who knows? They may have hit it off. So Dory and this man made contact by text, and did indeed swop messages over a short period. Then nothing. Were they both a bit shy, unsure of how to conduct conversations with someone they had not met? But nothing.

I bumped into him in town one afternoon, and after exchanging pleasantries, asked how he was getting on with Dory. Perhaps to break the ice we could meet up as a foursome for a drink one evening (me with whoever I was with).

Then he texted her, just 'BOO!' *Was he trying to be funny?* Dory thought, and got a bit frightened, so their conversations ended there.

Not a great success, and enough to make her a bit wary of this computer thing, but she would give it a go.

Over a glass or two of wine, we went online to open an account for her. Like my beginnings, we decided to go for a paid site, as one tended to get more 'honest' men on them. So we decided to give eHarmony a go. We spent over two hours setting her up on this, opening an account, creating a profile, and having to pay a fee of thirty pounds. A lot of questions about Dory herself, then five questions about various scenarios.

If you could take a dream getaway, where would you most likely spend a week? For Dory, a log cabin in Scotland, open spaces. What would he say?

Your idea of a romantic time would be? For Dory, a romantic break at a castle or spa, relaxing, walking, love in the air.

What style of dress do you prefer? For her, smart casual when out.

How organised are you? Dory, well ahead of the game... beat that, chaps.

Lastly, are pets an important part of your life? Most definitely, especially dogs, we'll keep pussies out of it!

There may be other questions to answer in time, but Dory was up and running, just waiting for her bait to be taken, waiting in anticipation, eye on the float, any movement, any replies yet.

I left her that evening eagerly awaiting the first nibble, motivated that she was about to make a catch, and hopefully it would be her Nemo.

But as she hadn't been on a date for so long, then the doubts set in, the worries, the apprehension about what would happen when someone replied, and if she met any of them, all sorts of questions came flashing into her mind.

No sign of any bites at the beginning, so she went to bed. But Dory couldn't sleep with all these thoughts going through her mind. She did especially have two big phobias – dentists and dating – oh, and anyone called Dave. Therefore, Dave the dating dentist was a definite non-starter, and if he smoked as well, I don't need to say any more.

She tossed and turned in bed. *Fifteen years, that's scary. Bloody hell, that's scary, but I've got to be brave. Others can do it so I can too.*

Eyes closed, but then, *Oh s—t, what shall I wear? Text Gill. Oh, it's so late but I have to have an answer.*

She texted me, but then answered her own question. Casual – jeans, plain, yes, and bright. But then, what perfume? So much to decide. She thought she was losing her hearing, going mad. This was supposed to be fun with a nice cuddly Nemo at the end of it, but if he was there she probably wouldn't get there, putting up so many hurdles. Winding herself up over it, she thought she was going to drop dead. Worry, worry, but then she reassured herself that if 'Undateables' could do it then so could she.

Yes, even the thought of dating was sending her crazy, to the point of reaching the end of her tether. This normally was one laid back woman; nothing would faze her.

Over the next forty-eight hours she heard absolutely nothing. No Nemos, not one lonely sole, zilch.

I went round again to see if I could help, see if there was an internet problem or anything else I could help fix. We were worried perhaps the Wi-Fi was down, but after considerable effort, did manage to get through to the site to be greeted with, "Oops! Thanks for stopping by, but at the moment we are currently upgrading our service, and we should be back online soon."

"Fucking hell," was Dory's prompt reply, and she went on to say she had a good mind to ring them and ask for her money back.

"Bugger it, forget the thirty quid, it has all put me off. Forget it, lost interest. It's all sending me towards a breakdown."

She was very disappointed with the service, and discouraged, she did ring them in the end, when I had managed to find an 0800 number for them, and someone actually picked up the phone the other end. There was a ten-day grace period on starting a subscription so Dory opted out with a full refund.

I persuaded her to try another site, Badoo, and in no time at all she was set up again, waiting for a catch to arrive. Oh boy, this was different. After only thirty minutes there were 'Nemos' queuing up at her hook – fifteen contacts already. A lot different to the other site, but...

Dory was just so picky, and the fifteen were soon reduced down to one. Their photos, they looked different from what they said in their profiles. Fifty-eight years old, her age range was forty-five to fifty-three, couldn't they read? He slipped through the net!

She was then worried she would have to go to hospital with a repetitive strain injury of her index finger from so much deleting.

I left her to it, a match, delete, a match, delete. We chatted over the phone over the coming days, but she did seem so picky that no-one got a look in, not even a chat.

She had been to a Burns Night celebration in the meantime with a girlfriend, and had sat opposite a nice-looking gentleman who was accompanying another lady. He kept looking at her. The evening finished and Dory never gave him another thought; he was with someone, though nice-looking and probably a bit younger than her. Then one day at work, she received a mystery phone call. It was him. He had managed to track her down – a little detective work and he had got the telephone number of her workplace so here he was. Dory couldn't talk for long as she was working, but the nuts and bolts of the conversation ended up with him asking Dory out for a meal. She liked dining out, and had admired his perseverance in trying to find her, so the answer – yes.

He arrived to pick her up, armed with a bunch of flowers. A long time since Dory had this from a bloke, a promising start, but who was the lady he was with at that other meal she had seen him at? Nothing to worry about, just an acquaintance who had asked him along to make up numbers.

They spent the time over dinner chatting, but he was very quiet, too quiet for Dory, which was a shame as she found him very handsome. Then, as the meal was drawing to a conclusion, he wanted to smoke. A big no-no, so as he dropped her back home she had to say thanks but no thanks. At least she could say she had at last dated, and it hadn't been as traumatic as she thought it would be, but Nemo wouldn't smoke.

Back online the matches continued to flood in, and the index finger continued to delete them. Just so, so picky, and she was sticking to her criteria for possible matches rigidly – age, smokers, all, there was no leeway on what she wanted in her man, and to her, she could find fault with all of them, and they weren't even dentists or Daves.

Six weeks on, she still hadn't even had so much as a coffee, let alone a bite from Nemo.

It could be time to try another site, and refresh her profile. We would meet up and have another go.

THE PERFECT CATCH

If I was still struggling in muddied waters to find that elusive catch, through the different situations and relationships I have found myself in, it doesn't mean that it cannot work for everyone. Indeed a very good friend of mine, although a fairly new acquaintance soon found his ideal mate from an online dating site, and if it had fish in its name, I don't know which one that could be.

Orca had been in a relationship for a few years with his then partner, having just been through a divorce (this is getting complicated, isn't it?) after what had seemed a long and happy marriage. Through career changes, he had been content but over time, despite the arrival of a wonderful son, he was starting to feel uncomfortable in this second relationship, not helped by incidents at work that had affected him emotionally, and would for some time to come. If he was retreating more and more within himself, what he really needed was support from his partner. Alas, none was forthcoming as she saw herself as the only important person in the world. As his mood deepened he became more and more withdrawn, though outwardly he still seemed his normal jolly self.

As can happen so often in these circumstances, he – they – became more and more friendly with other parents of friends of his son, and in this new social group found solace in another woman who was going through a traumatic ordeal herself. Their friendship developed as they would meet on the school run, and before long it would be a coffee, and spending more and more time in each other's company; there developed an emotional bond which grew stronger and stronger.

Over the course of a few weeks, he realised he was really unhappy and had to get out of his present relationship before he became too controlled and too depressed. Time to make a break, which was very hard because of his son, but for his own sanity it was time to move on. The big decision was made and whether you may think him right or wrong, to him it was the right thing to do. Men can be quite emotional themselves and be destroyed by inner feelings and discontentment, it is not for others to judge.

So leave he did, and surrounded by some very good friends who respected his decision, it was time to start anew. And this new life he hoped would involve the woman who had come more and more into his life, the only problem being she was married and about to join her husband on a distant work placement. They fell in love, big time, but their baggage for want of a better expression meant there were some very tough decisions to be made. Their bond grew stronger and stronger, which made life tougher and tougher, especially with what would inevitably happen – it would all come out into the open. Not wanting to dwell on this too long, after much heartache from both of them, they went their own ways, she choosing for the sake of her kids to keep the family together. A tough one which meant they parted as lovers in something that was never to be, but how he wished more than anything that it could have worked out, because he really did feel this was the first time he had truly, truly been in love. Men can cry too.

Days, weeks of feeling sorry for himself, broken-hearted, getting more introverted, life was a bitch. In time through the support of his friends, he slowly snapped out of it and realised he would have to snap out of himself. He needed to start getting out again, meeting new people, getting back to being his old self. But how?

You've guessed it, the Net!! But not of his doing. If he was getting more and more accustomed to the new wave of phone technology, it was a female work colleague who, herself using the Net to try and find a partner, set him up on one of these sites. An interesting personality, his profile soon brought results as he started chatting to several women who thought he may be their match. But after his heartache, it would take a lot to get him to do more than just chat.

Just a quick interlude to say that after some time, there was contact between the two lovers but only as friends, always there for each other if necessary but at a distance as they both moved on to new lives. Wonderful memories for him which he will carry with him forever, but it was not to be. And perhaps as fate took its turn, it all worked out the best for all concerned, especially for all the side issues that would have been created.

Life goes on, and as I got to know him better through a close friend, then he was encouraged to bite the bullet and start going out again with female company. And believe me, women did like him for his many idiosyncrasies – a 'Jack the lad', funny, interesting and very caring.

One or two dates with colleagues, acquaintances, and he was his old self. Dates were set up after chatting on the net, and life got, to say the least, more than a bit interesting again. More than a little interesting in some cases. Car journeys could get a little too stimulating, but hey, he was – is – a man of the world.

After chatting to one particular lady for some time, he felt there was enough in common that this particular one may have some future, and they should meet. She was a midwife so there was a degree of a mutual interest, something that would help break the ice. A rendezvous was arranged in the town where she lived, not that far to travel, but they would meet up in a hotel near the town centre, a nice old-fashioned type where they could chat and get to know each other better, rather than face to face. As he waited patiently for her to arrive, what would she really be like…? He would soon find out. She had said through the course of their internet chatting that she had a certain style of dress, which she enjoyed, but hoped he didn't find over the top considering their ages. Here was some interesting bait.

There he sat patiently in the hotel bar, waiting for

his 'date' to arrive. Anticipation, a degree of nervousness for this first online date, what was he expecting? And how he found out! Midsummer and there she was, thigh boots, the shortest hot pants he had ever seen, a loose blouse and there she was standing in front of him. All that was missing were the fish nets! Even he was taken aback, but there's no point having a Picasso on the wall if you don't admire it so, enjoy the view, enjoy the conversation, even if our man was a little overawed in the situation he found himself (and we are talking early middle age here). The conversation was good; she seemed a lovely lady at face value, single mum looking for a partner, attractive, and obviously a dress style that could only be described as exciting, very exciting actually.

Would he like to come back for a coffee? Yes, that would be nice, so they went back to her place, but when left in the sitting room while she prepared the coffee, he was greeted with a full-size nude on the wall, and yes it was her. Bugle out, and even for him, time to beat a quick retreat.

An experience, but all was not working out as he had hoped. Time to take stock again, and so came the decision to try and live by himself a while, learn to look after himself more, find himself more. No more of the Net sites for a while. See how it goes!

So the solitary life started, for four days! Well, he tried but couldn't resist seeing who was trying to chat to him on the net. And by chance, here was one who looked like she had a similar background in terms of her profession, some mutual interest there, sounded very genuine and perhaps life hadn't quite been as kind to her as it could have been.

FISHING THE NET

So, again the conversations started on the net; this fishing net certainly is getting a few bites. Looks like the solitary life will be shelved for a day or two, maybe more. There seemed a lot to keep these two interested in each other, and certainly on first contact online they seemed to be going in the right direction.

Our man has a keen interest in boating, and especially canal boats, and being somewhat of a perfectionist had designed and built a couple of his own. In fact, for his now single life, that was his chosen residence, a life on the water, so the appropriate place to be fishing the net!

I suppose there comes a time when internet chatting moves on to the next step of meeting up. So here we are, time to meet, and our lady thinks, and decides that as she has never been on a canal boat, this would be a good place to meet. Sounds okay, but then: "Can I bring my kids, two teenage boys?"

I suppose. Why not? My son could be there too. So, we will settle for that, meet the family, may as well see what you are getting (so to speak) straight away.

"Oh, and can I bring the dog?"

This is soon turning into Noah's Ark. Well, I suppose that will be a companion for my dog – this is turning into quite a date! Pussies, what next? I don't think so. Well, they are not that keen on water.

Well, it looks like the rules of engagement have been set, meet the whole of the neighbouring town in one go and you know that there are no dark horses hidden in the cupboard. The date was arranged and if it had strayed very, very slightly from what was expected, this was going to be an experience.

So, date and time set, and having given directions to the boat, our man waited for what was going to walk over the water. The car pulls up, and out she steps, and her sons, and the dog. Where will this go? At least there was an absence of hot pants and no sign of the photo album, so no revealing 'snapshots'.

The Angel Fish, just arriving, Orca's next internet date, was quite an old hand at this online dating, and I don't want that to sound disparaging to her. Angel, too, had lived a, shall we say, disappointing life. A lovely lady who it could be said had been unlucky in her choice of men. Through no fault of her own, her long-term relationships seemed to sink under the murky waters of failure. Here was a lady who had strived hard to achieve what she wanted, and worked her way through the ranks of her job, reaching the upper echelons of where she could be in her chosen profession. Her career was a success story, but her home life was often there to disappoint her, dampen that sense of achievement. Through divorce, she had found that she had to rebuild her life, succeeded, but then as a second marriage hit the rocks, every time she seemed to be getting somewhere, life would deliver another blow to her self-esteem. She had so much to give to life, but there always seemed another setback around the corner.

But now she was free, free to live her own life as she pleased. Children nearly grown up, it was time she could start concentrating on herself again.

Angel would set herself targets, goals, those challenges that make you feel so much better for trying, even more so for succeeding. Through these she would meet new friends, female friends, and form lasting bonds with them, always being there for each other. Many of these she met doing a charity ride across the sub-continent. An arduous task, but the challenge was set, and Angel was going to defy the hot, arid conditions, and reach her goal. Friendships made, and a lasting reputation as a karaoke singer.

Like me, she was tuned into technology, social media, Facebook, and so Internet Dating seemed a logical progression for her to try and obtain the thing that was missing in her life – a lasting relationship. Again, a lady like myself who in the course of her work, had antisocial-hour shift patterns, so the opportunity to go out at anyone else's convenience, was not always practical. But she had a free spirit, and wanted to go out into the big wild world, experience new things, succeed and share the experiences, these new adventures, with a man. The only way she could see to do this was to find said man on the net, chat, and if a mutual compatibility, meet up and see where life takes them.

She had been on the net for some time, on and off, chatting, messaging, and having the odd rendezvous with a gentleman. But Angel wasn't succeeding in finding this lasting relationship. She found (like me) the men who weren't quite honest about themselves.

A date with a man invalided; he couldn't get out of his car without help. Nothing wrong with that, he deserves the same chance as everyone else, but why couldn't he say something about it before they met? If Angel had known, then she would have been prepared, but it came as a complete surprise, and there was a feeling of a lack of trust from the start.

Perhaps he felt she wouldn't meet him if she knew, but Angel was not that fickle. From past experiences with men, she just wanted honesty. If there was a slight feeling of guilt, she also felt let down once again, and it wasn't the right way to start out on a new beginning.

Like me, she had come across scammers, but had realised what was happening from these sweet-talking blokes on the end of the line, in time that there was at least no financial cost to her, even playing them along for a while until the scammers had to admit they had been found out. Then they revealed how they were employed to do this, find what they thought were vulnerable ladies looking for love, and a bit of lovey dove chat would hook them to send loads of money, for some made-up emergency.

Yes, Angel had seen most of it all trying to net her fish, and was starting to feel more than frustrated that she couldn't move her life in the direction she wanted it to go, certainly in sharing new adventures.

Then this guy came on her site, Orca, and he sounded fun. To begin with, their professions, not the same, but in the same line, would give them a lot in common. A good start to chatting online, yes, Angel and Orca would have plenty of time to get onto hobbies, holidays, general background, but here was an easy icebreaker. They worked in different counties, under different authorities, so their paths hadn't crossed in their respective jobs. But it would give each of them an insight of their daily routines, the stresses each had to cope with, the disappointments, the heartaches and the joys. There would be a lot of common ground that would give them a good start in finding out about each other.

Yes, Angel thought, this guy, Orca, did sound fun, and could offer her experiences she had yet to try. He had a canal boat; she had never done that before, although her father did sail yachts. He had a motorbike. Again, she would like to try that, ride pillion, wind streaming through her hair. No, that was silly, she would have to wear a crash helmet, so forget the hair. Perhaps she could even learn to ride a bike? That was something she had always wanted to do.

No real commitments, free and single, Orca did have possibilities. He had done charity events, 'Run for Home' with Heart FM, raised a lot of money over a three-year period, just like she had done her cycle marathon in India.

There did seem a genuine hope that this guy was the real deal, as long as, and she had been there before, what he said about himself and his profile pictures were the real thing – present and correct.

They chatted online forever, an eternity of probably four, five days and soon reached the obvious conclusion that they should meet up. Orca had a few days off with his shift pattern and was living on his boat. Why not suggest that she should come over there, see what his lifestyle was really like? But supposing he was not all he seemed, was there a risk of a lady going to meet an unknown man in the middle of nowhere, in his own home? Risky, could be very risky. She had a teenage family, so when he agreed to meet up, and it would be on the boat, Angel asked if it would be okay to bring her two sons along as well, might as well meet the family all at once, then when they got home they could take a vote on whether to see him again. He, Orca that is, had no problems with that suggestion, the more the merrier. They could take the boat for a short trip along the canal, grab a bite to eat at a pub on the bank, then get back to the mooring.

The only problem was that he would have to disappear in the late afternoon, as he had another appointment. Fine by Angel, it would be a natural conclusion to the meeting. No awkward goodbyes, just time to go now as you have something else planned. What about the dog, could she bring him too?

All was good; Orca had his dog on board, but hopefully they would get on fine. A bit of doggy company for his old fella would do him no harm, a break from it being just him and Orca.

They had a time, and they had a place, a first meeting was arranged, and as Angel drove into the middle of nowhere, she wondered what the day would bring, along with the two sons and the dog. Luckily she had no cat, nor a rabbit!

They had come to the gate, down a short track and they would be at the canal. Nervous, just a little. But Angel had the troops in the car with her; safety, comfort in numbers, and now she was driving down the track, there was no turning back.

Waiting, perched on the stern of his boat was Orca, and as Angel drew closer was relieved to see he was the man in the photos. He came over as Angel opened the car door, smiling warmly as she got out and the formal introductions started, after all there were four here that hadn't yet chatted online – two teenagers and two dogs, who luckily didn't seem to want to launch into a pitched battle. A quick sniff of each other's bums (the dogs, that was), and they were friends, even if there was a slight disappointment one wasn't a bitch, especially a bitch on heat.

Orca showed them round his boat, very tidy for a man residence, made a cup of tea, more strictly described as a bucket of tea that he produced, thankfully gave a quick lecture on the safety and hazards of being on the water, and the merry throng set off in the sunshine, bound for a pub, and luckily no locks to contend with.

Angel positioned herself at the back of the boat, where Orca was steering – a lovely position to enjoy the sun, and more importantly chat and get to know this charming man barely a couple of feet from her. There was a bond straight away, as they made their way slowly towards their lunch. A mutual respect for what was around them. Peace, quiet and nature at its best. How perfect was this?

A bridge and then an area where the canal opened out wide enough to turn the boat around was reached, so the boat was moored and they were in the pub enjoying a pint and a good lunch. Everyone seemed to get on well, including the dogs now curled up together under the table.

Then the return trip back to the mooring and the car. Time passed so quickly on this journey, but conversation was easy, jovial and interesting. Could this go on longer? No, sadly they had arrived back at the mooring, and after another bucket of tea, it was time to go back across the county border and home. Orca did admit that his appointment was meeting another lady he had chatted to online, but he already knew that he would be telling her he had met someone else, and hoped, well…

That was very honest of him. Angel knew he wanted to see her again.

She and her boys sat down in the living room for a family discussion. What did everyone think? A count up, three hands raised in favour, oh, and a paw. Angel hoped Orca would be in touch soon.

Orca had that date that night as well, and he did go and see this lady, but he had someone to compare her with now, and although she was pleasant enough, he decided she wasn't on a par with Angel. He had to tell her that he had met someone earlier and he wanted to see where life would take her with this lady. Short and sweet; he had met five ladies from this fish site, and he thought, hoped, that he had found the person he was looking for.

Orca, never one to leave things in limbo when he could grab the bull by the horns, was soon in contact with Angel, telling her how much he had enjoyed their trip down the canal and meeting the rest of the family, including the dog, and hoped she would want to meet up again. That was the call she had been waiting for, and she was only too pleased to accept the invitation, but added that she would come alone. The rest of the family could stay at home and look after the dog. A bond had started between them, that both hoped secretly to themselves, would grow and grow.

The second meeting, this time for a drink in a pub, went very well. They had so much in common, so much to talk about, conversation was easy and their friendship was struck up. They wanted to see each other again, and again. They did live more than a few miles apart but as their feelings for each other rapidly grew and grew, distance proved no obstacle in their wish to see each other. Orca, who was best mates with a close friend, was soon round at his house, only a few days after telling him he was done with women for a while; now he was 'seeing' a lady again, a really nice lady and he had really fallen for her.

Romance blossomed, and it was not long afterwards, probably seven or eight weeks, that he was round at his mates again, telling him he was going to do something really stupid, after all that he had said in the past few months. His mate said, "You're going to get engaged, aren't you?" He had met Orca and Angel out on a couple of occasions since they had first met, and had seen the bond between them, how much happier Orca was now, back to himself for the first time in a long while. Yes, he had guessed, and guessed correctly.

When I found out, I would have to admit I was really annoyed; jealous would have been a better description. After that short time online, Orca had found his match, and was now engaged. Me, I had been floundering around all this time, had seen blokes for a lot longer than they had been going out together. Now, they were engaged, and me, I was getting nowhere – it just wasn't fair. An emotional reaction when I first found out, but looking at it in a different light when my jealousy had subsided, I was genuinely pleased for them.

Their relationship blossomed, went from strength to strength as they got to know each other better, spent more time together, whether on the canal or in

Angel's hometown across the county border. She was enjoying becoming a biking chick, holding on tightly to Orca's waist as they sped around the countryside on his seven fifty. She knew she would realise a dream with this man, of having her own bike; they would be able to cruise together, stop at bikers' cafes, use the open road.

They were becoming as one, talking of buying a house together, and doing it back in Orca's old home town. Angel having said yes, their wedding plans gathered pace, finding a destination to congregate their close families and friends; a small, intimate day – well, weekend – in a beautiful part of the country, then motorbike off to Scotland for a few days on their honeymoon.

As with anything, there were slight glitches along the way, but they rode through them all, and it was only some fourteen months after that first boat outing that they became man and wife.

They remain ever happy together, enjoying each other's pastimes, trying new experiences together, planning their long-term future together. They have a mutual respect for what each has to go through at work, the stresses and strains of their vocations, helping each other when they can. They actively involve themselves in each other's families, they are as one.

By all accounts it was a lovely wedding, where a small party enjoyed the company and binding together of this lucky couple, starting on Friday, and going on till they left for Scotland. I'm jealous of that too, but very happy for them.

I now see a lot of them, Orca and Angel, love the

relationship they have developed between themselves, and hope that one day I can obtain that too. From their angle, for these two, online dating did work. Plenty of fishing caught its reward with a massive catch for both.

Contrasting histories of online dating. Orca, a handful of dates, a tale or two to tell on the way, but only a very short time on a site before he found his match. Angel, like me, had experienced much in her online dating, some thoughts of success, but they were not to be. In the end, persistence paid off, and she was lucky enough at last to find the man she had been looking for.

A couple who found each other and clicked so quickly, and now have so much to look forward to in the future.

*

Starfish had recently moved to Shropshire, having finished uni, and now was about to start her first job. New area, new (first) job, new accommodation, new everything; life was looking a bit daunting. She of course had her colleagues at work, who tried to introduce her to the area, tried to welcome her, introduce her to new people and show her the ropes of her chosen profession that she was about to launch into. But they also had lives of their own, so Star was left on her own at times in the evening, alone in her flat she had rented while she served her probationary period. Life in a quiet village was far different from the hectic social and lecture life of being a university student. There was a lot of adjustment to cope with in her life.

She was working in a farming community, in rural surrounds, no big hub of social gatherings, and she needed to meet people away from work. Essential otherwise the stresses and strains of work provided no outlet for emotions, frustrations, anything, and she could see herself going into a descending spiral of becoming introverted and secluded – a far from ideal scenario.

She needed to get out and meet people sooner rather than later to be able to release herself, and have some fun. One of the best social groups in a rural community has for a long time been the Young Farmers Clubs, and in this part of the world there was one in most large villages or towns. Yes, she would end up meeting people she came into contact with on a daily work basis, but getting to know them better away from work would be no bad thing.

Decision made, she would join one of the local clubs, and having done that soon made a name for herself, in the best possible way of course, launching into public speaking competitions, national conventions, you name it, Starfish was your girl. It was like she was becoming a local celebrity; she was getting involved in everything, whether she wanted to or not. The trouble was that the YFC organisation does cover a wide range of ages, with an upper limit, which she was approaching, but also with a lot of teenagers, so although she was getting out and about, sometimes it was with a very mixed age group, sometimes where she felt like an oldie.

Starfish is an attractive girl, and got plenty of invites out, just her and a bloke, but she was not meeting the right person for a serious relationship, if that was even what she was looking for. In fact, at times, all this 'partying' was actually getting a bit tiring, even in her tender years.

She was enjoying it, but it was different from university life, and there was also the possibility that someone she might meet in the course of her work, could be the one who asked her out, and that could create difficulties, especially if she wasn't as keen on him as he was on her.

She knew she was going to have to cut her ties, though enjoying herself, and find another outlet to relax, and other circles of people to mingle with.

Star was backed into a corner. What should she do? She wanted to go out, but she also wanted to meet new people from different avenues of life. She wasn't going to turn her back on her YFC friends, but she would see less of them; it would not dominate her life so much in the future.

What should she do? One day when back home at her parents', and feeling a little down, a combination of being busy at work and not getting out as much as she hoped, she started talking to her sister about how life was treating her, and her need to get out more.

Sister, a wise old bird, suggested that she should try Internet Dating, if for no other reason, she could get a few free meals out of it. Star was a bit sceptical, the idea of meeting up with some random bloke who she had exchanged the odd word with on her computer was one, a bit daunting, and two, it seemed a bit mercenary that she would spend an evening chatting to this poor bloke, on the premise that she would get a free steak out of it, whereas he would be hoping for a bit more rump later. Maybe she could meet the right bloke, find a new circle of friends, but at this time, no – she was not over enamoured with the idea.

Whatever she thought, her sister was on the case.

The computer was on and she was on that fishing site, and – what! – she was putting Starfish up as bait. Profile, enter, there she was dangling on the end of a line, waiting to be hooked.

Flying Fish was a man of the world, seeing the world in the course of his job – a real high flyer. This meant that he was moved around from time to time, very much of no fixed abode. Mid-to-late twenties, tall, dark and handsome, but at this stage in his life, young(ish), free and single. There was no point in making attachments as far as he was concerned, tomorrow he could be someplace else. Emotional ties were not for him.

He got stationed near to Shrewsbury in the course of work – an exciting appointment? At that time, he did not see it that way; he was being sent out into the sticks, beyond the borders of civilisation. Why him? Why did he have to be sent to this place in the middle of nowhere? Just his luck.

He went where work sent him, actually didn't have any say in the matter, so there he was. He was having one hell of a time, out every night, wild parties, enjoying the local brew, and there were several. At this rate he would risk burnout, *except*, except it was the complete opposite. Yes, there were some good local brews, but company? Unless he walked down the road about a mile and leaned over the fence and chatted with some pigs, and they didn't want to come to the pub anyway, then there was no-one.

Oh boy. Was he grumpy, or was he grumpy? His mate, as all good mates do, thought he needed to snap out of this malaise, get himself out a bit.

What did he do? Yes, he put Flying Fish up on an Internet Dating site, and it would be no surprise that the chosen site was the fishing one.

Grudgingly, he said he would go along with the idea, and see what came up. He watched who came up, a match or not, chatted to one or two, but his commitment to the site was far from full, and was something he played with when he was really, really bored. It was better than talking to the pigs – just!

Starfish, in another part of the county, also payed due diligence to the site, when she could be bothered. The thought of that free meal was appealing, if only because around the area there were some very nice restaurants, and she would not be averse, coming to think about it, to trying some of them out.

A conversation, a date, the first free meal ticket. Very nice evening but this one wasn't for Star. Nice guy, but the chemistry wasn't there, but the meal was good. One to put back and keep fishing; there must be more out there looking for a girl like her.

One or two more conversations when she had time to look and reply back to them, one guy sounding quite interesting, talked of meeting up and then silence. Shame, he did sound a possibility for Star, but not to be. One of the other conversations did turn out to be a date – another meal, another nice evening, but again, not quite the right chemistry, even though they had a lot in common, and in fact if not dating, it would turn out that they would become firm friends, and still are.

Even friendships could develop from these dating lines, which was good in that it did not turn out to be just a cattle market.

Flying Fish now and again looked at the site his mate had put him on, half-heartedly checking to see if there was a fish on the line, one that was worth chasing after. It would take a few minutes, reduce some of the boredom of living in this last outpost of society in deepest Shropshire. Something caught his eye – a nice-looking professional lady, looking for a relationship, nothing serious to begin with, and see where it goes. Nice-looking girl.

The die was cast. He made some random reply to her profile, pressed the off button on his computer and went about his business again. Somewhere in the back of his mind, her profile persisted. He would see, though still not convinced of this angling game. At least it would keep his mate off his back; he was making the effort – just.

Star had been chatting away merrily when time permitted, and had in fact arranged another date, but short of free time, had suggested that this guy meet up for a quick drink before she had to go on to a work get-together in town, an organised pub crawl. The meeting, well she thought this guy again not for her, and after chatting for a while, made her excuses that she had to go on to her other date for the evening, a prior engagement with work. She would be in touch (Unlikely, she thought).

She met up with the gang at Ashley's, a wine bar in town, where there was a good mix of professional and reception staff, 'team bonding'. It was good to see everyone out of work, far more relaxing and informal and a chance to get to know everyone better. A G and T, courtesy of the bosses, the evening could turn out to be fun. Star mingled, chatted to her work colleagues, but then to her surprise, turned round to find her 'date' also there, as if he was still with her. Her boss, none the wiser, thinking he had come with Star, bought him a drink as well. He thought he was well in; it turned out to be a good evening out with a nice-looking lady.

Another drink, or move on? Majority decision that the next stop would be at a cocktail bar by the river. One or two of the staff chatted to this bloke, thinking he was with Star, trying to make him feel welcome, incorporate him into the evening. At the same time, Star was telling one or two of the others that she hadn't invited him along, they were supposed to go for a drink, then go their separate ways. He hadn't gone away, and to be quite honest was now becoming a bit of a pain.

The cocktail bar was busy, very busy, and one of her noble troop made his way to the bar, trying to remember the thirteen cocktails he was supposed to be ordering. Good effort, but it was obviously going to take a while.

'Star's' man was still there. This was getting embarrassing for her; she wasn't keen on him, there would be no further contact after the pub drink she had already decided, but he was still here, and sponging off her work colleagues. What would the bosses be thinking?

She was feeling more and more uncomfortable, and a couple of her male colleagues could see this, asking her if all was okay. She confided her discomfort, and that she didn't want to see the bloke again, and hadn't invited him along to the works part of the evening. Did she want them to 'get rid' of him? That sounded bad, but yes, she didn't want him spoiling her and everyone else's evening (others were now also uncomfortable with his presence, knowing what was going on).

Star turned to find the bloke being ushered out by the two colleagues she had confided in, nothing heavy but when they got him out through the door, they laid it down that he hadn't been invited, was spoiling Star's evening now, and to put it gently, f—k off.

He wasn't seen again, thankfully, with the bonus that when the valiant mate at the bar had succeeded in his order, there was one too many cocktails. Star gratefully accepted the offer to have the departed's drink as well. Good shout.

One other persistent follower, but she knew she didn't want to meet up with him, and then the cupboard was looking bare. But what was this? Someone she had chatted to some time ago, asking her if she would like to meet up.

Flying Fish had taken the plunge. If he was on this site, he may as well have a look at what was on offer, and this lady was niggling away in his inner mind. He would message her, see if she would like to meet up for a drink. Nothing to lose, and who knows? Plenty to gain.

Star remembered vaguely chatting before, that was all, but agreed to meet up with him. They would go to The Boathouse by the river, a nice spot especially in summer, where they could sit outside watching the world go by on the water. An ideal place for fishing, in fact.

Time and place arranged, she was going to meet him. But then it occurred to her, she didn't know his name. What should she do?

She emailed her best mate at work, asking her what she should do.

"Soooooo… I have this date tonight with some guy from PoF, but I hadn't been on for ages, and, I can't remember his name and it doesn't say on his profile. I can't go back through the message to find out. What do I do? Also we are going to meet at the boat house for a drink… Where do I hide my car in case I want to run away (the car clearly marked with work stickers)?"

Her mate replied, "Pretty sure not possible to hide the car," and gave a few options as to what to do about his name.

Tell the truth and explain you've forgotten.

Pretend you have an imaginary friend and make him introduce himself to them.

Hope he turns up in a shirt with his name on.

Start using a website that actually has people's names on, not much help for this evening.

Get him to add you on Facebook.

Star replied, "Right about van, one of bosses said it would be visible from space!"

"Just say, 'Hi, I'm Star,' and hope he replies with his name. Maybe he's a spy. You could run home from the boathouse, or run round to a mate's house round the corner, but not worth involving him at this stage."

This was starting to sound like an impending disaster, but Star replied that she would find a side street to deposit the car. The last date she had parked outside the police station. She liked the introducing herself angle, good thinking.

"Spy would be fun. Alternatively it could all go horribly wrong, then I wouldn't have to worry about the fact that I can't remember his name."

Her colleague replied, "That's very true, but you should be optimistic! He could be the one…" adding, "It's exciting, might be very fun."

A ridiculous conversation, but it hadn't solved anything. She set off to meet her 'spy'.

Outside The Boathouse stood a solitary man, who when she arrived looked as if he recognised her. Here goes.

"Hi, I'm Star."

"Hi. Flying Fish."

Thank God, he had given his name. That eased the situation considerably. It was a summer's evening, and a World Cup footy game. Not their cup of tea, especially if they wanted to chat, hard amongst a noisy football crowd in full voice, so though this was a lovely destination, they decided to look for somewhere quieter, which gave them the chance to talk as they made their way through The Quarry into town.

At last, peace and quiet, no football, and they enjoyed a drink together, chatting. It seemed as if there may be something here, thought Star.

They had enjoyed each other's company, now it was time to go. They got up, went out of the pub and faced each other. Star hadn't been in this situation before, what should she do?

She gave Flying Fish her phone number and said he could ring her if he wished. The evening was over, no running away, no awkward situations, and she knew his name. He wasn't a spy, or wasn't admitting to it anyway.

Time to wait and see!

The grumpy man, put on PoF by his mate, yes he did reply. He would like to meet up again, and they did.

It worked out for them. Though there were difficulties thrown up by each other's work, him moving away again with his, and her sometimes anti-social hours, they started dating. That sounds very old fashioned. They saw more and more of each other, and happily after a romantic evening at the opera, he popped the question.

Star was only too pleased to say yes, and now their wedding fast approaches. Jobs will make things tricky to start with, but they have a life planned out in front of them; they looked at the problems, found solutions, and will make it work for each other.

Good luck to them.

Two people who weren't that committed to this dating site, went on for a free meal, and to remove the grumps, but they found each other. Probably when they both started, they both thought it a waste of time but went along with it to please friends or family, but for them, online dating had worked.

Another perfect catch.

THE BLOW FISH

I was finding sometimes, more than sometimes, that the net became addictive, and rather than just finding a set time during the day, or early evening that I would go online, see if I had any nibbles, I would find myself online all the spare time I had. There seemed plenty of fish out there who wanted to play my line. Was I that desperate to find this man out there, my life partner to be? I think I probably was, and while they were interested in my bait, I would find more and more time to chat.

If I was still naïve in what I was looking for and sorting the nibblers from those with other intentions, those opportunist fish looking to take advantage of me in my quest for contentment, I was becoming more and more accomplished at spotting a hoax, a predatory fish hoping to scale my defences, looking just to get me in the sack.

The dirty talkers, those that would start their conversations with 'hello sexy', 'you look gorgeous in your photo' and 'I like the larger lady', these ones were looking to take the bait, and only once for a quick splash between my legs, a quick extension of their pole to catch me, and then throw me back from whence I came. They would hope to be satisfied – me, swimming against the current. I was learning to spot a lot of them. The distant photos, the topless photos taken in the bathroom mirror, all I was beginning to learn were giveaways for wham, bam, thank you ma'am! Men, not the ones I was hoping to find, they were trouble.

One or two, I would give them a chance to redeem themselves, show themselves in a better light, by letting them chat on, but if they escalated the conversation to say, 'when did you last have it?', I would pretend not to understand. If that line continued, then they had blown it. If I thought I might fancy one, then I may have played along a bit, teasing him, saying 'that's smutty talk,' or, 'you don't ask a lady that sort of thing.'

But still not in total command of guessing every situation, I would make the odd mistake.

Here I am chatting to what sounds a really nice man, Dan Pout, living in my town, sounds interesting and interested. Possibilities! So I continue chatting to him for a while before we arrange to meet for a coffee in a local pub.

The three-date rule is strictly in operation, but I am really looking forward to meeting him.

Dan Pout, a tall, handsome man, liked his coffee fully loaded. Initially I thought, *This guy is okay*. As we chatted, he told me more about himself, how he owned a B and B locally (goody, a man with property), and how the business was going, and where he wanted it to go. *I like his guy,* I thought. First impressions, very good, worth pursuing.

We continued to chat and an hour had soon passed, but I accepted the offer of a second cup of coffee. Nice.

As he brought it to our table, he placed it in front of me, bent down and gave me a kiss on my lips. Forward but nice, I am enjoying this meeting. Another quick peck, and he seated himself down again, but this time closer to my side. He was getting a little flirty, but I was enjoying it because I like kissing, and a good kisser really turns me on. But this is date one, and nothing more is on the agenda as far as I am concerned.

But he is a man, an unpredictable animal, and things suddenly took a downward turn, literally!

The conversation goes, "So, you like snogging?"

"Yes," I reply, "I think it is very sexy and a turn-on."

"Do you like sex?"

"Pardon?" Thinking, *Where the hell did that come from?* "Yes, with the right man, at the right time, and place. When we have got to know each other, I would sleep with the right man, I am like any woman. We enjoy our pleasures."

"Not all women like sex."

"Well that's a bit forward after just a kiss," I reply.

"Well just wanted to you to know," he said, "that if we went to bed together, I would want you to go down on me."

"Pardon!"

"I want you to give me head."

"Pardon!"

"But I will not go down on you, only you on me," he pronounced.

I stood up, picked his coffee cup up and emptied the contents into his crotch.

"I wouldn't go down there for you, and if you want to finish your coffee, then I suggest you suck yourself off!"

I abruptly about turned, headed straight for the door and didn't look back until I was back in my car, and driving out of the car park.

Whether he did enjoy the rest of his coffee, I don't know and don't care, but could imagine him bent over himself, tongue between his legs licking frantically into a frenzy. Blow fish doing a blow job, a different sort of selfie! He may have changed it into a takeaway, I couldn't give a toss, and never spoke to him again.

What a plonker, obviously was never interested in a relationship, just self-gratification. Not from me.

I will learn to spot these whales in the future; there will be others out there, but they won't pleasure themselves at my expense.

The search goes on, and undaunted, I will continue to look.

CLOSED SEASON

―――――≪◦❀◦≫―――――

The One That Got Away

So time to take stock of where I am and adjust my plans if necessary. I've now been fishing on the net for eighteen months, two years or so. I have had one or two nibbles, one or two escapes, but am I getting what I am looking for? It has been interesting, and I have got out a little, but haven't met the man I'm looking for yet, neither am I getting out as much as I would like, doing different things, or exploring new places. 'How can I change this?' I ask myself. Well I suppose there are always the singles clubs I could try! There are of course a vast number of these, some on a national basis, some just local groups. Some are well known and can be found on the web, who to contact, when and where they meet, others just by word of mouth, but of course to do this you have to get out and about to meet like-minded people who may know of these groups. And, not liking going to places where I know no-one, I would find it preferable to go to a social event with someone I know, firstly for me to feel more confident walking into a room of strangers, and be introduced to new faces, and secondly, I would never walk into a pub by myself anyway. A more mature woman, I just don't think it looks right.

So what shall I do? Searching the local rag, I do find an advert for a new singles group that has just started, concentrating on looking for new members from my home town, and the county town some fifteen miles away, plus surrounding areas. This could be promising; the opportunity to meet new people, get new friends, and who knows, maybe meet Mr Right. A new club, hopefully there will be no cliques, and as it advertises itself as a singles club, presumably there will be no couples. It could be open season!

There are a couple of telephone numbers given of people to contact if you are interested – one lady, one man who have set the club up and are actively now seeking members. Give them a ring, why not? I have nothing to lose. The man, I shall try him and see what he can tell me about the club, so on the phone I get and make the call.

Paul answers the phone and I introduce myself, and explain the purpose of my call. He sounds very pleasant as he starts to tell me about the club, and why he and his colleague had set it up, to get people together, to enjoy social events together without the demands and commitments that some of the more national groups impose on their members. A regular weekly meeting, socialising, in a pub halfway between the two towns on a Tuesday night, with another social night in my town every other Thursday is the basis of the club, and from there other events and activities are organised and can be signed up for, whether it be going out together for a meal, theatre trips, games evenings, whatever the members want to do, looking for a host to organise and welcome people to that event.

This sounds as if it may be fun and certainly there sounds the opportunity to meet new people, women and MEN. Worth giving it a go, I think so. But I am still apprehensive about the mature woman walking into a pub by herself bit, especially a strange pub. I explain this to Paul, who quite understands, and it is agreed that I will go to the pub and he will meet me outside at the appointed hour, so that he can take me in, and then introduce me to other members, old and new.

Tuesday night arrives, it is time to give it a try. Having given Paul a call to tell him I will come tonight, I will meet him outside the main entrance of the pub at eight fifteen. Agreed, so time to doll myself up and get out there and trawl the natives, like-minded singles of my age, and maybe, just maybe, there will be Mr Right there. Nothing over the top, just present myself smartly, some make-up, and yes that will do nicely for my first presentation at the club. It is mid-winter so when I get in my car it has been dark for some time. Never mind, even in this gloom, I can use my electronics, set the sat nav and I should soon be there. So pointing myself in the right direction, out of town into the countryside I head, looking for this pub which Paul has said is easy to find as it is right on the side of the main road. The only trouble is that once in the countryside, a post code can cover a wide area, where buildings are few and far between. I also probably haven't mentioned that my sense of direction is poor – well, very poor – and one should never take any notice of me giving directions, because if I said 'go right', it is almost certain that I actually meant go left, and vice versa. By which time, you will have gathered I am now lost. Murky waters down dark lanes. And of course when I ring Paul to tell him I am running late and am lost, I can't really tell him where I am for him to redirect me because I don't know where I am. Three quarters of an hour exploring a county I don't know, and even in daylight would not be able to tell you where I have been, but at last the pub appears before me.

But even after a couple of phone calls, Paul has long ago given up on me and returned to drink with his mates. So here I am, and I am now going to have to do what I didn't want to – enter a strange pub by myself. Well, here goes. I make my way in, feeling rather insecure and apprehensive. A large room with one or two people eating, and a large group of people in an annexe down the far end mingling and talking to each other. This must be the singles group, so tentatively I make my way down to join them. A man breaks off and approaches me (help!), but it is okay as he introduces himself as Paul. He had given up on me after my 'non-arrival', and it was cold outside waiting. He tells me a little about the club, and how it functions, lists you can sign yourself up for to join in social events, trips and social meals. After this, he says he will introduce me to a few of the other members and I can ease my way into conversations, and hopefully get to know a few faces, so that next time it will be easier just to walk in and say hello to those I have already met. I am also introduced to the lady who has helped start this group with Paul – a very pleasant lady, tall, well-spoken and easy to make conversation with. She also tells me about the group, and the nitty-gritty like joining, subscription, and the hope that if I joined, I too would host social events.

There were some twenty-five to thirty people in this annexe, but sadly for me most of them were female, and what men there were, were perhaps just a little over the hill. People were very friendly but spoke very little about themselves, the big intros being, "What have you signed up for event-wise?" Conversation, but you just felt everyone there was hiding something, a sadness in their lives, or, well, I just don't know. All we can do is give it a go and see what transpires.

Obviously not everyone goes every week, and different people may come in the following weeks. No obvious partners, but then it did say it was a singles club, some people just looking for company, one or two of the men obviously looking for the women of their dreams, but on opening night with these, that would not be me.

A cider and soon a couple of hours had passed, and it was time to wind my way home, this time the right way. So, saying my farewells, I said I would be back and then disappeared off into the night. Back home safely, I reflected on the evening, it had been okay and I had met some nice people, even if they hadn't been the right sex. Yes, I would go again next week, but would perhaps try and persuade a colleague from work, also single, to come with me. I then wouldn't feel quite so uncomfortable amongst strangers. To bed and dreams of what might be, I can only wait and see.

Seven days on, I have persuaded my work colleague, Linda, to accompany me, and so we set off to the appointed pub again for another Tuesday night session, I mean meeting. We have purposefully gone a little later so that hopefully there will be more people there, and more conversation. Familiar faces from last week, some come and chat, and Paul comes over to see how I have been, and introduce himself to Leslie. This guy is almost certainly out to catch a fish! Then we buy a bottle of wine between us and sit ourselves down at a table near the entrance to the pub. Some people come over and chat, one or two men especially as they haven't seen these two ladies before. I'll be honest – yes, we were enjoying ourselves, even if my man was not visible to me. A laugh over a glass of wine or two, we sat chatting to a couple of blokes and the club treasurer when…

Where did this one come from? Hiding in the reeds all night, this one certainly was worth me casting my line. Young-looking, had obviously looked after himself, had his hair (well most of it anyway), scarf round his neck, and coat tucked over his arm, but there seemed a mystery in his face, something smouldering behind those blue eyes. He seemed to know a few people as he made his way to the door, a pleasant smile, the odd word to his acquaintances as he passed them coming in our direction. But, there was a sadness in his demeanour which couldn't be hidden. A nervousness came over me as I felt this man was worth angling for, but it was soon apparent that Linda had spotted him too, and was also after a nibble. Action will be required urgently because he looks as if he is about to leave these waters, and return from whence he came.

How could I have these feelings? One fleeting glance and I find myself playing this fish, trying to draw him to my bait. How do I attract him? Is my bait the right one? He may be a shy feeder. Oh why do I suddenly feel so anxious, apprehensive, and unsure of myself?

Action! He has stopped to talk to the lady standing opposite Linda and I, so close but so far, but I will have to make my play now or else he will be gone. Well, what can I do? Smile at him, and... Oh no, that old cliché, "I haven't seen you here before," spews from my mouth before I have a chance to think about it. Well it's hardly likely, is it Gill? This is only the second time you've been. Why did I say that? But hang on a moment, he has stopped and turned towards the two of us. Do something. What? Offer him some of my wine and see if he will remain for a while. He does stop, and politely acknowledges the two of us. I may have him, so invite him to sit down. Yes, he will, and seats himself between the two of us. What shall I say to him? I'm never usually lost for words, usually loud and flamboyant, but my mouth is ahead of my brain and something comes out, and at least I have engaged him. But Linda is also trying – two anglers chasing the same fish.

He is very softly spoken, very quiet, to the point where it is difficult to hear him. Why should that make me think of this? I hope he is not gay. Sexy, tight-fitting, light blue jeans. Hmmmm! Think I've fallen for this one, but I don't know why. Trouble is that Linda is also interested. A professional man as it turns out – interesting for me, but for her also as his line of work may be of use to her. Use and abuse, everyone has a use somewhere! But now my gills are rising; this one is going to be mine, so hands off, Linda. I'll fight you for this one until he is reeled in and safely in MY net.

We spend a pleasant hour chatting, me drinking my wine but he was on his way out when so rudely interrupted, and is driving so drinks no more. Yes, he is quiet, and yes there is a mystery, a sadness about him, but he does talk a bit about himself, though he gets both barrels of me as I sell my wares, and never lost for words, I relate my life story (well, some of it anyway), while Linda tries to get the odd word in, but this one is mine. As with all things, it must come to an end tonight as both of us, all three of us in fact (I mustn't forget Linda even if trying to prevent her getting at this rare treasure) have a thing called work to go to in the morning, and he has already stayed an hour longer than he intended. What next? There is another club night in town (where he also lives), meeting up again in a pub, just socialising and chatting. Yes, we may both go to that. I certainly will be and can only hope that he does as well. The evening ends as he says his goodbyes to us, and to the others that he knows who are still about, and with that he turns as is gone off into the night.

For us ladies, we finish our wine and also then depart, a short fifteen-minute drive, travelling with a smug but hidden grin on my face as this 'catch' does look promising. Arriving home, I reflect on my evening by the pool. This could be a big one and I will have to play my line carefully. There does seem a vulnerability about him, something, as if he is scared and running, so if this one is going to be mine, then I must reel him in carefully, not striking too soon.

I snuggle under my duvet, a little puzzled as to why this exotic fish has had such an effect on me, if I have fallen in love with him already – I fear I may have done. I feel totally protective towards him, but that is probably to my own ends so as not to let anyone else get to him. Sleep, and dreams fall over me; this has been a worthwhile night and I dream of the future.

Tomorrow is another day, and as I go into work I feel a new, invigorated person, with bright new hopes for the future. Is it obvious to my work colleagues as I go carping on to them about my 'new man'? Steady Gill, you haven't caught him yet. But I am seriously tickling for this fish. Unlike me, and the technophile that I am, I didn't get his mobile number – that was unlike me! Oh well, next time, first thing I must do! There is a spring in my step, and I can't wait till the next meeting, club night tomorrow.

But that vulnerability he seemed to have, that distant look. I wish the hours away, but worry, will he turn up? Now, now. I am now feeling a little apprehensive, worried even, because I want everything to work out the way I want. So I will fret until I walk through that door and find him there.

And now I must also worry about those girly things – what shall I wear? Will I look too fat? Oh, the dilemmas of being a woman 'out on the pull'. Worries, worries. I'll go casual – ankle boots, jeans, shirt, and flying jacket. Let's go and see what the evening brings. Grab my bag and car keys and drive the short distance to the town centre and pub meeting place. Fingers, everything crossed that he will turn up, I get to the pub and enter in anticipation. Big turnout by the look of it. Paul and another man I have met on a previous evening, but no sign of my man. The pub is not busy and there is no real worry of me going up to the bar myself and getting myself a cider, and joining the other two. Sounds like these evenings in this pub aren't a great hit and may well be knocked on the head in the not-too-distant future. As I chat to the other two, all I can hope is that my wish will come true and he will walk through the door, and soon.

My wishes are answered. He enters, looks round and sees the three of us, says hello and goes to the bar to get himself a... looks like he is a beer drinker. He sits down beside me but is very quiet as the rest of us chat, perhaps showing himself to be the reserved person I had met a couple of nights ago. The evening passes, and as there is such a poor turnout, the other two don't stay that long, leaving just myself and him. Great, a chance to have him to myself and see if I can find out more about my mystery man. He gets another couple of drinks for the two of us and we move to a quieter, more out of the way part of the bar. Although I do more of the talking, but that is me, he does open up more and tells me more about himself, his job, his life, and his history.

Married some years ago, but now divorced, had one or two relationships but through the trials of life, had and was now suffering from depression, and at present was actually taking medication for it, though not that it was making a lot of difference. Something in common as I had been there after the breakdown of my marriage in Australia, and so could in part relate to what he was now going through. But at least a barrier had come down and he had opened up a little so I could now see what was behind those mystery eyes. Something to work on. For now, our evening is over, and early days. I know with his job now that he works nights sometimes so can't make the club next time, but from the program, I know there is a band playing in a pub the following week – Friday – which could be fun to go to, so we arrange that we will go to this. This time I do get his mobile number so I can contact him in the meantime.

Do I try and steal a quick peck before we depart, or just play safe and not seem too forward? I will play it safe, so it will be next Friday, and oh boy am I now looking forward to that. I leave feeling very content with myself. I have had him to myself for a little while, found out some about him, though he is still very self-protecting and there must still be a lot he is hiding, or keeps within. A flutter in my heart, it's home and to bed feeling very satisfied with myself.

Just eight days to wait now, and we will meet again. Linda has decided to come to the pub too – a heavy metal band are playing covers, which should be good, at a pub down by the river. A couple of texts, but he seems not very forthcoming on this; short and to the point, yes, no, and not a lot more. Despite this, I suggest that Leslie and I will get a taxi, and we will pick him up on the way, and share the fare. We then can all have a drink. All decided.

More decisions – what shall I wear? And more importantly this time, I must consider my undies attire, you never know what may happen! 'What happened to the three-date rule?' you may ask. Well let's see where this will take me.

Friday has come and am I excited or am I excited? Taxi booked, times sorted for pick-ups, all is good. This has been on my mind now since the last meeting, over a week ago. Clothing sorted, this time my ankle boots again, jeans, a smock top and jacket, should do nicely. Let the evening begin.

The taxi arrives, picks me up, then onto Linda's, and I think I may have made it clear this man is mine and only mine. Lastly we have to pick him up, and then go onto the pub. I may just have had a little drink to calm my nerves before I left, but now we are at his door, no turning back. A dark entrance, but I find the front door and ring the door bell, and he soon arrives, ready to go and looks just a little bit sexy. He's quiet in the taxi but it is only a short journey to the pub, just over ten minutes. A lovely setting even in the dark, the pub and car park buzzing with people and then the murky river running below, on its frontage. The pub is heaving, crowded and noisy, but we struggle to the bar to get our drinks, wine again for the girls and him with his pint. We find he is a little deaf and it is a struggle for him in all this noise, so conversation may be difficult.

We find the rest of the singles group who have attended, a dozen of us in total, and make the best of trying to chat as we can, while trying to hear ourselves think. And then the band starts to play, which means the doors are shut, and they are seriously loud. Great music, the legs are starting to move, hips swinging with the beat. But it is hot, very hot, as more and more people start to gyrate to the band. They take their break, the doors open and a chance to cool down for a while, and refuel. A good evening so far, and even if he is struggling with the noise, he does seem to be enjoying it.

The band starts again, and it is time to take to the floor, and this guy can move; very fit for his age, just keeps dancing and dancing, moving with the beat to Kings of Leon, 'Sex on Fire', and it certainly may be igniting! All good things come to an end, and it is time to make our way home, so I summon a taxi again. It will be a few minutes, which allows us time to go outside and cool off a bit. Linda finds some waif and stray who has drank too much and is now collapsed on the floor and takes it upon herself that she should nurse him, so even when the taxi arrives, she doesn't want to leave. The two of us depart and head back to his place.

Very forward of me, but I invite myself in for a coffee. I may have had a little too much to drink already, but now we are alone and with no external noise. We can talk, and if I try for a quick snog, then it will happen or it will not. Nothing to lose so here goes, and yes, he is quite responsive. The smell of is it Obsession, ramping up my ardour. It is not long before we have departed the settee for the spare bed, and oh dear, some of my clothes seem to have been divested.

The three-date rule?

Well, he was a gentleman, as far as you can believe in that he was not going to take advantage of me so early after we have first met. Bugger! So intimate was as far as it went, though I think we had a fair idea of the whys and wherefores of each other's bodies before we had finished. But if I had made a mistake, then I did find that he did find women in sexy underwear a serious turn-on, far more than naked women, and boots were the cream on the icing. My lime green granny knickers and matching bra were not quite what he had in mind about sexy underwear, and the jungle between my legs, well enough said. Work to be done there, might have to contact the forestry commission!

It's now three in the morning, and time to go home so I summons a taxi, and re-unite myself with my clothing, don't think the limeys will be welcome if left in this house. The evening has come to an end; I am not quite satisfied (it was close), but very contented and can tuck myself in with a serious grin on my face. Rampant rabbit won't be coming out to play tonight. We have arranged to meet again on our own, I look forward to where this may take us, fingers, everything crossed (well, they weren't earlier), and now to dream.

If this is a fishing book, then I am seriously hooked. Am I in love? I think so, but what it is about this man, I just don't know. Hook, line, and sinker is the phrase, but why? Is it his vulnerability, his quiet but polite ways, his profession, or just the total package altogether?

Yes, over the next few weeks we do see more and more of each other, both at the singles club (which he didn't want to give up, as to him it is a way of forcing himself to meet people to bring himself out of himself – anti-depressants don't seem to be helping at all), and going out by ourselves. Live pub bands were very popular with both of us, and for him despite university days, something he had not done a lot of, but thoroughly enjoyed. You could see his mood lighten to the beat of the music, the rhythm of the band, whatever type it was. I may have mentioned my love of technology, and if my phone and contract was better than anyone else's, it's because it was. Five thousand free texts a month, which if you work it out means one every forty-odd minutes, take night time hours and work out means one about every fifteen minutes, and this bloke was going to get them.

He went away one weekend with his long-time mates for a rugby and golfing weekend, and having talked about our liking for boots, I was going to use my time usefully by finding a pair. But did I need to give him a progress report every four steps? Probably not. I think at some stage over the weekend, his phone was chucked in the car and forgotten about. Yes, I did find and buy a pair, chains and all. I was very pleased with my purchase, but more of that to follow.

I felt things were moving along okay, seeing more of him, getting to know him a little more, though he was not the sort who would open up readily. We still went to the singles club evenings, did pub quizzes, at which he was a bit of a smart arse, except for music rounds. Actually, he put me on the winning team for a change, and every now and again I would come up with some obscure answer. Then one day he asked me if I would like to go to a burlesque evening at a theatre in Stafford. He didn't know what it would be like but thought it would be fun to give it a go. We could spend the night there, book a hotel, and make a weekend of it. I thought, 'Why not?' It was decided, this is what we were going to do.

I would have to apply my mind to this one, get some serious tackle and see how much he would take the bait. Hotel sorted, booked in at an old hostelry in the town centre, parking, and fairly close to the theatre. Easy to park, yes, this was going along nicely. But the old limeys weren't going to do me much good here. A shopping trip is needed again. Lingerie, and it better be classy. A trip into town by myself, and I soon returned home with my chosen wear. He won't be able to resist me! I shall make sure of that. Yes, I have chosen well and will collect my just rewards when the time arises.

The plan is that we will head off to Stafford after lunch, find the hotel and have a relaxing unwind before we eat and then head off to the show. A night in the hotel, and then perhaps head off for the day into the Peak District for an explore and gentle stroll, before another overnight stay in another hotel then heading off back home. It should be good and I am rather looking forward to it, more and more as the closer the day looms. And in his own quiet way, I think he is too. Not quite sure what to expect from the evening, but will take it as it comes and he will enjoy himself.

Even for a short weekend break, as is my norm, I have to take everything bar the kitchen sink, and that only stays behind because of the lack of room in my case. It's difficult for a girl – travelling clothes, theatre clothes, night attire, then something for walking and sightseeing, a choice of handbags, pairs of shoes, there is just no end to it. So I pack, change my mind, unpack and repack something else, an exercise repeated more than once before I settle on my chosen wardrobe. And if I'm not totally sure myself about burlesque, I do know that the stage attire is at least sexy, and that I must match as the evening progresses. I hope this doesn't sound like a seduction in the making! Okay, I admit it.

The day has come, the sun is shining as I await eagerly for the knock on my door that will signal his arrival to pick me up. He's here and with a quick snog I point him in the direction of my travelling wardrobe. He politely says nothing as my mound of bags fill his boot, next to his solitary bag. The journey will not take us that long, and we are soon in Stafford, trying to negotiate some difficult instructions on how to find the car park behind the hotel. Eventually we succeed, park up, and register into the hotel, him laden with my bags again. The room looks very nice as I open the door (he'll catch me up with the bags in a moment, bless him). Comfortable, roomy, and with a nice ensuite.

He does seem more relaxed than he usually is – good – but I have found out that he does like hotels; the luxury, comfort of being looked after. It will be nice to go downstairs again and get ourselves a drink and just unwind in the sunshine in the beer garden. It's early spring, but it is a gorgeous warm day. Just soak up the sun and chat, perfect, until we need to think about getting ready and having something to eat.

While I have a bath, and start preening my scales, he takes himself off for a stroll into town, and to ascertain the whereabouts of the theatre. Upon his return, I'm still sifting through my jewellery as to what suits best. Men, why can they get themselves ready so quickly? I am still floundering with my choices by the time he has bathed, shaved, dressed, and is ready to go.

I am as ready as I can be. Do I look drop-dead gorgeous? I think I do. So, down to the restaurant for a very pleasant dinner, and then the short stroll to the theatre. The meal was good and we chatted lightly about anything and everything, enjoying a nice bottle of wine while we dined. What were we to expect? Well, we are now about to find out as we wrap up the meal and set off to the show. I am a little apprehensive as to what we are going to see as I have never been to a burlesque evening before, but from what I gather it will be entertainers dressed up in various ages of lingerie and dress, with song and dance. Well I enjoy nice lingerie so we will soon have all revealed.

We enter the theatre lobby where the audience is intermingling, some dressed appropriately for the occasion, bodices, high lace-up ankle boots, old fashioned Victorian dresses, and that's just the ladies. I make a mental note that if we do this again, then I will dress appropriately myself, I will enjoy that. A drink and into the auditorium, and we wait in anticipation. The show starts with our hostess introducing herself, singing and dressed in her Victorian attire, leaving a little to the imagination, but as she introduces the other performers, they may start dressed but clothing soon departs their bodies, as they perform in their boned corsets, thick stockings, suspenders, with the odd breast (well, there have to be two) revealed to all. I wonder what he is thinking. Is it turning him on? I do hope so. The show progresses, and we even see one or two men also performing, though are they doing a lot for me? I don't think so.

FISHING THE NET

At the interval we retreat to the bar; a quick G and T goes down very well, as we listen to the rest of the audience reliving their thoughts on the show. The second half and our hostess finds one unsuspecting male to pick on, and keeps returning to him to carry on her teasing of him, but he takes it in good spirits. A grand finale, plenty to see, literally, as the cast flaunt their wares, busts of varying sizes – a good show.

If this was the ground bait, then it is now back to the hotel and up to our room for me to prepare my own bait. I disappear into the bathroom with my newly acquired tackle. Time to reel in my catch, or that's what I am hoping for. He will have a little time to kill as I prepare myself. Make-up and lipstick will need just a quick touch-up, a spray of scent, here and especially there, and now to put on that lingerie I had been into town for, to encourage my desires. The stockings, they take a little time to put on, trying to get those back seams dead straight, and clipping on the suspenders, not a common procedure I have partaken of in the past. Dressing gown on and here goes. I will vacate the bathroom for him to get ready for bed.

He has brought some wine up into the room, and a glass awaits me on my bedside cabinet. I cuddle up to him so he has a sample of what he is going to get, my firm, covered breasts pushing against his through my gown. I feel a fish rising, before ushering him into the bathroom to prepare for bed.

The lady awaits, as I slip myself in between the white ironed sheets. My line has been cast and now it is time to make my play. My bait is on the hook, I'm now the hooker.

The bathroom door opens. Good – no modesty as he enters the bedroom again, naked but smelling of heaven. Nice body, lovely firm butt, a hairless chest and the equipment? Well, I can work on that, I intend to.

It is time to reveal my bait, and I am rather pleased with myself, rather turned myself on. As I pull back the sheets to reveal my sexy attire, a well-cut purple bra with a little black lace over the top, matching suspender belt covering my hips and belly (I have had three children and am a bit conscious of this area, but it will not be revealed) leading down to a very skimpy purple thong. The stockings you know about already, and those newly acquired chained boots finish the bait. As he slips into bed beside me, I can see he likes what is in front of him. Good. Let the foreplay begin, and in no time at all, yes, there is a big fish rising, wanting to take the bait, as we buck and roll around the bed. The smell of man and woman, their different scents, fill the air. He too likes kissing, everywhere, so to say the atmosphere was getting steamy was an understatement.

This is going really well, I'm satisfied with the way the evening is going – very satisfied. If the burlesque was titillating, this is mind blowing as we explore each other's bodies, nothing left to the imagination. I'm so glad I've come and will come again, oh boy!

An hour and a half later, I'm f—d, and as we briefly untangle ourselves, he removes my boots and stockings for me. I put on a skimpy nightie, and it is now time to sleep. Yes, I am satisfied, very satisfied with how this has gone and look forward to more in the future. If catching my marline took the same amount of time and energy, that was hard, but this was pure pleasure, though there was something hard in it somewhere.

Goodnight and sleep well, and sweet dreams. I think mine may be a bit dirty, but they are mine and mine alone, oh good.

It's morning and I awake next to my man who then makes the morning brew, before laying down beside me again. After our exertions, I do feel a little stiff. Well hang on! It's not so little now, and I'm not going to say no, so you can use your own imagination as to what or who was served before breakfast.

A full English of course was just what was needed to fill in an empty space, and slipped down well as we enjoyed a breakfast together, and time to plan our day. On our return to the room, time to pack my bags and as I tucked my new lingerie back into my bag. Yes, that was money well spent. All done and he has to stagger back down the stairs with all my bags.

We then spend a little time in town, shopping and looking before departing for the Peal District and springs at Tideswell. We are blessed with a lovely sunny spring day again, as we enjoy the outside air, and the walk around the village, the craft shops, and then a nice lunch. It has been a nice leisurely day after the exertions of last night, and it is now time to return homewards, and to Uttoxeter where we have booked another overnight stay.

Again, a struggle to find the hotel, or more strictly the car park, and again we are booking ourselves into a room. A big room, with an annexe, plenty of room to put all those bags of mine again. We read for a while, but I need a rest, so settle down for forty winks while he goes for a walk in town to try and find somewhere suitable for us to eat tonight. On his return he says he has found nowhere other than Indians which he doesn't fancy, and we find that the hotel we are in will give us a nice meal. Just the two of us with an intimate window table, and a nice bottle of wine. I can reflect on a rather good day. I have enjoyed it – the company, the scenery and the... yes, that was very enjoyable. A nightcap and back to our room where I find he also has been shopping as he produces out of his bag a rather nice red bra and matching thong. I better try these on straight away, and they will probably go well with my stockings and boots again. I disappear into the bathroom and slip them on. Do I look gorgeous? Let's see what he thinks.

As all good fishermen do, having netted my fish last night, when the angling was finished, I had returned him to the water. But now, as I cuddled up to him I could feel a fish rising and I think it is the same one. What a piece of luck, different bait but he has taken it again. I can only help him out of his clothing and slip between the sheets again, and as our lovemaking continues, if not quite as long as last night, we have scaled the heights again. Wow!

Sleep and time to go home. Yes, it has been a good weekend, more than a good weekend, and I think I am seriously in love.

*

Spring passes into summer, and as time has passed I am spending more and more of my spare time with him. More and more of my clothes are ending up in his house, as I stay more and more frequently overnight. We cook for each other in our own different but accomplished styles. And as we seem to have a mutual appreciation of sexy lingerie, my bottom drawer is also filling up, plus a nice pair of black boots he has bought me, and they certainly get some use. I like my bed boots. We spend time together watching live music in pubs, walking (though I haven't his stamina), often finishing up in a pub with a nice pint of cider, and then back home for a rub down, or whatever else you may want to call it. Sometimes with the best of intentions we went for a walk but got no further than the pub car park, but at least over that drink we could talk and I hope bring him more and more out of himself.

There were family occasions, on both sides, big wedding anniversary parties, family weddings, and parents' birthday parties, but in all these, although he would support me and my presence when with his, there always seemed a sense of aloofness, desperation even, as if he would have preferred to be somewhere else, which I could only put down to his remoteness from his children, and a big discomfort from being with family members who said they were neutral through his divorce. Saying they were always there for both parties, always there to talk to and give help, but his perception was of them seeing him as the 'sinner' and taking his wife's side, ex-wife's side. This would send him into dark moods which he struggled to get out of and although I was always there to be at his side, it didn't seem to help. As they say, the silence was sometimes deafening.

But when he did snap out of it, he was a bundle of

laughs, and a great lover. But he was also having difficulties at work, almost verging on bullying, and although he enjoyed his day-to-day routine, back in the office was another story. Clouds were building around him and he was struggling to find a way out. He had seen a doctor for his insomnia, and if I had noticed, whilst lying beside him, he never slept for more than five minutes, verging on sleep apnoea at times.

But through all this struggle we still had some great times. If I would cook for him if he was working, and I was not, then at other times he would cook for me, and he was quite accomplished though he cooked from his head and never wrote anything down, so every recipe was a one-off, never to be repeated, though a slight variation may have been tried again. But whatever he did it was spectacular.

Whether it was me or him, I'm not sure, but one of us came up with the idea of intimate soirees, him and me in 'Café Frontroom', curtains drawn, a private table for two in the corner, candlelight, privacy and romance. Love it! He would bathe, change, and migrate into the kitchen to prepare a meal fit for a queen – ME – giving me an intended time for serving. That is for the meal, not whatever else you may think. Tut, tut! I would then go and prepare myself as he worked his magic with the food. Always three courses, fine wine, and produced to perfection, so all I could do was put the icing on the cake. At the appointed time as he placed the starter on the table, I would appear.

Those black boots (a must), hold-ups, black and sheer, a little thong and a negligee or some other suitably skimpy top to cover (just) my heaving breasts. All loosely covered by a black chiffon drape, just to cover everything a little, but not leave a lot to the imagination.

Let dinner commence; raise a glass (of wine) to a good evening, and tuck into my starter. The waft of his aftershave mingling with my perfume, these evenings can only go one way. A leisurely meal, interspersed with the odd snog, well there has to be some bodily contact, and then he is off to get the next course, arriving decoratively arranged on our plates. Pure bliss, and exquisite in taste. Good food, good wine, good company, and the hormone levels were rising. He was clever in his preparation in that when the meal had finished, all the washing up was also completed, the last few items while making coffee, so the rest of the evening would go uninterrupted.

After Eights? F—k that. I had better things to do than shove mints in, in my mind. I was there to be taken, and taken I would be! Whether it be up to bed, the settee, or the floor, afters were to be had, and they were. Without a lot of persuasion, his clothes would soon be a heap on the floor as we entwined our bodies wherever we had ended up, and after the pleasures of the table, the pleasures of the flesh were now taking over. And again, his stamina was something to behold as he brought me to the boil time and time again. This to me is what romance is all about. He would tease me, he would please me, but I always finished satisfied – well satisfied – and would want to make another booking for 'Café Frontroom'. Table for two, and in the same corner.

Why change a winning formula?

Before we met he had arranged a holiday with an old friend – eleven days in Portugal, in the Algarve in mid-summer, and with a little persuasion I managed to get him to change the name on the second ticket, yes, to me. I was really looking forward to this, and arranged another shopping trip for a sexy one-piece swimsuit, a couple of smart but light dresses for evenings, for those balmy summer evenings, and while I'm at it, I might just as well see what Ann Summers have in now.

We're ready to go, and as you can guess, my suitcase is overflowing again, and I can rely on there being some room in his, so no worries. I know where my extra luggage can go. But at the moment, some will remain hidden from his eyes, my little treats to come, for his eyes only, and he is going to love what he sees when my appointed time comes.

An early morning flight from East Midlands, after tucking into a nice healthy full English (breakfast, not what you are thinking) takes us up into the sky as the sun rises, and off towards Portugal. It is light enough to see the shores of England left behind us as we cross the channel, over the Normandy coast and head south over France before crossing the Pyrenees, and then the arid interior of Spain. Not a long flight and we are soon circling over the Atlantic Ocean before getting ready to land at Faro, the sun glimmering on the gentle ripples of a calm sea. We turn parallel to the sea and descend for a smooth landing, before departing the plane and going through passport control. Yes, we are on terra firma and I am away with him.

It is a return for him, several previous trips in fact,

and so it is easy to follow him (even if he is having to lug my case about as well), as he finds his way to the car hire place to pick up the pre-booked car we will have for the duration. Lucky for me, I am not a named driver so can be chauffeured about for the full eleven days. A little white four-doored saloon, with air-con, imperative in these mid-summer temperatures, just large enough to fit all my luggage, and be able to squeeze his in as well. We are self-catering in his friend's apartment, and it is a short run of just over an hour to our destination.

Through Faro, before heading west towards Alvor. Now a motorway running parallel to the old main road to the most westerly tip of Europe; the kilometres fly by, the sea to our left in the distance, and arid farmland to our right, dried riverbeds reflecting the heat of a Southern European summer; orange groves, with that wonderful aroma they give. We're getting close as we cross the Portamoa River, now with mountains on our right before descending, then reaching our exit point near Penina golf course, and we are there, driving through the newly built estate where the apartment is. Fresh, well-manicured, flowers, and a small car park next to the block. A well-trodden path for him, he unloads the car and managing the trick of negotiating the front door fully laden, escorts me up to our second-floor flat. Entering, I'm impressed – lovely kitchen, large lounge/diner, bathroom, and two bedrooms. A large balcony either side of the flat means there will not be many minutes where one will be without the sun at any stage during the day, and also overlooking a large pool with café close by. This holiday is going to be good.

As I have said, we are self-catering and so will have to stock up with food; he knows there is a supermarket a couple of minutes down the road by car, where we can get all we need. Breakfast we will need every day, lunch and supper we will take it as we go along. He will cook, I will cook, and we will eat out a fair bit as well. The decision now is to go shopping, or get out and enjoy that sunshine, which I can see he wants to do. I will go with the flow; sun, and we will do the food shop at the heat of the day, as a rest from the sunshine. To think it was only just over five hours ago that we were in England and now we are basking in temperatures, mid-eighties already, and it will get hotter. Decision made, he goes down to the pool area to find a couple of sunbeds, looks like from the balcony there is plenty of choice, and after having explained to me how to get there, I will follow shortly after at least starting to unpack. I take in the ambience of the place. Very nice, and the views from the balconies, the mountains in the distance one way, and the more residential area the other, overlooking the pool and I would imagine where the sun is going to set. Actually he told me that, because anyone who knows me will have prior knowledge that I have no sense of direction whatsoever, which means it could set anywhere.

I don't unpack much, but being a fair maiden in my skin, cover myself in factor 30 before heading off downstairs and to the pool, where my man is already into sunning himself. Looks like he may be a professional at this, prone on his sun lounger, skimpy swimwear and sunglasses. We have been up for a few hours now, so what better to do than to lie in the sun and think of – well, use your imagination as to what I may be thinking. It gets warmer by the minute as the sun moves more directly above us in a cloudless sky. He loves the sun. Me, from my Australian experiences, I am warier of it and so despite the factor 30, I am soon seeking his assistance to get a sun brolly to cover my body, a girl wouldn't want red and sore thighs later, would one? The bar/restaurant is only a few yards behind us for coffee, soft drinks, or a beer, so now and again he trundles off to seek refreshments for me, well, both of us, he is not quite a personal slave to me, yet! This sets the pattern of our days to come. Sunbathe after breakfast while it is still not so hot, taking in the odd excursion some days because we both want to see something of the country we are in, though some of it will be revisiting places of interest he has been before. The mountains, the Atlantic west coast, wherever takes our fancy. We have no fixed agenda other than to enjoy ourselves, eat, drink, and be merry, and of course my fringe benefits!

A couple of hours is enough for starters, so we leave our towels on our loungers and quickly throw on some clothes to go to the supermarket just down the road. It is big and looks as if it will cater for all our requirements – meat, fresh fish, fresh vegetables and fruit, and everything else we might want. It is so handy we only need to buy essentials and enough to tide us over a couple of days, then we can come back and restock. So a long shop for him, short for me, and we are back in the car and returning back to our flat, the heaviest items being that we have to buy our drinking water, and the containers were large and not that comfortable to carry (he told me).

We decide to use the pool café for our lunch,

where he reacquaints himself with Emma, our Scottish hostess, moved over from home a few years back to settle down with her Portuguese husband. Very friendly, but of course, she knows one of us from past visits. She is only too pleased to cook, and does special evening meals too, altering her menu each night. A strange habit of us Brits, we go abroad to these hot climes, and what do we order for lunch but a burger in a bap, and chips. I suppose the beer cools it all down, but again, lovely to relax in the warmth, though the sun umbrella is a must now as it is getting seriously hot. We dare not overdo the sun, especially on our first day, so it is nice to just talk and enjoy the heat, and relax.

For him now it is a return to the poolside, book in hand. Me, I will take a brief rest from the sun, unpack a little more and close my eyes in the apartment. A bit of a breeze has got up now, and a few clouds drift lazily cross the sky, quite normal he tells me, but it doesn't bring about any drop in temperature, very hot but comfortable. I enjoy my forty winks before rejoining him by the pool, where it is now easier to find a bit more shade, though if it was more crowded, one may not be able to get in the most desirable spot. A swim, he gives it a go; it is a large pool, and from the toe test does feel a bit chilly, but no messing, he just dives in to get the ordeal over with, and as I watch him swim up and down the pool on his front, on his back, he does swim like a fish, and I am going to reel him in.

He climbs out of the pool, and dries in the sun. Me, I will give the pool a miss today but promise that I will swim in the next few days. We have had a relaxing start to our holiday by the pool, not over-sunned but not wanting to overdo it, we clear up our pool kit and return to the apartment, relax some more over a beer, shower, and prepare to go out for an evening meal.

The evening is warm, an impressive sunset, and we go for a lovely meal cooked by Emma's husband. Quiet, only another couple eating there this evening, and we share a bottle of the local wine. On completion of the meal, we go and sit on the patio outside the café, enjoying, enjoying a coffee and each other's company before it is time to call it a day and get ready for bed.

How tired is he? I can only dangle the bait and see if he rises to what's on offer in front of him. Lucky me, he cannot resist my body and after a short time of 'wrestling' each other on the bed, we make love and it is time to sleep. I close my eyes, dreaming of happy times on our holiday and perhaps into the long-distant future. I am content.

Another morning and I am greeted by him making me a cup of tea, service with a smile, and he is naked as well. He possesses no pyjamas, and hasn't done for some forty years now. The sun shines through our bedroom window, as the curtains are drawn open and a gentle breeze blows in. He puts some shorts on and takes his coffee and his book out on to the balcony. Then he prepares our breakfast, eaten on the other balcony, peacefully overlooking the pool. Today will be another lazy day, finishing unpacking, and more time spent by the pool, or in his case both in and out of the pool, more reading, and lunch again on the café patio, enjoying a nice cool beer. The temperature is rising, beautiful blue skies, perfect holiday weather. We read some more, he swims more, trying to increase the amount he will swim more and more every day, hoping that when we will return home, he will have managed fifty lengths – impressive if he does it as it is a long pool.

An evening meal in, then a drive into the local town of Alvor, some six or seven kilometres away, just to explore and have a drink there. A walk along the main street, down to the fish market, obviously closed now, and to see the moon reflecting on a still evening sea. We can enjoy a quiet drink together, trying one or two bars, before party time begins and the pub singers start in various bars; the choice is ours as to what we want to listen to. Then back to the apartment where we can enjoy a nightcap before retiring to bed. And then the passion as the lights go out. But I am saving my best for other nights, that trip to Ann Summers, all still to be revealed.

So the tone of our holiday was set – lazy days going nowhere interspersed with days out, and evening meals at the café or going into Alvor. This is a fishing port, so seafood plays a big part on most menus, fish often cooked on a barbeque, while you wait, with some exquisite Algarvian sources, food to die for. Eaten and washed down with some lovely local Alentajo wines, especially the reds, these were great days.

One trip we took up into the mountains, climbing, climbing up a steep winding road to the summit where there was a large satellite station and panoramic views for miles towards the Algarve coast and the hills to the west, with reservoirs hidden in some of the valleys. On these quieter backroads we would find cheap restaurants serving the local speciality of chicken piri piri and chips at under half the price of those restaurants in the resorts such as Alvor. Artisan shops aplenty, even at the summit, selling anything from local pottery to thick woollen jumpers, obviously in preparation for winter.

Although not at the top of the world, there was a nice breeze up here, but one could see how arid these southern European countries can be, confirming the views from the plane as we flew into Faro. Huge Eucalyptus trees lined the roads as we drove back down the mountain, a picturesque avenue to meander through. We passed through a quaint little village boasting its own spring, coming from the mountain, worth a stop and a drink, again with its array of artisan shops, a postcard village square lined with bars and restaurants, even sardine restaurants up here. A spa village, with Sanatorium for the healing properties of the water, and a nice walk up the stream through the woods, scrambling over rocks and wooden bridges.

Time to descend back to sea level, but first stopping to book a table at a roadside restaurant called Rouxinol; he had been before and recommended it, especially with my time in Sweden – it was run by a Swede, Stefan, and his daughter. Mid-summer's day was approaching and they were having a celebration which my man thought I would enjoy as the food would be based on their country of origin. A nice thought, so we would go along on that special day.

This turned out to be an enjoyable evening when it came, a sedate drive away from the coast up into the hills to the restaurant. A very warm evening and by this stage we were starting to glow a bit from the sun; we were greeted by Stefan and seated in the shade of a large tree, enjoying the outdoor vista, like all assembled guests. I think we must have been the only non-Swedes there, but what the hell, we shall enjoy ourselves. Beer, more beer as it is so warm, and there are a few midges about to try and annoy us as we tuck into our smorgasbord, as more and more food is presented on the table. This takes me back, but I'm not sure if it is exactly his thing, especially when we, as are all the guests, are serenaded by an ageing gentleman and his guitar, singing Swedish folk songs (could have been singing anything for all we knew), strumming along as he sang. Not quite Status Quo or the bands we would listen to back home. Never mind, it all made for a pleasant evening, with an ex-(Swedish)pat community coming together to celebrate the summer solstice, and we were welcomed among them. And then as the sun disappeared over the hills to the west, in some ways the highlight of the evening was when the nightingales (apparently what Rouxinol means) started to sing in the trees around us. This is making me feel more than a bit romantic, so it is not the worst thing in the world when it is time to head back down the hill, and back to our abode.

This has been a special night, nice of him to think of my Swedish connections so I think time for that little red set to come out and yes, it is hot, but I will treat him to my stockings tonight as well. As I slip under the sheet, waiting for him to come from the bathroom, my passion is rising, and if our bodies were glowing before, they are boiling now as we explore each other, rising to a crescendo of lovemaking and ultimate satisfaction. Oh boy, have I had a good night, now satiated and satisfied, and am now falling more and more in love with this guy. With a grin on my face, we lie back. Sleep soon overtakes me as I dream of he who sleeps besides me.

Wonderful summer days. More days, part days by the pool, and it is now getting seriously hot, to the extent that especially in the afternoon I would have to retreat inside to get away from the sun for a while. I didn't want to be toasted. He would just find a brolly and in the shade would carry on reading. We got to know Emma and her assistant very well, and were invited to come along and share her father's birthday party with the rest of the family and other guests, and had the pleasure of spending a lot of time in the company of said father, a fascinating gentleman who came over to visit a couple of times a year. As the sun set, the meal was cleared and a disco started to play. As ever, my man was up on the floor and dancing, moving those tight cheeks to the rhythm of the music. Where does he get his energy from? I don't know, and I know he will save some for me later.

Another trip took us to Lagos, slightly to our west along the coast, where we would explore the harbour, the monuments to those Portuguese explorers of times gone by, Cabot etc., strange patios laid out to give you the impression you were standing on waves, going up and down as they ebbed and flowed, a funny and disconcerting experience that your eyes played upon you. We sat and watched as yachts, fishing boats, all sorts arrived and departed up the river to the marinas, and out into the open sea. One wonderful pub we found nesting in the fork of two streets, playing good music, and set on three levels, so we could sit on the balcony of the second floor watching the world pass beneath us. More of a tourist resort than Alvor, but very quaint. And as you arrived in town, there were large cranes working on construction work, and along the beams of the cranes there were nesting pairs of storks and their young, three or four nests, and also on the top of some disused chimney stacks.

Further along the coast, another trip is the most westerly point of Europe, Cape Vincent. As we headed off along the main road, it was for a change quite dull. Are we going to get a storm? But luckily the clouds started to clear, and we found a wonderful place to stop before arriving at the Cape, on top of the cliffs overlooking an azure sea below us, with the waves crashing in against the rocks. It was worth just standing and enjoying the beauty of our surroundings, standing there amongst the flowering yellow gorse, and one or two other small hardy flowers that would have to withstand the hammering of the winds. And when we did arrive at the Cape, despite the now cloudless and blue sky, how that wind did blow. If I wanted to get my man's clothes off, this was the place to be, wind-assisted. Obviously now, these places are made into tourist attractions, as well as the more functional needs of looking after shipping out to sea. A giant's chair, that we scrambled up on for the normal corny photo, though he had to give me more than a leg up to get little me seated up there, but no problems for his athletic prowess.

As we stare out there, far, far away is the next land mass, America, where those past explorers would have set off towards, centuries ago, not knowing where or how far they would be going, to the edge of the world. A place I would well recommend, though I don't know what it would be like in a gale in the midst of winter. Turning northwards, the wild rugged West Atlantic coast before it turns into sand dunes – a National Park, noted for its sandy beaches and good surfing. It is this way we now turn, to enjoy a beach and some sun, and some lunch on the way. There are many long stretches of sand along this part of the coast with plenty of parking, but most do involve a walk to the beach and the distant Atlantic, with its incessant rollers tumbling in and over the golden yellow sands. There is usually a stream or river winding its way across the sands to its final destination of the sea. One such beach we stop at, managing to park close to the sands, a stream running along the south of the beach, quite deep in places, otherwise vast open space with a solitary surfer's hut and café in the centre of it. We get our towels, books, and set off towards the distant waves, kit in his beach bag, and eventually on finding a spot to encamp we settle down to read and relax. But, he finds after this longish trek, that somewhere he has mislaid his towel and so sets off retracing his steps, to try and find it while I wait patiently sat on mine, reading. Sadly, for him, he finds the towel by the car, and then starts back towards me. He eventually arrives back and settles down himself, but in the middle of this beach, with no shade, and even with a sea breeze, it is seriously hot now, more than I can cope with, so I say we will have to go back to the car. Poor soul, he stands and trudges back to the car. Nice rest I allowed him to have, I will have to give him a little treat later.

More to the point, I hope he will give me one!

Thank God the car has air-con, as we head back down the coast and then turn east back towards 'home'. We decide it will be more interesting to head back across the hills, seeing many oak trees that the bark is removed to make corks for wine bottles, though we reflect on the ever-increasing number of screw caps now used. Another memorable day, which we will follow with a nice meal out and a little something later. I'm sure neither of us will turn it down.

So as bedtime comes, time for an outing for one of those little numbers I bought from Ann Summers, methinks. As he lies in bed, I make my arrival in a little matching red polka dot bra and knickers set, but how strange, there are holes in both bra cups and the crotch of the knickers. Well, I knew there were, and now to find out what he thinks, and from the look of his face, it's a hit. I slip in beside him and with the desired effect, the fireworks begin as we explore each other's bodies, and those parts exposed for his pleasure. How I like my sexy lingerie, and him too, ten out of ten for dress and the pleasures it brings me, as once again our lovemaking is long, passionate, and very satisfying.

As the holiday progresses, the temperature rises and rises, on a couple of afternoons exceeding a hundred degrees in the shade. Too hot for me to bake in the sun, but not enough to put him off, and with this, sometimes during our afternoons we would be separated, him by the pool and me in the shade of the balcony or having a nap. But in this time I could reflect on how much I am in love, and also that away from work and his life at home, he seems a new and invigorated person; no worries and so much more relaxed than I had seen him in the past. Am I a good influence on him? I hope it is me doing it.

Nights, as previously mentioned, were spent mainly dining out, in the café, in restaurants in Alvor, but especially in one beach restaurant that he in past visits had become quite a regular at, and had a very good relationship with one of the waiters who remembered him from before. Atlantida, set on the edge of the beach, with a few large sandstone rocks jutting out of the sand and the sea just in front – a lovely setting. Seafood specialities, nervous-looking crabs and lobsters in a tank as you walked in, hoping that you wouldn't choose them as your dinner, and trays of fish in ice from which you would choose what you wanted to eat. Then they would be cooked for you, usually over coals, with lovely Algarvian sauces, garlic potatoes, and a salad. The clams in garlic were gorgeous as a starter, then stone bass steaks. Our first visit there, we sat inside and enjoyed a lovely meal, so enjoyable we decided to return for our final night meal, but requested a table on the veranda. Booked and waiting for us.

For a change we decided we would go by taxi. Tonight I am going to look special, so the works came out; one very colourful long dress I had seen, showing plenty of bust, the full make-up, eyes looking stunning, red lips, and to finish it off, a multiple stringed and beaded white necklace. Do I look good? Oh yes, oh yes! When he sees me, he is stunned too, and as we enjoy a G and T on the balcony, glowing in our summer attire and well browned now, him a lot more than me, we link arms and stare towards the sunset. A pleasant taxi ride, where our driver tries to teach him some Portuguese, and we are dropped off outside Atlantida. Our friendly waiter greets us and directs us to the table he has selected for us on the veranda – perfect and very romantic on this wonderful summer's night; the waves could be heard washing in towards us, a very gentle and repetitive crashing as they break on the sands. A lovely, really deep pink rosé to drink, and I wish I could remember its name, as we select our meals for the night. The array of sea food, wonderful, and with our attentive waiter taking every care of us we settle down for a very enjoyable meal.

We take a break from the meal before our sweet, to take a stroll along the shore, removing our shoes/sandals as we dip our feet in the sea, and under the moonlight hold each other in our arms, a strong embrace and long, lingering kiss, the smells of the sea, and of man and woman. Bliss. I could stay in this hold, in his arms forever.

We make our way back to our table, to enjoy the sweet he has told me about and ordered, as we will have to share as it is specially prepared – a pudding for two. Effectively flambéed strawberries, in three different liqueurs, lots of sugar, all prepared in front of you, a great floor show. Rich but lovely, it slips down well, before we enjoy a coffee and a liqueur on the house. A truly memorable meal both for the meal itself, the romance, and the very special company. This will last in my memory for some time.

It is time to summon a taxi and take us back to the apartment for our final night. My man has looked after me well over these past few days, and it is only fair that I now return some of that pampering. What can I do? Well, I have one more Ann Summers outfit as yet unworn, and perhaps this is the time to get it out. What better way to look after him than my little nurse's outfit? Very tight, very brief, and a little white thong to cover those bits that ought to be covered but are not.

I put on my uniform, and now can only usher him into bed, tuck him in and settle him for the night. But first he must have his medicine. I don't think matron will approve of what I'm going to do next, but who cares? I slip under the sheet myself; I'm sure there is somewhere in the manual that says two bodies are warmer than one, and I can certainly feel the temperature rising now. And I don't think that is the only thing rising. Just what the doctor ordered for both of us, as we grapple with each other, not quite sure where the sheet has gone, but I know where we are going, and to an ever rising crescendo, I am satisfied over and over again. What a climax to a perfect holiday, but I have broken the rules of being overfamiliar with my patient, so I can only take my punishment, bend over and have my bum lightly smacked. Now I'm off duty, so I discreetly slip back into bed to cuddle up to him for the rest of the night. Magical.

All things must come to an end, and it is now time to return back to England. A sense of joy in me, but also a sense of sadness that all this has come to an end, and I wonder where life will now take us. He has seemed so much more relaxed, a different person, but all the stresses and strains of everyday life will soon be back upon us. Perhaps Portugal isn't for me again, the heat and laziness of it all, but anywhere else I will gladly follow him.

Home and summer meanders on. He still has plenty of holiday due, and so we are soon looking at spending another week away. In between we manage the odd weekend, an open air Queen tribute concert in one of our stately home gardens, with accompanying firework display, and he likes the look of one of the female singers in thigh boots; great entertainment followed by the usual wonderful night together once we are back in our hotel. He really knows how to pleasure me and perhaps I am starting to hint that we should make this a more permanent arrangement. I am spending more and more, in fact most of my time at his, and he is very much becoming my world.

WORLD RIVERS/BRINGING IN THE CATCH

He has never been one for cruises, totally dogmatic on the subject – doesn't fancy it, not going to do it. Somewhere I see an advert for Nile cruises, great deals, and ask what he thinks about that, and am surprised when he says yes, let's give it a try. Surprisingly for his online incompetence, he finds a deal even better than the one that I had found and so it is all booked for us to go late summer, flying Birmingham to Luxor, then seven nights on this mighty African river, heading down to Aswan, then back up to the Valley of the Kings, before departing from Luxor back to home again. This is going to trouble my wardrobe again; formal evening meals with appropriate dress, and day-to-day wear for exploration and just travelling on the river. Again, he doesn't let me down by donating part of his suitcase for my goods, his light summer clothing not weighing that much.

An early morning flight sees us arriving over the Mediterranean by lunchtime and then we follow the Nile down to Luxor, flying high above and the sight of this massive river, fertile on both banks for a narrow strip of land, then the Sahara desert stretching both ways into the distance. A truly, truly amazing sight, what a spectacular world we live in. A smooth landing then out into the heat of the day, and it is hot as we make our way over to the cooler air-conditioned arrivals lounge where we have to buy a visa, and then await our coach that will take us to our boat. A modern airport, but as soon as you get out, you experience what is the custom, we will find, of being hassled by Egyptians trying to make a buck, or more strictly, a pound sterling, for anything from giving you a piece of toilet paper to carrying your case to the coach, but as soon as they are paid, they abandon your case for you, or in my case, him, to carry the rest of the way.

A trip through Luxor and a brief sight of some of those wonderful Ancient Egyptian monuments, ruins of temples, as we pass by on our way to the boat. Expensive-looking hotels also, and we are there at our boat and ready to embark and be directed to our room, ours being at water level. There is something almost Victorian about the look of the room, the décor, except Queen Vic had no TV of course. After unpacking, our package includes guided tours to all the sights we will see; we opt to pay a not-too-expensive extra to be all-inclusive, and with that we take a drink out with us onto the deck of the boat, sit back and enjoy the sun. This is not a travel book, but there is something very special at the appointed time when all the mosques send out their calling to their flock, as these 'sirens' boom out from across the river. Then a Nile sunset, a case of now you see it and now you don't, timed by my man as seven seconds for the sun to touch the horizon, and disappear. A calm falls over the Nile. After recent troubles, Egypt has lost some of its popularity as a tourist destination and so not many of the fifty-odd cruise ships are in operation, and we are to learn that ours is one of the few that is nearly full.

It will be hot throughout, and although a dry heat, even now the sun has set, it is still very, very warm. A quick shower and after a long day travelling we will then make our way to the dining room after exploring the boat a little. A bar, and lounging area, with the rest of the room being a large dance floor, we make it a rule that if one foot touches this floor for any reason, then we have to dance, even if others think we are absolute prats, and dance we will, whatever time of day. We are going to enjoy ourselves. We will be on the same table for all meals, with the same dining companions, a couple from Yorkshire, probably slightly older than us, and a very pleasant young couple, all of whose company we will enjoy immensely over the next few days. Plenty of choice of food, excellently prepared, we aren't going to starve. And after the meal, back to the bar or mix with other guests out on the deck, looking out over the river, the lights spreading across the still waters.

It has been a long day today, and we have travelled many miles, the furthest south he has been, and we are tired. It will be just a cuddle tonight, as we return to our room, and despite the manful attempts of the air-con, it is still very hot, so much so that our two single beds put together, after a warm, very warm embrace will function as single beds for us to try and keep cool. Sleep will follow soon as I close my eyes, and dream back to those wonderful days in Portugal. Will my man be the same now on this different continent? Certainly over the past few weeks that tension had returned to him with his return to work. Just sitting out in the sun on the boat's deck, the barriers had come down again and he was getting back to the real man that I have fallen in love with, so head over heels in love. We will have a week of seeing the sights of this ancient civilisation that dominated this corner of the continent, their culture, history, and for my own satisfaction hopefully the rising of another power.

Sleep.

A new dawn, and we rise to a beautiful sunny sky, activity outside our harbour side window, and the real start of a new adventure. We meet up with our fellow diners for a delicious breakfast, the choice of what you could have, immense, and then after the usual morning wash and toiletry chores, we are all to meet up to be divided into our respective groups and meet our guide, our Egyptologist who will look after us for the week. A brief introduction from our man Omar, who gives us a quick talk as to what we will see over the next few days, and especially today, and we leave the boat to get a bus to our first stops, the temples in Luxor itself.

Only a short drive before we are at the first temple, the temple at Karnak, and we assemble inside the entrance in the shade of the building, for a briefing on all that will unfold before us. And then the tour begins, and as we step outside the real heat of the day hits us, and one is grateful for any shade one can find, whether it be behind a tall pillar, or any still-standing wall. We are told how these temples were put together, all manual labour, and if it wasn't quite right, then it would all be started again. An introduction into the hieroglyphics and their meaning, all fascinating as we realise what a civilised and forward-thinking people the Egyptians were. And then we can go off and explore ourselves, and it is here that we meet the modern Egyptian; a helpful policeman offers to take our photo, and we are grateful to have one taken together, but for him, even the law, they expect a tip. So every step of the way, we find these 'helpful' natives offering a hand, or trying to sell you some ancient artefact which must be at least a month old. Hassle, hassle, hassle! This mustn't take anything away from the wonderful surrounds we are in. Omar has already warned us of their persistence; we must barter, don't expect any change, be firm. If my man has one family streak, it is stubbornness, and he soon gets very bored with the hassle. He develops a cunning plan. Panama on, shades over the eyes and just walk, straight, ignore any banter and head straight for the appointed destination – nothing will stop him. It is not long before our Egyptian friends realise he is not going to stop, and start to leave him alone. Noticing this protocol, it is not long before he has a line of people following in his wake, heads down too, follow my leader and don't stop at any cost until he does. The temple of Karnak was very interesting and I could see my man's mind ticking over, trying to take in all that we were being told.

A short drive through town took us to the temple of Luxor, different sections, through a long line of sphinx set on stone blocks leading to the main temple. Now it was seriously hot, and we were glad of the still-covered parts of the temple ruins, protecting us from the sun. Again very interesting, as we walked around this ancient wonder. Lots of photos, the odd kiss, and on we explored until it was time to return to catch our bus outside the perimeter of the temple, and then of course the constant attention of Egyptian 'salesmen'. Donkey rides aplenty but there was a policy to discourage us from using these as it was thought there was some mistreatment of said donks – they were certainly on the lean side.

It all was very interesting, this after all is the ancient Egyptian city of Thebes, staked with so much history from all those dynasties that had ruled the area from here, but it was also a pleasure to return to the boat and get into the shade with a nice beer to help cool us down, before we settle into our first lunch on board. We could get seriously fat on this trip if we are not careful, the food is magnificent. The wine, one would have to admit is not that special, but anyway we do need to keep our fluid levels up, so long drinks are far more the order of the day. While we are enjoying this meal, the boat frees herself from her moorings and we set sail southwards down to Aswan; we will be on the move for some time. Time to explore the rest of the boat as Luxor slowly slips behind us on both sides of the river. We haven't visited the bow end yet, but that involves crossing the dance floor, so true to form, we perform a little jig as we cross it before arriving at the foredeck and can watch the river in front of us, slight breeze in our faces, but still grateful for any shade offered.

The Nile in fact isn't that deep for a lot of its length unless there are exceptional rains, but look behind the trees – sand, sand, and more sand, so that isn't going to happen that often. It is just exceptionally wide, with fertile lands either side, water buffalo coming down to the banks to drink, with their herdsman keeping an eye on them. A gentle ebb, as the flow is controlled by dams, especially the Aswan dam that we will be heading towards, our most southerly point on this trip. The west bank, more fertile land stretching away from the river banks, but on the east bank, soon into desert. My man and I sit in the bows of the boat, feet perched up on the rails, enjoying the river as we pass along, the occasional riverside village, and a few dhows passing along the river in the opposite direction, fishing or just travelling. The relaxation of water, I can't deny that in this bliss my eyes did close more than once.

We sail on through the afternoon, the gentle river passing around us, and we do see the odd cruise boat going in the opposite direction, but sparsely populated. We approach what looks like a massive lock regulating the flow of the river, but just before reaching this, from the western shore come a whole bevvy of little boats, opportunist traders with towels and other clothes that they wish to sell us, but having no access to the boat, all they can do is come as close as they can alongside, and throw their goods up to passengers who can look at what they have to sell, then purchase, pass on, or throw back. An interesting method of sale, and it is difficult to barter like this. Sadly, for them, most was returned back to them.

Dusk is falling and as we are close to the west bank it is not so easy to see the rapid sunset, so spectacularly seen from the opposite bank the previous night. The lock, as we pass through it, is very interesting for its size. I wonder how much the volume of water changes in our passage through this vast lock. Container ships are moored here as well, a mini port in the middle of nowhere. We progress further on, as we will right through the night, so it will be our dinner and then enjoying the night air with a nice drink or two, before settling down for the night in our room.

Am I feeling a bit randy? I think I may well be, inspired by all the 'pictures' on the tall temple pillars. I think it is time to enjoy a pillar of my own. Shall I be Cleopatra, and he let me sample his asp? Sounds a good plan, so I dip into my sexy lingerie drawer again to pull out a little something to seduce him with. We will endure the heat of the evening, as we devour each other under a sheet of my bed (a choice each night – he can come over to me, or me to him, an open invitation). But my little red set always gets him going, and hasn't failed again as our kisses turn into passionate embraces and as he enters me there is not only the smooth motion of the boat through the waters, but also of him inside me as we accelerate through the intensity of emotions reaching towards the final crescendo, and... that was wonderful, as we lay back in a warm embrace. My appreciation of Egyptian pillars is satisfied once again. It is too warm to embrace for too long, and as sleep consumes me, he sits by the window, just above water level, watching the water and the banks pass us by, left in our wake as we venture further south towards Aswan.

He looks so at peace with the world, love, and these beautiful surrounds, and of course he has me.

Another day, another sunrise and further south we have travelled, and he has enjoyed much of it as he has stayed, watching our progress; the early rising fishermen, the stirrings of life on the banks, of herons, egrets, all sorts of birdlife.

The usual routine of dressing, and then joining our fellow passengers for breakfast, but on our continuing journey to Aswan, we will stop at one astounding temple at Kom Ombo, a very impressive monument on the banks of the Nile, and we are entranced by again the details of the hieroglyphics. An insight into their surgical instruments, not a lot different from ours not so long ago, the documentation of caesareans being done. What an advanced civilisation this was those many centuries ago. This really was an impressive place, and we felt enlightened to have been there. But we have to go back to the boat for the last part of the journey to Aswan, taking lunch as we complete the journey and then venturing to the bow of the boat to see this major town as it approaches. And that of course means crossing the dance floor, which means much to everybody's amusement, a little dance again.

Aswan arrives and we moor besides other Nile cruise boats. The new part of Aswan is just above us, with a fairly major road going towards the main town – taxis, traders, and donkey karts much in evidence. A busy city, which we are now due to spend two nights, three days in. This starts with a trip to a Nubian museum, and our first sight of a mummy, amongst many other artefacts depicting this time in Egyptian history. A special treat for us when we get back on the boat, as after supper we will be having a Nubian night, with special Nubian dancers bussed in specially for this event. It has become a theme when we return to our room after our daily outings to find some ornament made out of a towel left on the bed – a croc, a swan, a flower. Clever people, our room attendants as it turns out, and wonderfully helpful, chatty and polite.

We find a seat for the entertainment (yes, we did cross the dance floor with a little jig), and wait for the dancing to begin. Music, then a massive bloke arrives on the dance floor and struts his stuff, as the rhythm of the music intensifies, and he comes to the climax of his routine. Volunteers are required as they will now join in the dance, and I have no hesitation in pushing my man forward, which he doesn't look too pleased about, but he is on the floor and can't back out now. Each volunteer is given a part to play in this routine, and now he is there, he joins in with gay abandon. Thrusting hips, they are good, and I will have some of that later methinks, and his rather sexy bum moving to the music. This has got everyone livened up and as the dancers disappear, the disco starts and the evening continues, partying long into the night.

And then to see that bum again back in my room, and yes those thrusting hips keeping me satisfied as I lay on my back and think of heaven.

Our days in Aswan continue as we are taken to see this great dam, Lake Nasser on its other side, and the nets that stop crocs from invading the Upper Nile. What an impressive structure this is, as it stands way above the waters either side, and with Nasser extending as far as you can see, into 'Nubia' and beyond.

Then we continue to Philae, a temple reconstructed on an island, as its original location was flooded with the building of the dam. A very impressive temple, now standing near but way above the waters of the Upper Nile, and here Omrn re-enacts an Ancient Egyptian legend for us, again looking for four volunteers, and guess who I push forward again, but he's up for this even if he is the crocodile god, and all sorts of nasty things end up happening to him for his earlier misdeeds. It's all a bit of fun, and everyone enjoys the show.

Afternoon brings us some downtime – relax, do what you want. We enjoy the sun and one of the other guides had said he would take a group of us into town to the bazaar if we wanted to go. Sunbathing, then yes, we would go on this trip. Long lines of stalls, just like a market back home, with the one exception, every trader was upon you as soon as you approached anywhere near them. If my man isn't a great fan of shopping, the final straw would be this constant bombardment of sales pitches, so we were back to shades on, eyes front, and keep walking until there was actually something he wished to view, some lovely herbs and spices, whatever, but his mood wasn't going to be budged until one shopkeeper did manage to stop us, and ask him why none of us would stop at these stalls. He politely replied that we are being hassled too much and if left to our own devices, are far more likely to buy something. He promised no more hassles. Word spreads quick in this bazaar, and it is not long before every stall we now pass, the words 'we no hassle' are muttered by the marketers. One can't help but admire their persistence and ready change of tactics. It was, though, a pleasant and interesting experience, and if you did want to buy anything you were expected to barter.

The next day there was an organised trip to Abu Simbel in the desert, or a trip around the islands of Aswan to see the birdlife, Kitchener gardens, and a Nubian village. We didn't fancy a long trip into the desert in a coach so opted for the 'local' Nile trip. Sadly, I was feeling unwell but encouraged my man to go regardless, meeting his guide Mohamed on the boat before setting off in a small boat to disappear amongst small islands below the dam, seeing all sorts of bird life in abundance; some birds such as bitterns that you know exist back home, but never see, but very obvious here. The Nubian village, fascinating, and the garden with its arboretum amazing, he returns back to the boat to see how I am, raving about the trip and how glad he was for opting to do this one. A shame I couldn't join him, nor do I feel that special to join him for lunch, before we depart back to Luxor and further up the river. We have to wait for those who have gone into the desert to return first, and it is now that is the only time we experience any sign of the troubles enveloping this country, as there are demonstrations outside one of the Ministry buildings, and a burning of the flag as the peoples demonstrate against the fact that a lot of promises made during the Arab Spring have not happened. Even then, the demonstrators are very polite to us, apologising, and being very grateful that we have been the first nationality to return as tourists to their country.

Eventually our fellow travellers return and we can set sail again. The bow does offer some shade now as we head north, and time for a nap here with my man, and to do some reading. While in Aswan, we had been treated to an Egyptian night, with belly dancers and swirling dervishes. For our part, we had to go to dinner in fancy dress, me as Cleopatra, my man, as so many of the other men on the boat (which was selling the outfits), in white Arab attire and wearing a fez. He also thought he would wear his shades, dressed as a 'seedy' Arab – think most people thought him a bit nutty. I wonder what these sheiks and alike do wear under their dress, remind me to find out later. But as our swirling dervish took over and whipped up the frenzy of crowd, I, yes I, volunteered to be a belly dancer for a short while. Then back onto the dance floor for the disco again, but he didn't think he was going to escape that easily as he was volunteered once again by moi, to play some strange potato game whereby he had to hit one potato along the floor with another attached to his waist by a piece of string, which again meant thrusting his hips forward to get the right swinging motion, to project said potato to the goal line. Yes, those hips can move, very good thrusts, but progress with the potato, non-existent. I have an idea that he better practice those thrusts on me, after I have found out what is under that white 'sheet', and it will probably be more satisfying if I am on my back.

So after the Kings of Leon's 'Sex on Fire' and I think it may be again, we retire to our room and no guesses for what happens next! (He didn't have a lot on underneath!)

One of the fascinations of this ancient civilisation is the division of life, so as sun worshippers, the good, everything on the east bank where the sun rises is thought of as the living, and on the west bank, where the sun sets, is the afterlife. While contemplating this, my man nudges me and points to one of the engine crew who has come out on deck; he looks remarkably like the Nubian dancer. Oh well, he could have fooled us. I wonder what the swirling dervish does on board.

The trip up the river takes us back to Luxor, and then on towards the temple at Dendera, a temple full of wonderful frescos. This will be the most northerly point of our journey, and for this part of the trip we are accompanied by a man with a machine gun situating himself on the upper deck, just in case we should meet any trouble. After Dendera, it is time to head south again and back to Luxor, for tomorrow we will visit the resting places of all those pharaohs, including Tutankhamun, of course situated on the west shore in the Valley of the Kings. The river is so peaceful, just the odd buffalo drinking from its banks, the odd heron, egret contemplating the art of fishing, and us. Blue cloudless skies, sunshine – sit back and enjoy it.

Our journey from Luxor takes us across the river to the west bank to explore these last sights of an ancient civilisation, a very developed civilisation, before we return home. A trip around a couple of artisan factories, making urns, pots, whatever else those men out there are trying to sell us, but these are more authentic, with a price to match. And on our visit to the Valley of the Kings, we are allowed into a couple of the tombs, but can only admire others from their entrance. This place is swarming with local salesmen, and the hassle is reaching fever pitch and does perhaps spoil the place a little, but the actual valley is amazing. The place of the afterlife. After that, we visit the temple to Queen Hatshepsut, on the other side of the ridge, a most impressive building. She was the queen who managed to fool everyone into believing that she was a man so she could continue to rule this great kingdom. A vast expanse of sculptured rock, great icons of their civilisation, then a long walk back to where our coach was parked and then other than one last stop at another monument, we were back to the boat and time to head back towards Luxor and our final night aboard.

Our last dinner, and a quiz and disco again and time to say goodbye to our great host and guide, Oman. We have got on really well with him, have tried to appreciate their culture with him, had a laugh, and I hope not asked him too many stupid questions. Certainly, my man has found him a great source of knowledge, to satisfy his ever-inquisitive mind. He has family troubles and has to leave before the evening is out, so we bid him a fond farewell. Actually, my man tries to sell me to him, perhaps for a couple of camels. I take the hump, but luckily the offer is turned down. We say goodbye, and return to the dance floor for one last time, dancing that is, and then back to the bedroom for one last night of Egyptian passion and lovemaking. Yes, it's that red set again. What it does to him, and then what he does to me, oh boy!!

We have a very early start as we have chosen to go on a balloon trip; up at three to cross the river and take off in a hot air balloon, as the sun rises over the Nile. We wait patiently as the balloons are inflated, the flames roaring away beneath them as they fill, ascending up in the air. Then it is time for us to board. So many of us in this one basket, eight sections holding up to four people each, but we get to be in the one close to the flame, and are slowly grilled as we go up into the sky. What an incredible sight, as the sky turns red and the sun rises over the Nile to our east. The Valley of the Kings in dull dawn light, and then rapidly illuminated as the sun sprints into the sky. And to our west, and into infinity, the Sahara stretches beyond our eyesight, something that will stay with me forever. Sadly, the following year, it was one of these balloons that ascended next to ours, that exploded in mid-air, killing all those on board as it crashed back to the ground. For us, a safe trip followed by a bumpy landing, as we hit the ground with a thud, caught by many locals, who as you may have guessed, were looking for a tip. Disembark, offer our thanks to our crazy Captain, and then it is back on the bus to our boat, and a well-earned breakfast.

Now we just have time to kill before leaving the boat to the airport, a delay there and a couple of opportunists again trying to con a quid out of us for a bit of loo roll, and eventually we are on board and then up in the sky. As we are arm in arm in our seats, as we climb higher and higher into the ether, we watch the sun set one last time for us over Egypt, that amazing red sky that all too soon disappears behind us as we leave this land and head back across the Mediterranean, and home.

A wonderful holiday, full of interest, humour, fun,

sun, and best of all, love, romance, and passion.

I want to be with this man forever.

Muddied Waters

We are back in this country after what was a superlative holiday, both for the country and the fun we had while in Egypt. I am well and truly head over heels in love with this man, and it was good to see how much more relaxed he was once again away from these shores. I have got to know him far better, but at times, he can still be withdrawn and introverted. He did come across a wonderful little ditty while upon the boat in Egypt which may just have changed his philosophy on life. He is still undergoing counselling for his depression, but now sees all in a different light, a far more positive light. I am now hopeful, more and more, that we can forge a life together. I am at his house more and more, and have moved more and more of my clothes and some other belongings in as well. Those well-used black leather boots now live there to pleasure him, and myself whenever the mood takes us, which is quite often, as our little soirees together still occur, plus more.

Next year will be a leap year, and I keep hinting that it will be my prerogative to propose. But here he seems to withdraw slightly, seeming to be afraid of that sort of commitment. Autumn comes on, and his progress is hampered by a nasty fall at work, aggravating a previous neck injury, with the accompanying headaches it brought with it. A setback, but we still have many enjoyable times together, walking, talking, dancing, and those nocturnal activities we have come to enjoy so much together.

We see a lot of some of his friends, another couple who have just found each other, and I get on very well with his best friend. An evening out with other of his friends, a lovely lady who has helped him in his troubles, just as he has stood by her in her moments of need – very good friends, nothing more. How we laughed when we saw Jethro live in a local theatre, and met him in the foyer during the interval. The whole house was roaring with laughter.

We had planned one last holiday for this year which would take us down to his favourite part of this country, the South Hams, to spend a couple of nights in a small hotel/pub very close to the coast.

But just before this, his best friend had got engaged, and they had only been going out for three or four months. I wasn't happy (I had said this earlier), especially as my man had known before, and had helped organise the proposal evening with him, having been sworn to secrecy. I was cross with him for not telling me before, and very jealous also, to the extent that after a nice evening out, when the news was revealed, I was really in a huff and there would be no bonking tonight. The tension was palpable, and I at the time didn't realise how hurt he was that he had kept his word to his friend about not telling anyone, and that I didn't seem happy for them, the happy couple, in my expression of jealousy. In later times, I would reflect on how badly I handled this, but I so, so wanted this to be me, and it wasn't.

Yes, I did come round and felt happy for them, and concealed my jealousy, but with that came more and more hints about us, and the leap year, and I could always go back to Australia where men would be queueing up for my hand.

We set off for Devon – a long drive, but well worth it when we arrived in a quiet beachside hostelry. After a long drive, all we really wanted to do was relax for a while, then walk on the sands – a lovely, sunny, late autumn day, with a slight breeze blowing off the sea, Burgh Island (the setting for Agatha Christie books which had been filmed on many occasions) in the distance. Shoes and socks off and a paddle in the sea. Yes, we can say we have been in. Very calm, just the gentle ripples of water passing up and down the beach representing waves.

We decide to eat in the pub we are at, saves driving down these narrow country lanes in the dark, but before the sun goes down we will walk over the hill and to the next village, and enjoy a drink in the Thurlestone Inn. He races up the hill, but me, I'm slipping and sliding, way behind him, full of excuses why it is taking me so long to be with him. As the sun sets to our west, over the sea, it is a beautiful sight, and as we reach the pub the light is fast fading. But we are greeted by a lovely roaring fire, and sit down for a pint of the local brew – me cider, him, his pint of bitter. Lovely. Then in semi-darkness, we retrace our path back over the golf course, across the fields, and hand in hand, having negotiated the down slope of the hill, we return to our pub. A quick bath, and then down to the bar for a lovely meal, and as we are by the sea, it has to be fish.

As we only have to negotiate the stairs later, my boots, stockings, and the red set (which you may now think are becoming infamous) can have an early outing, of course covered by skirt and blouse, but that is only for downstairs. We are spoilt tonight in also having a couple, husband and wife, who are also down on holiday but have said they would play their guitars and sing, and they were very good. Ballads, love songs, this is really getting me in the mood. We chat to them for a bit when they have finished their stint, then it is time to drag him upstairs to have my wicked way with him.

As we know, boots, stockings, and the red set, then he is mine, and so having revealed myself in a favourable position, I can now lie back and enjoy myself; the long snog, the tight embrace, and then as his fingers start to reach for those parts that are private, but now open for exploration, my excitement is mounting and mounting. Until that is, he does the mounting and as he enters me, I am reaching fever pitch. He teases me, plays with me, toys with me before we rise to the occasion together, a wonderful long climax that repeats and repeats and repeats. I lay back, totally pleasured. Wow!

The following day sees us exploring this wonderful coastline further, a stroll along the coastal path, past the Soar Valley, and onwards until a darkening sky tells us we should return to the car. The clouds disperse and we head to a lovely, picturesque village called Hope. What I would hope for – him! The afternoon takes us into Kingsbridge, a pub lunch where again I broach the subject of us, my plans for the future and some commitment, or else I will consider going back to

Australia. Sadly, again this seems to make him withdraw into himself. What is he scared of? We will let the matter drop for the time being.

Then back to our pub for a rest before we attack the hill again; back again to the Thurlestone for our pre-dinner drink. More informal for tonight's dinner, I will slip into a little something later. Again, fish, nothing else as we are by the sea, and up to bed. I will see if my fish is rising tonight again.

In Kingsbridge, I had bought myself a little fur jacket, so what better time to try it on? As he is reading quietly in bed, I make my entrance. How boring, I have put my boots on again, fishnet stockings (what else to catch him with?), and a small white thong. And the fur coat. That seems to have done the trick, and as I open the coat I certainly have his attention now. It could be hot in bed with this coat on so as it slips down off my shoulders, I slip between the sheets beside him. It is getting hot! The action begins, and all I can say was that if there was a gentle tide on the beach, here, the waves were starting to crash in, one followed by another as we satisfied each other's passion over and over again. We could be reaching storm warnings here. I can certainly now say, if asked if I've been to Devon, that have come there many times. Lie back and enjoy.

Strike, the line is Broken

A journey back the following day, stopping on the

Teign estuary to meet one of his long-term friends, and we were back home.

All I can say now, was that again he was a different person away from home – so loving, caring and relaxed, but we are now home and he has changed again.

A couple of weeks together, nice but I keep bringing up the subject of where we are going, because I know where I want this to go. He even introduces me to rugby when we go down to Worcester on a wet Friday night to watch a dull game against Wasps, not that I would be averse to being under a ruck with all those men, and see whose balls I came up with. I took much delight in cheering on Worcester as he supported Wasps, but back home under the cover of the duvet, I secured good ball and satisfaction was reached on all sides.

The ins and outs of it don't matter now, but from here, all didn't quite go as I had hoped. I don't want to dwell on it, as it made me very sad for some time to come, but after a night together with friends where I probably drank too much, everything came to a head. The following morning, who broke it off is open to debate, but he couldn't make the commitment that I wanted; his mental state still couldn't let him make that ultimate decision, and I wasn't prepared to wait any longer, despite my feelings being so strong, and so we walked away from each other.

How can I express how I felt? Sad, angry, disappointed, all words but none of them could explain the emotions. Lost dreams, the future I had envisaged that had just been lost.

I was heartbroken.

OPEN SEASON

The Goldfish Bowl

I was back where I started. I really thought that I had found the man of my dreams, Mr Right, and that my story was going to have a fairy tale ending, for me/us anyway. But it didn't turn out that way, somewhere it went wrong but I didn't know where. Did I put too much pressure on him to settle down, or was it that he, with his mental state at the time, just couldn't cope with a long-term relationship, needing to find himself before he could commit to anybody else? There was no point dwelling on it because it was over and that's the way it was. We went our separate ways, but where that would take us, only time would tell. He had a lot of searching to do to find himself, and though I didn't want to lose him, I could only hope for his own sake that he could find the answers and the life he was looking for. Depression seems to be a disease of our time, and different people will find different ways of dealing with it, and overcoming it. Others sadly don't and will suffer long-term or take more drastic action. I only hope that he will find peace of mind; he had taken large steps at the time of our relationship, but still had a way to go, though he had given up medication and was making big efforts to find his own answers.

But my life had to go on as well. I was devastated, cut up. I wouldn't say hurt, as I don't think there was any blame to assign, I just met him at the wrong time for him. But me, I had to pick myself up from this.

But I couldn't. This man was stuck in my mind, our relationship had consumed me. I had a clear plan, a map of where I was going, and it had been taken away from me. I was lost.

The goldfish bowl, I was swimming round and round in circles trying to find myself again, looking for a direction. In the back of my mind, I hoped he would see how good we had been together, and would come to his senses. That's unfair. I hoped he would want me again.

It was also just before Christmas, that time lovers should be together, especially that first one together. It wasn't to be. I don't know what my true emotions were, only that I was missing something I really wanted. I wasn't depressed, wasn't angry, just I suppose if there is such a thing, lovesick. But life goes on, I had a job to do, those things don't change. I still had to go out and earn a crust, however I felt inside, and just put on a brave face when there.

I had responsibilities there, I wouldn't let my wards down, and they occupied my mind fully when I was at work. But at home, and I was still lodging in my colleague's house, so often when I wasn't at work he was, and vice versa, I had solitude which was probably the last thing I wanted.

I needed to break myself out of this. How? How? With time to spare now, my free time, I would get in the car and drive down to Sussex to see my sister. Any length of spare time and I would be there. How she must have got fed up with me. "Hi, it's me again. Can I come and stay again?" But if she felt it, she never said it as she tried to point me in the direction of life again. What a wonderful baby sister I have, because she was wonderful. She introduced me to a DVD called 'The Secret', a self-help guide on how to succeed in life, obtain your goals, and reap the dividends from your endeavours. How many times did I watch this, and with that, slowly but surely came a belief that I would rise up from the ashes, and succeed. Thanks Sis, you put me back on track again, though it took a little time.

I was back on the computer, but not on my dating sites, no. This time back on my gaming sites, World of Warcraft. I spent endless hours on this when not at my sister's or working. It made the time pass, and kept my mind on other things than that man who had escaped my grasp, my love.

I was in my room by myself, usually in the house by myself, wasn't going out and let's face it, was in a world of my own, a world that I had enclosed myself in, and at that time didn't want to escape from.

But as I went through 'the secret' again, it slowly dawned on me, and with sister pushing, that I had to go out into the world again, show the world my assets, the real me, and then hopefully get the rewards for doing it.

To get myself out, I re-joined the singles group again (in the hopes that I would, one, get out and about again, and secondly, was there still a thought in the back of my mind that he might be there?). I went along anyway, paid my sub again, and then went round all the boring people that I had met before. They were not boring, just all had their own stories why they were there, and were probably just looking for company, but I was looking for more.

I went, paid up, socialised, and never went again.

I had not been on dating sites now for five months since we had split up, so way over a year in total. I wonder who may be swimming in the pond now. Is it time to find out? Perhaps it was. My heart had been broken, but despite that, I wanted, wanted, wanted to find someone to spend the rest of my life with – to love, to cuddle, to talk to and to look after, and him me.

With a little reluctance, and some apprehension, I was online again. But with two changes: I tried a different site, Oasis, and also I lowered my age range for the man I was looking for down to between forty-eight and fifty-five years old. I had been with my older man and in the back of my mind I didn't want to be let down again. I hope in all this I don't sound desperate for company, but I am a warm, loving person, with so much to give.

The other change in my life was a move into my own rented house out in a country village, far closer to work, and Shrewsbury would now become the hub of my social life if I could regenerate it. Of course I could, remember 'the secret'? A quiet village with a pub a whole, well, less than five minutes' walk away, and that's if I was going slowly. A small shop, some community, a new life for me.

My gaming continued and I did in fact meet someone through this, someone who I chatted to online as he joined our guild, our playing group for the game we played. Gaming in fact was big time, almost becoming addictive when not working, but it was nice to chat to this man though I never did meet him. His main interest was a different type of gaming to mine, and he did not participate in the guild that often.

I did hear of a birthday party in my old stomping ground, a joint party of some old friends, and I did decide it would be good to go along to this, little realising that one of the birthdays was of the one that got away – he was having it with three other ladies whose birthdays were within days of his. They had clubbed together to hire a disco, and put a small spread of grub on in a country pub, and when I walked through the door, was surprised how many people had come along to it.

It was over three months since I had seen him, but not knowing it was his party as well, I didn't know whether to expect to see him or not. A lot of old faces I knew, but then I had to bump into him. He was sociable, and not displeased to see me, and if I say it myself, I did look rather ravishing, but he was with a small group of people that he had come with, and did his host duties well in circulating amongst everyone there to see they were okay and enjoying themselves. And I did bump into him now and again on the dance floor, as he moved that wonderful bum about again to the music.

If I had started to babble a bit on the chat lines

gain, I was committed to finding the man of my dreams. I was also committed to go out and have a bit of fun. So, during the course of the party evening, I did start to receive a lot of attention from one particular guy, a charming bloke, a slightly rotund, long blond-haired (may have been from a bottle) bloke, who actually had arrived with the one that got away's party. Will, by name, and he did seem very willing. Jovial, kind, and very talkative, we chatted, danced, and got to know each other very well, though I'm not sure if I was trying to make someone else there jealous. Whatever my motives, this bloke, Will, was good company, and I really enjoyed his company. As I had said, I was dressed to kill, and so couldn't blame him for falling for me, and as things can when you have had a couple of drinks, a smooch dance number, arms encircle me, and a little kiss turns into a long snog. Hope someone is enjoying the show.

The show stopped when it was time to go home, both having to head off in different directions, both driving, so neither had drunk too much. As we left the pub, we did have a long cuddle as our lips met passionately, and it only seemed proper before we had departed that we had exchanged telephone numbers, and would be in touch.

It was not long until contact was made, and we had arranged for him to come up to my little village for the evening, a drink in the local and I would cook for him. I found out more about Will as the evening progressed, interesting stuff, which would answer a few questions as to long-term plans.

He did indeed live with a woman and his daughter, but wouldn't leave the family home for want of not losing his offspring, even if the relationship was long dead and buried. But he did go out a lot, most Friday and Saturday nights, in fact, and live the life of a bloke, young (well, not so young), free and single.

No long-term prospects here then, but he was fun, and I had been in the doldrums too long, so why not take advantage of this male attention and take all the advantages it may bring? And that it did later, as we climbed the stairs together, and he gave me what I had missed for a few months now which was a good fuck. He was good, took me to my limits, satisfied my carnal pleasures, and more, and then when finished would lie back with me in his arms and cuddle me, while he chatted about something, nothing, anything. He was fun, and a very attentive lover, and if this was the first of several trysts, I would look forward to them for the pleasure I knew I would get, the satisfaction that arrived between my legs, and never just a quick bonk, always some feeling of mutual respect and gratification.

A very touchy-feely man, we knew what each other liked, and responded accordingly. It was never going anywhere, but satisfied a need for both of us, while life meandered along.

But, I knew I was not the only one, he was a 'man of the world', and would get his pleasures wherever and whenever he required them. I would be one of many, but I didn't mind. I would continue to look, to search those waters of life, to find the chosen one when I found him, but knowing that I wouldn't go without while I looked. A sensible solution for me for the time being.

An irony though was that as this went on, he, Will,

also became close friends with the one that got away, often meeting in town with a group of friends for a couple of beers. Funny old world.

Back to fishing, and I found especially on this Oasis site there tended to be a lot of farmers, looking for a farmer's wife, and ALL the chores that brought with it – cooking, washing, cleaning, feeding the cattle, lambing the ewes, in fact everything you could imagine (well perhaps not quite everything as the poor dear would probably be too tired). I don't think this was really the life I was looking for, if I had to milk a cow, I would probably know which end to stand, but that would be about it.

Not a lot of takers there then!

Back on Plenty of Fish, and my net had been empty now for some time. At last, a bite as I started to chat to a guy, a bit of a wheeler dealer, and in time arranged for a meeting, the three rules back in place. Why not make use of my local? It would save me driving, though I could look as if I was going through the motions of travelling, and take the long drive just around the corner.

I arranged to meet Mark here, on meeting one (three-date rule) so no hanky panky, just a couple of drinks over an hour or so, and farewell. I found out that he would buy fire damaged goods, sets of posters, floor tiles and suchlike for a knock-down price, and then sell them on at a reasonable profit. As I said, a wheeler dealer, and doing okay at it.

We got through the three rules of angling and beyond, and I did start seeing him as a date, whenever our work allowed. No rush, but how did he feel about

Australia in his retirement? Something he had not thought about, but then why should he?

One Sunday lunchtime I did meet up with the one that got away, just for a catch up in the pub, and he was genuinely concerned of my welfare and happiness (though I don't think he knew how down I had been after our separation), and he was concerned that I was throwing myself too quickly at Mark, and that I should give him a chance to get to know the wonderful person I am, rather than putting him off with long-term plans on day one of our relationship. Also, knowing Will better himself now, he just said take care, and wasn't going to say any more than that; he didn't want to see me get hurt. Nice of him to care, but I was – am – a big girl now. He left doubting whether I would fit into the bra left on top of my ironing basket from what he could remember, and if only he had asked, I would have demonstrated for him, that I could. In fact I would have loved to show him the lot!!

Mark and I started seeing more and more of each other. I started going on business trips with him in his van, off to Scotland or wherever to pick up some merchandise, long day trips but good fun.

He asked my advice on his mother, and care as she was ill – terminally ill. I guess this was going down the lines of being close friends and confidants rather than developing into lovers, so in time it drew to a natural conclusion and fizzled out.

He would still keep in contact, to the extent that sadly when his mother died, he wanted to know the type of care she should have received in a home. Was there negligence? And also what should he do as he had found that his sister had been dipping into her mother's savings to her own ends. I was only too happy to help out with advice or anything that I could. But towards my dream, this was going nowhere, and never would.

But for me, I had escaped the goldfish bowl, the endless circling getting nowhere, round and round, feeling sorry for myself and my disappointment of losing the man I loved.

My course was clear now, swimming in a straight line, objective defined and clear. Go with the flow, enjoy yourself, but keep in mind your objective and don't sell yourself short.

The 'secret' – remind yourself of it if straying from your path.

Gill, you will find what you are looking for. No longer a fish out of water, you are now out to hook your prey again.

As they say, where there is a Will there is a way!

Snappers

After previous experiences I have described, a man's teeth are important to me, not only from the perspective of me getting a bite, but more importantly, in what they did to his appearance, whether it be a gummy smile, a gappy smile, halitosis, or just a row of broken and rotten gnashers staring at you. I had committed my decision-making as to whether I would meet up with a man, to whether I had seen his teeth. This didn't mean I demanded an oral selfie on first contact, but an up to date photo with a smiling face was always a good place to begin.

It was one of these photos, a snapshot of a gentleman with a broad smile on his face, that attracted me to investigate his profile further. If on a photo you cannot tell if they are all his, or the originals, at least it didn't look as if I would be meeting up with Jaws if we decided to see each other. So a conversation started up online which soon turned into a first meeting.

I think somewhere along the line, and perhaps it showed a slight lack of self-confidence, that he was quite surprised that someone as gorgeous as me had replied to his 'match'. So after an exchange of messages, I asked if he would like to swop telephone numbers, and from there we arranged that first meeting, a lunch date in a local market town, handy for me as I could call in to see my ailing mother before we met up. Suited me fine as I could accomplish two things while on a day off.

At the appointed time, I met up with him in the designated pub. He was easy to spot as a snappy dresser, and easily recognisable from his photo online, with that warm welcoming smile, and white teeth well positioned gleaming at me through his lips. *Good*, I thought, *at least he looks genuine and worth getting to know more.*

We had obviously found out a little about each other from online chatting, so he knew I was looking for a lifetime partner, my plans of a dual life here and Australia, and what my interests were.

As for him, Peter Pollock, I knew he had been married, and divorced, and now lived with his grown-up son in his own house in Wolverhampton. He was soon due to retire from his job as a Tax Inspector, and from there could pursue his lifelong hobby, and here was something that really interested me.

As we chatted over lunch he told me a lot about what he enjoyed doing, which was reconstructing models, especially of trains, locomotives, to a precision that was unbelievable. First a train spotter, now a train modeller. My hobby of course was gaming, and it felt good that if we were to see more of each other, then we could enjoy each other's company but have our own interests to pursue while together. More so in that his son's hobby was also gaming, though like others I had come across, he was another Xbox man. If not identical, we at least had something in common to talk about when Dad was not around.

Peter told me of a love that he had had since his divorce, a love that was not returned and they had ended up going their separate ways, he hoping she would change her mind, but that never happened. Here, I had an empathy with him from my 'one that got away'. But he did want to find someone that he could spend the rest of his life with, for love, for company, a meaningful relationship, and his son wanted this for him too.

This was sounding very promising, and I would have to admit even on meeting one, that I did feel very comfortable in his company. It had been a pleasant and informative first meeting, lunch with an intelligent, well-dressed, and kind man who wanted his life to go in a similar direction to that which I hoped mine would follow.

I want to meet this man again, and see where life would take us. We left the pub, and were about to go our separate ways when I reached up (not that he was a lot taller than me), and gave him a quick kiss on his lips. Surprised, he drew back, taking a step back as if he had been affronted.

"Do you mind?" I asked, to which he replied he didn't at all, but wasn't expecting it.

"Good," I said. "I will give you a ring." With that, I turned and was gone, but at last perhaps saw a little ray of light at the end of the tunnel.

It was a natural progression to ring him, and arrange to meet up again, and he was very pleased to get the call. I was interested in him, I was interested in his hobby, and he seemed a real gentleman.

We did meet up again, very soon afterwards, again for a meal in a local pub, a weekend which was easiest for him without work commitments, and for me when not down on the rota to work then. Yes, I was feeling very comfortable with his company and after these initial couple of meetings, it would become a common occurrence to have a little soiree with him somewhere in our locality. He always was very attentive, a real gentleman, would open doors for me, etc., made me feel like a woman.

Following that, he did ask me over to his house, to begin with just for the day, which I was comfortable with, and I would drive over on a Saturday morning with my Wi-Fi and laptop, so that when he wanted time for his hobby, I would have something to occupy myself with. He showed me his workshop, his tools, turning equipment, lathes, a multitude of precision instruments to recreate the trains he was making in miniature.

Sometimes, I would just sit in the garage, his workshop, and watch in amazement as he made these parts, valves, whatever was needed to get an exact copy of the real thing. He was so clever with his hands. I may just have wondered what those hands could do for me! But it was a real pleasure to watch a master craftsman going about his business. One could only stand back and admire the final product that he produced, and when all put together was truly, truly amazing.

Through his model making, he belonged to a local club of likeminded people, who would frequently meet up for a chat in a local pub to discuss how each other's projects were going, about conventions they would be exhibiting at together, and offering helpful advice to each other if they could. To be honest, it all went over my head, but they all made me feel very welcome, and were pleased to see Peter with a belle on his arm. At least I didn't have to sit there like a wet lemon, totally out of the conversation.

He was totally committed to his hobby, without that sounding like he ignored me, which he certainly didn't, but with that commitment, other things had tended to be ignored, like the house, which one would describe as functional. The front room, which he shared with his son, they would eat together, talk, watch television, but in a man abode, there were a couple of old chairs, faded cloth backs and wooden arms. Not the sort of thing that would inspire romance, and I think we were of an age where the only way for togetherness was if I spent the evening sitting on his lap – not that comfortable, and whether they would have stood our weight, the experiment never took place. I demanded a settee that we could cuddle up together on, and this soon arrived.

Bare floor boards, and if things progressed into a 'real' relationship, there was no way I was going to risk getting splinters in my arse, though no doubt there would have been some machine for taking them out and putting me back together, model that I am.

The kitchen, very outdated with a cluttered table, his son's hammerhead models lining up to be painted, Xbox games, you had to be careful when eating your full English so that you were not about to devour a dragon, an orc, or something more terrifying with your runny egg.

A woman's touch was obviously needed, but I didn't want to imprint mine too much on such a male preserve. Don't rock the boat Gill, not yet anyway!

It would be true to say that our lives together at this stage were very much dominated by his hobby, and no doubt with his retirement fast approaching, he would have even more time to play at it. That isn't to say that Peter neglected me; I had my gaming, would sit sometimes in fascination at the skill and precision that was employed in making these models, and felt it was good that we could share each other's company while pursuing our own interests. We would have evenings out having meals, or just going for a drink, and these not always with his modelling mates, though I did get to meet some of the other halves. Meeting different people is good, interesting, and broadens my experience of life so I enjoyed these nights out.

Over the course of these evenings out, we got on to discussing previous relationships, failed marriages. Yes, our past. We had both lived life and so had experienced different things, but where I always feel I am a jolly person and can laugh at anything, including myself, he, well he could smile and show off that well-kept set of snappers, but I would never say that he could let himself go, and really laugh, laugh out loud, belly laugh, crease himself.

He didn't talk much about his marriage, but did divulge more about this love of his life after separation. He had obviously been in love with her big time, but as I have said earlier, she did not have the same commitment to a long-term relationship that he did, or wanted. I am not really sure how the subject came up, but he did elude to their sex life together. I'm not sure how we got onto the subject as by this stage in our relationship, we hadn't even shared the same bed yet. But he did tell me that a problem that they had was that he was too big for her. Wow, hadn't heard that one before, and couldn't help myself from looking down between his legs. Was he a shower, or a grower? There was definitely some well-defined being lurking inside those trousers – yes, definitely a shower!

I thought to myself, *How small was she?* and it transpired that she got less and less keen on their bonking, which may have had an inhibiting effect on him. But more to the point, I was filled with GREAT EXPECTATIONS as to what lay hidden, and one day I would experience. Intriguing, yes indeed. Good sex is important to me, in any relationship I have, and over time I've had many disappointments, especially through the course of two marriages, and brief relationships since while dating online. I had also had one or two real studs, who could satisfy my every wish. Was this going to be another, possibly a real stallion from the bill-board reviews I had just received?

It was during one of the evenings out with his fellow modellers that I got chatting to a partner of one, and we started talking about relationships, especially between older people who had experienced life, marriage, and were now seeking a partner, a companion to spend their time with in the later part of their lives. She and her partner had been together for some years now, quite happy in the way they were going. But, they lived apart.

"Why?" I asked. "Surely the whole point was to end up together."

The answer was easy, that she was too set in her ways to have him in her house, and likewise so was he, though he did say he would try and change to accommodate her. Better to not spoil what they had, than risk union and a big falling out, so this was the life 'together' that they were happy to pursue. A different outlook I suppose, but not really what I wanted, and at least in Peter's company, I was comfortable, even with the lack of furniture and carpets. All that could change if indeed our lives would come together.

I suppose at some stage, the interest in modelling did start to diminish. Fun, I did enjoy the exhibitions, conventions that I accompanied him to, the new people one would meet, and being able to join in the success that his group did achieve. He would go with me, help set up the stands with his mates, and then devote some attention to me, even if it was showing me other models, the intricacies of their makeup, and their faults that he could see. Fascinating. Well, it wasn't really, but I could tolerate it.

It was after one local event that they had won again and were out to celebrate, that we did all have a glass of wine or two, and so unlike on previous occasions, I had exceeded my limit, and would not be driving home.

I always had an overnight bag with me, just in case this should arise, and so we ended up spending our first night together. It was only natural that as we wound our way upstairs, we followed each other into his bedroom. We each retreated into the ensuite in turn to get ready for bed, put our night attire on, and then under the dim light of the bedside lamp snuggle under the duvet, both in our pyjamas. This is sounding romantic, isn't it?

I was not ready for hanky panky with him yet, but as we snuggled up together I could feel this stirring below, rubbing against me. If my hand accidently brushed against his leg, yes, there was something pretty enormous lurking down there, in the depths of the bed. Again, great expectations when I will be ready to indulge in a more sexual relationship.

Sleep now, after a cuddle, but I shall try not to have nightmares about that conger eel I may just have discovered. He had enjoyed a successful day with his hobby; what he felt as my hand brushed against him, whether I added to his elation of the moment, that was for another day.

At least that had broken the ice and it could possibly mean that our relationship could now move forward to the next stage, a more intimate relationship perhaps. It was a long journey from my home in the north of Shropshire down to the smoke, to Wolverhampton, to do twice in a day, to him and back after whatever we had done during the day. We had shared a bed and so in the future, it would be nothing to spend the night there.

At this stage, he had never been to visit me in my little village house, living alone with my pet rabbit, Buzz Buzz, and I was happy there, participating when I could in village activities, pub quizzes which I enjoyed, and anything else I could. But weekends looked very much like being in Wolverhampton.

That's where we continued to try and develop our relationship, see if we could build on where we have been before, see where life would take us. Our days were spent doing our own thing, our own hobbies, passing time with Peter's son with his gaming, and him showing an interest in mine. Then evenings, out for meals, the pub, meeting his mates or sometimes I would cook for both of us.

But a girl does have needs, and if he had already whetted my appetite with tales of his manhood (too big had to be a good CV, would impress most girls), and that quick brush of my hand the first time we had shared a bed, then I wanted to experience this thing, get to grips with his sexuality.

He certainly wasn't pushy about sex, even perhaps being a little shy on the subject. But I felt the time was right, and I wanted to try.

So it was that on one Saturday evening, when again we had retreated to his bed, dressed in our pyjamas, that I thought it was time to take the bull by the horns and see what would happen.

As we cuddled up to each other again, him thinking to exchange goodnight kisses, I reached down between his legs to find this eel I had brushed before. This was no eel, this was a snake and it was big. When fishermen say their catch was this big, this one really was this big, if not bigger – a real monster that may take two hands to control. As I stroked it there was an immediate response as it uncurled itself and raised its head into the air.

If we were in only half light, I knew I had never encountered such a monster before. On the thin side, but it was big. *This should be good*, I thought to myself, as Peter responded to my attentions, holding me closer without seemingly knowing what to do with me. He sighed as he was released from his jim jam bottoms, his lance thrusting forwards. If this was getting a bit like DIY sex, I slid my own bottoms down my legs and off over my ankles.

A positive response at last as responding to my gentle strokes, he mounted me (no foreplay for me but here goes, and if he uses his precision tool like he does for those of his models, this is going to be quite a treat).

This massive cock, the likes of which I had never seen before (and in my nursing days I had seen quite a few), entered my gentle lips, slipping, squirming through those gentle hairs as it headed towards its lair.

FISHING THE NET

But what! Having entered my inner recesses, it then behaved like a timid tom cat, exploring territories governed by the dominant male. There was a quick spray, a rapid retreat and that was it. Just as I was waiting to get aroused, that monster of just a few seconds before was already limply coiling itself up and going to sleep, its work done for the night.

I lay there in disappointment, and silence from the other side of the bed. I suppose I had to score it a two, one point for entry, and one for coming, couldn't give any more than that. If I had blinked, I may well have missed it.

Other than asking gently if there was a problem, no conversation followed, and frustratingly I turned over to sleep, hopefully as soundly as that snake.

It was in a reflective mood that I journeyed home the following evening, disappointed but also thinking of my needs, any woman's needs. I was going home to Buzz Buzz. Yes, I had checked I had enough batteries. Rampant Rabbit – yes, he was not the sort of rabbit you would ask the neighbours to look after while away for the weekend – was coming out to play, and when he entered my burrow, the earth was certainly going to move, and move it did. A girl has to have her pleasures, and I had just got mine, though not quite how I had hoped.

Satisfied now, I could sleep, but what will happen next time with Peter? I can only hope for better things, perhaps we need to talk. Next weekend we would be seeing each other again, and some tact and understanding may be required – certainly it can't be ignored. When will we try again?

At least I know though that I can always go home, and my rabbit will be pleased to see me. As long as I remember my AAs, he will be buzzing for my attention.

Life goes on, and if I had to make a decision on where I wanted our relationship to go from here, I could only give sex with Peter another chance, while we carried on our lives together, comfortable as we were with each other. The old routine of going over to see him at weekends continued, him modelling, me gaming and the evenings out.

We shared a bed, but though he never seemed shy of his body, there did seem to be a reluctance on his part to try sex again with me. I could go home to Buzz Buzz, but the real thing is far more pleasurable if you can find the right man (Harry, my friend with benefits, the one that got away, Will, they all knew which button to press to turn me wild), and I wanted to try again, especially with that snake waiting. But how to arouse him, that was the dilemma. I would have to try and seduce him, turn our pyjama cuddle into a night of passion.

My night arrived, and I couldn't be more blatant with what was required than arriving out of the ensuite, and immediately discarded my pyjama bottoms in front of him, before snuggling down by his side. Sidling up for a kiss, I moved his hands onto my breasts and as our lips met, hoped he would respond by gently caressing me, while my hands delved deep below the sheets to find and excite that huge snake. Things were looking promising as it stirred, starting to rise to greet me. He was showing signs of rising excitement, and I knew he did want to please me. He had started the countdown to launch his rocket inside me. Ten, nine, eight, I eagerly awaited take off as he got into position to mount me. On, four, three, two, I'm ready for him, and then one, we have lift off.

But we don't, there has been a misfire in his engine and the fires are quickly going out as his penis has lost power, and quickly resumes its normal state. My anticipation is… gone. Yes, Houston, we do have a problem. I lie there disappointed, him conscious of this but also subdued. We have to chat now, I think I have been here before. Remember Tom, and his cock cage? I don't want to be going down that route again.

It was a difficult subject to bring up, but after a careful introduction to the subject, he did have to admit that he may have started with that age problem of men, Penile Erectile Dysfunction.

I had now experienced this twice, and though sex was important to me, was I entering into an age range of men in my match group, where this may become more and more common. I hope not, and one hears of plenty of old couples still at it like rabbits, real rabbits that is. I didn't want to miss out, but it was only fair to offer some sympathy, some help if we could find it, to see if the problem was not insurmountable.

We both knew how to use a computer, and would go online to find out what we could about PED, and what could be done about it. A positive move that we hoped would be of mutual benefit, giving him the confidence in bed, and me the pleasure I so much desired.

We had done our research together, looking into this problem online. Remembering Tom from the past, I had suggested that he too should try a rubber band, but so as not to put all the onus on Peter, I decided that I would have to get myself a sexy little number, just to try and liven things up, and I do like dressing up, it always turned me on, increasing my sexuality. He surprised me, he came up with the idea of looking on Lovehoney.com, an online sex site, specialising in sexy lingerie, sex aids, and sex toys. How did he know about this site? Who cares? It had some wonderful stuff on it.

We both went on this site separately, him to get his band, and me to line myself up with a little surprise for to rouse his passion. I found a lovely black body stocking, fishnet, crotchless, with lovely black ribbon ties going always down the front. Very nice, I would feel good in this, I know.

Though ordering separately, our goods arrived at the same time at our respective addresses, and it was with excitement that I tried my new little number on. Sex on legs, though I say it myself. How could anyone resist me looking like this?

If there was ever pre-planned sex, then this was going to be it. Tonight's the night as they say, so after I had cooked a lovely meal for him, and we had shared a nice red, we retired upstairs. No jim jams tonight, I was to look a million dollars in my sexy new outfit. Him, he would have to bare all.

We retreated under the duvet, making sure first that he had a good view of what he was about to get; dressed like this I was even turning myself on. We embraced, kissed, and some form of arousal began. I wanted to whip that massive snake into a frenzy, I so wanted to embrace it in my inner sanctum, so my hands worked up and down it, goading it to reach for the skies, and the enter me. I was succeeding in my aim, and reached the point where he was as hard as mahogany, and it was time to apply the band. A bit of a turn off as he toyed under the sheets, not quite knowing how to put the thing on. Was it his size? I don't know, but there was a lot happening down below, and none of it to me. I suggested he put it round everything, his balls and his cock (he should have tried it before we were together), and at last I had a grip of this huge snake, firm and hard.

We were ready, and in great expectation I lay back, legs apart, ready to receive what I hoped to be heaven. Why wasn't anything...? No, it's happened again, the snake had lost interest, and despite the attentions of the band, was retreating rapidly.

I was so disappointed, I had waited ready for him in my lovely outfit, hoping, really hoping that he could satisfy me at last. My wishes, like something else, had gone limp. I turned to Peter – how did he feel?

He just shrugged his shoulders. It hadn't happened, and that was that.

I slipped out of my outfit, frustrated it hadn't produced the results intended, but I couldn't blame that on the stocking. At this time, I didn't know the turn on it would produce at a later date.

Where do we go from here? I thought. *We don't row, we are quite comfortable in each other's company, but I'm not getting the sex I so desperately seek to fulfil myself.*

I fancied a holiday, I needed a holiday; I hadn't had one for over a year. I wondered if this would light a spark in him, so asked him if he would like to go away with me. It was getting near the end of season, and we should be able to pick up a bargain somewhere. Whatever else, we were still comfortable in each other's company, and yes, he liked the idea of going away with me. If things weren't going to well in the downstairs department, then he was still looking, still wanted a lifelong partner for company and just sharing the things in life one wanted to do, preferably as a couple. We would holiday together, and as it turned out through the whole of my internet dating, my angling career, this was the only one, my Peter Pollock, that I actually went on holiday with.

A trip online again found us the holiday we were looking for, a rip to Greece, end of season, a real bargain on an all-inclusive package. I love my holidays and so was really looking forward to this.

It was time to go, and I was really excited, a well-deserved rest after a year of hard toil, and company would make it even better. Peter, in his normal polite way, too was looking forward to some time away with some company. Greece, here we come, and we departed there for sunshine, relaxation, and who knows, those 'Shirley Valentine' moments of romance in a foreign land.

A lovely hotel, but as we were to discover, it being end of season, things were starting to close down. The sun shone, the food was lovely, but some of the hotel entertainment was gone the week before, especially the shows, the cabaret, so no embarrassing Mr and Mrs competitions to try and avoid, no embarrassing questions about one's partner if we were pushed forward to participate. It would just be us and our own company to enjoy the warm evenings after our dinner, to stroll, to talk, and enjoy the odd glass of Ouzo or two.

Eleven days to discover ourselves. Days spent by the pool, reading, swimming, and then walking. Discovering those picturesque little harbours, drinking coffee, listening to the gentle lapping of the waves against the harbour walls, enjoying the slow pace of life and just unwinding. It was a pleasant holiday and it was nice to have Peter's company but other than the odd cuddle out walking, a kiss and cuddle in bed before we slept, that was as far as any romance went, and he didn't want to push it any further than that, even if the odd night I would think that a quick bonk would be good. He was content in this placid, comfortable-with-each-other relationship, and even when one evening we had a power cut, as in the hotel, not his working parts like before, then rather than doing the decent thing and taking me to bed, we just went down to reception where there was light, and read until power was restored.

It was time to go home and I can't say I didn't enjoy my break, I did, and it was nice to have company. But as we flew back to England, I was beginning to doubt the long-term future of our 'romance'. I would give it a little longer, but may have to call it a day. I was loyal while with Peter, it was only fair, and so hadn't gone online to see who else may be waiting to take my bait, but there was just a little wish to see.

Wrongly, the decision was made for me. My little

car, bless it, much needed for work to get me to and fro, decided that life was too much. Its big end went, and Peter valiantly came to my rescue, knowing one of his mates could fix it for me, and duly arrived at my home to tow my motor back to his, then his mate's. He would lend me his Postman Pat van, his red van that he would use to cart his engines to his exhibitions and shows. It even had Jess hanging from the rear-view mirror. Bless him, he had the van M.O.T.'ed and taxed for me, so my life could go on normally while my car was being repaired. How long this was going to take his mate had to fix, who knows? He was under pressure to sort his wife's car out first.

I owed him, and would obviously carry on seeing him, so my weekend trips to Wolverhampton would continue. I was grateful; I don't want to sound unkind but there was something still missing for me. Buzz Buzz was offering some satisfaction, but it wasn't the real thing.

I would try to get him to try the rubber band again. I know he had not seemed interested in sex, not even on holiday, but he would try again, knowing I wanted it. There's no point building up to a big climax here, and oh boy did I want one. I can only say we were unsuccessful again, my car's big end not being the only one that wasn't working – no pistons pumping, no spitting exhaust, just a rather flat tyre.

Disappointment again, there was only one last thing we could try, the little blue pill. I knew you could get them online, not from personal experience, but I knew. Peter, was more cautious, having heard the effect Viagra can have on some men. He wanted to go to his GP to get checked over properly, before trying the little tablet.

I can't blame him for that, but I had only heard good reports of its use. I was sure that if he took them, he would stand to attention throughout the workout I wanted to put him through.

The examination, okay, and issued with a private prescription, we were ready to give it another go. I could only get that body stocking out again to offer encouragement, and I did feel rather 'hot' wearing it. To bed and let's see what happens.

Nothing!

What? How could this fail? I don't think it can be me, I've never had trouble turning men on before. Poor Peter, what was going through his mind? I knew he wasn't that keen on sex, perhaps because he was nervous of the end result. Another failure, the stigma of his last partner not wanting sex, thinking him too big, the mental trauma of PED. He knew it was important to me and he couldn't deliver. Poor man, a feeling of sadness for him in not being able to enjoy the pleasures I could provide and wanted.

Bugger, it would be back to the corner shop to get some more batteries on the way home.

Progress on my car was slow, it fact like my sex life, non-existent, as autumn turned into winter. I think at this stage we probably both realised that our relationship was getting tired, and if it wasn't for the car we would have gone our separate ways. I know that sounds a bit mercenary of me, but there was no spark now.

The snows came, and even entered inside my car

as it patiently awaited the attentions that would get it back on the road. Mine and Peter's times together became less frequent, though I was still glad of the use of Postman Pat.

At last, finally my car was fixed, and was back on the road again. I could return PP and Jess back to Peter, to be used for his models. I was very grateful.

We did see each other once or twice more, but I think we both knew it was time, time to go our own directions. I at least owed it to him to tell him face to face, and he accepted what I had to tell him in his normal shrug-of-the-shoulders way, accepting his fate.

We parted on good terms. I was grateful for all he had done for me, and said that if we couldn't find anyone as lifelong partners, then we knew that we could spend our lives together, as long-term friends, knowing we would be more than comfortable in each other's company (but sadly sex couldn't, wouldn't enter into it). I wished him good luck in his hunt for the lady he was looking for, me, I was about to go fishing again.

Buzz Buzz would have to wait tonight, I needed to go back online, show my bait was in the water again, let the sport begin again.

I would always have sympathy for those men who suffered from PED, but it was hard for me to contemplate a life without the pleasures I desired, 'hard' maybe being an inopportune word to use. I certainly wasn't interested in the use of rubber bands and alike in bed anymore.

Time to move on, again on the trail of Mr Right!

Another experience, the longest so far. Again, it

hadn't turned out the way I had hoped, but the perhaps it was never going to.

Move on, Gill. All part of life's rich tapestry, and you have lost nothing but a bit of time.

GAME FISHING, SPINNING MY LINE

I would have to admit that I am not a great fan of sport, other than fishing, which other than my present interests, I have not done seriously for some years. If I have now found a bit of a passion for Rugby Union, and now trot off to see Wasps quite regularly, I am still not sure whether it is the game and its rather confusing rules, or watching all these hunks run around a field and into each other. Those rippling muscles, and for some of them (though not those sixteen men who push and grunt at each other, often falling flat on their faces only to stand and have to do it all again), their good looks. I certainly wouldn't mind some of them wrapping their arms round me and dragging me to the ground.

It would therefore be of no surprise that sport of any form (well, let's not discount man wrestling, but I'm not going to announce that online without making myself look a bit nymphomaniac-like), would not be on my list of interests.

Men, a different kettle of fish. A rarity, a man who

doesn't like sport of some sort, whether participating, or as in the age group I am looking for, they have hung up their boots and now are live or television followers, especially of football. Me, I hate the game, but that's something else one doesn't announce too readily.

It would be of no surprise that at some stage I was going to come across men interested in sport, and for me the sport was cricket. Yes, that riveting, quick-fire game that has you on the edge of your seat all the time. Vocal crowds, loads of singing and chanting, cricket was the game of a couple of men I started chatting to at different times, and in fact I think from memory was my only involvement in any sport in my dating days (other than fishing, which I persist at – I'll get the right one sometime!).

In fairness, I did actually know a little about the sport, as I has watched it as an army wife and when I was in Australia, and the television was always on with some match or other. I would have to admit that I did prefer the highlights though.

Needless to say, I was looking on the dating site to see what was about today, when I noticed this really good-looking chap had his profile up, and there was a match there somewhere. Yes, very good-looking, and about five years younger than me. Perhaps that was the match; he was in the age group I was looking at, and he, just perhaps preferred the older woman.

Well, he certainly looked interesting, and it was well worth casting out my line with me as the bait, and see if he wants to bite. No more than a, "Hello," and, "are you interesting in chatting?" and I left it at that.

Not straight away, but I did get a response, which I felt very flattered about, and also more than a bit surprised, because as I have said, this is a seriously good-looking man.

I was a little suspicious he may be married, as he put very little on his profile, and didn't come online that often. A 'shy feeder?' I looked for him online for a while, to see if he wanted to chat, but it looked like I was doing the chasing as it was always me who opened a conversation.

We did chat now and again, and it came up about one of his hobbies being cricket. I of course could tell him about my experiences of the sport in Oz, so we had struck up a topic we could chat about. Though not a keen follower of the game, it was nice to catch up on the sport, especially as it was so popular in Australia, and at times a cause of social gathering.

We had struck a chord, and I thought with this that we could go on and meet up, but for some reason or another, he was always putting it off.

I did know the name of the team he played for, a village team near Wem, and so it was on one sunny weekend off, and as I had nothing else to do, I thought it would be interesting to go and watch him play, be a cricket groupie for the day. Knowing the name of the team, it was simple to go on the internet to find the fixture list for his team, and so find out where he was playing on that day.

It was a home game, so all I had to do was to head in the direction of the village, and find a cricket pitch. Simple, or that's what I thought, even with the use of my sat nav to overcome my useless sense of direction.

I found myself driving down endless back roads, through villages other than the one he played for, endlessly searching for one bloody cricket pitch. One envisages all those wonderful pictures from days gone by, where the cricket pitch would be on the village green, benches around the boundary, and a road skirting behind the green. The village pub would also overlook the pitch so liquid refreshment would be readily on hand.

Not today. I didn't think I would be playing hide and seek with a cricket pitch, after all, they are not the smallest of items. I was getting exasperated, and was getting to the stage of giving up and going and finding something else to do in the sunshine, when purely by chance, and knowing me, I may have been this way today three or four times already, I stumbled on the damn ground.

I parked up near the pitch, taking due care with my car that if someone got too violent with the ball, it wouldn't be in range. I donned my shades and set off to view the game from the boundary edge, eyes scouring the pitch and pavilion for my man.

No sign at the moment, perhaps he is on the batting team, and is waiting in the pavilion? It looked as if I had swelled the crowd quite considerably by my presence, as I stood very lonely on the boundary, whatever other crowd there was, standing around the pavilion.

Hang on a minute, who's that over there, in the slips, having a conversation with a fellow fielder? It did look like him, and I thought he looked my way, so up went my arm to shoulder height and I gave a little wave. I must have been at least fifty yards away, and he took no notice, or hadn't seen it.

I tried again, but was very conscious of other fielders thinking, *Who is that weird woman over there waving at us all?* I guess I must have watched for an hour or more, subtlety trying to catch his attention while he was fielding, I was more and more certain that it was him, but couldn't be a hundred percent sure, from the distance I was away, and wearing glasses, my distance sight has never been perfect. He was obviously transfixed by the game he was playing in, to take any notice of the 'crowd', but I hope he may have noticed me, recognising me from my profile picture.

I thought it was time to go home, but I had made the effort to watch him, and had registered my interest. I hoped this would give me a chance of an innings sometime with him, chance for him to bowl me over.

I went online that evening, to see if he was chatting, available for a chat. I bowled him my googly that I had been to his pitch to watch him play.

He straight batted my opening shot with the announcement that he had been playing away, cricket that is, and that I would have been watching the B-team, the second XI.

Oops, did I now feel an idiot. Who was I waving to? It did look like him, or so I thought. He must have thought, *Weird woman.*

Stumped, or retired hurt, I felt totally embarrassed and ended the conversation. The series had been lost, and I never heard from him again, nor did I have the courage to try and speak to him.

Did he think I was a stalker? I suppose he would

have had every right to, but no more, no more trying to meet up unannounced. Stick to the gaming I know, but an interesting experience. I shall return to the selectors.

I guess that was a true rejection, of which I, up to then, hadn't experienced, but I had to put that behind me and carry on undaunted in my quest to find my man, a little hesitant as to whether crickets were now good bait. A slip on my part, not how to get a maid bowled over.

Sport would not enter my chatting for some time after that, it would have been interesting to know more about my handsome cricketer, but it was not to be.

It was therefore quite a while, before sport interfered again. That man of my dreams, the 'one that got away' was also a keen sportsman, though for him, after a successful hockey career, he now kept himself in trim in the gym, walked a lot, and played golf, but as with so many men as they get older, enjoyed armchair sport – rugby and football especially – rather than participating in anything too strenuous. He did enough to look good and that bum was always worth a second look, and a third! He was still in my thoughts a lot, and there would be the very occasional catch up in a pub, or a quiz. He was seeing someone else, though what he ever felt towards her I don't know. How could he resist me?

The nuts and the bolts of it was that I was still searching, searching for Mr Right, not knowing when he would appear again.

And so it was when looking through profiles again,

that I came across another rather smart-looking man, and as we came up as a match, there must be something that we could build on, and perhaps create a relationship, and a future. He seemed very pleasant and easy to chat to online, and it therefore seemed sensible to me to try and meet him.

He too was keen to meet up, and so we arranged to meet up at a halfway point between us, in Eccleshall, as he lived in the north of Staffordshire. Eccleshall is a lovely small town/village, with a few more than pleasant country pubs within its surrounds. A nice place to meet, with plenty of options of different locations to meet. As they say, variety is the spice of life.

Our first meeting, very civilised and if not formal was certainly a finding out mission. He lived with, and looked after his mother at home, when not working. A nine to five white collar worker, this gave him time in the evening to look after her needs, though she was not totally dependent on him. It sounded as if he was a kind-hearted and caring man, with a good job, and a nice-looking white car, the make I can't remember as I'm not really a car expert, but a nice motor. Possibilities, yes, though I didn't really want to become a carer as that was my day job.

A pleasant first meeting, just a pleasant hour in a pub and we went our separate ways, but this guy I will contact again in the hope that he too will want to meet me a second time.

Yes, he did, and as the location seemed to offer plenty of choice, then Eccleshall it would be again. It was only three or four days since our first meeting, but it was good to meet up again. A different pub, but they all seem nice here. He was easy to talk to as we passed the evening chatting away, finding out what he wanted out of life, my ambitions of a life here and in Australia, the holidays I enjoyed, other places I hoped to visit. He told me of a woman he had been seeing but she didn't have the same commitment to the relationship that he had, and they had gone their separate ways. I'm not sure about the Australia thing, but there did seem grounds for encouragement that this could progress further.

We continued to see each other over the coming weeks, once or twice a week, for a drink or a pub meal, and seemed to be getting on very well. Just like the 'one that got away', he was quietly spoken but always the perfect gentleman, looking after me, helping me into my seat, escorting me to my car, and then a quick kiss or peck on my lips. No snogging or groping me on the park bench (damn!).

The evenings were starting to draw out, so we would be able to walk as well on our rendezvous, as winter moved into spring. We had enjoyed each other's company on weekdays to begin with, but did start meeting up on some Saturday nights as well, but of course everything did have to fit in with my work rota, my four days on, four days off schedule.

Summer was fast approaching but with those evenings drawing out, his hobby, cricket, yes, that game, had come to haunt me again. Not a game that you play at three o'clock, and are back home after a pint by six, six thirty, but the whole afternoon and early evening, plus the pint – very time consuming. He was committed to his sport, and with that was tied to these weekends of cricket, umpiring. Worse, for me anyway, was that he had given up playing and was in fact an umpire, of reasonable standard and so very much in demand.

Where would that mean that I would fit into this? Back to weekdays, or late Saturday nights to meet up, and we hadn't got as far as staying over at each other's.

Over the past few weeks I had been seeing quite a lot of him, and so anyone else had been put on hold while I saw where this was going. With the start of the cricket season, I felt I was on a turning wicket where cricket seemed more important than me. I had to look at the fixture list, the list of his umpiring appointments, to see when I could possibly see him to spend a reasonable amount of time, rather than a quick couple of hours in the pub halfway every so often. It was great he was so devoted to his sport, and so much in demand, but I wanted him devoted to me. If I was looking for Mr Right, it is essential that I can get to know him, but how can I do that if I never see him?

He would go off to his matches, and ring me when he was finished, usually quite late in the evening, so there was no chance of a meet up. I guess I was starting to get a bit bored, but as I was seeing no-one else, when he rang and asked if I fancied meeting up, then the answer was usually, "Yes." But that early interest was fading; all he talked about was his cricket, the decisions he had made, dodgy snick behind the wicket, bowled him, but I just spotted his front foot had strayed over the popping crease. All very exciting for him, but not to me.

One night when we were meeting for a drink, he did ask me if perhaps on one of my free weekend days off, I would like to come along as well. Obviously he would be on the pitch the whole game, but we could have a quick chat between innings, and then after the match had finished, we could go for a meal on the way home.

Give it a go, I suppose, show some interest in his main hobby, and perhaps it wouldn't be then such a one-sided conversation. I agreed and so on one sunny Saturday lunchtime we set off into the country in search of the match he was officiating in. He knew where he was going, and easily found the ground. He was then in his element as he knew a lot of the players involved in this game, and immediately was greeted by them, and his fellow umpire for the afternoon.

"Would like you to meet Gill? She has come to watch today," was about my lot in introductions from him to his mates. I certainly didn't feel in, definitely out here, and no need for an umpire's review. He said he would see me later and was gone, into the dressing room, emerging in his white coat and straw hat, very much the part. This was his environment, certainly not mine, as he strolled out to the middle, placing the bails on the stumps, and waiting for the captains to toss and decide who would be in now, and who would be in later.

For me, at least the sun was shining, and there was a bar in the pavilion, but I would have to ration myself as we couldn't have the umpire's girl singing 'inappropriate songs' from the boundary edge, if she had downed a cider or two too many.

Best I could do was to find a nice deck chair, sit down with my cider, and enjoy the sunshine and the game. Some hour and a bit later, I woke up, and not a lot had changed. He still stood upright behind the stumps as some young tyro came running in, hurtling the ball towards the poor bloke holding a piece of wood in his hands at the other end. The occasional sound of a snick, and everyone would leap into the air, shouting, "Howzat!"

He would shake his head knowledgably and say, "Not out." Perhaps he had been asleep like me? This rapid action continued to the extent of being on the edge of my seat, I dozed off again, only to be awoken in the distant future with a cup of tea thrust in my face, and to be asked if I was enjoying it. As you could see, I was scintillated, but showing some interest, did ask why that bloke who had been throwing the ball at the bloke with the wood in his hand, had a long red mark down the inner thigh. Did he have a rash or something? I was really getting into this game. He patiently explained that he had been rubbing his balls, so he could shine one side and be able to swing better. *Swing?* I thought. *Swing? Isn't this supposed to be a game of cricket, not some gay affair for public school boy swingers?* He gave me one of those looks that men give women when they think we are stupid but don't want to announce it out loud.

He beat his retreat, saying he had to get ready for the second innings. What, another cider? *Sounds good to me,* I thought, and I settled down as those that were in were now out, and those who were out, now in. Try explaining this to my granddaughter.

The afternoon drifted into evening as people were out and others came in, ran up and down between the wickets a few times and then walked back to the pavilion, heads down as if someone had just told them they were sleeping with his wife.

Then real excitement, my man, the umpire, removed the bails, everyone shook hands and headed back to the pavilion. After all that excitement, it had been a draw. I could have wet myself with the excitement of it all, especially after a couple of ciders and not knowing where the loo was.

We had a quiet journey home, stopping for a pub meal, as he tried to explain the intricacies of umpiring, and cricket, and winning draws and losing draws. Uh! Je ne comprends pas.

I don't think I had disgraced myself, but as we parted company with that usual kiss, I was thinking, *Is this for me? I want someone to treasure me, not stick his finger up and say I was out.*

He would ring and we would chat, but for me it was the end of the series, it was stumps and the end of the season.

Bloody sport, bloody cricket, back to fishing the net for me. Cricketers, a WIDE from now on, with no extras.

I did hear from him some months later, seeing if I wanted to meet up for a meal, but I was not bowled over this time. I was starting to see someone else, so struck him off my fixture list.

THE HADDOCKS AND THE HADDKNOCKS – LOOKING FOR NEMO

So what of Dory? We had become really good friends, and if my attempts at fishing the net had at this stage been unsuccessful, I was only too willing to give my advice to her, so that she may be more successful than me, and not make the same mistakes that I had. Yes, she had been deterred by the initial lack of success, the responses she had received from the first sites she had signed up to, the non-connection with the paid site she had tried to begin with. She hadn't dated for a long time, but wanted to start now, and thought results would come quickly. They hadn't, but let's face it, she was a mere novice of a few weeks, whereas I had been fishing online for some years now, but for one reason or another, hadn't got the serious bite that I wanted, to take out of the water and take home with me, to mount in my living room, to keep and cherish (and by mount, I don't mean bonk in my living room). I felt there was some nervousness in her when she went online; she was too ready to press the delete button, but she had been hurt in the past and didn't want to put herself through that torture again, so it was easier to cross them off right away than see what they may have to offer.

We saw each other frequently, when we could, when our shift patterns allowed. I had set her up on sites originally, and wanted to help her all I could. We hoped that someday, we would both be successful in our quest, and would be able to go out as a foursome with our respective fellas, to go out to dinner, theatre, or even go on cruises together. But at the moment, one thing was missing – a man, for both of us!

Having got a lot of bites, but none she felt like catching on other sites, we thought we would try her on that Fish site, see if there would be any change. She would stay on the other sites, you never knew what may turn up, but time to try something new.

I had become her self-styled personal advisor on fishing, fishing the net that is. We needed to get together again on the computer to set up this other site, with the fifty thousand questions that would have to be answered to set up her profile. We arranged another coffee meetup at her place, gave ourselves the whole afternoon to get Dory set up again. Coffee, yes, but were we becoming 'coffee snobs'. Is that something we should put on the profile? None of your rubbish for us, only decent, proper coffee, and see what response that brings.

So over coffee and cake we began the long process, chatting while we did it, me asking the questions and typing in the answers she gave me, that the site demanded.

Name, height, hair colour, eye colour, all the questions I had answered myself a long time ago, but now again for my blue-eyed blonde friend. I would say, while we answered, filled in these questions, we did have a laugh at the same time, and I was impressed by how honest she was with some of her answers. This was unlike some of the supposed matches she had already received from other sites, though some of them, she did wonder if they did ever read her profile. Still a big no-no for her was smoking, no way did she want smoked fish. Like myself, she had given up the foul weed some ten years earlier, and now hated being in the company of smokers, the smell of stale cigarettes and tobacco. Yet, how many men still replied, wanting to chat, wanting a date, yet when Dory raised the point about smoking, they said they would do it, smoke, away from her, go outside. 'It wouldn't be a problem, she wouldn't notice,' other than the smell. This was one thing she wasn't going to compromise on.

On the questions, on the answers. Average build, wanting fun, open to new adventures, liked dining out, the theatre, outdoor pursuits.

Dory had just joined a gym, tried to work out two to three times a week; she had become a 'GYM BUNNY'. Bunny hops, star jumps, squat thrusts, she was at it. She was a fun person, but was serious in wanting a relationship. Marriage, not sure yet, but certainly a regular fella to enjoy her life with. She was single and wanted to mingle! She worked hard, two jobs and everything else to fit into her life, but was beginning to find this internet dating like a third job.

She had enough work to last her a lifetime, or that is how it felt, but as I had found in the past, all this could become more than addictive.

Ping! Another message comes through from another site. She had been chatting to a guy who had come online. It was obvious from their conversations that he had some sort of disability, probably was autistic, and he was only eighteen years old. But he kept on coming back. I suppose it was something for him to do, someone who talked to him. Why Dory did chat she wasn't sure, perhaps she just felt sorry for him if he was lonely, whatever, but he kept coming back as if he fancied her. Dory got to the stage when she had to point out, as the lad got more suggestive, that she had a daughter older than him, did he realise her age? And that he should try and find someone his own age. She didn't want to be rude, just honest, and wished him good luck looking for a girl his own age. Dory never heard from him again.

Another, now this one really was an interesting guy. A handsome-looking bloke from his profile, good job as some sort of company director. Dory had some good conversations with him. He wanted to meet up, BUT, he wanted to come round and be her maid for the day. He wanted to pick up some tips on being a housemaid, imagine. This good-looking bloke was a cross dresser, who wanted to come and clean her house for the day. She had no problem with him being a cross dresser, but was this really the person she wanted to meet? She wanted a man, not a man dressed as a woman.

A few years ago, Dory had been in Manchester for a hen party, staying in a hotel, and it just happened that in the same hotel was a cross dressers' convention. She had been sitting by the bar having a drink, when a good-looking woman – well, man – came and sat next to her on a bar stool. If she was a good-looking woman, then he must have been a good-looking fella. Fishnet tights, a short leather skirt (nice legs), skimpy blouse with a red bra underneath, very fetching. They chatted through the evening, and he/she got drunker and drunker and as he/she did, then as men do, his legs got wider and wider apart to show, well you can guess. He/she eventually put his hand on Dory's knee and said he really liked her and would like to go upstairs and have sex with her. No thank you! So Dory did have a thing about cross dressers. Nice people, but...!

She didn't want this fella cleaning her bedroom and pinching her Chanel, going through her undies drawer. Imagine, she thought, going out to dinner with her 'man' because she loved dining out, her possibly in smart trousers, blouse, heels, and him in a dress and heels. Then coming home to bed, going out with a woman and then making love, sleeping with a man, taking their knickers off together. If you'll excuse the expression, fuck that! Well you wouldn't know what you were f—g! No, not for Dory, but what a waste to her of such a good-looking bloke. At least he was honest about what he was, and good luck to him. Dory would do her own cleaning, and wear her own dresses (and knickers).

But here were two examples of her frustration. This was becoming like armchair dating – she had never, as yet, got out of the front door, let alone the back door.

Back to the profile. We decided between us that there would be no mention of Dory owning her own house, because from her past experiences, she had been inundated with men wanting to chat, and it would usually turn out that they were foreign, wanted somewhere to live, sex, and money. Dory was turning into a dating virgin, but she was not going to be used, and not mentioning the house would hopefully cut a lot of these men out, all these that were wasting her time. Being foreign wasn't a problem, like the Frenchman who came online to chat, likeable enough, lived in Birmingham, and was collecting badges left right and centre. Most liked person, most matches, he was doing well. The only badge Dory would get at the moment would be the pickiest woman, but a badge is a badge and she would wear it proudly. No, it wasn't being foreign, it was the thought that she would just be used as a convenience, be taken for a ride (and still be a dating virgin!).

We went to put her photos on this fish site, all taken in the past three months and showing her off as a blonde bombshell, but found some were upside down. Was that why she wasn't getting any dates? She was being seen from the wrong side? Easy to resolve, and they did show her at her best, anyone should want to be with her.

As some of this went on the site, there would be some instant replies, though not that pleasant. One guy, saw her pictures and comes on asking whether she's naughty or nice.

Where was this conversation going? "Nice," she replied.

Calls himself 37. "I'm 37, and would like to be

naughty with you, Dory."

Dory asked him what he called being naughty, rolling in mud drinking Fizz?

"Well, Fizz yes, but not rolling in the mud."

It was Dory's first night off in six, she was tired and could have done without this but tried to remain polite. "Why not mud? It's good for the skin, and fizzy after." Why was he up so late?

37 was sad they weren't going to get naughty, adding that he was just about to play with himself, have a wank as his cock was hard.

She really didn't need this, so politely tried to end the conversation, saying she would leave him to it then, be careful and happy days. It had been a pleasure, at least for him anyway.

What did she mean? He hoped she would have some naughty pictures, to which Dory said she was sure he could entertain himself. She was sure he would have some magazines.

What a waste of space. What wankers, some of these men; why did they waste her time?

We put Dory on as a fun-loving person, decisive, honest, good in a crowd, a leader if needed, liked to be taken out to dinner (and a bottle of wine would certainly get her socks off if supplied), the life and soul of any party. Slowly but surely, a picture of her was being fed into the computer by me, that when complete, at the press of a button, would produce a life profile of her, that would sell her to the world (well, at this stage, any date would be nice).

So here was Dory, after a couple of hours of

tapping keys on the computer, and there were still questions to answer which I would leave her to do herself. I started reading the profile out but decided she should read it herself, and she could agree or disagree out loud as to what had come out of it. There was certainly a lot of it, but the gist was of it was that here we had a confident, good at interacting lady who enjoyed mixing, and was very relaxed with people, and with talking about herself. Yes, Dory agreed with that. She was good at relaxing other people in a crowd, making them feel confident when mixed with a group, and people would look to her as a friend and for leadership. She could command difficult situations, basically a good egg.

They wanted a word to describe her. Dory thought 'fantastic' was the most apt, but this was not on the list to tick the box, so we had to go for something else. Yes, it was very long-winded, but she agreed with the character they had portrayed her as. "Why lie to any of these questions?" she thought out loud. White lies were just like fake orgasms, though a chance of one of those would be a fine thing. She thought she had presented herself as an open book, and let's be honest, from her profile, she had to be the most desirable woman on this or any other site, in the age bracket she was looking at.

Common sense told her she only had to lie back (again, chance would be a fine thing), and wait for the shoals of fish to arrive, knocking on the door of love. Yes, Dory, just lie back and wait for it to happen. If the right man came along, then she could ease back on work, because as she had said before, this dating was like a third job, and she was starting to get exhausted.

So in a nutshell, we had this attractive, blue-eyed blonde, confident with people, and now looking for new things in life. She liked a drink, liked fine dining, so was only too happy to be taken out for meals. Self-sufficient but was now looking for a long-lasting relationship (marriage, not sure yet), had been on the naughty step for too long so hadn't dated for a long while, and sex, well a bit here or there was okay, a starting point anyway. But no smokers and no men who were just out to waste her time. And of course, she was a gym bunny, and really getting into this fitness thing.

Things were ready to roll; she had been getting very demoralised about this dating game, was thinking of coming off the site, as after all this time she still hadn't got off the starting blocks with this. Her time had been wasted by some men, they had just been rude (one bloke came on saying if she had cake and coffee, he was feeling horny and would be round in ten minutes), and she just thought of them, in her Yorkshire accent, as just wankers! She had been frightened of dating; it had been so long since she had been trying it, but now, now she WAS ready for a date, and wanted to get started.

She had made us another cup of coffee, better than tea for me as I could drink coffee cold, but certainly not tea, and as this had taken so long and for her, still wasn't finished. We sat back and took the chance to relax and talk about other things.

But the computer was soon hot. *Ping*, a reply. *Ping*, another. *Ping*, and yet another, and after just a few minutes, she already had five people wanting to see her. I pointed out to her that on this site she did have a third option, not just yes (a heart) or no (a cross), but here she could also have a maybe. She wouldn't have to make a decision straight away on those she was unsure of, just press maybe, and Dory would have time to reflect on him being a goer or not.

First one, claims to be fifty-two years old (Dory had put her age range as between thirty-five and fifty), but looks a lot older, single, and had been on and offline with this dating for a few years. He played in a band, and now after a twelve-year relationship that didn't turn out how he hoped, after some time, he didn't want to be single anymore. Could be a maybe, though he does look older!

Man of fifty-eight, wants easy-going woman (hope he doesn't mean or think Dory was loose), who makes people laugh – that's Dory – and would cook and enjoy meeting friends. I trust we are not talking threesomes here, and Dory was not stuffing anybody's chickens for them. No, this guy sounded too old.

Man of forty-nine from Birmingham, looks nice from his picture, muscular, a bit of a hunk, very athletic-looking. Self-employed, and seems nice to begin with. But he did look older than the age he had given. There were tell-tale signs here to me already, and give Dory her due, she was spotting them as well. He opened up, "HI HUN," and went on to talk about spring and the fall. He was American, and I had seen this before, it had SCAM, SCAM, SCAM written all over it right from the beginning.

Even Dory said, "Gill, this is going to be a scammer isn't it?"

"Yes," I said. "I think it almost certainly is." So a press on the cross button straight away.

But at least Dory was getting some replies. We had been at this along while now, and it was really time I should get back home. We bade each other farewell, and would get together soon, in the next few days, and review how she was now doing, what replies and types of men were nibbling. Dory was getting eager for a date, wanted to get out there now, but didn't wanted to see time wasters, or dentists, or Davids.

By the time that I had reached home, my phone was hot with text messages from Dory. It would appear that we had baited the riverbed well, and now the fish were streaming in, wanting to have a nibble at her. Even though we had tried to be careful with how we portrayed Dory, hiding that she was a home owner, a woman of means, she still got all the 'matches' from people who could see her as a nest egg, those still living at home with their parents (and were forty-five years old plus the rest), Moroccans, Americans, Londoners, and of course the smokers. Why didn't they read the bloody profile? Now Dory was in danger of a repetitive stress injury to her index finger, as one by one they were deleted. Yes, lots of replies, but to her, lots of time wasters.

For a lot of the men who were messaging her at the same time, she thought about holding a coffee morning and inviting them all round together, so she could choose at her leisure. But then she thought coffee may be a bad omen, it would be a beer morning instead – bittersweet! Would they all come for coffee together? Far more likely for a beer, or two, or three – a Shropshire Lass. Then she could save meeting for a coffee for a first date for the chosen one, or if he was no good then the next and the next. After all, us ladies were coffee snobs!

For the moment, I had done all I could to help; we had spent considerable time together trying to set all this up, first on the paid sites, then a couple of others, and now the fish one. Now a lot depended on Dory, how ready she really was to start dating again after all those years, and all it involved considerable time online looking, chatting, filleting the good from the bad. The ones she would chat with, those where there seemed some mutual compatibility to pursue and try and take forward, the time wasters and the rude ones. How would Dory react if there were rejections? She certainly had a larger than life character, would be the life and soul of any party, but this was a different ball game to her, with faceless characters (where you assumed the photo you would be looking at was actually the real image of the person who may interest you).

At this stage, I wasn't sure how committed she was to it, to fishing the net. She was already a busy lady, and there were times when she couldn't pursue her interests online because of work, and the need for sleep in a demanding job, her second job, and of course she was now a very keen gym bunny. She had already had a lot of interest on a couple of the sites but had only been too quick to press the reject button, without giving them a chance. Or, was Dory just expecting the perfect man to come along, staring at her from a computer screen? I rather fancied, if he was that special, he wouldn't have been online dating. Was that being too negative? Dory herself was fantastic (in her own words, but yes, she would be a great catch for any man), but then it is always harder for a lady than a man, to get out and about, especially by herself, to meet new people.

I could only see how things progressed from here and offer support where I could, but probably from the outset, our goals had been different. Dory wanted to start dating again, get out, dine, meet new people, and see where it took her. Me, from the outset I had been looking for someone with mutual interests to share my life with, the rest of my life. Fingers crossed we would both get what we wanted, and then we would be able to go out together, but as a foursome, holiday together. Exciting thoughts for the future, especially as already she had booked herself in to be my bridesmaid, when that day should arise.

I would always eagerly await our next meeting to catch up on where she had got to. Coffee at mine, coffee at hers, and maybe a little shopping first before we switched the computer on. Was she getting a little down with it all? Yes, I think she was. Eight weeks she had been doing this now, and she still had not got off the sofa, no date, so hadn't even got off the starting blocks. She was beginning to think she would be drawing her pension before she would be going out on a date.

"No thank you. I don't smoke, haven't for ten years now, and won't be starting again, so not smoking in front of me, or anywhere within two miles of me. No, it won't work." Dory checked her profile and sure enough, as she thought, it definitely said no smokers. Why didn't these blokes read the profile more carefully? Did some read it at all? They were wasting her time; the time she could be at the gym destressing as she really enjoyed her newfound role as a gym bunny (though she would only be too pleased if some guy would be there feeding her lettuce).

Then some real hunk would come on. She would show me his picture, and I would have to agree, what a body. Okay, a few tattoos, but with a body like that who cares? But, and I'm not sure why, no conversation would readily develop and her frustrations would continue.

But then out of the blue, there was one that wanted to chat, and he sounded interesting. Dory's finger hovered over delete, hovered while she thought, and then moved away from delete and passed maybe, and went onto a yes. Be bold, Dory – give it a go. There would be no commitment at this stage; chat, see where it takes you, and if a date materialises, good, you have got off the sofa and out through the front door. Perhaps, having got one in the system, you will find it easier to chat again in the future, and have a more positive outlook to it all.

So Dory gave it a go, chatted to this bloke who came from the West Midlands, right age bracket, had done with having a family, all had flown the nest, a good job, car, all sounded good. And he was foreign, but now had a British passport, had lived here all his life but that was not an obstacle to Dory. If he was nice enough, and ticked all the boxes, no – it didn't matter. He was a true Brit but any nationality, as long as he was genuine, it didn't matter. Things were on the up, or that was how it looked. I was really pleased for her, firstly for chatting for some time with a bloke, and secondly, she had got out of the habit of deleting them straight away.

Things really were looking up; he had asked her out for a date, and she had accepted. He wanted to take her out to dinner, and she seemed quite keen. A date at last, she rejoiced! Time to take this forward which meant exchanging telephone numbers. He would need to know if he was to pick her up, or where to meet, a date, time, and rendezvous. Dory gave him her mobile number, and anticipated the call.

It came. She answered and there on the end of the line was the Yow accent of the West Midlands area, just west of Brum. For her, a real turn-off. She couldn't stand that accent, however gorgeous the face of the mouth it came from was. Think of an excuse, quickly – she couldn't. All was arranged, she had a date, but she still couldn't bear that accent. She knew what to do. She would, when she spoke to him, say she had thought about it and the difference in their ages was too much, too much of a gap. So no, thank you very much, but she had thought better of it and changed her mind. Is that not a woman's prerogative? Yes it is!

She had had a date, and now she didn't. Progress, well at least she had got beyond the computer screen, talked to someone, but still a dating virgin.

Yes, now the messages were starting to come in. She had one guy from Wolverhampton come on and started chatting, and without Dory replying, was giving precise instructions as to where he lived behind the... (I won't tell you unless you want to pop round there as well) and she could check it out on Google Maps and then pop round for a... no thanks.

Another guy came on, sent a message to say hi, then a couple of days later came on with this rant about how sick he was that he messaged ladies but they never had the courtesy to reply, how rude they were, and why were they wasting his time.

Dory, for once was moved to reply, saying with rudeness like that, it was the reason some didn't reply. He had looked at her profile, so she had looked at his, that was all. How when she said no smokers, yet loads still tried to message her – scammers, false pictures, people who were just after one thing, no honesty, and then you get rants from men like that.

No reply from him, so Dory messaged him again, saying that proved her point. She had looked at his profile, and he had a wedding ring on. Was he wasting everyone's time as well?

He did reply, offering some sort of apology. No, he wasn't married, but wore his grandmother's ring on his finger, definitely not married!

Well why didn't he wear it on another finger then, or change his picture? He said he had been on this site now for some ten months, but had got nothing but scammers, bitches, and heartache from it.

Dory wished him happy hunting, thinking that would be the end of it, but he did message again thanking he for her reply, and saying he was going to take himself off the site.

The last Dory saw, he was still on. He had been rude, very rude, but had apologised. How much of the truth was he telling? Or was he too just trying to take someone along for a ride.

There were those who would message, and when

looking at their profile, their photo would show them with another woman. Tactful. Was it so hard in this day and age just to take a selfie of oneself, your real self, and post that?

Dory felt it was like going to a fairground and trying to hook one of those ducks as they went past, trying to win a fish, a goldfish in its plastic bag. That is what this dating game seemed to her at the moment. Yes, again she was beginning to feel a bit downcast about it all. Would she ever get a date, chat to someone who sounded genuine and nice? She had lost her confidence with the whole process, her opinion of men on the sites, a lot only after one thing. Well, shitheads was one word she described them as.

Yes, Dory was still an armchair dater, a dating virgin.

IN SEARCH OF A LOST SOLE

I didn't seem to be getting very far with this fishing lark, had caught a few, thrown most of them back, or they were just some creeps wanting sex, probably cheating on a wife at home, or not getting enough from her, and so looking for easy sex in a group of women who they thought were 'up' for it. Mr Right was proving very elusive, bar that one unforgettable man, but that was not meant to be, and I was moving on, swimming with the tide, looking for fun, and still that catch I wanted to make.

And there was an idea, swimming with the tide, what better place to catch a fish than from a boat? It wasn't going to be dating online, but what about trying a cruise? Surely there must be others like me who found the life on board fantastic – fine dining, shows, different ports, and plenty of opportunities to meet new people, single men, who may also be looking for a catch.

I needed a holiday, so thought what better than to take myself off on a cruise? It was August and what better time to go for a trip on the Med? Yes, I would do it. I chose a trip around the Greek islands, incorporating one Turkish one. I took myself off to the shops, any excuse, to get my wardrobe, a new cosy to show my wares off to their best in the sunshine, and nice shoes and handbag to go with my glad rags for the evening events. Sun protections, because being of fair skin, I needed to look after myself – all was got, packed, and ready to go.

Airport parking, and I was on board a plane, heading south, to the sun, to the sea, and fingers crossed, to my love. My flight took me to Crete to board my boat, my cruise ship. The normal embarkation, up the steps to get on board, and a photo with the Captain.

He looked okay, I wondered if he was taken. That would be a whale of a story if I could catch the Skipper. I was shown to my room (not by the Captain, I wasn't going to get that lucky that quick!) and was impressed by the comfort on offer. I had gone all inclusive, so all my meals would be taken care of, I just had to remember that I did want to be able to get into that lovely swimsuit, without too many bulges leaking out, and increasing as I overindulged in the cuisine on offer. I enjoyed the wonderful views from my room, looking out across the blue carpet we would begin to glide across when we left port. I went off to explore the ship, walked around a couple of decks, and ventured towards the casino for a quick look, but alas this was closed, at least until we had left port – licensing laws or something. My initial thoughts of the ship were most favourable.

It was time to dress for dinner, and see what there

may be to catch, to net and live happily ever after with. Would the trip serve both my wishes, a holiday, and a mating ground, to find a man? I spoke with the maître d', a Frenchman, or he could put on a very impressive accent, as to what table I would like to be on. Well, next to the Captain of course, but failing that, I didn't want to be alone, so would it be possible to be put on a large table with other single people like me? The first night it was just pot luck, go on a table and hope. The next night and for the rest of the cruise I would be on the same table with hopefully seven eligible bachelors, all drooling over me, wanting my attention, and if things went well, my body, and of course my heart. I hoped for better things the next night and went off to enjoy the show, and have a quick flutter at blackjack before retiring to bed.

We were on the move, sailing off, and as I drifted off to sleep, I hoped I may be sailing over the horizon to my dreams, a life on the ocean waves with the Captain, a rich shipping magnet – my Mr Right.

Breakfast could either be formal, or taken as a buffet, which as I was alone, was my choice. Our first day at sea would be literally at sea, a day to unwind, enjoy the sun, and get to know the ship. I decided to encamp to what I saw as the most likely best fishing ground, a chair by the pool, in the sun. Loaded with my book, my sunglasses, and suntan lotion, I arranged myself carefully on my lounger attired in my new swimsuit – meat on the slab. Watch the sun, Gill, because you don't want to be red meat. Not my first cruise, and the reminder of the feeling of being free, breeze in your hair, sun in your face, all those feelings why I liked cruising so much. It was a day to unwind, and that's what I did. I had presented myself on show, and hoped that come dinner, I would arrive at my table to find HIM there waiting for me. I was content, I was cruising, with all the luxury it gave me, and the chance to enjoy myself later, at dinner, watching the shows and then in the casino. Life couldn't be better (well, if Mr Right were next to me it could be). Relax and enjoy.

Evening came, and after dressing suitably, I headed off for my dinner in anticipation of who I would be sitting by, who else would be on the table. The maître d' escorted me to my table, to my destiny, and presented me to my dining mates… seven single women, oh whoopy. I wanted to sit with my prospective mate, not the competition. Pleasant enough, but I had enough thoughts of my own, of what I wanted to do with the Captain. I didn't want to hear theirs.

And so the day-to-day routine of the cruise started and went on much the same; we would sail by night to our next island, where after breakfast we would leave the ship to explore whatever island was next on the list. Tourist attractions, shops, local markets, all of which I enjoyed, except I was still by myself. On one island, I even took myself off for a long walk alone, along the shores. Was I reminiscing of Shirley Valentine, and hoping it may happen to me? Alas, no it didn't, but I did like the scenery, the pace of life on show in these places, and the friendliness of the locals. Sitting watching fishing boats bob up and down on the calm harbour waters, a wine, a frappe in hand, it certainly was a peaceful existence.

Then back to the ship, set sail onto our next stop,

the next port of call for the following day. Dinner and listening to what my seven companions had done in the day, and me still wondering why the Captain hadn't tried to sweep me off my feet. I felt positive he must be thinking about it. Meal over, and then to the shows, which were very varied and were excellent, and then either to the casino, or a game of bridge. Maybe there would be someone looking for a 'partner'.

My birthday would be when I was on board, so for a treat, I booked myself an excursion, a daytrip on a small boat, to a lovely cove where we could bathe in the sea, have a barbeque on the beach – it would be fun. Something to really look forward to, I was going to have a wonderful birthday.

Happy birthday Gill, I had my normal buffet breakfast and was preparing to go on my planned treat when, OMG – disaster. Descending between decks, I slipped, slipped very badly from the bottom steps and fell heavily on my right knee. Did I scream, as I crumpled up in a heap on the deck with a sprained ankle and knee that was swelling by the second. At last, I was the centre of attention, but this wasn't how I meant it to be. Fellow cruisers, and men in white uniforms surrounded me, trying to look after me, take care of me. I was sat up and a wheelchair arrived for me, which I was put in and taken down to sick bay.

My knee was now, well, enormous, and the medic after examining it said that he wasn't happy with it, and he wanted me to have an X-ray. Sadly, the island we were visiting was small and had no facilities so they would have to take me the following day to a hospital on the Turkish island that was the day's destination. Luckily my holiday insurance would cover this, though I would have to reclaim it back when returned to the UK.

He gave me fruit teas while I remained in the sick bay for a couple of hours, then returned me back to my room, equipped with crutches and bandaged leg. What a birthday treat I was having as my mind turned to the day I had planned, and a tear ran down my cheek.

I was getting attention at last, but this kind I could have done without, as I became a hermit in my own cabin, the hours only broken up with attendants bringing me my meals. At this rate, I was thinking I would have to lower my goals. At least they were coming to my room, so forget the Captain, I may have to get my leg over with one of these, except my leg was too bloody swollen to even contemplate such a manoeuvre.

A painful meal that night as I tried to eat my dinner, kindly brought to my cabin, with one leg up but my knee so swollen that it was difficult to have it out straight to rest it. No cabaret, no casino, no chance to meet up with the man who wanted to give me a birthday treat I would remember. It was no consolation I would get a refund on the trip I didn't take, this had to be one of my worst birthdays ever.

An uncomfortable night for me, but in the morning we were safely docked in Turkish waters, where I was wheeled down to a waiting car that took me to the hospital. Would there be a language problem? Well, the Turkish I knew I could write between this word and my next. But things were looking up, just look at the interpreter they had provided, who had driven me to the hospital in a Merc, and now would care for my every need, and would translate for me as I went through X-ray and on to the appropriate medical care. I could have been signing my life away, and my money also when I had to pay for my medical attention that that I was now getting, but my dishy man looked after me, getting me over every obstacle which was put in front of me – not easy with a gammy knee.

I was fitted with a knee brace and given crutches. No major damage, and time would be the healer, if only my travel insurance would carry on paying for my EVERY need, which I'm sure my helper could have given me. Alas, the injury would spoil the rest of my cruise. I wouldn't be able to chase fish on one leg, nor enjoy the scenic beauty of the Greek islands we visited. Hobbling to dinners, then onto the shows, but at least with one leg sticking in front of me, I did get the prime spots for the shows. The casino, again, wasn't much fun with my impediment.

Poor miserable, unhappy Gill. This trip hadn't worked out how I had hoped in terms of romance and enjoyment, and I was restricted to the insides of a cruise ship, except the few places I could get on deck on one leg, and to be quite honest, if I looked dishy in my new swimsuit before, the swollen appendage rather spoilt the effect now.

At one port, I was able to hobble down the gang plank to some shops that were quayside, but that was all I could manage. I did decide though, that I would endure the pain and spend what time I could in the casino, and did play some blackjack on crutches. I avoided losing an arm and a leg, even made a bob or two to keep my spirits up.

It was time to go home, as we sailed back to Crete, and then departed to the airport. I wasn't looking forward to a four-hour flight back home, but would have to do it. I would no longer have the attentions of my handsome assistant to look after me and had been very kind to me. I would have liked to give him something, well I wouldn't have complained if he had given me something. I bade farewell, and was soon up in the sky returning back to England.

I had to pick my car up and drive home, which under some pain I did manage. That was it, home, one or two good memories, a large credit card bill for medical expenses (which I would get back), and a bloody painful knee.

Again, my fishing exploits, or attempts at fishing, were cast to the wind. I bet the Captain is still thinking about what he had missed out on – he had the chance! No rendezvous with desirable bachelors, no holiday romance, nothing.

In fairness, it was the first cruise I had been on when I hadn't met up with a lot of other people, and socialised with them. I will cruise again, but next time and in the future, I will have a man by my side to escort me to dinner, dance the night away, and help me be lucky at the card table. My cabin wouldn't be lonely again.

But, I still have to find that man, and am quickly running out of ideas. Like a trawler dragging its net, I would have to cast mine again far and wide, so back home it was time to switch on the internet and fish again!

HOOK, LINE AND SINKER

Like me, there were men out there, fishing the net as well, with the same aim as myself, to find a lifelong partner, some who just wanted instant sex, some friendship, and some who wanted to marry you as soon as you came up a match.

We have already met Joe from some way away, who met me, wanted me to come over, and then became more and more demanding of my time, to the point of obsession where he wanted me there all the time, moving in, giving up my job, in fact my whole life that I had back home. Too much. I wanted to find Mr Right, but not change everything that I knew. In such a short space of time as well. He was well and truly hooked on me, and I had to end it as the same response was not coming from me.

I started chatting to another man, Bob Smelt, in time, who actually turned out to be very local, living in the same town as my parents. He was younger than me, but was keen to meet me. That was not a problem for me, meet sooner rather than later to see if there would be a spark between us, and as he was local then it would be easy to arrange. We could meet before or after I went to see Mother.

We arranged to meet in a traditional old fashioned teashop in his own town, and meet we did over a good old cuppa. First impressions, he seemed very pleasant, very attentive, reasonably good-looking, but probably a bit overweight for a man of his stature (but that had never really been an issue for me, a man with a little extra poundage), towering a couple of inches over me at about five six. He worked part-time now, a clerical worker, due to having some difficulties with his back, but was strongly involved in Trade Union work at his job, and was a local councillor. A political animal which I am not, but as long as it is not thrust down my throat I don't mind. He knew I was a care worker, and did offer to see about me joining a union, but kindly, no thank you.

It also turned out that his daughter was training to work in the care industry, and he wondered if it would be possible that I could help with parts of her course. Not a problem again. It had been a pleasant chat over a cuppa, and we were going to see each other again, so it wouldn't be a problem to help his offspring.

This was the first of several meetings over the next few days; he was a gentleman and would change his working hours to accommodate mine, and my visits to Mum and Dad. These dates would usually be for lunch in and around the town he lived. He was diabetic, but controlled it just by diet, so food was a thing of routine for him, regular intake at regular times, but fitting in seeing each other never created problems in his control of it.

It was becoming more and more obvious that he was falling for me big time, and couldn't see enough of me. He did introduce me to his daughter, and I did help her do a part of her study on dementia. She was very nice and I was only too pleased to help her in her job progression. Bob would also help when he could, dropping her off on her thirty-minute care calls when he could, and she needed his help. He couldn't do enough for her or me.

He had a lovely car, a motor he was really proud of, very comfortable to help his back, but also having heated seats that, it being winter, he would always have on, again to ease the discomfort from that lumbar problem. It would have been bearable if he didn't have them on their highest setting, which unfortunately with his diabetes, then meant that he would omit a strong ketotic body odour – not very pleasant while we were driving, especially as the windows would stay shut. It was a very distinctive smell. Whether he noticed it or not I don't know, but when he sweated, I knew all about it.

He was so proud of me, of being with me, taking me for lunch, dinner, wherever, and would parade me down the High Street on his arm, very old fashioned, showing me off to his friends and acquaintances. Because of his politics and being a councillor, he knew everyone. He lived in a flat above one of the shops in the middle of town, so would only have to walk out of the place to bump into someone he knew. It was nice for me to be put on such a pedestal, but worrying he was so smitten with me so quickly, and certainly his feelings for me were more at that time than I could reciprocate. We did exchange kisses, the odd peck on the cheek from him in front of these people just to show them I was his, but at this stage romance had gone no further.

It was February, and it was Valentine's Day. He wanted to take me out for a special dinner, picking me up and treating me like a real lady. A candlelit meal in a local restaurant, it was nice. A lovely steak, and as the evening was drawing to a conclusion, he presented me with a Valentine's present, a lovely make-up compact. I examined it in my hand, admiring its sleek lines, but turning it up, found the words, 'Gill, love Bob X' engraved on it.

It was too much. I was very grateful, and kissed him in thanks, before we went outside and he took me home in his car. Heater full on again, that smell, it was becoming too much for me.

He dropped me off at my house, kissing me and telling me how much he loved me, before reversing the car and returning to his flat. I stood outside my home in the cold air. What a lovely kind man he was, and he was falling for me hook, line, and sinker.

This may sound like we had been seeing each other for some time now. It was only a fortnight, our 'romance', but we had crammed a lot into that short time. I wished I could say that I had the same feelings for him as him me, but I didn't, and found it harder and harder to return his affections. On top of that, I was really starting to hate that car, the heater, and that horrible body odour.

It was only fair to tell him where I was, to be upfront that I didn't have any feelings towards him other than friendship, before his feelings would get hurt. I didn't want that as he was such a gentleman.

Tomorrow I would ring him. I did, and was totally upfront on how I felt, telling him what a lovely man he was, thank you for the beautiful present, and I that really appreciated his attention. I told him I knew he was really smitten with me, but I didn't have the same feelings, so would love to be his friend, help his daughter if I could, but there would never be any more than that. It was a shame, but I hoped he would find Mrs Right soon as he was so nice. His reaction, a bit like a scolded puppy, taken aback, "OH, OH," but thanking me for my honesty, disappointment, and wishing me well in my search.

I didn't want to hurt him, but could see him thinking wedding bells. He would do anything for me, but was just not my type. Such quick feelings in such a short time, I really did hope that he would find his match, and I do still have the compact.

Time to move on in my mission, to find that right fish, wherever the bloody thing may be hiding.

Artie Dace was the next online, and it took him only a little nibble at my bait to want to see me, meet up for a coffee. We started online, but he was keen and it was the following day that he wanted to see me, again in Newport. This Newport thing was becoming a habit, but was very convenient for me to go and see Mum and Dad while I was there. By this time, I had also got to the stage where I thought, *See 'em quick and then continue, or cross them off quick and move on.* My life clock was ticking.

So another coffee shop in a local town – they would all be knowing me soon – and a midday rendezvous. I got there early, parked my car up and had a quick wander around the shops first before going in, buying myself a coffee and then finding a table in a quiet corner where we could chat.

I waited patiently for his arrival, and bang on the appointed minute, he pulled up outside the coffee shop on his bicycle, dismounted and chained it to something outside the window. This looked promising! We could date on a bicycle made for two, except it wasn't, so looks like I would get the handlebar to sit on. Doesn't that bring back memories of Butch Cassidy and the Sundance Kid? Don't jump the gun, Gill.

He entered the coffee shop, removing the clips from his trousers and tucking them in his pocket. There he stood in the doorway, smart trousers, shirt and tie, but the trousers belted halfway up his midriff. To finish the outfit, a V-neck sweater. I could recognise his face from his profile, so I waved at him and said hello.

What the photo hadn't shown was a rather portly gentleman, and rather on the short side. Never mind, we all carry a pound or ten extra, and I was no exception. He walked over to my table, bent down and pecked me on my cheek. *A little forward,* I thought to myself. *We'll be bonking under the table in five minutes at this rate!*

But I suppose it fitted with the image, the real image of what was standing in front of me – a real blast from the past, well, even before my time, and a bit. The bicycle clips, a twenties-style hairdo, cut straight and even, side parting and gelled down with... Brylcream? Could I smell BRUT as well?

He took a seat and ordered a coffee himself, and we introduced ourselves properly, and got onto talking about ourselves more. He placed his mobile phone down on the table in front of him. *How old was that?* I thought. *Must have been made the year after they went cordless.*

He came across as a very nice man – intelligent, interesting, informative. He told me that he enjoyed ballroom dancing, and how good he was at it. We had a long chat about that, a subject I knew very little about, not quite the boogying that was more my style. We should give it a go sometime, he suggested, a quickstep if ever I saw one. He had stopped at the moment, but it was something we could try together. Other than that, he liked his garden, grew tomatoes, and lots of flowers. He worked as a kitchen hand in a local pub on the minimum wage, doing the washing up and general clearing up. He had wanted to retire but every time he talked of cutting his hours, they would ring up and say they needed him to come in as they were short-staffed. An inkling crossed my mind that he was a bit naïve, not so savvy as first impressions gave me.

Our coffee cups were getting low, and with that, as our last sips departed down our throats, it was time to end our first meeting. We got up to leave, and he invited me around to his house for Sunday dinner. *Why not?* I thought. It was early summer, and it would be nice to see him in home surrounds, see the garden he talked about and find out more about him. Yes, I would love to come. He told me he lived just down the road, gave me his address which I entered in Notes on my phone (don't think his would have that capacity, even with the cord attached), and with that he put on his bicycle clips and went home. Me, I went off to see Mum and Dad.

An interesting first meeting, Artie seemed very pleasant, and I would look forward to finding out more about him when Sunday came around.

I thought I would dress up nice for our dinner, a nice skirt and blouse, and of course my make-up. I would more than do. *Ravishing,* I thought to myself, and with that, set off a little early to see Mum and Dad first. Dad teased me about who the latest on my conveyor belt was, but always having my best intentions at heart, and knowing I wanted to find someone to love and be as happy as he and Mum were, he wished me good luck as I left them, off to dinner.

My sat nav took me to his house. I parked and stepped out of the car, standing in front of a very smart, medium-sized detached house in a nice-looking area. Impressed? Yes I was. I walked down the path to the front door, about to knock, but Artie had anticipated my arrival and opened the door to greet me, and usher me in.

Through a small hall and into the front room, he welcomed me into his home. It was a large room, but there were ornaments everywhere, all shapes and sizes; this must be a nightmare to dust (why is that the first thought of us ladies?). The dining room came off this room, with a separate kitchen behind it.

He offered me a chair, and when sat down presented me with a glass of wine, which on tasting was rather good. Dinner wouldn't take long, all was in hand, he said, so we could chat for a while before he served it all up.

He was a difficult man to gauge, was Artie. On our first meeting we had discussed interesting things which gave a thought of a little sophistication about him, but now he came across as of average intelligence, and his job he told me about in the pub, wouldn't have struck one as him being a high flyer. He also spoke of being a Trade Union rep. Yes, another one (I must remember to wave the red flag whenever out in this town), yet his job suggested probably not. He was washing up in a pub kitchen. Was he playing me, or just very vulnerable?

Enjoy the wine, Gill, and let's see where we go. I looked around the room at all those ornaments – little ones, big ones, of all types and shapes. He told me he had looked after his mum until she died, and so then had all her ornaments. Then he looked after his brother until he sadly passed away, and had all his, then became carer to his father and then inherited all his. They were everywhere, I was surprised I didn't have a gnome sitting next to me on the settee, there were so many of them, and they craved for space. I suggested perhaps he could divide them into four, and have a different display with the changing of the seasons. No, he must do what he wanted. I didn't want to interfere, but again thought, *Wouldn't want to be dusting this lot too regularly*. He seemed very set in his ways and if this was the way he liked it, that was his decision.

He left me to drink my wine as he retired to the kitchen to continue with his preparation of dinner. Through an opened door, I could see a pressure cooker and a frying pan on the go; I wondered what treat I was about to experience.

He led me into the dining room at sat me down at the table – I was about to find out. It was my favourite; how did he know? Overcooked cabbage and potatoes from the pressure cooker, minute steak cooked for fifteen minutes, fried hash browns, and onion rings, all served with the most wonderful red wine. My favourite, as I said. I love red wine.

We continued to chat over this delicious meal, my taste buds being assaulted by this culinary delight, and the red wine which really was out of this world.

I enquired whether he was renting this property. I hope this doesn't sound too mercenary, but we may as well get the facts sorted straight off. He had bought the house. Wow, that was good, I said, but wondered how he managed that on such a manual, low-skilled job. He told me his father had owned his house and had told Artie never to get a mortgage on a house, but to take out a loan, as he said that with a mortgage the bank could repossess, a loan they could not. Whether that is right or not I wasn't sure, but this man had done incredibly well to buy a really nice house which was his and his alone. His brothers, he had two, had not known this, and he had bought it when he was looking after his parents. When they had died, his brothers said that the house must be sold and the proceeds divided out equally, but he said no, and much to their surprise proved the house was his. His older brother had died, and his younger one didn't need the money anyway as he had built up his own business, owned a factory, and so was rich in his own right, and didn't need the money. Yes, it was his – all his.

So here I was having dinner with a man of means, a man of property, a nice chap who had never been married, had probably missed out on a lot of life as he had looked after his family in illness. But he did now want to go out more, and although it was only our second 'date', and it was early summer, he wondered if I would like to accompany him to a function that his brother organised for the whole family every year, a trip to the theatre in Birmingham in three months' time. At this rate we should be married before Christmas! There would be a meal, wine, and a show – they were going to see 'Wicked' this year. He told me he had never taken a lady before, but would be honoured if I would accompany him.

I told him I would love to come, noting it down in my diary for the future. He said he was going to pay for the tickets and the meal, so I said it was only fair that I should get a hotel room for them, a twin-bedded room, and that I would prefer to drive. No problem, that was all sorted. Something to look forward to, and he certainly seemed pleased that I had agreed to go.

Back to dinner. The delights of the first course put away, he then served up apple pie and cream, which we ate and then retired out into the garden and sat together on one of those swinging chairs, enjoying the warm afternoon sunshine.

He started to chat about a lady he had seen before me. She sounded a bit of a con artist, making Artie buy her a mobile phone, and give her money in exchange for a kiss and a cuddle, and more if he obliged with the cash, she would sleep with him. Now I knew he was vulnerable, even suggesting to him that he was a little naïve, but he just asked me what naïve was!

It had been a delightful, and interesting afternoon, even if the dinner hadn't quite titillated my taste buds (the wine made up for it). It was time to depart, and as he walked me back to my car he put his hand in mine, turned me and gave me a big kiss on the lips. I think this guy has really fallen for me as well. I must read the Trade Union manual about what it says about dating Gill Finn.

I went away in pensive mood; a nice bloke but vulnerable, naïve, not worldly, but had property and would be devoted to me. But he was falling for me too quickly, and was probably inexperienced in women and attaining all their desired pleasures. Much to think about. A long work shift was coming up so I wouldn't be seeing Artie for a few days. I did also wonder, as he seemed such a technophobe, how he had managed to arrive with his profile online on one of these dating sites. Maybe, probably, his sister had set him up.

I went over to see Dad a few days later, and realising I was not getting as close to Artie as he would have wished, nor seeing a long-term loving relationship developing between us at the moment, I was wondering how I could tell him that I didn't want to continue seeing him anymore. I told Dad about him, whose opinion was that with a nice house here in the village, a man of property and handy to visit him and Mum, I could do worse. It seemed a good match, as without being too blunt, time was slipping by. Yes, a very good match.

We will meet the man of my dreams a little later on, but at this stage in my dating career, I had already met him. Artie came nowhere near him, but to be honest in my mind no-one was going to be him or surpass him. Yet we were apart, and with no future as it seemed of re-establishing a relationship, I was in clear waters, and did need to find another fish. Could Artie grow into this role? Should I give him a chance? That was a question I honestly couldn't answer at this moment in time.

We continued seeing each other on a regular basis, but I knew in my heart of hearts that he wasn't the one. I would be fishing again soon, but had to let him down gently. I decreed that I would tell him, but would add that I would like to stay friends. But he was getting more and more possessive of me, wanted to spend more and more time with me, thought he loved me and that we were the perfect match. Again, he had fallen for me hook, line, and sinker. Why am I so desirable, so gorgeous, but not yet to the man I want to be with? I decided that before I told him about wanting just to be friends, I would at least try ballroom dancing with him, as he said he was good at it, and it may give him more confidence to try and sweep me off my feet.

I did have a heart to heart with him though, or should that be an Art to Art! I felt even at this stage in our relationship, that I could have taken him for every penny he had if I had wanted. If I had asked, he would have produced. But I never would do that to anyone, that just is not me, so I explained to him that he shouldn't buy anyone anything. He was very vulnerable and knew nothing about fishing in these deep waters, where there are sharks out to take you for all they could. He must be careful. I think I had got through to him, I really hope he understood, and that I would appreciate his company without being lauded with gifts, and though I didn't say it, certainly not a wedding ring.

Onto dancing; Artie said he had done it for some years, and was good at it but had given it up, spending time on his ailing close family, and when at the club he used to go to, his female partner had hurt her leg and could dance no more. She had given it up, and with circumstances at home, he did so as well.

He decided that our first venture would be at one of those tea dance type things. We shuffled round the floor, progressing in the same direction as everyone else, and everyone seemed to know Artie, also welcoming me with a friendly hello. I could see that he knew how to dance, but I didn't know how good he was other than the fact that my toes were all still intact, uncrushed by false manoeuvres as we twirled (well, that would be an exaggeration), around the dance floor. The shuffle turned into a few steps, proper steps as he showed me a few basic moves, and it was here that I did create a bit of chaos, bumping into people as I tried to conquer what he was trying to teach me. The first experience over, he dropped me off at home, and to go with the image he gave with his dress and hair style, it had to be in a good old Moggie Minor saloon.

No bruises, trampled toes, I had got away with it.

He rang me, suggesting that if I had enjoyed it we could go along to a couple that taught dance – a free lesson to see if I wanted to dance or not. I would give it a go, so we booked ourselves into a dance lesson at a local sports centre. We arrived, and were shown a few basic moves, how to address each other, which of course Artie knew already, how to move as one, how to dance. I was given a bit of individual tuition, and then joined up with Artie, but whether it was him or me, or both of us, we kept on going wrong, couldn't keep a straight line.

Well actually I was doing okay, but our instructor kept on shouting at Artie, "You're doing it wrong! Straighten up, you're wrong again."

It would seem that he was not as good as he thought he was. It all was turning into a bit of a disaster, and I was feeling more and more awkward as he made more and more mistakes. I didn't have to be brain of Britain to know that this wasn't for me, but at least I had tried, had given us a chance of having a go at something together, something that if it worked we could have built on and pushed our relationship forward.

Dancing, I will stick to the twist, and shake my hips; if I move my feet too much it could all end in disaster on the floor.

It was decision time, make or break. To me, without seeming arrogant, I had seen the world. But Artie seemed unsure of the way of the world – naïve, vulnerable, almost lacking intelligence if that wasn't being too unkind. There was almost the perception of some learning disability. I wasn't sure, but whether there was or was not, he wasn't the one for my long-term plans.

It was heart to heart time, so I told him to his face that he wasn't Mr Right, the partner for life I was looking for. I would like just to be friends and nothing more. He was very disappointed; he had really fallen for me, and thought I was his match for life. He was in love with me.

I had promised to go on the theatre trip with him, and said I would still do this. He asked if I would pretend to be his girlfriend in front of his family at their do. I didn't want to upset him so agreed we would go just as we had planned all those weeks ago.

Over the next couple of weeks, it seemed as if he was slow to cotton on, almost as if we hadn't had that conversation, frequently texting me, and if I didn't answer then ringing me up. Yes, he was hooked on me, didn't seem to get the message, made excuses for calling – it was getting a little awkward. But I said I would go to the theatre, and I would do that for him. I did feel a little sorry for him, his caring for his family, his sheltered life, and being used as slave labour.

The day arrived. I drove over to his, and he drove us into Birmingham to find our hotel. I had showered and everything before I got to his, so that life in the hotel room would not get too complicated. The hotel was in China Town, so handy for our evening, no need for taxis, we could walk. I hadn't taken much luggage, just a nice dress and shoes, pyjamas, and my wash things.

I wanted to go shopping in China town, so Artie tagged along behind me, carrying my shopping for me back to our room. Then time to change, trying to squeeze into my dress in the tiny bathroom, while he changed in the bedroom. Time to go, and he did look very dashing in his dinner jacket. As we arrived at the theatre and went up to the private room we were dining in, we looked quite the couple.

We were a group of about eighteen, adults bar a couple of late teenagers. I had only met his sister from all of this group before, but Artie proudly introduced me to all the guests. His sister whispered how pleased she was to see Artie and I together, but I had to tell her the truth, we were acting a lie for his sake. She was disappointed that he hadn't found his lady after all. I suspect it was her who had set him up on the dating site in the first place, and she was lovely lady, working in the same line as me.

I told her he was too set in his ways, was not the one for me, and I could have fleeced him for anything I wanted. But, I wanted him to be happy in the future, though it wouldn't be with me.

We prepared for our pre-ordered meal off an à la carte menu, though as ever I couldn't remember what I had ordered.

Artie was the perfect gentleman, very attentive, introducing me to all his family and armed with photos of these guests he had taken the previous year, which he showed everyone. He gave me a print of him in his attire from then as well.

Champagne and wine flowed as we sat down and enjoyed a lovely meal, lots of conversation, joking and laughing, only his sister knowing our true relationship.

Then it was time for the show, Wicked, which I wouldn't say I enjoyed totally, but at least Artie had company. Half-time drinks back in our private room and then the second half, the show ending, and all departing their separate ways.

We went back to the hotel, my promise complete. I

said that I was going to go out to a nearby casino for a bit of sport before retiring, so changed back into my travelling clothes. I left him in the room, and was gone.

An hour, hour and a half of blackjack, during which I didn't gain, but then I didn't lose, but I enjoyed it, before returning to the hotel and our small room to find Artie tucked up and snoring away.

I had left my clothes folded on the bathroom windowsill, so dressing wouldn't cause any complications. Breakfast and home, back to his to pick up my car and go.

That was it. A couple of texts, then phone calls. "Your friend Artie here. How are you?"

I told him I was seeing an old flame, which was true, and hoped he would find someone himself.

He was very nice, but not for me. I fancy he probably was a virgin, in his sheltered life. I genuinely did hope he would find someone to share his life with, fingers crossed for him.

*

"Hi Gill. This is Henry Sturgeon. I liked the look of you in your picture."

Yes, I'm fishing again, and this one could be caviar! Back online, this is my latest catch. Well, at last it seems to be taking the bait hard, with more than a few nibbles. This one, Henry, a nice-looking bloke on his profile, young-looking but with a few wrinkles, and having his own business. There was no point wasting any time on this one, he had taken the bait, so play him and net him quick.

We arranged to meet for coffee, my normal intro,

to see if there was any possible future in seeing each other more. A striking man to see when he pitched into the coffee shop in town at the appointed time for our assignation. Very well dressed, smart, fit-looking, I liked the look of this one.

He lived the other side of Shrewsbury from me; actually we were quite a few miles apart, but town was about central for us to meet up. A very well-spoken man, he told me about the big house that he owned in South Shropshire, and that he largely worked from home. He was in a partnership with a friend and colleague, undertaking very important work in the aero-industry, which involved travelling a lot around the country to rectify and amend any manuals essential in the safety and maintenance of the flight industry. Once in the RAF, he knew his subject well, an expert, and if you will excuse the pun, very much a high flyer.

He was a busy man so an hour over coffee then he was back to his business, but did invite me out to lunch, the invitation of which I was only too pleased to accept. We didn't hang about and met up a couple of days later, the advantage of him working from home being that it was easy to pop out for a couple of hours during the day, though he could get called away at any moment, as he or his colleague had to be available all the time.

He filled me in with more details of his life. Married but estranged from his wife, a Swedish lady who now lived in Switzerland, and sadly had mental problems. He didn't foresee any way that their lives would be coming back together again. He essentially lived the life of a bachelor. Except of course he was going online, looking for a lady.

What were his motives? I have to admit I was very interested in him, a man of property and of money. What a gold digger I may seem, but there is no harm in looking for a secure future.

Things were moving fast and after the lunch, he invited me to his house, to see where he lived, and find out about his lifestyle. The journey from me to him, well over an hour, but as I found his residence and drew up outside, parking my humble car next to a very smart-looking Audi, I could only be impressed by the look of this large building before my eyes. I could cope with all this! He showed me in and after a coffee, gave me a tour of his property. Four large bedrooms, large fitted kitchen, dining room, lounge, ensuites all over the place, and the furniture was just out of this world. And of course there was the hub of his business, a well organised and well fitted office with all the essential technological mod cons. Was I impressed? Yes I was.

But he was thinking of moving further south, better positioned for his job, and was looking at houses right now. He had another viewing the next day of a house he had very nearly completed the purchase of, and asked me if I would like to accompany him. Yes, please. I wasn't working and would only be too pleased to offer my company while he travelled down, and could offer my advice, a woman's touch, on what to do in this house when he had completed. We settled down, watching telly for the evening, and did indulge in our first petting and kissing session. It wasn't a very good program!

I was being good, and was sticking to my two-week rule, so after a while, it was time to return home after a long snog on his doorstep, taking in the smell of what seemed very expensive aftershave. He would pick me up in the morning, and we would drive down, have a look at the house and then have something to eat. It would be a nice day out, and I was looking forward to it.

I as waiting for him eagerly when he pulled up outside in the big Audi. He told me it was a bargain that was too good to resist so he had bought it for a snip at fifty-five thousand. Did I hear that right? Yes I did, this guy really has got money! *Well*, I thought as I sat back in the passenger seat and we cruised down south towards the Home Counties, *I could certainly cope with this kind of luxury, right up my street.*

We arrived at a large four-bedroomed townhouse, fairly modern with a large conservatory. He opened the front door, obviously it was already his; beautiful house, solid oak floors, smart fitted kitchen, and four large bedrooms. I was very impressed. Having shown me around room to room, we came back to the kitchen. He turned to me and said, "Do you fancy living here then?"

Did I hear that right? Was he asking me to live here? I hadn't known him many minutes and here we are in, for me, foreign territory. That was quick! All I could do at this stage was to say what a lovely house it would be to live in, but my job was in Shropshire and I couldn't risk giving up everything yet to move to a strange area, and leave my parents who needed my help.

Was I giving up a chance in a lifetime? Was I mad? But there were too many uncertainties to ponder, the fact he was still married was one issue. But was I turning down what I was looking for? This guy, Henry, could be Mr Right and he certainly was a big fish by all accounts. Don't rush, Gill. Let's just see how the water flows for a bit.

Back to Shropshire in the Audi, watching the road whiz past, sitting in luxury, and he wasn't offended, and continued to chat about himself and his plans for the house.

We agreed we would meet up again in a few days when my next lot of shifts were done, and with a long kiss in the front of the car, adieu, and he was gone.

I was looking forward to our next date. I was going to drive over, and as I had passed the two-week rule with him, I knew I was going to spend the night there so I could have a glass of wine or three. There were no pyjamas in my bag either. After trying for a long time to get over the 'one that got away', I had decided I was going to have fun, and fun included... well, you know.

I arrived at his house and knocked on the front door. He shouted for me to come in and find him in the front room. There he was on the settee, watching sport on the telly. And the settee was all there was there! He told me that things were moving fast with the other house and that all the furniture had now gone other than what I could see. Sadly, for him, the beautiful kitchen centre he had made out of very expensive timber was fixed and couldn't go with him when he moved.

The settee was a sofa bed. "That's not very romantic," I said. "What about my back?"

He left me there while he went to get a take away, and then we settled down on the settee with our fish and chips, and a bottle of red wine. Not the perfect combination, but it was fun, and having finished eating, we cuddled up together, before getting down to some serious kissing and cuddling.

We both knew what was going to happen tonight so while he opened out the bed and found the duvet, I went to the bathroom to attire myself with the minimalistic negligee I had brought with me. Back in the living room I slipped under the duvet, waiting for him to join me. No messing, he undressed in front of me to show that body without a bit of spare fat on it, and lay down beside me. I wanted him, and he wanted me, so it didn't take long before our kissing got more frenetic and our embraces more passionate, pulling each other towards ourselves, and then releasing ourselves so that our hands could explore each other further. That expensive aftershave wafted over me gain, filling my lungs with the scent of a man – sensual, arousing!

There waiting for me without a lot of persuasion stood his manhood, growing as I coaxed it gently up and down, He, too, caressing, stroking my breasts, and then feeling for that ripening blossom between my legs. He was upon me and then inside me, gently thrusting in and out, adding all the time to my arousal, his loins working in unison with mine, until I felt that whoosh as he came inside me, and then me following him, as my muscles gripped him inside me. Satisfied? Yes I was, yes we both were as we untwined and lay back to capture our breaths.

He was good, not that good but I needed him

now, and wanted sex. If I had continued my scoring, a good six, not a seven, but we satisfied a need in each other and that was good. A long kiss and sleep overtook us.

We continued seeing each other over the coming weeks, it depending on where his work took him, whether he could drop everything for a couple of hours for us to meet up for lunch, for a drink, and yes, the occasional bonk when we had the opportunity.

His final move was dependent on when the I.T. equipment could be installed in his new house, but even then he would still be around and wanted to see me more and more. He had heard his wife was heading back to Scandinavia, and that would effectively be it, though he was reluctant on the matter of divorce, not wanting to lose his fortune.

We started to walk together more and more, though it would generally be a place of interest, historical site, garden, or suchlike. Wonderful walks around the meres at Ellesmere, enjoying the evening sun before dining somewhere.

One day he took me around the Cosford Air Museum, of interest to him with his job, and because of that far more interesting for me as he could explain the exhibits better, making it more meaningful. That was a long day, especially as my foot attire wasn't quite what was required; nice fashion shoes but not for walking in all day. Did my feet blister; I now have a proper pair of walking shoes. Lesson learnt? Despite the blisters though, I did enjoy the day very much, in fact I enjoyed all his company a lot.

He would show me more of what he did at work,

what he prepared for others to work from. So much in the industry depended on him to get it right. He impressed me with his fashion dressing, and his manicured nails, something I hadn't seen with any other men I had been with. Our occasional nights of casual sex continued and I enjoyed them. He did for his age perform quite well, though not in the league of 'the friend with benefits' (remember him?), Will, or the 'one that got away', but I was getting over him, and with Henry I was having fun, seeing a side of life I hadn't experienced before and beginning to feel like my old self again.

For over three months we saw each other on this basis – company, sex, walks, generally enjoying each other's company, and I knew he wanted me.

But despite the circumstances he had described to me with his wife, I did wonder what my future in his life would be. Was he really Mr Right, really the man I wanted? Yes, if he wasn't married, this would be wonderful, but it was complicated. We lived the life of two free people getting together, BUT one of us wasn't free.

Then he heard that his wife had decided to come to the UK to live, or that was her plan. Henry couldn't see a problem in that, he so wanted to be with me. They would still have separate lives. We could still be together.

He could set me up in a cottage of my own, and he could then pop in when he wanted. Bonk, bonk. That's unfair, we would have enjoyed sex but he was more devoted than just that, and would have wined and dined me, spoilt me.

I would have been his mistress, hadn't been that before, and really that wasn't what I wanted. He wanted me, a good screw when he wanted, me, his concubine. I liked the fast car, the perfect gentleman, the change of lifestyle. Yes, I did look forward to seeing him whenever I could.

But...

But, did I love him? Was he really Mr Right? I had to be honest and say no. A funny thing, he was always smart, and whether because of that or not I don't know, but whenever I was with him, I always wore matching underwear. Even if it were my granny drawers and bra, they would always match.

Sadly, I was having to say no. I could have imagined myself here, but it was not the way I saw my life. He wanted me, really wanted me, again hook, line, and sinker, but no, the life wasn't for me. He accepted my decision, disappointed, but I guess he would have had many affairs before me, let's face it – he was married and going on internet dating sites, and probably would have many more in the future.

We had had many good times in that short period, but time to say goodbye and we parted as friends thinking of what could have been.

It was only afterwards that I thought to myself I could have had it all, what had I turned down? But would I have got bored waiting for him? What sort of a life would I have had waiting? Would I have lost my friends, having to drop dates with them at short notice because he would say he would be arriving expectantly? I made the right decision, I know I did.

*

Three men, all desperate for me. The best I can say was that things were looking up, at least I knew I was desirable, even if Mr Right had not arrived online yet. Yes, all three had gone hook, line, and sinker for me. That's a compliment for me.

Patience is a virtue when you are fishing. I have had some serious bites, but I will wait a bit longer for the big one, the one I really want, he must be out there somewhere. The bait is good. Patience, Gill, patience.

*

It would be strange that all three of these men, dismissed from my net and largely forgotten about other than for the experience, would surface again quite expectantly. In their own way, they were taken with me, and very quickly, but each in turn didn't offer me the whole deal I was looking for, especially Bob and Artie, who were somewhat boring and had very sheltered lives. Henry was different, a gentleman, but married.

It would be some months before each in turn would try to make contact again, which I suppose disappointingly for them, meant that they hadn't found Mrs Right either. First Artie, ringing me because he thought I had tried to contact him, wishful thinking. Then Bob, did I fancy going out again? No thank you, my circumstances have changed. Then completely out of the blue, some three years later, and strangely enough when I was just thinking of him, but for other reasons, a text from Henry. How was I and what was I doing? Was he going to try and get hooked again, remembered me as the good screw he thought I was? Again, I texted him back as to my present circumstances, and asked how he was doing. I never heard back from him.

Yes, all three of them, hook, line, and sinker in falling for me.

With them, I must move on, I have a fish to catch.

The Sting Ray

My life was changing, and had gone through a bad spell. I was enjoying my work, but was starting to get the odd twinge in my back. I was looking for at least a little stability in my life, a base to build my life from, so I had spent some weeks looking around properties in Telford, to find that little somewhere I could call my own, a nest to go home to. After some weeks of searching, I had at last found the place I wanted to buy, and had got myself a mortgage, so things were looking on the up. I was close to my family, both parents, son, and grandchildren, so was giving myself the foundations of a life I had craved for since leaving the area all those years ago to go to Australia. I was going to enjoy watching my family grow, and be there to help Mum and Dad when needed.

A date was settled for completion on the house, and I was ready to move.

But that twinge was getting worse, and I was finding some of my duties more and more onerous. The girls were helping me out by mopping floors for me, but lifting was becoming more difficult. Yes, life was becoming painful. It was one evening about ten days before I was due to move that during the course of work, the pain became unbearable. I finished my shift in agony, and after struggling to get in the car, I set off homewards. It was too much, I had to stop and call Shrop Doc who directed me towards the orthopaedic department of the hospital. I was seen and told to go home and get on my back, and the only reason to get up was to go for a pee. I was prescribed suitable painkillers, and obeying instructions, was flat on my back for the duration.

But I was moving house. Bless my son who did everything for me, sorting my bed out in my new home, to which I retreated and stayed, still on my back while my trapped nerve sorted itself out over several weeks. Morale was low, I didn't know where anything was as my dear son had just moved my goods in and put them somewhere that he could find a space. I wasn't in a position to do much about it until I was able to start moving about, and then I had to make sure I didn't overdo it, or lift anything that might jeopardise my recovery. It was a disappointing time, the start to my new life, but I had to grin and bear it.

And of course, what about dating? What about my fishing, my quest for the person to spend the rest of my life with? Which at this stage would have been in bed, on my back, and not having a lot of fun. There are some things you can do on your back, but fishing isn't one of them.

My computer was by my side, when isn't it? But dating was off limits, Mr Right would have to take a rain check until I was back on my feet.

It was many weeks before this happened; luckily I

had enough money to survive, but life was very much on hold. At last I was deemed fit enough to go back to work, and with that my hunger for love was rekindled, it was time to look on the net again, see who was out there wanting to take a bite.

I cast myself on the waters again, available, keen and willing, and I wanted some fun. I couldn't take any more lying down.

It was not long before I was chatting again, and one particular bite was more than interesting. Ray, his name, sounded a nice genuine guy, looking for love, happily talking about his family, his daughter especially, and also what he did for a living.

Like me he worked nights, doing twelve-hour shifts in the gambling industry, sitting in front of three computers, following all the sports going on at that time, accepting bets, and moving higher risk gambles onto bigger operators.

With our hours so similar, it gave us the opportunity to chat regularly, which over a two- to three-week period we did. This man at the end of a line, he and I were getting very friendly so it seemed a natural progression for us to swop mobile numbers to open different lines of communication. I had, as you have seen before, used WhatsApp, and so it was this that we progressed onto, enabling us to chat quickly, and be able to exchange photos.

It was very early one summer's morning that we tried to make contact, coming to the end of one of his shifts, and me up early with the birds. Yes, he had managed to reach me, we were in a position to start exchanging messages, so a hello from me and a hiya from him and we were away.

Straight away he sent me a picture of a teddy with a heart. Ah, how sweet, and I in turn asked if I could have a photo which I could put on my contacts list. We talked about who were our phone providers, different but not a problem, but I did get a lot of free minutes etc. on my contract so this social media chatting wasn't going to cost me anything, so we could talk lots.

Out of the blue, the compliments started flying from Ray. "You're gorgeous," he said, commenting on my photo on the chat line. I said I wasn't but thanked him for the compliment, on a photo taken a couple of weeks before.

He persisted, saying he like older women, I was gorgeous and I shouldn't argue with him, and the kisses were being added. I was flattered, accepting his comments, adding that I liked dressing up, but never got the chance.

This was looking promising, I thought to myself, so told him that I would come off the chat sites in a few days. I just needed to thank the other people I had been chatting to, especially a disabled gentleman, I didn't want to appear rude to them. To my surprise, he said he would remove his profile straight away, adding that I needn't do mine as he trusted me, he liked my femininity and more kisses. Our relationship was now six minutes old. Nothing like a whirlwind relationship! Already past twenty kisses, this was real snogging.

He was gone from Badoo, he was mine. Boy was I flattered – wow. I added his picture to my contact list, him protesting that he was 'not that special, Hun xx!' I had never had a chap come off as soon as we had started chatting, he was the first. We had chatted for what seemed most of the night, though it wasn't and it was nearing home time. It was getting cold in my work place.

He agreed that the night had flown, he had enjoyed chatting, acted on impulse and had a good feeling about me.

Impulsive, nice. Romantic.

Yes, he agreed, he was an old fashioned romantic, loved a lady to be a lady, hold doors open for her, holding hands, and giving compliments. More kisses.

We exchanged pleasantries about what time we left for work, how long it took to get there, and what car we both drove. We were nibbling to find when we could talk next as work was coming to an end. I was keen to speak to him again as soon as possible and said I would ring when I got home as he wouldn't go to bed straight away.

He told me to text him when I was awake; it took about twenty minutes for him to drive into work. Okay, yes, I would do that, and by now kisses were flying with every message, after all our romance was getting on for an hour now.

I had to finish my paperwork before I left, so wished him a safe journey home, and told him how much I had enjoyed our chat, and really looked forward to hearing from him later, followed by more online snogging.

He would text me before he went to sleep, returning my kisses.

I finished my paperwork, sent a quick text to say with my memory, I may ask all the same questions again to which he replied his memory wasn't so good either, and that we'd speak when he was tucked up in bed. I drove home with a big smile on my face. Is this it?

I got home and texted again, just tucking into breakfast before bed. I was getting a hot water bottle ready to which he replied he could be that. He told me he was in bed, and when I climbed in too, my bed that is, he joked we were in bed together so soon lol!

Daft bugger, but he sounded fun, had a sense of humour which I liked. I told him I thought we sounded as if we were quite suited and that I really looked forward to when we could meet up. Sleep well and dream of me, I suggested. He would, he said. He would see me in his dreams. I hoped he would be a gentleman when we met in his dreams, to which he replied he was always a gentleman. An exchange of kisses, smiley faces, and love-torn looks, and we were apart.

Me, I was very happy and soon ready for sleep. Night-night (though strictly day-day) – my lights went out.

By mid-afternoon I was awake and just texted him to say as much, would have a shower, catch up with Dr Who and looked forward to speaking soon. An hour later I texted again asking if he was awake yet. I was cooking my dinner, but really eager to speak to him again.

It was some twenty minutes later before I got a reply. Yes, he had slept well and just woken up.

Kisses.

Oh good, I liked his kisses, saying to get himself ready while I finished my program and dinner, and would phone later. He was not properly awake, said okay, and would speak later. He didn't usually eat before work as he could take sandwiches with him, or pasta which he could microwave here. I told him he needed more than that, I should be cooking for him, but to let me know when he was at work, when it would be convenient to speak.

He told me he was a Trekkie fan, used to hide behind the settee when he was younger watching Dr Who, sent me some kisses, asked if I could speak at work which I couldn't as it was against rules but could text, and was gone after I said I would ring in an hour.

No reply, I have to go to work now. I left a message for him to ring me. I texted that I was doing my hair, asking if he liked it long, adding that he must be working hard.

Two hours later, finally a reply. He loved long hair, loved to run his fingers through it, and give a little tug in the act of passionate love. I told him that long hair can be a bit annoying in the act of making love, gets in the way, but he replied he would hold it back for me.

Not enough hands, I said, but he chipped in that he was a man and would have hands everywhere.

Could he French plait, while making love? Yes, he could, piece of cake, but inquired that we were talking hair on my head. Hey, this is getting interesting – a polite gentleman, with other talents.

We contacted each other briefly over the next few

hours; he was busy and I had my jobs to do at work as well, but I hoped that later we could continue where we had left off the previous evening. At last he said he would be quieter in about fifteen minutes.

At one in the morning we restarted our conversation, touching on favourite foods. Him, Indian and Italian, which was good as I make a mean curry, but he did not share my love of seafood. I asked him where he lived and he told me he shared a house with one of his work colleagues who owned it, but at least it cut the bills. We exchanged a couple of photos of our families, then straight to the point I asked if it would be okay for me to come over to stay when we had seen each other. No problems as long as his colleague said it was okay, hadn't happened before but he would very much like that.

Back onto family snaps, then I'm back onto the subject of beds, my preference for high quality sheets, washed weekly, to which he agreed that there was nothing better than a clean bed. I went through my washing habits, ironing and other household chores, and being a mature woman, my habits wouldn't change. Not a problem to him, nothing would change him from the person he was and so he wouldn't want me to change for him.

We covered a lot about each other over the course of the next half hour or so, my household habits, family, what we liked to drink, and then the big question.

"When do you think we could meet?"

He checked through his work schedule and was free September 5th, ten days' time. Yes, me too, that's a date. He could come over for the day and book a hotel in Telford for the night. He checked online for possible places to stay, but didn't know the area well enough to know where to book so I said I would look for him. We got onto holiday destinations; he didn't like visiting the same place twice, but where would I like to go? He had always fancied Canada. We joked about dressing up on a cruise ship, him in uniform and medals, me, I love dressing up, and in stockings and suspenders.

He liked the idea of that, he should be so lucky.

I wasn't having much success with hotels – booked or too expensive. No, nothing. So I suggested he could stay in my spare room; if we didn't get on he could go home. I felt we were doing very well chatting and getting to know each other, and didn't think there could be any problem. Nice, he thought. We could go out for something to eat, get a bottle of wine and get a taxi back to mine, sounded good.

I thought we were doing really well, sounded compatible, and I couldn't wait to see him. I would love to meet up earlier if I could, I suggested, but he explained that he already had commitments in Scotland seeing an old forces mate before then so, sorry but he couldn't let him down, but couldn't wait to meet me too. He would find out about me staying over, hoped it would be okay because if we got on well on the 5th, no reigning in, he wanted to see as much of me as possible.

Good, me too, and I was free at the end of the month for a few days, so would be lovely to spend it with him if he could.

By four in the morning we were getting quite intimate, talking of cuddles, and him calling me his perfect woman. Sexy, personable – that's me!

Forward of me but I asked him when the last time he had made love to a woman. Three years, and how long for me? I told him of my friend with benefits, how it worked when we were both unattached, a couple of hours here and there. I hoped he wasn't upset, and hoped I wouldn't need one when we had met up. He was shocked, he said so, but I told him not to be. A girl has her needs, and I was nice and honest.

"At least you know I'm not a virgin," I said.

He was glad I had been honest and told him, and I assured him I would never have secrets if we were together. As for the bedroom, I would be gentle and help him. He told me he loved to kiss and cuddle and found it a big turn-on.

I had to ask about his teeth. I had to know. Due a check-up next month, he seemed perfect, and he washed his cock. "What? Oh my word," I said, shocked, but I made him smile.

We had work to do, but over the course of the next hour, texts, quick-fire questions, pants or briefs, left side of bed or right, stockings or tights, big pants or not, perfumes, aftershaves, Sunday roasts, so many little questions. He liked nylon, loved the feel of it on a lady's legs. On our questions went, finding out every intricate little detail about each other, and so many of the answers made us sound so compatible. In bed and out of it.

Our evening's work was drawing to an end, time for him to leave and me to finish off, do my paperwork and hand over.

He was home, me still finishing, but as he tucked himself up I sent him kisses, and hoped we would be cuddling soon.

I was really having good feelings about all this. The fifth couldn't come quick enough for me. We had found out so much about each other, seemed happy in each other's company, as much as you could on a phone, and sounded sexually compatible, all sounded good. And I could improve his diet for him as well if I could have him near to look after. I'm so excited! Lucky my phone is unlimited as we had just spent the best part of seven hours chatting on it. It was going to be worth it.

*

Day three of our romance, our relationship, was about to begin, though with our work patterns, our days were starting late in the afternoon. I had just arisen from my slumbers; Ray, I would guess had been up a little while and would be thinking about going to work again soon. I couldn't wait to chat to him again, so was soon busy texting.

He was already on his way to work, he told me, to which I was cross and replied that he should not be driving and texting. I would text him later, but he was teasing me and told me he could take pictures too. Stop, I told him, but he joked that if he stopped he would never get there. I meant texting and added that I had only just found him, didn't want to lose him already.

He told me he was already there, at work, and was pulling my leg. I told him I was texting all my chaps I had been chatting to and would be off the site tomorrow. He didn't mind whether I stayed on or not, my choice. I was pleased with the way we were going, and could always go back on if we didn't click, but I was confident we would.

I texted him later to tell him I was off to work, and he joked, no texting while I was driving, bless him. He told me he had a boiled egg and soldiers for his meal. I really needed to take him under my wing and feed him properly, I couldn't wait to be looking after him.

We resumed again a couple of hours later, and he told me he had a dilemma; his mate in Scotland had organised a reunion with some of his ex-mates, so that would delay his return to see me a couple of days, but that would take us to Sunday, when we would be able to spend more time together. He could cancel. I didn't want him to give up his other life, so Sunday would be fine, I had ironing and some painting to do. I couldn't lie that I was a bit disappointed, but he had to keep his contacts.

I told him I was ironing at work, and again joking, he said ironing and texting at same time was dangerous.

I finished that and we resumed, him being very romantic with something he texted me. Oh, how I loved it, felt looked after, cherished, and wanted to return his love, look after him. I had never had the texting repartee I was having with Ray. I asked him if he believed in love at first sight – we both did, and I thought we could have a great future together, enjoying life, travelling, love. He said that I was the first woman he had warm feelings for in a long while, and felt we were well matched. This could be love at first text!

We were back onto twenty questions; what sweeties did he like? Did he snore (he had sleep apnoea and did snore so slept with a mask on, so no kissing in the middle of the night unless I kissed him somewhere else), and then we were onto each other's beds. Well, not literally! I had a king-size, him a three-quarter sized bed, and he had asked his mate if I could stay, so he may have to invest in a bigger bed. If all worked out he should, would, look for his own place, so we could enjoy our privacy. TV in bedroom, would be good.

"Let's see how we get on first," I said, but felt confident all would be good. We would know in less than two weeks now and I couldn't wait.

Our conversation was interrupted by me having to change a colostomy bag, so romantic, and of course not mine, but that was work. Then back chatting, telling Ray it felt like he was my boyfriend already. He asked if I was his girlfriend. The little heart strings were fluttering in me.

He explained his work pattern to me; he was doing extra shifts at the moment as his work colleague was on holiday, then a break, then he would be away. He would have done fourteen nights running, then to Scotland.

I was worried our contact would break, that he would go off me, but he assured me all would be fine, he was smitten. We could reflect on where we were, and all seemed good.

We were well into the night again, three thirty, and

going strong. There would be the odd break in the conversation while I attended to the needs of my cares, then back on texting each other.

We were running out of questions about each other, but carried on. The colour of my eyes, he asked. Blue. Do I have good legs? Yes, and feet.

Perfect, he thought. I sounded ideal, but I told him I had had three kids and hated my body, couldn't wear a bikini because of that, though my boobs were awesome, 38D. I had put on weight when I had given up smoking, and they were the result. Yes, awesome, and now I liked decorating them in sexy undies.

He assured me I would feel ten feet tall on his arm, we were a perfect match and we would have the best life ever if I liked him. This was making me feel so happy, to have met someone to spend time with, who sounded so brilliantly compatible, and so romantic.

We went on to talk about education, him from the University of Life, then onto our choices of book to read, again sounding very similar in our tastes. He could read my Kindle when we were on holiday together, IF we had time for reading, when on our cruise! I told him he would love cruising – the sights, fantastic food, the casino, and the shows on board. We talked about gambling, casinos, playing poker and blackjack, which I enjoyed, then his knowledge of the dogs and gee gees, days out at the racing. We could go to the Melbourne Cup, that would be good.

We were dating apace here, planning our future, talking of improving our wardrobes for this life we were going to lead together. I was feeling that the rest of my life had started, I felt alive again, revitalised. He sounded so romantic, talked of showing me off, how proud he would to have me on his arm. He had sold himself to me, made me feel appreciated. I really wanted this man.

We chatted about what I would do while he was away – cinema, house work, and that damn X Factor was starting again. Then, he reminded us both that he would need directions to my house for his return journey, for our meeting, our date at last which I couldn't wait for. I forwarded him directions, Google Maps, etc.

He asked if he could shower when he arrived to freshen up, then we could start our first date, a clean beginning, and to start with there would just be him and me, no early introductions to family, just us to get to know each other, to fall in love (if I hadn't already).

Our shifts were drawing to a close. I had some chores to do, back to check that colostomy bag, yippee, and Ray was about to sign off and return home to bed. We had chatted most of the night, and felt really good about how we were going.

I texted him when he was home, tucked up in bed, hoping he would dream of me. He would, and I would blush if he told me what he dreamed of me the previous night. Whatever it was, I wanted it!

Soon it would be day four of us. Tea time when we rose from our sleep but I had suffered with tummy ache, so had been uncomfortable and not dreaming. Ray had, nice dreams he said which had him making tents in the sheets.

I would be well enough to go to work, then the end of this run of shifts. The first time our shifts didn't run parallel, I had a couple of days off and so my hours would revert to normal, live during the day, and sleep at night. We wouldn't be able to chat through the night like we had in our relationship so far. That would be hard for me because I had enjoyed his company so much. He assured me every day was bringing us a day closer, and I was on his mind every minute of the day.

We would exchange pictures even if he was worried about his tum, but I suggested sexercise would soon sort that out, something he sounded very keen on to lose weight, and I blushed, felt a bit hot under the collar, but could offer my services with pleasure. Three years a virgin, did he like lovemaking and could he keep up with me after so long? He hoped he could, he did enjoy sex, love, and hadn't lost the urge.

Having got sex out of the way, what would I feed him before he returned home after our date? Full English, yes, would be good, but no tomatoes and he did like beans, which I didn't. I told him of my love of ice cream, wine, sweeties, which was probably why I was overweight, but when we were together, we could work it off. I would look forward to working it off with him.

I had to get some sleep before work after my disturbed slumber, he was off to the shops to get something to cook himself, so we signed off until we could talk later.

We were both back at work again when we next spoke. I was feeling grumpy with my tummy, still not happy, but had to get on with work. He had not eaten yet, to which I said I would be starving but he quipped I could eat him.

"No comment on the grounds I would have to shred myself," a phrase he had never heard before, which I explained meant no-one would ever know.

He tried to cheer me up with a joke. "What do you call a lesbian dinosaur? A lickalotapus!"

That made me smile, I felt happier.

Tonight we then went onto talk about our favourite TV channels, our shift patterns as to how our rotas would fit in with each other, how it would affect our seeing each other and us holidaying, and how good he was going to be in the bedroom. He was keen to show me. I added, "No pressure."

I said I was only joking, I meant painting and decorating, to which he replied that I wouldn't be disappointed, I would be painted and decorated all over. The evening/night was going quickly now, and he had cheered me up. We even got onto talking about religion, though thought we had sinned too much to worry too much about it.

Then it was back to my chores before we contacted each other some hour later. I thought I may have to leave early as I was still not feeling too good, but would let my work companion get some rest before I departed. I would miss chatting to him leaving early, but he comforted me in telling me that we had covered a lot of ground in our few days, and he couldn't believe how good we sounded together. We would have to go steady the first couple of meetings, but was sure we would be fine. I agreed, we looked fine on paper, but we would explore each other properly in person, and any worries we could try and sort out. And then the bedroom, we would respect each other, it could be perfect first time but if not, we were both adults and it was something we could work on.

I was getting impatient for him, nervous for our first meeting, our first…! But when we met, I would be nervous, but happy with my big teddy!

We got back onto the subject of beans, and if I ate them I would probably let off in the middle of the night. Remember the snoring mask, I could fart as much as I wanted and he wouldn't notice, as long as it wasn't too noisy. This conversation was going downhill.

I was cold and feeling unwell; it was time to finish, and go home early so I would wake up my shift partner now. Ray wished he was there to look after me. When I got home he had sent me some pictures of him showing off his tattoos, and his hairy body. Loved them. I would send him some pictures of me when I had slept and showered. It was time to sleep, or try, and so I said my goodbyes, wishing he was here to cuddle me. He, my perfect man, me, his attractive lady, and he feeling really lucky to have me.

"Sweet dreams 'hunny', and hope you feel better when you wake up."

"I hope so too, lovely man, and will be dreaming of you. xxx."

It had been a manic four days. I was happy, I thought that I had found my man at last. Having gone to bed feeling ill, and managed to get some sleep, I woke up refreshed, but still feeling a little bit crook. What ground we had covered over our time chatting, what we had found out about each other, and I couldn't wait to meet up. Not long now, but for me it was still too far away. Yes, I felt very good about things, and really had a gut feeling we were so perfectly matched that only good could come from all this.

But, no message so far today. I had got up, still feeling poorly but on the mend, had done a lot of my housework, been to have my hair trimmed, done my shopping and had put the washing in too. Well organised, but no message, I hoped my phone wasn't on silent and I had missed Ray.

At last, late afternoon and I finally got a message wishing me a good morning, and he hadn't wanted to disturb me in case I was asleep. How thoughtful of him. I thanked him, my lovely man. He had woken up dreaming of me; again, his bedroom was turning into a camping site, the tents he was erecting. But it was nice that he thought of me.

I told him it was a pity he could not just jump in the car and come and see me, but he reminded me patience was a virtue. I had none, and pushed again, I really wanted to see him, NOW. I was finishing a bottle of wine I had opened a day or two ago, but again wished he was just around the corner.

He suggested that if I carried on pushing, I would spoil it all, he couldn't get to me any quicker.

I changed the subject, asking when he was travelling up to Scotland. Monday morning after a quick sleep.

A strange predicted text went his way where I called him Gregory, not that I knew one. Where did that come from? Damn phone, but he joked I wouldn't call him Gregory if we made love.

"If?"

He toyed with me, but I ended up saying I hoped we would, no ifs.

I didn't hear from him until he was at work. I asked if I had upset him, but no, and he wasn't a sex pest or pervert, and wasn't going to just jump into my bed soon just for a quickie, just to satisfy his lust.

I was going out so telling him I didn't want anyone else but him, I was committed tonight so he would have to watch telly at work. What would he have done if he hadn't met me?

He would have been watching TV, but he would occupy himself okay. We talked briefly about hates, my fear of spiders, but they didn't worry him, and then exchanged our thoughts of our feelings for each other, how I looked forward to have someone to love and look after and to have someone love me. He too, but asked me again to be patient, our time would soon be upon us, and he couldn't make it happen any quicker. He had four more nights to do, then his trip, then me.

He had made me feel happy again, and wishing each other well, we kissed and said our goodnights.

"Lovely, lovely man. Xxxxx"

The next morning, I was up and feeling better, and had received a text from Ray that he was home from work and gone to bed. I was sorry to have missed him, but had thought of more questions for him. What films (type) did he like? Sofa or chair, tea or coffee, eat in front of TV or at table, any body piercing? And I hoped he was dreaming of me.

He stirred late afternoon and we were chatting again; he had received my pictures I had taken and sent him, liked the look of the redhead he saw, but I had to tell him it was a bottle, I was naturally a mousy brown. Sexy, he said, and he couldn't wait to hold me close.

He had to leave early for work that night as he had to pick up a colleague but would ring later. He rang from work an hour or so later, saying he loved the sound of my voice. I hoped he didn't think me impatient again when I said we would have to phone more often, especially when he had travelled up north. He hoped he would do his best but reception may be very poor.

We chatted generally for some time about my gaming, his TV programs, wanting each other to hold and cuddle, and more, and then as I wasn't working it was my bedtime. I promised I would be dreaming of him, lovely dreams, wished him goodnight and told him I was missing him already.

The next day was my trip to the theatre in Birmingham, so we wouldn't be able to chat much. This was the date I had with a friend, a date I said I would honour some months ago, not to let an old friend down. I had said I would go with him (Artie, remember him?) to a family get-together, meal and theatre to see 'Witches' – that got lost in translation. No – 'Wicked'. Ray was shattered after work so I told him, my big teddy, that I would try and speak later. I would try and do a little shopping in Birmingham, then the show. I would try and get my friend (Artie) to take some pictures of me in my glad rags and forward them to him. When he was awake and had seen the photos of the dress I was to wear he thought I was gorgeous.

I managed to reach him at half time in the show and then again when it had ended. He asked me if I had enjoyed the show.

"No."

Why? Because I had wanted to be with him. I told him I was just going to the local casino to play a bit of poker. "Texas hold-ups?" he asked. Oh, I wish I was with him now.

I played a little blackjack and won a few pounds, then it was time to return to my hotel and sleep. I told him I would go into the Chinese quarter and get some ingredients to cook for him.

"I don't like Chinese and I thought we were eating out," he said.

Yes, we were eating out, but he would love my cooking.

He was busy, his busiest night along with Saturdays so it was time to send hugs and snogs to his gorgeous sexy lady, and from me to him, my lovely teddy man.

Our next day, I returned home and took my granddaughter shopping, looking for some school shoes. I eventually spoke to Ray mid-afternoon. He asked if I was having a good day. Yes, I was, but it was better now I was speaking to him. Eight days now until he was here, I was thinking, and him too. I couldn't wait. Next Sunday we would be working out when we would next meet up, between our shift patterns, and life would be wonderful.

He went to work, and we started again. What had he had to eat? A sandwich, that's not enough. I really ought to be looking after him. We chatted a little more, then it was time for me to go to bed while he continued a busy Saturday night shift. xxxxxxxxx.

Another day had passed, another day closer to meeting up.

When I spoke to him the following morning, Ray had been busy all night and was about to go to sleep. I told him I was cooking a roast for my son, girlfriend, and granddaughters. I was missing him but now only seven days to go; cuddles and kisses and sleep well.

I spoke when he had slept, asking whether he would try and get a couple of hours after work before he left for Scotland. He needed to and would, which reassured me and I wouldn't worry so much. I would be in my work house later, would be busy but we would get a chance to speak at some time. He at work, and me again, these nights at work had led to long conversations before. I looked forward to that.

It was about one in the morning when we had a chance to talk. I said we hadn't asked many personal questions; he hadn't asked because he didn't want to scare me away, was his answer. Down to the nitty gritty, I asked him how many partners he had had.

Sexual? About fifty, he guessed. And me?

Married twice, and say another seven, so nine altogether. I added that I did enjoy making love, more than just having sex, it wasn't the same. I told him how surprised I now felt, that I felt so close to him.

His turn. I asked which his favourite position was for making love, most satisfying. He told me all positions were good, but best for climax was the woman on top. He loved foreplay, exploring his woman's body all over with his hands, caressing her breasts and reaching, exploring that lovely area between her legs. Oral sex was a turn on, both ways – he had a healthy sexual appetite.

He then asked me how I described myself in a sexual sense – adventurous, reserved, or prudish. I told him I don't do all orifices, one of them is for things coming out of, not going in, but I did love sexy undies, stockings, etc. if he liked. I was now feeling a little randy, more than a little randy, and could feel a moistening between my legs, wow! He too at the mention of stockings, which he liked, and had to admit to a bit of a stiffy while he was texting.

He wanted to respect me when we met so thought it perhaps better if he went home that night, but I said no way, he would be tired. He said he didn't want me to think he was only after one thing again, but I assured him that we were both adults, would go with the flow, and I would probably want him in the morning as well. We talked of how in our own ways, each had made the other come alive again, it was a wonderful feeling.

Then back to 'dirty' talk, asking me about dressing up. I told him about my sexy nurse's outfit from Ann Summers.

I recalled making love in the swimming pool in Oz, but then he told me he had done it on Westminster Bridge in broad daylight, he had been in a threesome, and a foursome (not on Westminster

Bridge, that may have held the traffic up, but another time). Something his wife had wanted and he just went along with. I had never done that, and didn't want to share him with anyone.

I did tell him of a candlelit dinner in my undies, and then we had made love, had a Crunchie, and, and had made love. I had shaved my privates, but didn't when not with anyone as it was itchy. He liked hairy so said I wouldn't need to.

We went on to talk about him coming, our meeting at last. What would be his first words to me?

"Hello," he said. He would need to freshen up, have a shower, and then our time would be our own. We chatted on through the night about all sorts, it was lovely. Any more confessions, about family, and then his journey. I asked him to text when he left, stopped for a break, and when he got there, I wanted to know he was safe. I was really looking forward to Sunday now, our meeting. Happily, I was off the sites now I had found him. It was fate that Ray had only been on a week and we had found each other.

We said our goodbyes for the night, our work done, and would go our separate directions, thinking of our conversations this night. Yes, he had made me feel randy, and I would be reading his messages again in bed. Look out Buzz Buzz! Ray, he told me he would be thinking of our talk as he drove to Scotland.

"Safe journey, my lovely man."

I was working so the rest of the day was in bed, sleeping, while he would get a few hours then be on his way. I woke in the afternoon, and first thing was to check my phone. No messages, so I texted to ask how the journey was going.

Still nothing, and it was getting close to the time I needed to go to work, so I tried again. I said I was worried I hadn't heard from him, was getting a little worried, was missing him.

Still nothing so it was gone ten when I tried again, asking if he had arrived safely.

Nearly an hour later, at last a reply, that Wi-Fi connection was poor, so the message would be sent at some stage when there was better connection.

I got that one, though what time it was sent I don't know. I replied I was missing him big time, but glad he had arrived safely because I was worried. I quipped that Ray was to make sure his mate didn't fix him up with anyone because he was taken.

The next day, random texts from me. I was on my way home, was having my breakfast, time for sleep, and I wished I could chat.

Nothing.

I hoped he would get in touch after my sleep, but no, so all I could do was to text hoping he was okay, that I was struggling without messages, hated it. Then I was off to work again, and still no reply. I hated it. After all our chats over the previous days, now zilch!

*

At work and it was gone midnight. I had decided that I hated Scotland, would never live there as the internet connections seemed so poor, far worse than overseas. Australia was far better.

I texted again just as I was leaving work, when I had completed my handover, then again to say I was going to bed. It would be my last night of shifts again when I went to work this time, messaging this and that. I was still missing no messages, getting fed up with it.

It would soon be time for work, when at last a message came through. It was Ray; he had hire an hour of internet time to send a message. I thanked him for paying to speak to me. I said I thought he had been sucked into a hole in the universe, of an undiscovered technologically deficient culture.

He was having a great time, though missing me loads and couldn't stop thinking about me.

That was good.

I told him all I had been doing was work, work, work. He should check the million emails he may have got from me.

He told me he was knackered the first day, and had slept a lot, but today he and his mate had chatted, been to the pub.

I hoped he would stop at a services when on way home, to let me know and give me some estimated time of arrival so I would be ready for him.

He told me he had read all my messages again, and had bored his mate with them, which I said was lovely. Well I was his gorgeous, sexy, lovely lady, he said, to which I replied it was good that he was as keen as me. I told him that I had showed my friend at work his photos, and she was really happy, but hoped I wouldn't end up with a broken heart.

"Why would I want to break your heart?"

"She was worried about me, knew how long I had

been talking and just wanted me to be happy."

He understood, but after our chat it was now time to sign off so I could get to work. He told me again he was thinking of me constantly, and I him, and I was missing our chatting.

Love and hugs, he was gone for a while.

He messaged a little later to say he would be in touch before Sunday, and asked if I wanted it in the car.

My days of it in the car are over! Lol.

The next day was a quiet day again; the odd message from me saying how much I was missing him, glad he was enjoying himself, and now I was off, just waiting for him, and really looking forward to Sunday.

Two more days to go, and he would be here. I was feeling a little nervous but really looking forward to it. I messaged him to say that if he did meet anyone in Scotland, to let me know. I didn't want to be hurt, didn't want him to meet up with me and me be smitten, then for him to have to choose between the two of us. It wouldn't be fair, I was just trying to be practical and save myself from being hurt.

Why my self-doubt now? We had travelled so far together. I guess I was really starting to feel nervous, in anticipation. I sent message after message of self-doubt; I remembered he had said he had met someone before but she wouldn't move in with him. Was I trying to prepare myself for a fall? I don't know, but I really was looking forward to our big day, so close now.

Mid-morning, he came through; he had paid for internet access again. I told him to sort through his emails, I was ironing, had three things to do then was his. Six minutes later, *coo-e*, I hear. He had been reading my last mails, and assured me there was no-one in Scotland.

Great, I said. Just wanted to give him a get-out clause, though I was sure he didn't want to use it. He said that I wasn't going to get rid of him that easily.

I was grinning now, and told him so. I was so pleased with his reply and told him I may lock him in the downstairs loo, to keep for my pleasure when required. He joked, was I going to tie him up? Kinky.

That was more like it, our conversation was fun again and I knew he wanted me. We resorted to talking about the breakfast I was to cook him, and what I was going to do today – cinema, shopping.

His time had run out, and he was gone, but not after telling each other we were missing each other.

I continued to send the odd message through the rest of the day, before later in the evening he was back. He told me he was a little drunk, but the pub did have Wi-Fi.

I told him I was so looking forward to having him… to breakfast. For breakfast, he answered, and his sausage did taste good. He had been drinking lager. I said it took a lot of lager to get pissed, then he would be going to the loo all the time. Don't drink too much, you have a long drive on Sunday morning, don't be sloshed. What time was he thinking of leaving?

He had his reunion the next day and told me he was just practising drinking tonight, but no, he would not get sloshed. I was his priority, he would be not up late.

I was worried I was nagging, but I cared, hoped he would take care, and said that I was now off to bed, but would be kissing him lots in my imagination.

Sleep well, my lovely man.

I was not sure if we would be able to talk the following day, so just sent a few random messages. Tomorrow would be the first time we would meet, I would have to admit to a few butterflies, but I was so looking forward to it.

Later. "I am looking through my knicker drawer. I have a few bits and bobs I haven't worn for over a year. Do you like fishnets?"

He had Wi-Fi – he came on straight away telling me he had nearly choked on his sausage, he would love me in my sexy undies.

I told him that fishnets were for the bedroom, or perhaps a fancy dress party. Normal stockings for going out.

He was going to get a sleep before his thing tonight, but was getting excited about tomorrow.

"Me too, babe."

Time to go again, with a message from him telling me that he couldn't wait to hug and kiss me, to snog me, and so much, much more…

I was excited, very excited.

The next time I would speak to him was probably when he was on the road tomorrow, COMING to me. I did text him during the evening hoping he was having a good time, but wasn't expecting a reply.

Ten the next morning was my first message from him, he was stopped in Cumbria having a coffee, hoped to be with me about lunchtime.

"Ok hun."

I busied myself doing my hair, tidying the house, waiting for him to arrive.

An hour later, Knutsford.

He's getting so close now, about an hour away.

Thirty minutes later, stuck in traffic!

Midday, in the town centre.

"Good, you will be here in a minute. I'll put the kettle on. I'll look for you through the window."

He drove past my house, but I recognised the car he had described to me, and was able to direct him back to where I was waiting by my front door. Two last texts.

"Hello sexy xxx."

"Hello sexy xxx."

He was here.

Here he was at last; this was the moment I had been waiting for. He got out of his car, shut the door and walked briskly to the door where I was waiting. Dressed smartly in jeans and a shirt, he looked good and his pictures hadn't lied. Yes, I did like the look of my Ray. From his six foot he bent down and kissed my lips, wrapped his arms around me and kissed me again. It was a warm, but strong hug. I was in his arms at last.

After, I don't know how many, possibly two thousand messages over the past three weeks, here he was at last standing in front of me. We had, over that time, quizzed each other on any and every subject we could think of – our favourite food, TV programs, dress, ranging to how many partners we had had, our sexual preferences, fantasies, there weren't many stones left unturned as to what we didn't know about each other. Except of course, how would we actually get on in person? Face to face, side by side, the real us, with no phone screens to hide behind. Yes, at times I had sounded impatient in wanting this meeting to happen, but he had said this was the first chance with his work commitments, and his reunion he had to attend, and he was here at the first opportunity he had after that, driving all that way today to see me.

Yet now, I don't know why, I suddenly felt nervous, shy, apprehensive. This was not full-on Gill, the person I really am. Why now when I have craved for this moment over the past few weeks, craved to meet the man now standing in front of me? Was it because in all that we had gone through, all we had learnt about each other, and some had been very intimate, that I was sure the man I had wanted, been looking for all this time since the one that got away, was now here waiting to be asked in? For all my fishing experiences, when the bait was about to be taken, and I should have been ready to strike and reel him in, I was caught dawdling. Silly me.

"Sorry Ray, come in. I'm Gill, oh silly me, you already know that. I'm really pleased you're here, hope you've had a good journey."

I was flustered. Come on Gill, you've been waiting for this, show yourself off in your best light.

I ushered him into the sitting room, and sat him down, while I went to make him a cuppa. That gave me the chance to settle myself down, get back to normal Gill.

I sat myself next to Ray, held his hand, and we chatted about his trip to Scotland, the reunion, and how it was to see his old mates again after so long. I was relaxing now in his company, and he seemed no different from the person I had chatted to, texted over these past few weeks. In fact, the person I thought I may have fallen for. He was chatty, funny, and interesting, and very attentive towards me. The odd kiss between our conversations, a cuddle or two, I liked this, all seemed as if it would be so romantic.

He had said he may want a shower when he arrived, just to freshen up after his long drive, so I showed him the bathroom, and the spare bedroom where he could leave his bag. I had already made the bed up for him so that we could spend as much time as possible getting to know each other. The rest of the afternoon would be ours to enjoy together, to walk in the town park, walking hand in hand enjoying the sunshine, the smell of fresh-cut grass, the flowers, the birds singing, all around us as we went into our own little world, just me and him. It all was what I was hoping for, there seemed a natural affinity between us and as the time passed us by, I felt more certain this was the one.

Back home to freshen up, then to open a bottle of red. We continued to chat away until it was time to summon a taxi to take us for an evening meal at one of the town gastro-pubs. Not the world's best menu, or food, but over more wine, who cared? We were together at last, laughing, joking, toying with each other, the chemistry between us building and building towards some sort of nuclear fission. Eating, holding hands across the table, completely oblivious of anything going on around us, this really did feel romantic and was everything I had hoped it would be. What did we eat? Who cares? Can't remember because to be quite honest, it didn't matter because we were so engrossed in each other's company.

We were having our first date, though it seemed we had known each other forever, and now it was time to go home, back to my house, depart to our separate rooms to sleep, then in the morning cook my man, my Ray, his breakfast and sort out when to meet again, where, what to do, plan our future, if that wasn't running before we could walk. All felt good.

We hadn't finished the wine we had started before we went to dinner, and we thought it seemed a shame to waste it, so while Ray poured us a glass, I got myself ready for bed, slipped into a little nightie under my dressing gown, and re-joined him downstairs.

You probably don't have to be a rocket scientist to guess what happened next! We of course drank the wine!

We had enjoyed the evening and each other's company; we did seem to get on very well, and there was certainly romance in the air. We kissed tenderly, then more strongly and then more in a frenzy, a real snog that went on and on and on. It was getting too hot in my dressing gown, and Ray only too willingly helped me slip it off from around my shoulders, down to remove my arms from the sleeves, and we were full on. Not snogging anymore, this was passionate, well, wrestling. His shirt of course had to come off to reveal those tattoos, and that body hair he had boasted about, that I could run my fingers through. He caressed by breasts, stroked them, tweaked my nipples, which were becoming more aroused, firmer and firmer. As my fingers ran through that body hair, down, down, until with a little loosening of garments, I could feel that stiffness he had talked about when we were texting before. Yes, we were full on, arousing each other. He said he liked foreplay, and he was getting it, his manhood now entrapped in my playing fingers. All this before I sent him to the spare room to sleep.

But now his hands were exploring, gently caressing me, working their way down, one down my body, the other up my leg, until they both met at my... His fingers were now running through that hair I had nurtured, hidden from mankind, but in this nightie, plain for all to see (though no-one else should have been looking). The temperature was rising, coming to boiling point, but I had my virtue to think of. It was time for bed, I wasn't going to let him have me on the floor of my living room as a first taster.

We let each other go, and retired to our beds. Okay, he didn't, as he followed me into my room, and the wrestling restarted on my king-size. Yes, we had sex, we made love, nothing spectacular, but we did it, and then cuddled up and slept.

No hanky panky in the morning, we got up, and I cooked him his breakfast, with a couple of sausages. We chatted, we kissed, we ate.

It was nice. I had broken my two-week rule, but we had learnt so much about each other, and now had learnt about each other's bodies. All seemed good, and we thought we both had something to look forward to. The start of a life together, it certainly seemed a strong possibility. I was happy, more so than I had been for a long time.

Then, it was time for him to go, he had jobs to do – see his mother, get ready for work that evening.

A long goodbye as we cuddled each other in the hall, a long, lingering hug while we kissed, until next time.

Then he was gone.

It's Monday. I'm up and ready and looking forward to the day ahead, to the future.

Started my day's texting.

10:35 am - Gill Finn: Fantastically, happy lady. sitting here waiting for your text xx

11:05 am - Gill Finn: Hey you???

11:13 am - Gill Finn: Have you taken your tablet Hun xxx

11:15 am - Ray: Just home got bit of running round to do xxx

11:16 am - Gill Finn: I know Hun. Just wanted to know your home safe xxx

3:25 pm - Gill Finn: Sweetheart xxx I am putting my phone on silent I will try to get 40 winks.

So much to talk about tonight xxxx

Speak soon x 🖤🖤

3:30 pm - Gill Finn: Thinking about you xxx

5:32 pm - Gill Finn: Hi you. Xx Kisses

Have you managed to do all you wanted to do?

7:37 pm - Gill Finn: You at work??

8:55 pm - Gill Finn: Just about to leave to drive to work xx

9:28 pm - Gill Finn: At work!!!

you busy?

Xxx

10:08 pm - Gill Finn: So no messages?

Does it mean you do not want to meet again?

10:15 pm - Gill Finn: Please just tell me xx

10:19 pm - Ray: Gill have had bad day today and am really sorry but I don't think can meet u again. Can't go into detail but may be able to in future if u want to remain friends. I can't tell u how much of a great time I had yesterday and I hope u don't think I just used u for sex cos that was not the case. If u don't want to keep in touch, I understand and am very sorry that things have turned out this way. I will not be returning to badoo by the way as am not looking for anyone else xx

10:21 pm - Gill Finn: Omg.

Please tell me why?

10:22 pm - Gill Finn: Please.

10:25 pm - Ray: I can't right now sorry

10:31 pm - Gill Finn: There is nothing you can say that cannot upset me as much as I am upset now.

After the last 3 weeks of continuous texting and then meeting up.

Are you still married??

It's not fair just to leave me like this.

Really not fair.

10:32 pm - Gill Finn: I thought we were doing fine.???

10:33 pm - Gill Finn: You cannot just say nothing

10:34 pm - Ray: Gill don't make this harder than it has to be this is not how I intended things to work out but it has I am not married and have no intention of getting married again

10:35 pm - Gill Finn: Nor me. But why?

Tell me. Bossy?

Demanding?

I have to understand please.

10:36 pm - Gill Finn: Was it because you got hurt... In a very private place?

10:37 pm - Gill Finn: It's not fair just to drop me without an explanation.

Not fair on me.

10:38 pm - Gill Finn: At least if I know the truth I can except it.

10:39 pm - Ray: Please Gill I can't say right now because I haven't got my head round it myself. Don't want to have text tennis all night

10:41 pm - Gill Finn: Head round it?

Just say I will then put it down to a lesson.

I need to know if I have done something wrong?

10:42 pm - Gill Finn: I really want just to understand and if you don't want me then fine.

If you're not ready for a relationship that's fine too.

But I do not want any more "friends"

10:46 pm - Ray: Ok no friends but no relationship either just put it down to me being fucked up

10:50 pm - Gill Finn: Will you just tell me!!! "fucked up" is not a reason.

I just want to understand.

You should of been honest when you were at mine.

I asked you several times are you / we doing ok are you happy.

You should have told me then.

I could have told you ok fine go in the spare room.

I do feel used now.

10:51 pm - Ray: Sorry that's all I can say. And all I will say

10:53 pm - Gill Finn: Well good bye.

That's why I should not go with the flow.

10:54 pm - Ray: Take care Gill x

10:58 pm - Gill Finn: Don't do this to anyone else. It would be cruel.

10:58 pm - Ray: I won't and I didn't mean to do it to u please believe that

10:59 pm - Gill Finn: Well you have and I have had

enough.

10:59 pm - Ray: Will say goodbye then

11:00 pm - Gill Finn: Don't bother

I will wash the sheets Tomorrow to take away, you, your smell, your, your seed.

11:50 pm - Gill Finn: I am still not happy and feel you owe me a full explanation.

You have probably finished the best thing that ever happened to me and you

You owe me, to try to explain why xx

12:27 am - Gill Finn: Are you ill???

12:27 am - Gill Finn: Is that why???

12:28 am - Gill Finn: Tell me please xx

12:50 am - Gill Finn: Please tell me. Are you scared??

It's not fair to leave me guessing.

09/09/2014, 1:00 am - Gill Finn: Is it your diabetes??

My brother was injecting from aged 16, till he died from lung cancer from smoking.

I know you were going to your nurse.?

Now I am thinking all the wrong things.

You cannot tell me now but might be able in the future.

You must be ill???

Or it's me. If it's me I want to know so I do not make the same mistake.

1:02 am - Gill Finn: Want*

6:29 am - Gill Finn: I would like to see you this weekend.

Please x

7:21 am - Gill Finn: Good night. Please be happy. Please contact me and tell me what's wrong...... I am not going back on to Badoo yet.

Xxx sleep well. X

8:49 am - Gill Finn: Sleep well xx.

My world had come to an abrupt end, again. Gill, how do you feel? Numb, absolutely numb. We had had such a good time together, we had chatted for so long, we had met, we had wooed, we had loved, and now for some reason that he won't tell me, nor can I figure out, it was all over.

What had I done wrong? If anything. I know I had seemed a bit pushy, impatient before we had met, but we were fine yesterday, last night. I didn't understand, couldn't get my head round it, and wanted to know so that I didn't make the same mistake again, or could help solve whatever problem he may have. I wished, hoped, wanted to know, but nothing was forthcoming.

It was doing my head in. I thought I had again found love, a future, someone to spend a life with, and it had been taken from me quicker than I had found it. I was confused, sad, angry, every emotion because I didn't get what had just happened.

I would never know what went on his mind to do this, to do this to me. Was he in trouble? A mystery I would never solve.

But then, as I reflected more and more on what had taken place, the events of the past few weeks, a feeling, a suspicion which in time has grown into a realisation that I had been had, literally, and I had fallen for it all.

This bloke, this predator, had come online, looking for honest women who were trying to find their soulmate, and a future, and he had preyed on me.

All that soft soap, sweet talk, how we sounded so compatible 'hun, my sexy lady', how he dreamed of me. Then, he explored my emotions, my needs as a woman, and we allowed each other to go into more than personal details. He had turned me on, turned me on online, and I had accepted it all, taken it all in by the spoonful.

Yes, he had groomed me, led me up the garden path until I wanted him, had to have him. I had let him into my house, wanted him in my house, and then I let him fuck me.

He had got what he wanted, groomed me for sex, had it and now that was it, he disappeared.

Was he married, and not getting enough, or just some bastard who preyed on susceptible ladies, looking for a happy life?

I was annoyed with myself. That two-week rule was there for a reason, I put it there myself, and I let his sweet-talking bastard break my own rule. I have learnt another lesson. I thought I could spot the sex predators, but this one was there to sting, stingray.

Bloody men, bastards... but I still wanted one, I still wanted a soulmate, a life partner.

Back to the pool, back to fishing, I would go back on the net, chastened but undaunted. Experience.

Yes, I was hurt and confused, but I had satisfied a woman's need for one night at least. Him, he could put another notch on his belt. He said he wouldn't go back online, but who knows? Who may he be next time, if there is a next time and I'm sure there will be – Billy Bass?

Bastard, forget him.

"Carry on, Gill. There are bigger fish to fry, and you make sure you get one."

Jack Dempsey

(A cichlid fish of Central America, noted for its aggressive nature, and strong facial features, like the boxer.)

I seem to have been on this sport for an eternity now, casting, reeling in, throwing back tiddlers, avoiding predators, searching, ever looking for that fish that continues to escape me. Have I missed opportunities from when I have been seeing someone? Others may have looked and found me unavailable. Who knows? But my resolve is to find a Sole Mate, so I will continue my search. I know I have met the man I want to be with forever, but it was not meant to be. For whatever reason, it didn't work and I had to move on.

It was not to be, so I cannot stay marooned in those still, gentle waters, hoping above all hope that he will come searching for me, so that we can be together again. No, Gill. Time to move on.

And so, here I am back on Plenty of Fish, back on Badoo. Looking, looking, there must be someone surely.

Sitting in bed, I am looking through profiles again, hunting. Is this me the predator now, me turning into a shark? Reject, reject, this one has possibilities, reject, very interesting, what about this one? Stop. What about this one? Yes, worth pursuing. Like a shark, I am following my nose, the scent of a kill, the food of love. I'm after him.

The profile, looks good, show I am interested on encounters, post my heart, wait and see what happens. Will he show any interest in my bait? Respond so that I can start going into a feeding frenzy?

Good, he has shown an interest, nibbling, and now I will just wait to see if there is an attempt at contact. Lurking in those dark waters of my room, I wait and wait for that scent, the signal to go forward.

Here it comes, the signal, the pheromone of an interested fish. He enters the chat line, looking for contact back from me. Strike! The message has come, and I am ready to reply immediately, strike and draw him in, and maybe capture him forever.

I separate him from the shoal of other fish I have been chatting to, drawing him to my lair, as we exchange chats, swopping information about each other. Jack Dempsey, from his picture profile, a handsome specimen, retired, single (or so he says), and reasonably local.

The encounter, the initial interactions, circling, probing as to what each is like begins, and builds.

He sounds nice, and at this stage as we chat generally on the net site over the next few days. There is a feeling of warmth building between us. I reel in the other lines I had out, and place them back in the tackle box, ready for another day if needed. For the time being he has my sole attention. Feeding him line, drawing him in, giving him slack then again playing him in.

All sounds good, and after some three weeks of this, he suggested that we could try WhatsApp, a vehicle that we could use to chat, swop text pictures, and could see when we were writing back to each other.

I'm good with that, being a technophile, can't wait to start. We had started another line of communication, just the two of us in our own time and space. Easy to pick up on my smartphone, so I was always available unless driving.

Little did I know the murky waters I was now heading into.

He's on, here we go, our own private conversation, though of course I can keep all this messaging for as long as I like.

"Hello naughty Gill," he begins.

That was not what I was expecting as his opening gambit. Where did that come from? Was this the man, so polite, I had been chatting to before?

"Hello," I reply tentatively.

"Do you have any naughty pictures, naughty Gill?"

"Nope, never have, never will. Sorry."

Shit, where is this going? I think to myself.

"Lol," he replies. "At least we can begin to chat on here now… or… naughty Gill. X ."

"Good. Just going to eat, will be right back."

"Okay," Jack replies.

Ten minutes later I reply, "Am eating at the moment, but I don't send photos of a saucy nature as I am connected to a drop box, which shares all my photos. Lol."

"Oh, I never went on a drop box, I don't know what a drop box is. Come off… drop box that is. Lol."

Do I believe him? I don't know, I'm sure his computer knowledge would give him some idea of what I was talking about, and he was just trying to be evasive and see what he hopes for.

I tell him I am just chatting with my sister. Messages cross in different contexts as we swop, typing our messages sometimes at the same time. A drop box allows me to share photos and documents with my family and those friends I wish to. I am thinking I can't be bothered with this bloke, but will persevere a little longer, try changing the subject.

"It's a storage system for photos and files. Why would I come off? I want to share photos with my sister, but I don't want her to have pictures of a risqué nature, that some bloke may want. What's your name?"

I of course already know it, but this may divert the conversation to something more sensible. I continue, "I'm out to a jam session tonight."

"Jack, my name is Jack. Where?"

"Hello Jack. In a local village."

"Oh, do you live there, in the village?"

"No, not there but close by, about a ten-minute drive away."

"So the last time you had sex was three months ago?" he asks.

He's back there again. I have only managed to get him off the scent for a couple of minutes, so ignoring that comment I continue, "I have my own house, a three-bedroom house. And I have a lodger too."

"Male lodger?"

"Approximately three months, but I do have a friend with benefits," I reply.

"Female friend with benefits you mean?"

"No. A female lodger, and a male friend with benefits. When was the last time for you?" I ask, trying his tactics.

"A few months ago. So you can get sex from your male friend?"

I think he is shocked. "That's what a friend with benefits is for, if we haven't been seeing anyone for three months and both want to meet up, there we are."

"SO you are good at blow jobs then? X"

That was below the belt. "I'm not going to answer questions like that. All I can say is that it ruins a good first meeting. Sorry."

"Oh."

"I'm not a prude, but you're a bit tacky… are you

in your own home or not? I am not into text sex or phone sex, the real thing is best, lol, but we can talk about cooking if we want to continue," I carried on.

"I live in the countryside near Shrewsbury… it's a cosy flat."

"Ae you buying or renting?" I ask.

"What's that got to do with anything?"

Touchy, touchy. In my head I think he must be married and just looking for a quick bonk, but I can't be sure. He doesn't seem very comfortable now with this conversation, what's he hiding?

"I'm buying as due to having a good pension, it would be a waste to have to use it to pay rent when I retire. LOL, it took your mind off blow jobs, works every time," I chip in.

"I'd like to have sex with you," David says.

Didn't take him long to come back to this subject.

"I expect you would. It's a natural thing. Coffee first though. I might not fancy you, and you might not fancy me."

Jack says, "We'll be alright."

"Hope so."

"Hope you suck and lick nice," he adds. "Lol."

"Stop it or you will not get any for four weeks. I have to go now and get ready. Where I am going there is no internet. But I would like to chat again, soon."

"Perhaps. It's also… not nice to hear you have a friend with benefits."

He is shocked, but is he is only after one thing?

"I'm not the one with all this smutty talk, and all that. It shows I'm not just after you for sex, lol. But I'm sure if you had a friend with benefits, you wouldn't be making these suggestive remarks. Now if we have gone through my two-week formality, and I liked you, then that would be a different matter," I say.

"Lol."

We have had an hour's conversation, and it's time for me to go. I'm not sure about this David, but have offered to talk again, but he is not getting me in the sack just like that. I will have to see where this one goes. I'm looking for a relationship, not a quick bonk.

I have decided that I am not going to out after all, I'm feeling too tired. I thought I would try him on speaker phone, so I speak on the recording app on WhatsApp. I want to hear his voice so I say I am happy to carry on chatting if he wishes to talk to me. But he doesn't, has he an accent he is hiding, or is he married. Back to the narrative on the app.

"What are your hobbies?" I ask.

He replies, "Look on my profile on Plenty of Fish."

That was a bit terse. "Okay," I reply.

"I like growing things."

"I know you grow lovely vegetables extra, what about holidays? I am thinking of going to Australia in the autumn, I am going to book my tickets later in the week."

"Who's going?" he asks.

"Just me at the moment. I am going to Queensland. If I decide to move back to Australia, then that is where I would live, close to Brisbane, the Gold Coast. My best friend is there, and my son."

"How do you have the money?"

I reply, "That's for me to know and you to find out, if we end up together!"

He wants me to tell him but I reply, "You were not forthcoming about your flat."

"Okay. Put your information on Plenty of Fish about Oz."

"So, your favourite holiday place then?" I enquire.

"I like Australia too."

"Have you been?" I ask, and then there is a lengthy pause from him. I wonder why.

"Apart from your lovely garden, sex, and Australia, what do you like to watch on TV?"

"LOL. Lots of things I like to watch. Yes, went for a month, loved it Gill."

"So where did you go?"

"Queensland, Sydney. Back in 2007."

"That's just when I was coming back. That was just after my divorce over there."

"So how can you afford to go there or consider living there?" he asks.

"I will tell you one day, but I have lived all over the world. I studied in Australia, so I can walk into a job over there. My son is in the forces in Queensland, my best friend lives there, and rents a house ten minutes away from my son. It would be easy. Nosey!"

"LOL. Wow."

"Wow what?"

"That's impressive, but why live over here, in Shropshire?"

"Family, my son and granddaughters are here."

"I like a quiet place in the countryside," he chips in.

"I can afford to go out there and spend three months a year in Australia when I retire. But I do not want to do it on my own. I need to find a partner who will be able to afford it to, for us to share thus time together."

"You won't find a partner. Not if you've a friend with benefits... a fuck buddy."

He is obsessed with this one, won't let it go.

"Are you shocked that I have a friend with benefits, and am willing to admit it?"

"Yes."

"After the things you have typed. I do not believe that you are shocked. Better to have a friend who knows what you want, can be trusted to be clean and safe. I'm not a bed hopper. I think you are jealous, have you never had such a friend? And, we are adults with needs!"

"I'm certainly not jealous, adult with needs, not for me!"

"SO you take yourself in hand, pleasure yourself? I think that it is unusual that it is not for you, after your smutty talk. If we had a short relationship but knew we were not for life, if we needed company, were without a partner, then what is the harm? A film, a bottle of wine, and…!"

"I'm not after that kind of a relationship."

"Nor am I, that's good then. I am looking for someone for life, to look forward to doing things as a couple. Enjoy cooking together, for each other. Holidays, living our lives together. I don't like being on my own, I was married at seventeen, was mad at seventeen, and now want Mr Right. At the moment, I am here and still need to look after my parents when necessary. If you're looking for a life partner, want cuddles, and more, then meet me for a coffee. Nite."

I have laid it on the line, what I am looking for, why I am on these sites. How will how respond? What are his intentions? If he wants to meet me, then is he after the same life relationship as me, or just another bloke after a quickie, probably married? *Watch this space*, is all I can think to myself. Bedtime.

It's after breakfast, nearly coffee time. I've been up and about for some time, readying myself to go out.

A noise. My phone.

"Morning Gill."

"Good morning, closer to afternoon. Got to put my make-up on, then out to visit my parents."

"Me, tidying up. Just back from town myself."

"Do you fancy meeting up today? I'm off to visit Mum, then will go down to the town centre. If all okay, then could meet you there."

"You can visit me in the morning, tomorrow

morning. You can drive? Only takes twenty minutes, if you know where you are going."

"To where?"

I reply, "Tesco shop for coffee. Am always careful where I meet for the first time. I like crowded places, less likely to be murdered! I worked in Shrewsbury, start my new job at the beginning of next month. I'll be driving for a while now. I'm at the hospital to see mum."

An hour passes and I write I have left the hospital and going to the town centre, enquiring if he is busy.

"No, if you want you can come over to mine for an hour, you're very welcome. I don't rape and I don't murder, anyone, at least not the first time! Think it over, Gill."

"A murderer would say that. LOL." An hour has passed.

"I'm not, don't be silly Gill."

"I don't expect you are, but this two-week barrier that I have, LOL, perhaps this meeting could be, say halfway. Do you drive?"

"Leave it then."

"Okay. I am sorry but I will not put myself in a situation I have no control over. I think we should meet halfway, if you do not drive, then there are always buses and taxis, I could meet you on a bus route. Also, if you're retired, and I am working full time, and you want ME to come over to you! I don't think we will get on very well."

I'm beginning to think this David is very selfish.

I add, "I like to look after the person I am with, and not run after them. I also have to be close to my house due to my dad waiting to hear about Mum. I do believe if we are making reasons not to meet halfway, then we will not be suited to have a great life together. I hope you find someone to love you."

Jack later replied, "I can't be bothered with this two-week safety barrier. Crock of shit! I drive, I don't need a bus or taxi either. I said come for an hour. I'm not doing all this ballshit."

"No worries then, bye."

That's it for me with this bloke, not contacting him again.

Tomorrow comes, and there he is on my app again.

"Would you like to meet at Tesco's, Shrewsbury, for a coffee this morning?"

I ask, "Why have you changed your mind?"

"I don't mind Tesco's. Our cooking skills are very interesting, as we both cook... you may find my amount of spices interesting!"

Is that innuendo again from him, cooking or more ballshit?

"Your cooking skills you mean?"

"This phone, it does change words, I only notice when sending them. If you want to meet at Tesco's for coffee, just say."

Is this him being up front?

"That's fine, but I can't today, won't have time as I'm booked in at the Vaults with some female friends.

A birthday and we are out in the town together, so I'll get back to you."

"You're confusing me. Are you coming into town on your own, or with mates?"

"I am sharing a car, and a room with a friend, a twin room at the Vaults."

"That's not about meeting me as a person, that's about you coming into town with your mates, and fitting me in somewhere. Sorry but no!"

"Okay. But think about it this way, I'm working full-time nights, and look after my parents part-time. It's a meeting to see if we click, not an hours snogging session or quick blow job — you wish. I'm sure I can spend an hour away from them, my friends, not a problem. But no problem."

"Your words tell me a lot about you. Me, me, me. Your life is all about you. An hour at Tesco's this morning would have been fine."

"And if my mum hadn't been coming out of hospital today, that would have been fine too!!!"

"That's life. I think I'm just saying about time restraint, you have twenty-four hours to lounge about, I have a lot to fit into mine, so you could be more accommodating with your time." I was trying not to be blunt. I also thinking this Jack Dempsey more than a bit selfish.

"Tell you what, just find another good cook, or should I say another fantastic exotic cook, you can lick, suck, and blow with. I can't be bothered with this; I am too busy!"

"LOL," Jack replied.

That was the last I heard from him.

That was three days, well spent, wasted, who knows? Why did I carry on chatting to him? He was so aloof. Was he married, or was he just after my body? Fuck Gill, and farewell.

I shall never know, but can only reflect that I should be choosier, follow my instinct more on my first thoughts on these blokes. Do the ones not looking for a relationship (what I want), but just to get me into bed, stand out a mile? Certainly they seem to show traits to look out for in the future.

Life is a learning curve; this fish has escaped again, scales intact, off to search out new waters.

Dory, Tickling Trout

So what of Dory? Was she still trying to catch her fish, line fishing as it were? We were still in regular communication, met up as often as we could, as best friends do, when our shifts allowed.

Yes, she was still trying to hook her big one, me helping her where I could, trying to fit it in between her main job, part-time job, and gym bunnying. There was a greater determination to succeed in what she was trying for, despite her despondency at times, especially when she felt her time was being wasted. But a bit of moral support and encouragement did her the world of good, and we would often joke about some of the messages, conversations she had

had, both on Badoo and the fish site. In fact, it was entertainment in itself for us, and if she was still searching, then at least if she could see the funny side as well, then it couldn't be getting her down too much. If in my early days of this fishing online I had found it addictive, to the extent it was dominating my life, at least Dory wasn't obsessed with it, and didn't let it get in the way of her normal life. Though she realised if Mr Right did come along, then she would have to make adjustments to that lifestyle, or risk burning herself out. And of course, there would be the fringe benefits, of which she was getting none at the moment, nor had she for the past three years, but hoped that they would come as well, especially if she offered a good meal. Better things to come, but she had done without for some time, and could manage a bit longer. The most important thing was to find someone she could enjoy time with; that corny old saying, share the important things in life, and see where life took her from there. She would look forward to a dinner out, a trip to the theatre, holidaying with her beau, and anything else the companionship would bring – only good things of course. She had plans, and wanted to fulfil them, hoped she would, and was getting impatient to get them on the move.

She would joke that if it was just a life partner she was out for, then as in my three-date rule, her first would be coffee, second out to dinner, and the third just head straight up to Gretna Green. Job done, sorted, and we all live happily ever after.

At least she was getting some interest now, and collecting badges by the handful. Not only the most picky, but now also the most likes, most looked at, and the most popular, more to add to the collection. Likes, she was now over a couple of hundred, but a lot, especially in her early days, had got the thumbs down without really looking (maybe a sign of her lack of confidence in herself and the thought of dating again). It had only been seven or eight weeks now that she had made herself 'available', so she had done well. Now I had to just persuade her to look more closely at some of them, look for the tell-tale signs of scammers, time wasters, and with some, try chatting just to find out more about them. You never know, there maybe one or two you would like to try going out with, and see where it goes.

So Dory was back online, and promising not to be so picky. There would be dates out there somewhere, and with the amount of interest she was getting, all those likes, then even if she did delete most, there would be some she had now decided she would talk to.

So, along came a Spanish gentleman online, put her down as a like, a very big like, and so Dory did enter into conversation with him – a certain Juan Fishing. This guy was a charmer, straight away calling her beautiful, and his beautiful dream girl. Pictures had been exchanged, showing him just out of the sea in the Canaries, where he had been fishing, diving with a harpoon. Everyone's fishing! This got them onto talking about the photos people put up and how genuine they were, or were they taken up to ten years ago? Then if they did meet up, they would be in for a big surprise. This Juan was talking of hoping, wanting to meet up in a couple of days for a coffee, on one of his days off, and this suited Dory as well, as that fitted into her rota. Juan was concerned that Dory didn't think his pictures genuine, and assured her that they were. Dory said she believed him, but all the fakes around were the reason this was called the 'dating game'.

Juan told her that he thought her a very interesting lady, and that he was keen to meet up and prove himself genuine, with natural enthusiasm, charming, positive, and romantic. Dory told him that he would be the first person that she would meet, and looked forward to it, and if they found that they weren't suited, then perhaps they could just become friends. They agreed that would be a nice option, and then got onto how many dates he had been on.

None, was the answer; he had chatted to a few, but whereas Dory was full of conversation, others don't talk much, which he didn't like, but Dory, those beautiful blue eyes and long elegant hair, sensual lips, 'a real dream, xxx.' Dory said she was just a working class girl taking care of herself, who enjoyed the good things in life. Only last week she had been to the gym with Chanel on her jacket, and someone had stolen it. Her friends joked that only Dory would wear Chanel to the gym.

Juan asked if there were any other men asking her for a date. Six in fact, but he hoped that he could be the first in/on line. Juan was really pleased that they were going to meet up; Dory joked that all the other ladies had disappeared off site, which only left him as the available catch. Juan was going to dream of her, especially if all these other women were disappearing. Dory joked she hoped she would be the last lady standing (though she could think of some fun while not standing), a bit like the sales, you get the bargains first before anybody else. She was off to the gym, gym bunnying again, bye!

Juan was worried he didn't get any replies to his messaging for several hours, but Dory had gone to work now, doing nights. She did reply in the end but Juan was worried she would be dreaming naughty and dirty about these other men who wanted to date her. She assured him she would be awake while working, but as the conversation progressed she realised his words were becoming more random, as if he had been drinking, as his conversation turned more and more to what he hoped would be happening with these other men, and it was getting ruder. And it got worse as he hoped that she would be given a 'hard' time by these men, having her, devouring her. This conversation was getting spooky, very spooky, but Dory tried to remain polite. But he still wanted to meet his now princess, tomorrow, very persistent.

Dory was trying to get some sleep after work, and when she came back online there was a strange message on her screen. "Messages you send to this chat line and calls are now secured with end-to-end encryption." What the f—k did that mean? It had appeared on his screen as well, but was first on Dory's just before he had tried to call her earlier. Juan said he would try and find out what it meant the next day.

Dory was starting to feel a bit creeped out about all this, the way his conversation had gone and now this. It was starting to knock her confidence again. Was she speaking to yet another potential scammer? She had rung me about it and I thought it all sounded a bit strange. Was it the start of what I had been through in the past? We decided that Dory would tell Juan that she was coming off the fish site, which Juan was happy with and thought they could carry on chatting on WhatsApp, as he did seriously fancy her. He was desperate for her to send him pictures of her, but she was backing away now, returned his calls less often, running away. She was knocking this all on the head. Enough. Somewhere, some Juan could smell a rat.

The delete button was pressed again, he was gone.

A little flustered again, but not put off with fishing online, she continued and was happy to chat to others. She was starting to get sort of addicted to her armchair dating, when along came another Spanish guy, this time from Barcelona. They chatted for a while as well, interesting conversations, but then slowly there seemed to be a pattern emerging in what he said, his mannerisms. Dory had seen this before, Juance too often. He wanted to meet for a coffee, but Dory did point out that Barcelona was a long way to go for a quickie – cuppa, that is. She suggested he find someone closer to him, and decreed that was the end of that conversation. She was finding he was stalking her online, as he appeared as different personas on several occasions, but he was recognisable.

Move on, Dory.

But now she wasn't put off, she was keen to get back down to it, get online again, and see what else was lurking in those dark, murky waters of the man pool.

But there was more dark still to come on the

horizon. If Juan had become a pain, and kept reappearing in different guises, my Indian gentleman who I chickened out of a date with (because of his accent) was now starting to message me again, and again and again. They were both giving me a bit of grief. I was talking to various gentleman, and, and… there did look as if a date may be on the horizon, then someone who started to message me, was starting to become a regular as well.

This guy was from Liverpool. He kept popping in and out of her messaging, trying to chat, then while we were together, and I was left with her phone this guy came on again, inviting Dory offering to take her to a sex swingers' party in Liverpool. Hey, let's skip the coffee and get right down to it! I showed Dory her message, and she politely replied that wasn't the sort of thing she was looking for, she just reiterated that she wanted the good things in life, to get out and about, and enjoy the company of a nice fella. He came back sounding a little bit angry and that Dory needed to spice her life up a bit, get out and about a bit in his world. He went on to say that he had gone out with a cross-dresser (Dory could nearly say, "Me too."), and had quite enjoyed some of the sex. His conversation was getting more and more sexual, and he sounded – was – very persistent.

Dory told him, each to your own, but it wasn't for her.

What was coming next? Not him, we hoped, but he did what we definitely weren't expecting. He said he was going to send a picture of him sucking a black cock, to which Dory replied that she would rather he didn't. The reply shocked her as he said that he was going to report her for being a gender offender, then he started looking at all her photos. Dory deleted all her photos straight away, and we debated whether we should be reporting him.

That wasn't a nice experience, something she, and to be honest me as well, could have done without, and fair dues to Dory, she did dismiss it all very quickly, but it did give us both a big question mark over the site that he had appeared on.

What could we do? Well, we did what girls like to do and went for a bit of retail therapy, off into the town centre. Dory was getting frustrated, and let's face it, it was now over three years since her body had been invaded by the opposite sex, and it was this frustration that took us to the toy shop.

I myself frequented Ann Summers quite often, in fact I would have to admit that some of my best bait had been bought there, but Dory was more interested in the pet department. Full of courage, she went straight up to the attendant, and enquired what she had in the way of rabbits. A very helpful lady, knowing all her animal husbandry, was soon introducing us to Rampant Rabbit, who came in his own waterproof sleeve, though Dory didn't want a swimming rabbit. He was apparently a very popular rabbit, orgasmic to the extent of being morgasmic. This was good sales talk; he had superior rounds of vibration, and climax technology, whatever that may be. We had heard of cruise control, but this certainly sounded far more exciting, this was definitely looking like number one for Dory, and she already had a hutch to put him in. What's more there were no batteries, no Duracell bunnies running out before she would reach the finishing line. Rampant bunny was starting to sound more exciting than gym bunny. Oscillating motion, this was going to be an orgasmic awakening. And it was half price, two for the price of one, though she only had one hutch. This was a real turn-on. The lady even explained how his soothing tones could stimulate a partner as well. She certainly knew her stuff. Practical experience?

She was persuaded and couldn't wait to get the young rabbit home, and house train him. We hadn't seen many violet-coloured rabbits before, perhaps it was a new breed, and it wasn't long until we were reading how to look after the young chap. His stomach was empty so the first job was to recharge his batteries. Forgot, he didn't have any – recharge his energy cells so he could pursue an active life, and he and Dory could enjoy each other's company. Oh, and the sleeve. Yes, they could shower together.

Like any new toy, we were fighting over it to see how it worked. "Fucking hell, Gill," Dory exclaimed as she couldn't find a way of getting it open. Rampant's light was flashing meaning he wasn't quite fully charged and therefore not quite ready to give his all. We were searching for the hole to connect him to the mains (please don't report us to the RSPCA), and get him fully in the mood, because then he would be quick, slow, quick, strictly not dancing. In our excitement, we hadn't read the instructions. Well, with sex you don't either, do you? Just make it up as you go along, or do what Mum told you, but Mum didn't mention rabbits! In the end we had to plug him into the computer to boost him, only hoping that he wouldn't download all his activities, get a virus and pass it on. Dory wasn't interested in any form of violet rubber Myxy VD.

I was sitting on them, and with their re-emergence we were able to get the poor rabbit sorted out. He was in the mood, going round and round, sounding like a Black and Decker. Omg!

Dory noted that regular inspection for damage was necessary, her or the rabbit – it had been over three years now.

We made another coffee and sat there drinking it, admiring this fine rabbit, upright with his ears 'pricked'. Dory was sure he would become a very accommodating housemate, and would be well satisfied with her purchase.

They looked longingly at each other; a cuddle would come soon enough, BUT, she had a date to prepare for.

Yes, a date. Dory was really going out on a date. She had changed her line, and was forever chatting now, starting to get hooked like I once was. The man pool, she was going to float in until the right one rose, took her bait, and her wait would be over.

She had been chatting to one Matthew Grayling for some three weeks now, and was enjoying the conversations with him, so was very pleased when he did ask her if she would like to meet up with him, perhaps go out for a drink for a couple of hours. Yes, a bite at last at what looked quite a tasty morsel. He was a mere forty years old, could be a real toy boy here, and single, allegedly, so this could be quite a catch.

After I had left her, she had a little time to prepare

for the date. Rampant, quietly in the background, was quite turned off by this idea of dating, and could think of better things to do, but Dory seemed very keen, so a hair wash, sort out a little sexy underwear (just in case, she was keeping an open mind on that one), and then lastly apply some make-up. If the date was arranged for eight o'clock, Matthew was picking her up, then she was ready nearly an hour earlier, waiting in anticipation; she was finally getting off the sofa. How time can go slowly when you are waiting, twiddling her fingers, pacing up and down, if only Rampant could offer some sort of conversation. But eight o'clock came and there was no sign of Matthew. The minutes ticked by, and through all her hope and the effort she had put in to show herself off to her best, he had not arrived, not a word from him. Was she going to be stood up? What would that do for her newfound confidence in herself?

Still nothing. She looked at Rampant and he at her, but no, Dory, there's a time and place for everything, and he would come, she knew he would.

Finally, nearly an hour late, there was a ring on the doorbell, and Dory rushed down the stairs to greet her 'date'. She opened the door, and there stood Matthew; she really was going to go out with a man after all this time. But the man standing in the doorway didn't quite look like the man she had chatted to and sent his picture to her. Sure enough it was Matthew Grayling, but this guy was a bit overweight compared with his image, and perhaps looked a little worn. He was here and ushering her to the car, so it was going to happen, a real date with a real man.

A short drive took them to a local pub where he went to the bar and bought a couple of beers. Dory was a Yorkshire lass, and liked her pint of Real Ale. Time to find out more about each other, like to begin with, why was he late? Not a good start to a future together if all worked out. Why? He really was a youngster compared with her, and if the pictures were a little flattering to him, his age was what he said it was. Time to research into his background. He lived with his father who had suffered a stroke. Dory wasn't sure if this was this evening (in which case why had he deserted him?) or sometime in the past. He lived with his son, and his father in town, with no woman to be seen anywhere. He had commitments, as he spilled out his life story, had lived with a woman for some time, but had found her quite a hateful person, especially to his father, and blamed her for the stroke. It had taken him some years to free himself from her, so now there were the three of them, the three men (one was seven), living together, but he had to help his father a lot in the evening as well as his fatherly duties to his son. His life was full, and to top that he was devoted to football, with his son, and running a junior football team which the son was in.

Yes, his life was full and Dory wondered where she, or any other woman would fit into his lifestyle. She supped her ale as any good Yorkshire lass would do, listening as Matthew told her more about himself, and then she told something of her own life to him – her job, gym bunnying, but deciding not to mention her new housemate who had moved in today.

Time sped by, and having arrived late, Matthew

couldn't be too long, as he would have to get home to check on his wards. Pints finished, they returned home to her place, pulling up outside her front door.

Dory wondered what the next step was, admitting to herself that even if the picture had lied slightly, she did actually fancy this Matthew a little. Pulling up and stopping the car, he turned and told Dory he was sorry he was late, and had enjoyed her company, but it did underline what he wanted from a relationship, why he was online. He could only ever spare a couple of hours in an evening, there would never be any nice dinners out, not the good things in life that Dory was so looking forward to with her 'new' man.

His two hours were, and he was quite open about it, an hour chatting, and an hour's sex. *Gosh, it's been so long, does it take that long?* Dory thought. He was looking for, and what he thought Dory was, was a bored housewife looking for a bit of fun and a bit on the side.

Dory explained that she wasn't that, she was looking for a man to share the good things in life with, this starting to sound a bit repetitive with the men she had talked with, dinner dates etc., and whatever may follow.

Even if he wanted her to be, he said he was glad that she wasn't just a bored housewife, then he leaned over and tried to kiss her, well to be honest, snog her like an eighteen-year-old. Dory didn't want that. There was no future in this, a young son, an invalid father, and football, well she had never been to a football match and was quite happy to keep it that way. No, sadly Matthew wasn't for her, and to make it worse, when was the last time he cleaned his choppers? His breath stank, she had to push him away.

He seemed quite annoyed now; the evening was coming to an abrupt end, Dory bidding her farewells and disappearing quickly back into her house.

She had been out, but success? No! At least he had been honest about looking for bored house wives for sex, but why couldn't he have said that three weeks earlier and not wasted her time chatting when there would not be the outcome she wanted? What both were looking for were worlds apart.

She looked at herself in the mirror, reminding herself, reassuring herself she was a good-looking woman, and sooner or later the right man would come along.

She wound her way up the stairs to her bedroom, stripping down to her sexy undies. She felt another presence in the room, waiting in the half light – Rampant Rabbit – and in her sexy undies he was getting turned on, he wanted to find the hutch he had been offered. Now there was a buzz in the air, and Dory experienced something she hadn't had for too long, far too long.

If the date hadn't turned out how she wanted, then at least the day had ended in a most satisfying way. She turned her light off and thought of sleep. Rampant, now still, waited motionless for another time, another time for her to come with him.

That was Matthew, and along with the West Midlands gentleman who was starting to become a bit of a pain, and the Scouser with his black cock, Dory was beginning to have doubts about this particular site, Badoo. I told her that she should be careful and think of her safety with some of these men, should consider reporting some of them, especially the one getting very heavy.

She did go back online, and found that he had deleted himself, though no doubt he would reappear as someone else, but she would not be around on this site anymore, if he did reappear. She would go off Badoo, and we would put her on another paid site, Match.com when we next got together. Ann Summers would also soon be launching a site, Snuggle Bunny, may be worth a look, and Rampant would certainly enjoy that one, and of course my Buzz Buzz.

Dory was still chatting away merrily on the fish site, and was getting more and more experienced in spotting the different types of men on here, those looking for the bored house wives, the scammers, and the rest.

Then to cap it all a bunch of flowers from Mr West Midlands – he wasn't giving up, but Dory wasn't interested. A nice treat? No, as the flowers were words, not the real thing, and went...

Forget-me-not, flowers since I can't get you out of my mind since the first day I saw you,

The Red Poppy, as I will remember you forever,

And finally, Poison Ivy, because you look gorgeous but can be deadly.

Wow, was this guy keen, so poetic, and persistent, but not for her.

*

She was now a compulsive chatter, but as she

talked to Rough Collie, Chitty Chitty Bang Bang, and more, there did sound as if there were some genuine men out there looking for something like what she was also looking for. If she did joke to them about whether she could finish her coffee before they rushed up to Gretna Green, there did sound as if there were some honest upfront men, and she was now talking to them.

Is Dory about to meet, have a date with a Henry Higgins who wants her with her accent to be Eliza? It could be an interesting game of role play, but more of that to come. Well, perhaps at a later day.

In the meantime, Dory is confident, and going to give this fishing lark a real go. No longer a dating virgin, she has got off her armchair and out the front door.

Her and that fucking rabbit will be satisfied, they are on a mission.

REFLECTIONS ON THE WATER

I was in a room the other day, having just finished a meeting with other member of staff and a couple of blokes from an outside agency, when we got talking about how we met our partners, or in my case, prospective partner. The two words, 'Internet Dating', came up in the conversation from one lady, a youngster in fact, who had just got engaged to her first catch online. The conversation continued, and slowly, one by one, everyone in the group bar one admitted to either actively fishing at the moment, or had met, caught their fish online. If people are reticent to talk about this form of dating, it is surprising how common it is and is used by many people for finding a partner or for getting a social life. In the distant past, before the invention of computers, it is in fact how my parents met, through a dating agency, and have lived happily together ever since.

The net has now taken over, and one frequently reads or hears on other forms of media how older people have met up through internet dating, whether by their own volition, or because their caring children have wished them to find another partner for companionship in their dotage, because they have sadly already lost a partner, but still have plenty to give, especially to another lasting relationship. A happy side of this new dating game, and good luck to them all, for now and for the future that they have found happiness, company, love again and can look forward to years of happiness together.

The younger generation are also using this form of dating more and more, but whether it is to find a lasting relationship or just a date, a one-night stand, or just convenient non-complicated sex, I don't know, but in these days of social media, Twitter, messaging etc., is the touch of a screen just a lot easier than that old-fashioned method of communication, talking to people face to face and discovering each other personally, rather than having it all printed on a screen? Social interaction may be something of the past in these electronic, technological days we live in. But life is becoming more rushed, more stressful, and maybe it is a sad reflection of life that we find it hard to find the time to explore the one thing that nature is all about, finding a partner, finding a mate to breed with. What is the main purpose of all species? Maintaining the future of that species is for us now squeezed between work, pleasure, travel, and so many other things, that we don't give ourselves the time to actually communicate in the way that we have developed through evolution. So social media and the internet take over, a convenient and ready form of access to anything you may want or need. And of course it opens avenues of contact that you would never have dreamed of thirty, forty, fifty years ago.

More people about, higher divorce rates, easier travel to places you are unfamiliar with if that's where work takes you, creates demand for ready contact with other people, people who may be in the same position of yourself.

That is where I found myself, when I came back home to the area I had spent my early years, but now a woman of the world, and my hometown a greatly different place from where I had grown up, married, and had my first two children. I had experienced a lot in my travels, had seen a lot of the world, but being back home by myself, and starting a new life when in my fifties, was something very different, and something I thought would be very hard. I now knew virtually no-one other than my son who still lived here, and a couple of siblings who now had their own lives, and my ageing parents in a neighbouring town. I had missed them on my journeys, and would now be close at hand to help them if needed. It was a fresh beginning, but I was desperate to learn from my mistakes of the past, forge myself a new life and find a lasting relationship, to see me into old age. Despite two marriages, I still hadn't found that special one, and now I was determined to find and be with him for the rest of my life.

I had already met my last partner through computer games, so was well averse to using the modern technology to help organise my life, and it was a logical step, especially as it became more and more advertised to use this form of communication to try and meet people in this lonely town I had moved back to. Being of an age group where most were either married or in couples, it was a daunting prospect to go out by myself in the hope of bumping into the man of my dreams. More so now that our streets become more dangerous for people and especially women out on their own. I hoped that the net would at least give me the chance to find out something about the people I hoped to meet, and if there was a mutual attraction, we could arrange to meet at a safe place for a woman to be, in broad daylight, giving a safe exit route if required.

However, even this cannot be guarantee to be safe, and convictions are now quite common news these days, where men have lured unsuspecting women into traps, and harm, where they have innocently arranged a date to find they were meeting up with a devious and dangerous sex predator.

In setting myself up online, I had endeavoured to protect myself as best I could, making my rules on dating, though I didn't always stick to them as closely as I should have done. But my three rules of dating were there for self-protection, and thankfully up to this day I have received no physical harm, nor have any of my friends and acquaintances who have also used this form of dating.

But the dangers are out there, and we mustn't forget them. Watch your back ladies, and I don't know but there may be similar risks for some men dating as well, especially if they are a little naïve.

I have been internet dating now for some seven or eight years, and can reflect on some interesting experiences, some where I have been hurt, some that have been an education, and some that are best forgotten, part of life's rich tapestry but where I should have been more subjective. Where I should have followed my own rules, in actual fact.

But for me, at this time, my internet dating has alas got me no catch. If my reflections have been grouped under 'Fishing the Net', then it is because to some extent it has been like fishing, and as both Dory and myself have thought, it is like a game, teasing, tempting your 'prey', your fish, with whatever bait you may think suitable, the aim being to catch your man. Like Dory said, hooking the duck at the fairground, and if successful you come away with a goldfish. A game but with some of the dangers I have mentioned above.

I am approaching being a sexagenarian. If that sounds appropriate for me, and yes I do like a bit, but through my fifties I have tried this fishing game as I thought it the most likely way of finding my man, catching my fish, to mount (there I go again) as my keepsake in the cabinet called home. Did I want a man to stuff (or more likely him, me), preserve forever? Yes I did. Alas, my years on the net to this time had been unproductive. Yes, I had been out with a few men, but relationships were few and far between. I had chatted to many men, on different sites, different types of men, varied backgrounds, but I think on reflection that I could stereotype them into not many different groups, and over time have been able to categorise them early on, and I would say that Dory is reaching this stage too.

Paid sites, free sites, and the fish site, I would say that there didn't tend to be a lot of difference between them, though I may perceive that if men were paying for it, internet dating that is, then you probably did find that there were more genuine men on these sites.

In my experience, I did find groups of men who were genuinely interested in finding a partner. But, and it is a big but, they were of similar age to me or older, and had lived by themselves or with aged parents for most of their lives. I found that they had lived very sheltered lives, had little experience of the type of life I wanted to lead, and basically they were on the whole very boring. Sadly, most of the men I had met at the singles groups I had been to, I would class in the same category, though they may have had the misfortune of losing a partner in the past, and now seemed incapable of kick-starting their lives again. It was like they wanted their lives and social activities all organised for them, they were trapped in a time warp, and seemed incapable of getting out of it, or unwilling. There was nothing like going out on a 'date' and spending the whole time talking about the man opposite's past, former lady. They were stuck in a rut and seemed reluctant to get out of it, and though wishing them the best for their future happiness, they were not for me. I wanted – want – to live, go forwards, not look backwards the whole time.

The likes of Artie, yes, he was kind, and was what you would class as a good man, but he offered me nothing other than devotion, and twenty-minute cooked minute steaks.

The likes of him, I could have taken for a ride, and taken him for as much as I could have got out of him. But that would have been no pleasure, and would not have given me the happiness that I was looking for. No doubt there would be ladies out there that would have thought differently, but no, not for me.

Secondly, there were the men who may have had a partner, married or otherwise, and had lost them for one reason or another, like myself divorced twice, and like me were seriously looking for a new beginning, and I suppose this was the pool that I was hoping that I could fish in, and with the right bait could catch the one I really craved for.

Was I unlucky, or just using the wrong bait? But in this pool I seemed unsuccessful. I did get a couple of bites, and did see a couple of gentlemen for some time, but there always seemed some sort of hindrance to it being a lasting relationship. It may have been that if I had met them in five, ten years' time, we could have had a very happy relationship, shared each other's company, holidayed together, been there for each other. We could have been very contented. Whether we would have lived our lives between here and Australia I don't know. They were very devoted to me, would have done anything for me, but that was where the problem arose. More strictly, where it didn't rise.

Though I say it myself, I had looked after myself; if a little overweight, my skin was still good, smooth, my red hair flowing over my shoulders to my perfect breasts, good legs – I felt proud of my body and liked to enjoy it with 'members' of the opposite sex, that is not saying that I'm a nymphomaniac, but if I hadn't enjoyed sex when I was young, I certainly did now. It had been a huge disappointment to me, when in these couple of relationships, when we had decided to sleep together, and then go a bit further, my jaunts under the sheets had finished in frustration for me. As the moistures in my inner body would start to flow, I would lay expectant that some hug sea serpent would find my cave, enter, explore, in and out with the flow of the tide, and would release his tadpoles deep inside me, would want to come visiting again, arouse me, excite me until I too was spent.

But no, a quick sniff at the cave entrance and there was a limp retreat back to where he came. He would lay back, spent, talk about a minute steak again. Me, I would lie there unfulfilled, unsatisfied.

Penile erectile dysfunction I would read is a common problem in older men, and I don't want to sound horrid in demeaning those that suffer from it. For many reasons it is becoming more common, and as men get older the chances of them suffering from it increase. For some, it may be due to illness, others the stress of the hectic lives we live these days, others it may be mental. I am not an expert and don't wish to be, and I suppose the psychological effect it must have on your partner if it keeps happening to him, must be profound. Maybe there are some who think a quick in and out, and they have done the business, they are satisfied and are content to lie back and drift off to sleep thinking they have given their woman a good sorting, but a lot, it must be very demoralising, and either they give up or resort to the little blue pill to see if that works. The problem can't be dismissed lightly for those it affects, and I presume the medical profession will try and help wherever they can. It is a shame that these men can't enjoy the bed pleasures I like so much when with the right man, and yes, I would have to admit there have been one or two of those mentioned before who knew just what to do with me. Pleasure verging on bliss, and I wasn't quite ready to give it all up while my body still had that craving.

I suppose if it arises (or doesn't more to the point), then it is a problem you have to discuss with your partner and see if there can be some solution to satisfy all, and in honesty I had gone through this line when the problem occurred. But I still had my needs and they weren't being satisfied.

Trips to Ann Summers and online to Love Honey had provided goods, but not the solution to my encounters (even if they would in the future). Did I want to be driving round the countryside with a key in my handbag, deciding when I wanted to release the little prick, waiting then to see whether he was too shy or not to pop out of his cock cage, whether I or he would have to find a rubber band in the drawer and toss for who was going to apply the thing around his balls? No, sad for him, but if I saw he was hung like a stallion, I wanted him to perform like one as well. Ride, baby, ride!

No, really nice and devoted blokes but sooner rather than later, my frustrations would have become too great, so sadly these blokes were not for me. I do genuinely hope they find the happiness they are looking for, but it won't be with me.

There seem to be a group of men out there, and probably a likeminded group of women as well, who just think of themselves as the greatest invention to women ever created, and it was their duty to put themselves about as much as they can. Whether it be married men looking for a bit of extramarital pleasure, or men just out for a good time, their conversation would probably soon give them away, becoming very intimate 'baby, x', very early when chatting, very often with false pictures of ten years previously, and soon becoming very suggestive, smutty in the way they chatted. I had more than my share of these, Dory too, but in time one could recognise them fairly easily. My three-date rule was to try and find these out early, and after a time, I would try and meet up sooner rather than later, see these guys, find how genuine they were and could then discount them. I have described some, and I would try and get them off smut to a more sensible line of conversation if I could, but it would not take long before the smut reappeared. I really hope that I didn't encourage some of it, the conversations I had with Elvers Rose, for example, but I found out to my cost in one case that sex was all they wanted. I was had, literally, but it seemed common that many men looked at your – my – photo and if they liked what they saw, all they were interested in was bedding you. It often turned out that they hadn't read your profile, just thought you were a bored housewife looking for a bit to brighten your life, and they were only too willing to oblige.

Come clean, Gill. I did have one or two friends with benefits, but it was more than just sex, and I do keep in touch now and again with some, as friends.

Yes, it would seem there are plenty of sex predators fishing online, some serving a purpose for frustrated women, others just out for their own gain, regardless of a lady's feelings. Plenty of broken hearts.

I of course had my gentleman who just wanted to set me up as his mistress, and had the money to do it. Cheaper than divorce probably, but I wouldn't have been happy for long, waiting at his beck and call, that wasn't for me.

The nibblers, the stalkers, even the ladies who would chat to you, hoping for a little more than just a dabble. Probably nice people, but again not for me.

Then there would be the perverts, out there for self-gratification. Internet flashers, 'cybersex', those who quite honestly I would lock up, but certainly need reporting to the managers of these dating sites, and to be banned from them. If I had wanted to watch porn, I would have done so but to see, or have thrust up on you some tosser wanking off on screen in front of you, that is not what I started fishing the net for.

But the most dangerous of the lot were the predators, the sharks, the pike, the piranhas. There would seem to be a growing industry in computer scamming; how many people do we all know that have been scammed in some way or another, especially on the telephone or online? Generally, it will be financial scamming, trying to get access to your credit card numbers, bank account numbers, mobile phones, so that they can move money away from you without you realising what is happening.

Internet Dating is no exception. There are sharks out there out to get you, and that is male and female sharks. I hope I am wise enough to spot them now, but again I have been had, both financially and sexually, and it is here that although I would consider myself a woman of the world. Then on these occasions, I have been more than a little naïve, falling head over heels in love with someone I have never even met before, and realising what was happening too late.

If one Googles Internet Dating and scams, one finds no end of especially women who have been had. I suppose those scammers, those sharks, see a pool of vulnerable, lonely women looking for a soulmate, just as I am doing. A surprising number of them will claim to be American forces personnel, overseas, fighting the good fight, just as Samuel Johnson claimed to me. They will tell how they are posted away from home, are lonely, would love to find a partner, and the dating sites give them the opportunity of meeting people they otherwise wouldn't have done.

It is not long before they are calling you babe, sweetheart, wooing you online, and you are falling for them. They are saying all the right things you want to hear when you are desperately trying to find your mate. They are warm, loving, apparently open about themselves, have seen your picture, flatter you, tempt you. They are real pros, and if you don't know it, they are probably lining up several traps at the same time.

They will look for signs that you have money. With me, I was setting up my own business; they didn't know that it was in its infancy, there were no financial resources behind me, but the print said 'business woman' and they thought, *We'll have some of that*.

Then they build you up, build you up, more and more, increasing your confidence in them. They flatter you more, and like me, you find yourself falling, falling, madly in love with them. I have to admit, I was fully taken in, and now look back on how stupid I was, falling so head over heels I love with someone I had never met. Besotted, lost sleep over him, didn't eat worrying about him. For us poor women who are taken in by all this, we are dragged in so much that we are sinking. Promises that when their tour is over, they would come and visit, perhaps holiday together. Yes, we were setting up our future, me and this American soldier. The rice man, he took me in for a long time, and I had been scammed already, they are all very clever, and us women fall for it.

Are we so desperate for a man, for male company? Yes, it would appear that we are. Oh dear!

And then the sting comes. When they think we are well and truly hooked, WATCH OUT!

It would not be for me to lecture everyone on Internet Dating scamming, especially as I had been a victim myself, not once but nearly twice, and luckily for me, I didn't have much money so I couldn't send my 'brave' American serviceman very much, but if I had had it, I would have done; he had taken me in with his tales of love, the shop he was going to start in London, and our future lives together.

Luckily, the rice man scammer, I got wise when I spoke to him. His story was not fitting with what he had told me before, and I managed to escape unscathed. But, nearly fooled again.

Romance scams are now big business, run as profit organisations, with a well-structured hierarchy, run from internet cafes, very often in West African countries – Nigeria, Ghana, the Ivory Coast. There will probably be teams working their prey, usually coming over as American servicemen abroad. They have no close family, no-one to share their love with, and it is not long before they are sweet talking you, the love of their lives. In messaging them, you often get strange replies as you may be talking to someone different to the last time, delays in answering you about their homes, as they go on the internet themselves to find the correct answers to your questions.

Very often strange names, or names you know but spelt in a funny way. So many clues that they are false, they are about to scam you, but in their speech to you, they are taking you in, and as in my case, you find you are falling in love with them, these men you have never met, only seen pictures they have sent. But these are almost certainly false as well, using false photos, which may even be of people that have been scammed before. This really is like fishing as they hook you and draw you closer and closer to their net.

You are in love with them, and sooner or later arrives the sting. Tales of hardship, they have been injured in active service, they need money to pay their hospital bills, so that it will be all the sooner that they can come over and see you, to cement their relationship with you. There may be a package they want to send you, something valuable which needs to be 'smuggled' into the country by some helpful courier, as in my case, but they need money to offer a bribe or two along the way. You are in love and can't say no to them; you are well and truly hooked, and subscribe to their wishes. Others will get you to go out to visit them, to these African countries, and wanting to meet the man you have fallen in love with, you go, you meet them, and even if they are not quite what you were expecting, you love them and want more. You visit again, and get drawn into this scamming yourself, becoming an accomplice. They really have got you.

A friend of a friend, yes, a bored housewife, nearly gave up everything in terms of her marriage and wealth as she started chatting to an African gentleman, indeed went out and visited him, slept with him, gave him money on the premise of a bright future, but luckily just in time, realised what she had already was not so bad, and knocked Africa on the head. It was a close call, and she got out just in time.

Angel, again was nearly taken in by one of these scams, but got wise to it, but was interested just to see where it would go. It reached the stage where the scammer realised that he had been found out, but continued their conversation, telling her that he was working for the Government of his country, preying on vulnerable women, to extort money out of them – it was a job to him.

It has become an industry, and probably for the opposite sex as well, especially with Eastern European beauties offering themselves to vulnerable men, looking for a future, a relationship, but, send them some money for some sick relative, or their flight over to the United Kingdom so that they can meet up.

Agencies are set up to investigate the scammers, which may in fact be scammers themselves. Yes, a huge industry built up on screwing people over in their vulnerability of wanting a partner. Some can get so drawn in that they become an accomplice to the scam, a criminal themselves, and place themselves in a position difficult to get out of.

I'm not an expert, and like so many others, can only read up on this business online, and I would suggest anybody, especially in my age group, should do some research online into scammers, so that they scan spot the all-too-obvious tell-tale signs, and try and prevent the heartache and financial loss that may ensue.

A hundred-odd quid, it could have been more if I had had it. I didn't, I was lucky.

There is plenty on the net, read it and save yourself a lot of grief. I can't believe how naïve I was, very nearly twice. Please don't make the same mistakes I did. I was heartbroken, then felt a complete ass.

You can check out GIs on service lists; very often payments are asked for through Western Union. Check the account is genuine. Protect yourselves, ladies. If you have taken the trouble to answer all these questions for your profile, then spend a little time looking at the possible scammers after you.

A different sort of scam I suppose, but those out there who are just grooming you for sex. I was again had, literally, and can't really offer any advice on how to spot them, other than perhaps they are a bit too good to be true. But more heartache.

These days there are many sites, choose what you want, whether it be men in uniforms, for men, Russian ladies, Thai ladies, there is probably a site for anything you may be looking for. I stuck to what I thought were the main dating sites, some paid, some not, and I suppose I got a good mix of men on them – scammers, perverts, those just looking for sex, thinking us all bored housewives, all sorts. Dory, new to this angling sport, now also finding the same sort of men that I did, but with one difference, or to start with anyway. I have to admit, I love technology, the bee's knees, and I became addicted, to the point where it was taking over my life, chatting to so many men, hoping, really hoping that the next one would be the one for me. My fishing days would be coming to an end.

Angel, Orca, Starfish, yes they did find their match, and I, if jealously, can only wish them the best for the future. Dory, if a bit reticent to begin with, deleting anybody and everybody, also now finds herself, well, not quite as addicted as I was, but let's say compulsive. If she was nervous about this dating game to begin with, now she has got into it, chats a lot, has got off the sofa and has at last dated (and of course now has a pet bunny).

I should not, of course, forget to mention those men out there, fishing themselves, like me, and Dory, for that perfect catch. A life partner, like me, someone to enjoy the good things in life; like me, someone to share a bed with and enjoy those carnal pleasures that our children think us too old to enjoy; like me, those genuine, sexy, really nice men, who want to spend half their year in Australia, want to cruise, want to love ME. But all I can say in this category, for me, WHERE THE FUCK ARE THEY?

I would have to admit over these years that I have been fishing, yes, a couple of relationships, and I have laid myself open (again a couple of times literally), blinded by my wish to find the perfect man for me – it has not been a great success.

I know many women, and men, have found their match dating online but not me, or Dory (a novice at the moment). Is there something about our age group, the fifty-somethings, that men just think us frustrated, and just want a good bonk? WE may enjoy sex, but that doesn't mean that is why we are on these dating sites. As Dory would say, allow me to finish my coffee before we lay ourselves bare. Are there so many men out there that just think it their duty to give us 'frustrated' women one, satisfy us and just another notch on their belts? It would appear there are.

Where does that leave me? I really want to hook a man, I want a life partner, but where do I find him? I can't walk into a pub and say, "You, I want you, now, but it is commitment for life." In fact, I can't walk into a pub by myself full stop. It would be like opening the door and saying, "Who wants it? Who wants it now?" No, not for me or any other 'lady'.

What shall I do, continue online, continue my search, float my bait out to the pool I want to catch in?

I probably am becoming a little disconcerted by this method of fishing. I seem to catch a load of sharks, but not the fish I am after. Would Ann Summers' Snuggle Bunny site be any fun? Would that find me what I am looking for, or, knowing what their line is, would I be just offering myself as a 'bored' housewife, looking for a bit of fun, dating yes, but finding a lasting relationship? I don't know. There is someone I know who does really like what Ann Summers has to offer me, who liked me dressing up, so whatever way I decide to go, it is a shop I will be frequenting still – a very good bait shop!

Gill, it is time to take stock, review your life plan, change your strategy. Is there any better bait to offer?

FISHING THE NET

Taking stock takes me back to somewhere I have been before, a perfect (especially if you look at his bum) fish, that I have so nearly hooked before, but let him get away.

I know, though, that for all those fish I have hooked before, put back many of them, that this one would not be caught on the net. I would have to devise some other plan, because in my heart of hearts, for too long this is the one I have wanted.

I have tried a bit, of course, fishing, to have some fun, to try and get over him, but as hard as I search for what other shoals that may lay deeper in my pool, like a shark, his fin circles above water, reminding me of his presence.

I have to admit to myself, I want him, I want him mounted, I want him in my special plaice, and I am going to make one last cast to see if I can hook him, or try and forget him forever.

The sun shines over the waters, making it easy to reflect on what might have been, what has gone on before in this dating game, and what I really want from it.

It has taken a long time, but now my goal is clear. I'm out to catch the big one, and I think I know what sort of net will get him.

TACKLE, BAITS AND LURES

Through all this, I had met one man that I, whatever else I did, couldn't get out of my mind. I had been with others, some even to try and get him out of the system, to go out and have some fun, but my mind always came back to him.

He had got away once, should I angle after him again? And this is where, Gill, you have to be honest with yourself and admit he is the one you want, and have wanted ever since it didn't work out. One thing is for certain, he was a technophobe, and I wouldn't get him on the net, or any other type of organised dating system.

We had kept in contact over those, for me, lost years. We swapped birthdays, and would meet up every now and again for a catch up, a drink, or sometimes a pub meal. He showed concern when I was on my back (the spinal complaint, not what you thought), seeing if there was anything he could do to help, and had offered the occasional bit of advice about not selling myself short to some of these men I had seen. If he kept his own life to himself, he was a changed person from the one that I had gone out with and fallen in love with. Now so confident, so sure in where he wanted to be going, he had in that lost time to me, found himself. And his bum was still just as gorgeous.

In jest I had threatened to drag him upstairs, but it had never happened. Did he want me, did I want him? The question never arose as we continued our separate lives. That said, I did enjoy catching up, seeing him from time to time, even if I was looking, fishing in different waters.

But all else had failed me, where was this man who was going to woo me, love me, and be by my side for the rest of my life? I ain't found him yet, and seemed to be swimming against the tide in making any progress in finding my catch.

So Gill, you have made the big decision that you are going to go after the one that you have wanted ever since you first set eyes on him. There was nothing to lose and plenty to gain if it came off, to try and recapture the one that got away.

Go for it, but you may have to play a different game to the one you played last time; it will take more than a bit of ground bait to entice him to your hook, then strike and reel him in, into that waiting net, into my arms.

I was going to have to give a lot of thought to whatever strategy I decided on to land him. May have to play the long game, and wait patiently for him to approach into my pool.

It was a long, hard decision; I didn't want to set

myself up again, only to fall and be hurt again. Last time was the wrong time, it certainly was for him anyway, but whereas he had moved on, resolved a lot of the issues he had had with himself then, by all accounts, for me, it had been a long, hard, and painful time to get over him, if I actually ever had. My sister had been brilliant and had introduced me to the Secret, which had helped a lot, and perhaps it was because of this, that my decision would be to try again. It was certainly something that I still wanted, and if I didn't try, then I wouldn't succeed in my mission. I could end up with someone, though it was all falling a bit flat so far, but would I regret always that I was not with the one I had let slip through my finger before.

I guess that was it, I was going to try and would have to find a way of wooing him back. I knew there were things that made him back off before, me being so full on, perhaps not giving him the space he needed to be him. He hated technology, even TV, which I enjoyed so much. He had his own very individual tastes and ideas of how he wanted, and with his newfound confidence, how he would spend his time. It takes two to tango, but I would have to let him be himself more, not force myself up on him too much.

The problem now would be how to make all this happen. I would have to plan carefully to hook him, and the first task would be to arrange a meeting. If I could do that, then perhaps I would be able to think of a bait that he couldn't refuse to take.

As ever, the biggest obstacle to my plans was my shift pattern, especially knowing his work, to find a convenient time for both of us to be free wasn't that easy. I knew he also enjoyed quite a heavy schedule at the time, so finding that date was going to require a bit of patience.

I decided that the easiest way to begin this process was not the internet, but the good old telephone; send him a random text to make contact, and see where that would take me. I suppose I was a little nervous, but nothing ventured, nothing gained. Here goes Gill, and fingers crossed.

At the time, to get myself out a bit more, other than when I had the chance to go out with the girls at work, I had joined another singles group, who met up at least once or twice every week, and was less structured than the one I was in before, where I had met him, but did have some of the old members from before, along with a new set of people I had never met before. Obviously, I had joined to try and find my man, a man, but had found it gave me company but no new bites. It gave the opportunity to see who were members online, and a little about themselves, so I had gone along for better 'sport'. Up till now, yes, it had got me out, but in finding a new beau, no, nothing. The girls at work were even getting frustrated that there were no new chapters in my continuing saga of finding a life partner.

An aside, but that along with the continued use of the dating sites was producing unproductive fishing.

The random text was sent, my plan was under way. Just a question asking him how he was, how work was, and how his parents were, as they had moved up into the area now. Press button, sent, now wait and see. In the past when I had contacted me, sometimes I would get a quick reply, other times in may be a day or so, sometimes even a week or longer. I would have to be patient, and see how long it took him.

This time he was very quick with his reply, as usual not giving too much away about himself, but more asking about me, and suggesting that we should catch up again sometime, a drink or pub snack, whatever I fancied. Well, I knew what I fancied but it was too soon for that, so yes, a drink would be nice.

"WHEN?"

Not wanting to sound too eager, but it couldn't come soon enough as far as I'm concerned. When? When? I would tell him my next group of shifts and see what he wants to do. Message gone again, now the anxious wait.

This time the reply wasn't so quick. Two, three days passed and nothing. How obvious was it at work that I would keep checking my phone, waiting for that reply, waiting, waiting?

I busied myself in my day-to-day life, working, my housework, and gaming. Yes, for me World of Warcraft was a hobby, and I spent plenty of time on it, and though I say it myself, am rather good at it. Though it didn't seem to be working for me, I also kept an eye on my dating sites, see who was checking me out, messaging me, and still with an open mind because my master strategy may not work – see if there were any I may fancy a nibble at.

I could only wait on him now, hope he would get back to me soon. I really wanted this date to happen, the sooner the better, so I get to move on to the next part of my plan. Scheming bitch! But hey, nothing tried, nothing gained!

At last, a reply. He had been very busy, his job could involve long hours, sometimes working day and night, and so at times he could get very tired. How was I fixed the following Wednesday? He could manage then or the following night, but the Wednesday would be better.

I checked my diary, hoping that work would not get in my way, and thankfully I was free between shift blocks. We were going to meet up, but I mustn't seem too eager. "Yes, that would be nice. What did you have in mind?" I enquired. I know what I wanted.

Again, a wait before he came back to me, suggesting a bar meal down by the river. If it was nice we could sit outside over a beer and food, and enjoy the summer evening sunshine. Wonderful, that sounded great to me; we had arranged to meet, and that was the first part of the plan completed.

It would be a catch-up again, always nice to meet him, but obviously this time I had other motives. It had been a while, and I'm sure we would both have news to tell each other, of what we had been up to over the past few months, and it probably was three, four months since we had last met, though there had been the exchange of texts now and again. He hadn't even seen my new house, so, yes, quite a bit to refresh ourselves about each other. I had something to really look forward to, but, Gill you mustn't raise your hopes too high as nothing may come of it, despite your little plans.

I went on my way, happy. What had I to lose that was any worse than what had happened last time we broke up? It could only be the beginning of a new exciting chapter in my life, or the permanent closing of a book. At least I would know one way or the other, rather than keep hoping.

With my sense of direction, I suggested that he pick me up, trying to give clear instructions on how to find my house. With my right often being my left, I hoped I had got it right, left, oh I don't know. I just hoped he could find me.

I wasn't going to overdo things when the evening arrived, it was just to make contact, see how the land lay, and plot my best way forward. Yes, I was excited about meeting up again, but I had to try and keep that to myself, and try and play it cool. Gill the cool chick, there's a novelty.

No fancy dress tonight, a nice blouse, see through with a black tunic underneath, but it did show enough of my boobs just to remind him what he had been missing these past few years. Yes, more than a bit of cleavage to tempt, and tease.

That should do nicely; a reasonably tight pair of jeans, and to finish it all off, some nice light tan slip-ons with a bit of a heel. A quick spray of perfume, and a touch of lippie, that should do nicely, and of course with my hair down how he used to like it.

I was ready for my date. Was it a date? I'm not sure. No, at this stage we will just call it a meeting, a night out with an old friend.

I waited patiently, ready before I needed to be, but just like old times, almost bang on eight, there was a knock on the door, he was here. I opened the door with a broad smile on my face, and if there was a little flow of excitement between my legs, well that was my secret. He had even bought me a bunch of flowers.

Wow, I wasn't expecting that, and accepted them gratefully, returning a quick peck on the cheek.

Good, he didn't run away from that. Fingers crossed my night would work out as I had planned. As he went back to his car, I collected my handbag from the living room, locked the door behind me and went over to where he was holding the car door open for me, a little skip in my step, unnoticed by him. Still a gentleman, and if I had a quick glance behind him, that bum was still perfect. Good, that did please me, and a thought crossed my mind how those tight muscles had serviced me all those months, years ago, and I hoped would do so again. He hopped in beside me, started the car and drove the short few miles down to the river, crossing the old bridge and turning into The Woodbridge. It was a pleasant evening and we would be able to enjoy some of the sunshine before it disappeared behind the trees. He hadn't changed in his choice of beer, always looking for something he hadn't tried before (hoping the same didn't apply to his women as well!), and me, a refreshing cider. We found a table close to the water's edge. I sat and watched as those firm thighs straddled the wooden bench, again hoping that they may again straddle me in the not too distant future.

We chatted, about nothing in particular – how work was going, he was in a particularly busy spell at the moment, and had suffered a lot from his neck and back, going back to a time he had fallen badly when we were going out before. Not anything I had done to him I might add, but now there were regular visits to a local chiropractor to try and sort him out. The stresses of his job on his body were beginning to take their toll, but retirement was still a distant vision as he strived to make ends meet. I told him about my job, though not a lot different from the last time we had talked, the people I worked with, of which Dory was one, but he didn't know any of them, so it largely went over his head, other than the antics we got up to on our girls' nights out.

It was time that we ate, so we moved inside, finding a table where we could talk without being drowned out by other people also dining. We ordered and waited for our meal to arrive, nothing particularly special, but I was enjoying meeting up. Talk of family, his parents, children and granddaughter followed, all of whom I had met at one stage or another in the past, but some time ago now.

Over food, I told him about my house, lodgers, holiday plans, and then… why did you mention it, Gill? Why start talking about my dating? Why, why? I was trying to get him back; it was unlikely it would make him jealous, we had been apart so long now. Why did I have to bring that up? Yes, in the past I had told him and he had even proffered advice as he often thought, as when I was with him, I threw myself at the next available man, was too full on to the point of being off-putting. He often had said that I was a wonderful person, but I didn't need to throw myself at men, let them find the real me themselves.

He didn't seem to take a lot of notice of it. Why should he be that interested anymore? So the best I could do was to quickly change the subject. Holidays. What was he doing this year? Me, I was going to Australia in the not too distant future to catch up with my son, even consider if life wasn't going the way I had planned, to use my dual nationality to return there for good. I had often said that if I couldn't find my love in England, then in Oz, there would be plenty of men chomping at the bit for a bit of me.

You're doing it again, Gill. You want this man, are out to get him, yet you are talking of leaving the country permanently. Get back to the plan.

"How's your meal?" A good fall-back, as I tucked into a slightly chewy steak. He was fine and just carried on chatting. He too was away soon, a holiday in the sun to unwind. How jealous was I of all those ladies who could admire that bum again as he stretched out in the sun. My mind was on a Mediterranean beach ogling him, wishing I could be rubbing factor 15 on those thighs, hoping I might get one later. Lovely thought, but back to him. Yes, he was going away with a lady friend, for a few days – ten or eleven – and he really needed the rest. He was looking forward to it.

Lucky bitch, I thought. Was this going to stop my plan in its tracks? Time to regroup, a wee break to get myself together again, offering my excuses, and would return shortly.

More composed, I sat down again, relieved and back in control of myself. Go forward, Gill, as if sticking to Plan 1. Thrust your cleavage forward, regain his attention, keep his eyes on you.

He was driving, so had reached his limit, but I slowly downed another cider as we enjoyed the sweet course, and our evening was nearly done. Again, he opened the car door for me, to let me in and if my bust brushed against him, I'm sure it was only accidental.

The position was held for what seemed an eternity, letting him feel the warmth of my bust against him. Yes, definitely accidental, then I lowered myself into the car. I realised that I had the short journey home to achieve my goal, put my plan into fruition.

That journey passed oh so quick, and before I knew it, we were home. Should I offer him coffee? Yes, see if I can extend the evening a little longer, but he declined the offer. Were my plans falling around my ears?

One last chance before he was gone; this was supposed to be a trap, a lure, to get him again. It came out in one rush, words delivered perfectly, if unplanned like this.

"Would you like to meet up again before we both go away, my treat (yes, that's what I was really hoping for now, this time)? A meal, we could find a band, and then if you liked I could put my boots on?" Did I really say that? What will he think? That was really laying myself bare, and he preferred me with my little red set on.

Oh dear, I have said it, now what will he say? Could I have destroyed my chances forever? I didn't dare look into his eyes, but would have to face him, see his reaction. Would the tyre marks be left permanently on my drive as he sped to get away as quickly as possible?

No. He turned to me and said that he would like that, not emphasising whether it was the thought of the meal or me in my boots which he wished for. Let him know possible dates when, and we could finalise it. Yes, would be nice before we went away. The trouble was that from what I had said earlier, he may have taken it as a last goodbye. I leant over to thank him for the evening, give him a kiss on those lips, let him smell my perfume. Oh dear, I almost lost my balance as my hand reached down onto his thigh to steady myself, well okay, it may not have been his thigh, but it did feel hard. I gave him a quick snog, removing my hand, and opened the car door, stepping out quickly with another lingering glimpse of my cleavage on show.

He reversed off the drive and was gone. I fumbled for my keys in my bag. Yes, he said yes! Fuck, he said yes, I almost had a climax on my own driveway.

As I got back into my living room, I reflected that my evening had been a success; he was going to go out with me again. The mention of boots, my nice black boots that had pleasured him in the past, hadn't put him off. Now all I had to do was to find a day that would suit us both, before we went on our respective holidays. Do that, go out and hopefully at the end of the night I would know if we had a future, or whether I would have to try fishing in Australia, and with some of those Australian men, it certainly would be coarse fishing.

As I put my PJs on (he wouldn't want to see me now) and slipped between the sheets, I felt a surge of excitement again. It would do no harm just to send a quick text to thank him for the evening and to look forward to our meal, and afters in the not too distant future.

Sleep would be enjoyed that night, my plan was working, so far!

I slept well, but now had things to do, hoping above

all hope that having said yes, he would go on this date.

I needed to plan my wardrobe for this evening when it occurred. I needed the right bait, I needed the right tackle.

I had decided on a dress for a change, show off my legs, and if there had been a mention of my boots, then a dress would be better, especially as it was summer. What I really needed was a little something special underneath, so the nibble would turn into a bite. A trip into town was called for; I needed to go into Ann Summers for that special little outfit for me. The next day off, I was there looking through their wares. Somewhere in this shop was going to be the bait I needed.

Whilst I was looking, though I didn't recognise him to begin with, staring through the window, was the Italian stallion, though perhaps he may have been better described to me as the Italian gelding. He came in and said hello, luckily not asking any embarrassing questions on what I was trying to purchase. His Cornetto may have melted if he had seen. We talked briefly, it was nice to catch up, but I had other things on my mind, bigger fish to fry.

We went our separate ways, but I did say we should keep in touch, just in case. Now Gill, that really is keeping your options open! I was a lady on a mission and just needed that okay for all to go ahead. A text came, saying how much he had enjoyed the evening, swopping news, and giving a suggested date that if I wanted to treat him, then how was that day?

Of course it was okay, a Sunday night, but I was really looking forward to it. It was going to happen, and I could continue my plans.

The day he had suggested was still a couple of weeks off, but I was getting excited, the possibilities of a bright new future. A hiccup came along the way as his work commitments got in the way, but I was only too happy to make it another day, even if it couldn't come soon enough for me. But it would have to be after our respective holidays. A shame it couldn't be sooner, but it was going to happen, that was good. A fresh start?

I could wait if I was going to get what I had wanted. After all, I had waited these past four years.

Our arrangements were in place. A meal at Oddie's, and then listen to a local band playing there that night. Then back to my place for the boots and his belated birthday treat.

It would be a long few days until this evening came. I had arrangements that day with a singles group I had joined, but I would get out of that. This had the potential to be far more fun, and I wasn't going to miss it for the world.

Now all I could do was wait. The bait, the tackle, the line checked and all in place. All Gill had to do now was wait, wait for the evening to come, and from that line at the start of Gladiator, 'release hell'. She had no intention it would be hell; her time was to come shortly.

Everything was in place other than just checking by text all was okay and if he still wanted 'the boots'. Silly question, he loved me in my boots, and they were on offer tonight along with the trimmings.

The time had come, it was nearly time to go. He

would pick me up, no worries about driving because he wasn't going to drink any more than the safe limit. Work again; oh, I hope that isn't going to curtail our evening from all I had planned.

He was to pick me up at seven thirty, we would eat and then listen to the band, and then...

I put fresh sheets on the bed, I wonder why, and made sure my lodger was out for the night. Luckily she was only too willing to oblige, failing that I would have had to suggest the evening finished at his place, but as far as I was concerned this was going to be a home fixture. I had prepared the pitch and was determined it would play out my way.

Pitch prepared, it was now time to put my kit on. I had chosen a purple dress I had made myself, just above the knee, and yes, I was going to show enough cleavage to keep him interested again. Stockings and a pair of comfy shoes, the boots would come later if the evening went as I had hoped.

Red lipstick, and a spray of Angel perfume. I was ready for him, thought I had covered all possible escape routes. I was ready for him, and this time I was determined he would not get away.

A knock on the door, he was here to pick me up. I would open the door and this match would begin. I had prepared my ground bait well, the tackle prepared, the lure was ready.

This was serious game fishing. I knew my prey and I was about to cast myself to the depths to reel him in, never to escape again.

Let the match commence!

WADERS, NETS, THE END OF THE LINE

As Gill's eyes gently opened, she felt a warm breeze against her face coming through the open bedroom window. The curtains moved gently as the warm air wafted past them. Silence could be heard all around, just her in her own bed, peace and tranquillity on this warm summers morning. The start of the dawn chorus broke the silence; it was that early, was it? She must have slept, but obviously not for that long, but here was a feeling of contentment, and excitement in her as well.

Had she dreamed again? Was it in her imagination the evening that had just passed? She lay in her bed, wondering, thinking of what she thought had just happened. Had it been for real?

As her eyes circled the room, she saw memories of the previous night, her stockings now hanging limply over the end of the bed, her underwear strewn over the dressing table chair, her purple dress hanging on a coat hanger on a hook on the door. What was her thong doing hanging from the light shade? She smiled to herself, recalling the previous night, a night of love and passion. She pulled the sheet up over her bare breasts, and snuggling under the bare cotton, she closed her eyes again, trying to recall the events of the past few hours, what had seemed like a perfect evening.

*

Yes, the offer of meal, some live music and the boots had been accepted, and she had just texted to confirm that boots were still on the menu. The bait was ready, she was ready for him and waited expectantly.

Always punctual, there was a knock on her door; he was here. He had come to pick her up. Fingers crossed for the evening, she went to open the door. Gill had offered a taxi, but he had an early start the following morning so said he was quite happy to drive, not drink. Though it was Gill's treat for him, it wasn't an issue. Locking the door behind her, should she give him a quick peck? It wouldn't hurt so Gill risked it, let him smell her perfume, smell the Angel on her, feel her breasts rub up against him. He smiled and ushered her towards the car, opening the door for Gill to get in, a gentleman. A polite thank you as she got in, making it only too obvious that she had stockings on. Really laying the ground bait here and hoping it was working. Admiring that bum again as he walked round to get in the car, they were off for what she hoped would be a successful night's angling.

It was a short journey to Oddie's, where their evening would begin. Gill had booked a table for them so as not to be disappointed; they would eat then listen to the band who were playing later.

He offered her a chair, and tucked her in at the table, then sat next to her rather than the chair opposite. Why not? She wasn't driving, so ordered a bottle of Merlot for herself, and him a Shropshire Lass, hoping it wasn't the only one he was going to enjoy tonight. He liked his local beers, but could make it last and would have a sip of wine later, so she wouldn't have to drink the whole bottle herself, else she would be on her back. Actually, she thought that's what she was hoping for, but she did want to enjoy it, the whole evening, the whole experience!

The wine bar wasn't that busy so chatting was easy without being drowned out by noisy neighbours, and Gill was pleasantly surprised by how relaxed he was; so much more confident about himself, far different from the man she had gone out with some four years ago. Conversation was easy, they had both been away, herself having just returned from Australia, and not being sure she had enjoyed it that much this time (times, situations change and she could not now see her future there, whereas before the trip she had considered returning if life wasn't going in the direction she had hoped), and he from a holiday in the sun, Greek island, and had enjoyed it thoroughly. Holidays are always a good way of breaking down barriers – food, experiences, trips, and this man in front of her, just as she had remembered from their own holidays together, certainly bronzed up well. He enjoyed his sun and also told Gill lots about the inland Greece, enthused about it in fact, away from the tourist industry.

Time to order their food, nothing too

sophisticated here but enough to whet the appetite. A shared starter was enough to begin with, Thai fish cakes, spicy but nice before a more basic main course, but it didn't matter what the food was. Gill was pleased with the way the dinner was going, the chance to catch up, reignite their friendship to hopefully a closer bond; in fact she was hoping for much more, and at this stage he wasn't giving her any grounds to think she might be disappointed.

There was of course no harm now and again in leaning forward, flaunting her cleavage, or if her dress should just happen to ride up her leg a little, oops, there was another glimpse of the top of her stocking. It didn't go unnoticed, good! He drank his beer, Gill drank her wine, they ate, they chatted, they smiled, they laughed. Yes, Gill was pleased the way things were going.

She was not going to pass up a sweet, but he did, as he had often done in the past. As she tucked into her Eton Mess, she smiled to herself that she would serve him up his dessert later and a sweet tooth wouldn't be needed.

The meal was over and the band was starting to warm up, and as it happened it was a band that he knew well, followed them a lot. They had in fact seen them when they went out before, though he explained that the lead singer had departed from the line-up Gill knew, and that their genre was now more Irish Rock/Folk, but whatever mood he was in, listening to them would always relax him and take him away from the worries of the world. Sounded good to Gill, it was nice to see them play again after all this time, and he obviously had got to know them well, having a chat with a couple of them before they launched into their routine. The place was a lot busier now, louder, more crowded, so to begin with he and Gill were quite happy to stay at their table. They could see something of them, and could certainly hear them.

A set of various of their own songs, yes, the music of The Endings came back to Gill from four years ago. Some cover versions added in as well, they were very good to listen to, then launching into a Waterboys track which seemed highly appropriate to her evening, listening to the lyrics:

I wish I were a fisherman
Tumblin' on the seas
Far away from dry land
And its bitter memories
Casting out my sweet line
With abandonment and love
No ceiling bearin' down on me
Save the starry sky above
With light in my head
You in my arms
Woo!

Yes, they did seem quite apt for how she had felt, her fishing over the past, well, many months. Thoughts of the sea, Portugal, Devon, where she had been with him before. And now...

Gill, enjoy the evening, don't reminisce about what may have been. 'Her' man was certainly enjoying the music, and she could see him itching to get up and get closer to the action; the feet were tapping, and that bum (wow, that bum!) was looking like it wanted to move to the music.

The Endings stopped for a short break, Gill paid the bill for the meal and they collected their glasses and made their way closer to where the music would recommence in a few minutes. And back The Endings went into full swing, songs, Irish jigs, the wine bar was now really behind them, as they generated a wonderful atmosphere, getting the whole audience behind them. Sophie sang some Amy Macdonald covers, played her violin, Verna led the beat on her drums, Paul on his banjo, Ciaran providing wonderful vocals, and Jim at the back on his bass guitar – they were wonderful. What's more, someone's hips were really swinging to the music, mesmerising Gill with those firm buttocks, moving side to side, gyrating gently, certainly turning her on. Her mind was starting to turn to other things, other things those buttocks could be doing, and that involved her, later, the catch about to happen!

A great set was drawing to an end, an Ending in fact, and it would be time to go. 'Her' man bade them all farewell and would catch up with them soon, would look forward to it. Gill hoped she would be there with him, but for the next couple of hours had more serious fish to fry. It was time to go home, and well done to him, he had stuck to his single pint and half a glass of wine. That was good because she could offer him a drink now, knowing he was well within the limits to drive home when their evening was finished.

Back to the car, no harm in her walking arm in arm with him, and before she got into the opened car, kissing him (go for it, Gill, squarely on the lips, while letting his body know she was there) on his lips then slipping onto the car seat. No, another flash of those lacy tops of her stockings, all ground bait and soon time to try and hook the fish she had been after all this time.

It would be hard, when he had got into the car, not to put her hand on his... sorry, that was supposed to be his leg, just to say thank you for introducing her to the band, who had made her feel very welcome alongside him. It did feel as if it was rising, ready to take the bait, below the flies something was stirring. Perfect.

It was only a ten-minute drive and they were back at Gill's home, and of course he was coming in. So far, Gill had ticked two boxes, a meal and an evening out. The boots were still to come if he was still interested, and she was pretty sure he was.

If this had been a well-planned fishing strategy, all was, in her opinion, going extremely well. He had taken the ground bait, and she could feel him rising ready to take her hook, her bait, all that was needed now was to change the bait she had used to attract him to the one she would hook him with, complete the catch, her perfect catch, though any thought of stuffing the prize... No, she wanted him to do that to her.

He had never actually been inside her new abode,

so when they got back there it only seemed polite to invite him in for coffee or something else, and show him round. Gill unlocked the door and led him in, firstly into the kitchen, pointing out the kettle, where the coffee was, and also the booze. Next stop (how blatant is this, Gill?), the bedroom.

It was now or never, get laid or say goodbye. Muddy waters, but she knew what she should do, get in and go for it. Waders and a net to catch her fish, if he gets away, she had done her best, and it would be time to search new waters, because this fish would not come back again.

She took him upstairs, showed him her room, her bed, her most private room. She told him to get them a drink from where she had just shown him, bring it up, surprise her, she would be there in a minute. Oh, and for him to make himself comfortable.

Gill retreated into the bathroom; her trap was laid, what would he do? She heard the sound of him going back down the stairs. Good, no sound of the front door opening and closing behind of him, she must prepare her main bait.

She readied herself, listening intently for the sounds she wanted to hear, which were basically the sound of footsteps coming back up the stairs. There they are, she could put the bait on the hook, the hook she can now admit is her, her Gill Finn.

Setting the bait actually took longer than she thought, but if she had prepared her pitch as intended then all the plans would soon come to fruition. She was ready. She made her way along the landing, hoping for what? Well, she knew what she hoped for, but what would reality be?

Fingers crossed, half-light in her bedroom, and yes, her lodger was out as she passed her room. Here goes Gill Finn; she looked round her open door. He is in bed, her bed, what a cheek! Not at all, that's where she wanted him, that was the bait she had laid. A drink ready for her, and him, sitting up but snuggled under her duvet, he looked up, looked into Gill's eyes.

That was a lie, she didn't want him looking into her eyes – well, not quite yet. She stood there in front of him, and he was going to be hooked. Ann Summers had done well, for what the Italian stallion hadn't seen when he spied Gill through that shop window was the little number she had just slipped into, she thought that was the right phrase as she stood there looking totally irresistible.

A gorgeous black basque, teal frontage, revealing some but not all of two, though she said it herself, superb breasts, a zip at the front to release the little buggers if they were feeling naughty or wanting attention. She couldn't say the thong was black with a teal front, because once you had got past the front, there wasn't a lot left to be black.

Deep waters, require waders; she had found those black boots that he had found so sexy in the past, and of course to catch him, inside the boots, had slipped out of the sheer black nylons into a pair of black fishnets. Gill was there for the taking, if he wished, and if there was a giveaway, as she wasn't aware she had left any pole in the bed, the duvet seemed to be fast heading towards the ceiling – he was aroused.

He had made a gin and tonic for her, sitting on her bedside cabinet, so as Gill slipped in her side of HER bed, she took a quick sip, before throwing the duvet off. It would only be a hindrance, and she was now showing her wears so it was only right that he should rise to the occasion and do so likewise. In fairness to him, yes, he was certainly rising.

To say the atmosphere now seriously smelled of Angel, battling with his Obsession, was an understatement; most heavenly, but if Gill knew he loved that smell, that scent, he was going to bathe in it now.

She slipped in beside him, switching her light off to leave them in the muted light of the landing, seductive in this angelic atmosphere. She snuggled into him, kissing him gently on his lips before reaching down to find what she was looking for. It was there and seemingly ready for action. Her hand found his, directing it down her leg to the feel of net, then leather. 'Her' man, this is what you have dreamed of for four long years, and now, here in boots and stockings, she was now his. Please, please take her.

They embraced, lips meeting lips, kissing, hers, at last finding his, those she had longed for so much over the past four years. Hands explored each other's bodies; she felt, stroked, it was really him. His hands ran over the smooth silk of her basque, touched the zip, and moved on, rounding her breasts. Gill let out a gasp in expectation, but his hands moved down her side, down further, over the silk of her thong. Another gasp, but as his hands again explored down her thigh, over the mesh of her nets, and pulling her leg up, down to the feel of leather, the boots he loved. An inner smile as those few minutes ago, in the bathroom, pulling one, then the other net up her bare legs, rubbing her hands over them herself, adjusting them up her legs then pulling the boots over them, attaching the suspenders from the basque. He was now enjoying that same sensation as Gill had then, just as she hoped he would.

If she had started this evening, a cunning strategy, her the fisherman, the hunter, him the fish, as she lay on her back falling more and more under his spell, the roles were now being reversed. The hunted was turning into the hunter. Back up his hands came, back over her oh so private parts, stroking, exciting her. This is what she wanted, had dreamed about for so long, and it looked like reality was soon to take place. She was enjoying this so much, laying unable to do anything else other than kiss, and reach down from time to time, a quick stroke to be sure what she had wanted was waiting for her. In her past, things had turned limp here far too often, and it wasn't going to happen now, she wouldn't let it happen now.

Back up her body his hands moved, stroking, caressing, back up to her breasts again. Her nipples were hardening. Gill undid the zip a little but he promptly pulled it up again; they would come out to play when he said, and not before. She was helpless for him, laying, waiting in anticipation of what was going to happen.

She could feel a moistness starting between her legs, if this was arousal then she wanted more. But how much more could she take? She was like Pavlov's dog, responding to that gentle touch, deep down, salivating from within. He was playing her cleverly, an expert angler, giving her line, reeling her back in again, more line, then bringing her once again closer to him.

Was he ready now? Gill's zip opened a couple of inches, and he bent down, licking her nipples before kissing each in turn. Another gasp; it was really happening to her, and as she pulled the zip down more, she wasn't going to miss out on the full attention of his lips, teasing her nipples. What an investment this outfit was – thank you Ann Summers. Gill would be back again, she promised herself, but not for the time being, she had other things to do.

She wanted him more and more, now, inside her. Her evening was reaching the climax she had intended, as he kissed her breasts, his fingers now reaching under her thong, exploring her inner depths, that moistness that was seriously reaching flood proportions, Gill's ardour positively gushing.

"I need you inside me," she uttered helplessly. "Now!"

He was playing with her. Down he went, between her legs, his tongue now exploring her... it was too much, she was his, she could not resist any longer. "I'm going to come," she muttered, and she did, big time! A tingling shuddered through the whole of her body, right down to her toes. WOW! That was good.

But he knew Gill from before, knew if he played her right, she wasn't finished yet. Back up came his lips to hers, leaving a finger where his tongue had been. He was teasing her, toying with her, and knew she would enjoy every minute of it.

But what about him? Men have always liked to mount her, wham, bam, they came and were satisfied, often leaving Gill unfulfilled. But not he, he was here to give her the ultimate pleasure, and was. How long had they been in bed now? Ages, yet he had not seemed interested in himself, just her, just satisfying her. And he was arousing her more, more and more. He was going to make her climax again, come again in his arms, and there it was again, the gentle shudder running through her body again.

He stirred, gently moving his body over hers, her legs parted – at last he was going to enter her, erect, powerful, slipping into that moist sultry and now, very welcoming place. Sliding gently in, out, and in again, finding her sweet spot over and over again. Gill's body writhed underneath him, in unison with his body motions, on and on. She was hooked, gone, his, totally his, as over the coming minutes he played her in. Time for the catch; she could only help him, drawing her legs up round his body, her nets ready to envelop her big prey. This one wasn't going to escape.

This was bliss, as she came again, and again in quick succession. Her game was spent, hook, line, and sinker. He had her, literally, and Gill hoped oh so much that her efforts would be rewarded. She could mount him (well, that could come another time, she hoped) as her new specimen fish, the one she had always wanted since the first time they had met.

Had he finished with her. To be honest she was now totally fucked, was in ecstasy after what they had just done together, happy to now lay in his arms, dreaming of what the future may hold for her, for them together.

Of course he had to go, which she didn't want him to, but he had said that all along. They chatted, though Gill was dreamy, and it was time for him to go. She watched him get out of bed, pull his knickers then jeans up over that lovely bum, that had been servicing her so well just before. He helped her take those boots and stockings off, then fully releasing her from her basque.

"You couldn't have chosen better," he said before bending down to give Gill one last kiss before bidding her goodnight. It had been a lovely evening, he added, thanking her for the meal, the whole evening, it had been fantastic. He would be in touch. "We must do it again, soon."

Gill smiled and agreed, it had been sensational. She would look forward to hearing from him, seeing him soon. Next time she would promise the red set, locked away for so long since she had last slept, been with him. A glint in his eye, he said he had thought of her many times in the past in that little outfit. He blew her a kiss, pulled the duvet back over her, turned and was gone.

*

Sleep came easily that night as she snuggled under the duvet. Dreams of hooking trout, casting out to see catching barramundi, fighting with marline, netting a few tiddlers, and of her specimen fish. No nightmares of pikes, piranhas, cock cages. Dory occasionally slipped into her dream, hoping she would find her Nemo, hoping her fishing the net would be more successful. After all, Gill Finn had made her catch, trying another form of angling. She slept contentedly, slept well, she was happy.

Then her eyes gently opened. Silence, other than the shimmering of the curtains in the breeze. But what was that bloody noise? Sod it, it was the bloody alarm clock. Wearily she turned that horrible noise off. Rolled over to switch the alarm off. She wandered into the bathroom, naked, switching the shower on and standing under the warm, running water.

Bugger, bugger, had it all been a dream? She did need a man in her life, a man of her own to share her life with, to make these dreams for real. To be bonked when she wanted, to love and to be happy.

Gill made her way back to the bedroom. But as she reached the door, surveying the scene, her boots were by the side of the bed, stockings laying wearily over the top of them. Her purple dress was hanging from the back of the door, her teal thong was draped over the lamp stand, and that sexy basque, yes, it did lay unzipped at the end of the bed.

She pulled the duvet back, the smell and signs of sex, long and enduring. The ping of her phone, a message – wonderful evening, thank you so much, and really looking forward to next time.

It was for real, it had happened, no dream this time. Gill's face lit up like it hadn't for a long time, well not since last night in fact, but a long time before that. Was she happy, or was she happy? She had managed to catch the fish she had wanted for so long. Now to dream, dream what sort of a future they could have together, but no rush, plenty of time to plan together, see what else Ann Summers had to offer, to please him, toy with him this time. A sense of fulfilment at last.

Stories of Dory would follow, but for the time being she thought of herself and her catch.

I wish I were a fisherman...
Tomorrow I will be loosened
From the bonds that held me fast
That the chains that all hung round me
Will fall away at last
And on that fine and fateful day
I will take thee in my hands
I will ride on the train
I will be the fisherman
With light in my head
You in my arms.

Gill had been the fisherman, she now felt free, liberated from the inhibitions of her past few years as she thought she had got what she had wanted all along – him!

If this had to be a fishy tale, then as she reread the text to herself, she smiled and let out a small giggle as she got to the end of the text, signed 'Rod'.

Le Fin.

Book also by Rod Wood available on Amazon:

KILLIMANJARO, my GOAL, my STORY –
November 2015 (in Kindle and paperback)

Republished as:

KILIMANJARO, my STORY – June 2016
(paperback, monochrome)

Printed in Great Britain
by Amazon